The
Collected
Stories
of
ANDRÉ MAUROIS

The
Collected
Stories
of
ANDRÉ MAUROIS

Translated
by
Adrienne Foulke

WSP

WASHINGTON SQUARE PRESS, INC.
New York • 1967

Second Printing

Library of Congress catalog card number: 67–17359

*Published by Washington Square Press, Inc.,
630 Fifth Avenue, New York, N.Y. 10020.*

PRINTED IN THE UNITED STATES OF AMERICA

An Imaginary Interview
with André Maurois

"You are much better known as a biographer than as a novelist and short-story writer. Do you yourself attach more importance to your biographies?"

"No. Actually, what you say is true only in the United States and England. In France, Italy, Spain, and even in Russia, my novels—*Climats, Le Cercle de Famille, Les Roses de Septembre* —have been best sellers. As for my short stories, the eminent French critic Edmond Jaloux wrote that "A number of them will have a place in all French anthologies," and Russian critics have mentioned Chekhov in connection with them. That pleased me, of course, because Chekhov is one of my favorite writers."

"Who are your other models?"

"I admire de Maupassant, but I've never tried to imitate him. Temperamentally we are too different. My ideal would have been to write stories worthy of Katherine Mansfield's, but there again I lacked her poetic sensibility. I've felt closer to some of Dorothy Parker's short stories. In recent years I've liked Salinger very much and, in Italy, Giorgio Bassani and Dino Buzzati."

"Have you been influenced by the French *nouveau roman*— for example, the work of Robbe-Grillet or Michel Butor?"

"No. All my fiction was written earlier than theirs, but I am in sympathy with the fact of their searching. Art is never completed, never immobile. To be a passionate admirer of Balzac and Stendhal doesn't prevent one's appreciating the *nouveau roman.*"

"Aside from Balzac and Stendhal, who have been your masters?"

"Flaubert, and especially Proust. There again I recognized a temperament quite different from my own, but Proust taught me to dig deeper. I amused myself once by writing perhaps a hundred pages in imitation of Proust. I called the pastiche *Le Côté de Chelsea,* and in it I had Proust go to England—he never was there, you know. When he was young, Proust pastiched Flaubert. It's a very good stylistic exercise."

"So Proust is one of your masters?"

"Yes. Less so, however, than the great Russians—Tolstoi, Turgenev, Chekhov."

"Not Dostoevski?"

"Not Dostoevski. I've read him, I consider him a great writer. . . . But I'm not at home in his world. On the other hand, with Tolstoi I feel very close to myself. And then, for the fantasies (there are several in this collection) I had Pushkin in mind—'The Queen of Spades'—also Edgar Allan Poe, and occasionally Voltaire. When I was starting to write, I was enormously taken with the short stories of Kipling. But none of this is to say that my own stories are of the same caliber as the work of my models. A writer's intelligence sets him a goal, but the moment he sits down to write, his own aptitude takes command. Let's suppose that Pissarro and Sisley admired Van Gogh. If one had set them down in front of a wheatfield, what would they have done? A Pissarro, a Sisley—not a Van Gogh."

"Have you done a Maurois?"

"I hope so. I have certain ideas about the short story. The genre has laws of its own: relative brevity, otherwise it becomes a novel; ergo, a plot that is rather narrowly limited as to time and space; often a shock effect, an abrupt upset toward the middle or at the end—as in 'Thanatos Palace Hotel' or 'The House.' But the genre can take very different forms. In Katherine Mansfield's stories, almost nothing happens. A state of mind, the special complexion of one instant of ecstasy or despair is the only subject. Salinger suppresses narrative almost entirely. Everything happens via conversations in which banalities and ramblings make the whole point. . . . There is a *nouvelle nouvelle,* just as there is a *nouveau roman.*"

"Do you consider the short story a minor literary form?"

"Not at all. A small canvas by Vermeer is no less beautiful than an immense Rubens. 'The Queen of Spades' is a masterpiece. I've written stories that are only three pages long but I could have expanded them to novel size. Max Ophuls wanted to make a full-length film based on 'The Corinthian Porch.' To me a short prose poem seemed right for such a subject. It's for the reader to judge."

—ANDRÉ MAUROIS

CONTENTS

The
Collected
Stories
of
ANDRÉ MAUROIS

Reality Transposed

MY FEELINGS ABOUT ROBERT FABERT had always been mixed. I didn't like his cynicism but I admired his verve. His plays irritated me, although I recognized their dramatic impact. His egotism offended me, yet I was always touched that he chose me as his confidant. His morning telephone call—interminable, on occasion—put me out of all patience, but if he went three days without calling me, I missed him.

This particular morning, he was pressing and to the point:

"Drop whatever it is you're writing, there's a good fellow, and come on over. I've something urgent to tell you."

"Look, Robert, why do you impose on friendship like this— not to mention my patience? You insist on seeing me maybe three times a week, and more often than not it's for the most trifling, silly thing. I've just started an article. Let me have a life of my own, will you!"

After five minutes of discussion, I realized I would lose less time by going; if I'd said no, he would have kept me on the phone the whole morning long. He was living near me at the time, and fifteen minutes later I walked into his study. He immediately assumed his most flattering manner. From long experience I knew that a compliment from Fabert was an investment. What dividend was he after now?

"I've just finished your piece on Ménétrier, old man," he said. "It's a gem, a model of penetration, of taste and style! You literally are the one critic we have—"

"Thanks. What is it you want to ask me?"

"Well, uh . . . I don't know whether you happen to know Mme Astier—Mme Adrien Astier."

"You introduced me to her yourself. Very beautiful."

"Isn't she! Rather middle-class, of course, but she has such sparkle, such freshness, and do you know, she's even witty. . . . In a word, I'm mad about her."

"For two months or two weeks?"

"Time's got nothing to do with it. The point is, right now I can't see anything else in the world but her. . . . Now, there's a chance, a once-in-a-lifetime chance, of taking a trip to Spain with her. . . . Yes, she wants to see Andalusia. Her husband—he's got business interests in the Far East, you know—is going to be away for two months. Everything could work out to perfection—but there's Odette. Poor little Odette, I'd given her my solemn word I'd spend Easter with the family, at Beauvallon. I've not paid a real visit to her and the children in three years. She's going to be terribly disappointed."

"No doubt, but I don't see why you—"

"Why I bring this up with you? Because you're the only person, old fellow, who can help me out in convincing her. If you were to explain to her that since my next play is placed in Spain—"

"You have to take a Frenchwoman down with you to collect local color. Oh, no! I'm not undertaking to explain that to her. Don't forget, I am Odette's friend as much as—or more than—I am yours. If, as you say and as I'd like to think, Odette trusts me, it's because I've always been loyal to her. You're proposing that I be disloyal."

"Disloyal! Not at all, old man. I feel, on the contrary, that as a friend of Odette you will be doing her a service. Think for a

minute. . . . Let's suppose that she objects, that she makes a
drama out of this little interlude. What would happen? Our
marriage could be wrecked. Poor little Odette, that would kill
her. And who would have murdered her? You!"

This man of the theater knew how to play a scene. I soon
saw that once again I would have peace only if I gave in.

"All right. I will see Odette, but I don't promise to argue
your case for you. I'll simply present it. And that's all."

"But you won't oppose it? That's all I ask. . . . I'm going to
call Odette now. I'll leave you alone with her so you can talk
more easily."

I tried to win a delay. No such luck. Like the heroes of his
plays, Fabert was greedy and overbearing. He pressed a button,
lifted the receiver, and said to his secretary, "Ask Mme Fabert
to come to my study, please." Then he got up and left the
room. A few minutes later, Odette came in.

"Why, Bertrand! What a delightful surprise to find you here.
What have you done with Robert? He just called for me to
come down."

"Yes, my dear. That was so that you and I could have a little
talk."

"A little talk? What's all the mystery? Robert gave you a
message for me?"

"Exactly."

Whereupon I set about trying tactfully to prepare her for the
bad news. I said that Robert was exhausted, that I was beginning
to worry about his health, that the new play wasn't coming
along well, that he needed to be alone for a few weeks in the
milieu he'd chosen for it. She listened to me, smiling at first,
and then she broke out laughing.

"Dear old Bertrand!" she said. "What trouble he takes to
inform me, without breaking my already broken heart, that
Robert wants to go to Spain with his latest conquest and that
he'll be leaving me alone for a month."

"What do you mean? . . . You mean you knew?"

"I didn't know, no. But I was expecting something of the
sort, and your roundabout little speech—it wasn't too hard to
see through, you know—simply confirmed it. Which is all to the

good. Because—now imagine this, Bertrand—I need a month of freedom, too."

"To go with the children to Beauvallon."

"Not at. all. To go to the Greek islands with a very dear friend who has invited me. I'll leave the children with Mother and enjoy my holiday away from husband and family in peace. Don't look so stunned and upset, Bertrand! Don't you think I'm capable of making someone fall in love with me?"

"Yes . . . Why, of course . . . But I thought you loved Robert, that you were miserably but faithfully in love with him."

"For a long time that was true, and even today I'm attached to Robert. I admire his genius—if not his character—and I tolerate his caprices. I also consider that I have a right to some compensations. You don't agree?"

"Well . . . well, yes, of course. And who is your lucky traveling companion?"

"Bertrand, dear, I am more discreet than my husband."

"And what in the devil do you want me to tell him?"

"Very simple. Tell him that the message you were asked to give me upset me utterly, that you comforted me very adroitly, that you advised me to forget my disappointment by taking a cruise in the Mediterranean, maybe with some woman friend or other, and that you left me disconsolate and in tears, but resigned."

"Do you expect him to believe that?"

"Robert has the most amazing capacity to believe anything that flatters his vanity."

She was right. He not only accepted the reply and the plan but proceeded to play out for me, in all sincerity, a tender little scene in which his wife was the pathetic heroine.

"Poor little Odette. She's wonderful. I don't think, old man, that in our day there is another such example of a wife's self-denial. Imagine, sometimes she goes so far as to say to me, 'Tell me about this woman you're in love with. Everything that touches you concerns me.' Ah, I can just see her cruising through the Mediterranean, going alone at night to sit in the prow of the boat, looking at the stars, and thinking of me and my happiness. . . . Of my happiness with another woman!

You can say what you like, old man, but I think it's a much finer thing to arouse a feeling like that than passionate jealousy."

"But *you* are jealous," I said.

"Wildly."

He sat for a moment, thinking, and then he said, "You know, that would make a good opening scene—the scene between you and me, then the scene between Odette and you. . . . Complete self-sacrifice, but understated. . . . Of course, you—you the character, I mean—would have to be in love with Odette. You'd try to take advantage of the situation, but you'd come up against the purity of this extraordinary woman—"

"I had no such idea!"

"I realize that. You know Odette. But in the play . . ."

He went to Andalusia, and Odette went to the Greek islands, coming back bronzed and bursting with health, exuding happiness. I saw them both in June. After lunch, Robert took me into his study.

"Well, I'm doing that play," he said. "It's all set."

"What play?"

"What play! The play we talked about, the one that opens with the scene where I'm talking to you about Odette. . . . Title: *The Victim*. The first act's finished. It was easy enough to write, actually. Reality supplied practically everything I needed."

"Reality? That could be rather dangerous. I hope you transposed it."

"Naturally. I know my trade. Transposition comes instinctively. I made the hero—that's me—a kind of Don Juan painter. I made you—in the play I call you Bernard—a romantic—"

"Where's the transposition? You *are* a Don Juan and I am a romantic."

"Yes, yes, but all the specific details are different. The difficulties begin with the second act. I really don't know where I'm going at that point. Bernard, I think, will try his chances. He'll be on the point of succeeding, because Juliette—that's Odette in the play—wants revenge. . . . Then, at the last moment, her better nature will assert itself and in spite of her resentment, her love will win out."

"Her love for you?"

"Obviously. . . . That leaves the third act. I'm still in the dark there, but it seems to me that the hero's mistress and her husband should be brought into it. . . . This husband would be preparing some kind of—some kind of retaliation or other, and Juliette, throwing herself between him and her own rival— or between him and the hero—would save him. Save the hero, that is."

"You don't find this a bit on the melodramatic side?"

"If you tell it flatly, as I've just done, yes. But everything depends on the execution. My characters are contemporary people, they speak our language, they behave the way you and I would behave. . . . That is the essence of theater. Dialogue saves everything, and I don't hesitate to say that when it comes to dialogue, I don't have to be afraid of anyone."

It was true that when it came to dialogue he had not to fear anyone, and I gladly admitted as much. Then I asked:

"And Mme Astier?"

"What Mme Astier?"

"The Mme Astier you went to Granada with, the one who's at the bottom of this play."

"Oh, Pepita. . . . Yes, Pepita's the name I gave her because we were in Spain. . . . She was a charming creature."

"Was? What's happened to her?"

"How should I know? As far as I'm concerned, the episode is finished. I suppose she found a Pepito. But she will live on in *The Victim*. . . . Ah, I will have to see her again, poor Pepita, for one or two details. . . . She had the most delicious way of kicking off her mules when she was going to bed. . . . I'll ask her to act that out for whoever'll be playing the part."

The summer went by. In October, I heard that *The Victim* was going into rehearsal. Jenny Sorbier—she was young then, but already a famous actress—was to play Juliette. Fabert often used to ask me to come to rehearsals of his plays. Not that he considered I had any special competence, but he thought a fresh eye might be better able to detect any false notes. I was always glad to go; I love the theater and the hardworking in-

formality backstage. One day, I went by invitation to a rehearsal that turned out to be stranger and more hectic than
any I'd ever seen. The theater was empty, dimly lit, and Fabert
had me sit beside him in the orchestra. He seemed worried.

"I don't know what's wrong," he said. "It's not going right.
Usually Jenny understands what I want before I've half said it.
But this time she's fighting me. . . . She even blows her lines
sometimes, which for her is unheard of. I'm really annoyed.
But you'll see for yourself."

The stage was almost bare. An actor came out and sat down
at an Empire desk; he was playing the role of Fabert. He had a
short scene with his secretary; then the girl announced the
actor who was playing me. I felt very strange as I listened to
him. Fabert had used my own tricks of speech, and he'd
coached the actor in some of my characteristic gestures. The
dialogue struck me as fast-moving and natural. Then Jenny
came on. I listened with passionate interest, first because I had
been one of the actors in the original drama, but especially
because I was wondering how Fabert had imagined the conversation. After all, I knew how it had gone. But he believed that
a despairing Odette—or Juliette, rather—had made an anguished sacrifice for love.

And this was precisely the scene Jenny launched into. "You
can't understand," the Juliette character was saying. "His happiness is my happiness. His pleasure is my pleasure. . . ." And
so forth and so forth, all in a style that, as Fabert had warned
me, Jenny was bungling badly. Two or three times he interrupted to ask her to put more feeling into her lines. She
seemed to try, didn't succeed, then she got rattled, and when
the author made some further comment, she lost her temper.
She came over to the apron, shielded her eyes from the foot-
lights, which were blinding her, and tried to locate Fabert in
the empty hall.

"Are you there, Robert? . . . Oh, yes, I see you. . . . Who's
that with you?"

"Bertrand."

"Oh, well, come up, both of you. I must talk to you."

"After rehearsal," Fabert said. "Cue!"

"No. There's not going to be any rehearsal. We have something to get straight, the author and I, and I'm not doing a thing until I get an explanation."

"She's out of her mind," Fabert said to me, with an air of complete conviction.

"Why do you say that? Jenny's the most intelligent and the most conscientious actress in Paris. Whatever she wants to say to you deserves to be heard."

"What can she have to say to me? She should play her part the way it's written. That's all there is to it. . . . I'm no novice playwright who asks his actors for advice."

Up on the stage, Jenny was growing impatient.

"Are you coming or aren't you? Because I—"

I took the initiative and said:

"We're coming."

I pushed Fabert, grumbling and muttering, toward the temporary little ladder that connects the stage and the auditorium during rehearsals. At the top, Jenny was waiting for us, side book in hand.

"So?" Fabert said. "What's wrong?"

"What's wrong is that I cannot—*cannot* read these lines. Your woman isn't real, or at least she isn't for me. . . . I don't understand her, I don't feel her, I won't play her. . . . What? . . . Here is a woman who's just been told, and told very clumsily into the bargain, that her husband is going off with another woman. She adores her husband, but her only reaction is to say, 'All right. So long as he is happy, I am happy.' It doesn't happen like that! . . . Look here, Robert, God knows you've known women, countless women. Have you ever met one who, if she were really in love, would go around bleating like this sheep?"

"Only one," he said proudly, "and that's the one I'm recreating in *The Victim*. As a matter of fact, this scene that you say is unreal happens to be authentic. For once I've taken everything from real life, and by a stroke of good luck, I've got an irrefutable witness. It's Bertrand here, who in real life talked to the woman you're playing."

Jenny turned to me.

"So you're responsible for this foolishness!" she said. "You heard answers like these? It's not possible. . . . Either the woman was an idiot—in which case it's no role for me—or she was playing a game, pretending to be the noble martyr while actually she was preparing for a glorious fling of her own. In that case, she would be human again, but it would be another play."

I was in an embarrassing position. Jenny was right a hundred times over; her artist's intuition had discovered the attitude of the real-life Juliette. But I couldn't tell her so without at the same time betraying both Robert and Odette. I kept still.

"Well, say something!" Jenny said. "Did you know this Juliette, yes or no? And if yes, how do you explain her?"

I don't remember exactly what I answered. I remember beginning sentences I never finished, and trying helplessly to humanize the character and justify her in Jenny's eyes without compromising her in Fabert's. The whole business must have been pretty lame, because Jenny exclaimed triumphantly:

"There, you see! . . . Bertrand doesn't believe in Juliette's purity, in her resignation, any more than I do!"

"I didn't say that."

"You don't dare say it, but you let what you mean be very clear."

A moment before this, Fabert had stepped apart. I looked at him now, and his expression startled me He was striding back and forth across the stage, shaking his head violently, running his hands through his leonine shock of hair, or furiously biting his fingernails. Suddenly he came toward me, pointing at me with his finger, and his eyes were black with anger.

"I see now!" he said. "Jenny's telling the truth. *You* lied. I've behaved like a schoolboy. I appealed to the lover of Odette for help that only a friend could give. Because I believed you were my friend. . . ."

He burst into that famous neighing laugh of his, a theatrical laugh worthy of a Lemaître or a Garrick. It was my turn to become angry.

"I was your friend, I still am, but I am also Odette's friend— her friend, not her lover, and you know that perfectly well. Is it my fault that you put me in an impossible situation?"

"So you admit that Odette told you something you kept from me?"

"I admit nothing at all. I simply say that my position between the two of you was not easy."

But he was no longer listening to me. He walked upstage, muttering something I could not hear, and then he came back toward Jenny and me; his face was relaxed, almost smiling. He put his two huge hands on Jenny's shoulders and looked down at her with admiring tenderness.

"You are a great artist," he said. "Very great . . . You understood just by your actor's instinct that what I was asking you to say was not true, wasn't even believable. And I, who am also a great artist, now that you've shown me the way, I'll take it—against my feelings, against my own pride. I've seen the truth in a flash. And I'm going to recreate it. . . . It will be really fine. . . . Now I've got to rewrite the play, but I promise you that this time you'll have a role that fits your stature, a part you'll love."

"I'm sure of that," Jenny said, and she seemed genuinely moved.

"As for you," he said to me, "as for you . . . Well, you're going to help me."

At that moment, the stage doorman looked in timidly and said to Fabert:

"Madame asks me to say that she's outside with the car."

That famous laugh once again.

"Madame is here, is she? Ask her to come in."

A moment later, Odette appeared, all delighted.

"Well, today I'm allowed in," she said. "You, too, Bertrand! Is it going that well, then? . . . Hello, Jenny."

Fabert looked at her, shaking his head.

"You are a little minx," he said, "but I love you. And you love me. . . . Yes, whether you like it or not, you love no one but me. I am going to write, my dear little Odette, the finest play of my life."

"I don't understand a word," she said, "but I believe you."

Fabert did not work often; he wrote one play a year, and he would finish it in three or four weeks. But while he was at work, he gave himself to it entirely. First, he would tell his plot to everyone he met, trying it out for effects. He was a good storyteller; he would imitate the voices and mime the expressions, and he found his inspiration in the movement of the story. Then, when he felt sure of his scenario, he would dictate the scenes to a secretary, who was trained to catch his words on the wing as he strode up and down his study, taking the role of each actor in succession. Then he would reread this first draft and, at that point, would sometimes consult me. The new version of *The Victim* seemed to me excellent. With surprising courage, he had gone to the farthest point in a situation that for him was painful. It made for strong, convincing drama, with various comic aspects that relaxed the tension and provided good contrast to the highly charged scenes.

I was not present when he read the script to Jenny, but I met her a few days later.

"Have you read the revised script for *The Victim*?" she asked. "It's really good, isn't it? For the last two or three years, Fabert's subjects haven't said much to me. His characters didn't seem human, but this time it's hats off! . . . Real as life, hardly stylized at all."

"Satisfied with your part?"

"Delighted with it. It's easy to say, to live. . . . No problems."

Rehearsals went smoothly and quickly. Fabert asked me sometimes to drop by, and now and then I would run into Odette there. I had not seen her again alone since her husband had discovered the real situation. When they were together, at the theater or at parties, they appeared perfectly natural and made no allusion to any disagreement between them. Presently the opening of *The Victim* was announced. An aura of success already enveloped the play; the stage personnel—the wardrobe mistresses, stagehands, electricians—were full of confidence.

The first night was a triumph. Jenny was a great favorite with the public, and the critics, who often used to reproach Fabert for the slightness of his heroes, recognized that in *The Victim* he had gone more deeply than ever before in depicting human passions.

After the twelfth and final curtain call, friends rushed backstage. As I made my way with some difficulty along a crowded corridor I was listening to the conversation of the people milling around me. Many of them had identified the models.

"Amazing, isn't it! . . . What? . . . Why, Jenny even talked like Odette Fabert."

"Yes, and it's all the more remarkable because they don't resemble each other at all."

"And Bertrand! . . . Eerie! . . . Down to the very way he walks."

"Careful, he's right behind you."

When the wave that was bearing me forward broke and deposited me in Jenny's dressing room, Robert and Odette also were there. Some woman friend, whether out of clumsiness or malice, said to Odette:

"I recognized you right away."

Odette's laugh was as light as it was sincere.

"Me?" she said. "Why, I don't play any part in the story."

"What do you mean? . . . Why, Juliette—"

"Juliette no more resembles me than you do the Lady of the Camellias."

She turned to Fabert, who, standing beside her, elated by his triumph, was accepting congratulations with Olympian serenity, and she murmured:

"Did you hear that idiot woman. Some people have no idea what a real work of art is."

"Dear Odette," he said.

And, bending over his wife, he kissed her.

Mme Astier, who was out of town, had received two complimentary balcony seats, but she did not attend the opening of *The Victim*.

Darling, Good Evening!

"Where are you going, Antoine?" Françoise Quesnay asked her husband.

"I'm going as far as the post office. I want to send this letter registered and also walk Mowgli. . . . The rain's stopped. Toward Menton the sky is lifting; it'll be clear soon."

"Don't come back too late. I've invited Sabine Lambert-Leclerc and her husband to dinner. . . . Yes, I read in the paper that they're in Nice for a few days. I dropped Sabine a note."

"Oh, Françoise . . . Why? I can't stand that man's politics, and she—"

"Don't grumble, Antoine. You're not going to tell me you find Sabine unattractive! When I first met you, you and she were on the verge of being engaged."

"That's right. And I don't think she's ever forgiven me for liking you better. I haven't seen her for—oh, it's been fifteen years. She must be a middle-aged matron."

"Sabine is no matron," Françoise said. "She is exactly three years older than I. And in any case, it's too late to be sorry now. Sabine and her husband will be here at eight."

"You might have asked me first. . . . Now, why *have* you done this? You know how I dislike it."

"Enjoy your walk," she said cheerfully, and quickly left the room.

Antoine felt cheated of his quarrel. This was his wife's habitual tactic: she would walk out before the argument could begin. As he strolled along the garden paths of the Cap, between the angular, oblique pines, he thought: Really, Françoise is becoming insufferable. She knew perfectly well that I wouldn't want to see these people, so she took care to keep her little plan to herself. . . . More and more, she's resorting to this device of the *fait accompli*. And why is she inviting Sabine Lambert-Leclerc? Because she's bored being alone with me and the children. . . . But who was it who wanted to live in this corner of the world? Who practically forced me to leave Pont-de-l'Eure and my business and my family, and to retire? Retire at my age! And when I didn't want to.

Whenever he undertook a review of his grievances, it lasted a long time. Antoine had loved his wife passionately; he still loved her sensually and, one might say, also aesthetically. He could spend an entire evening and never weary of watching that delicate nose, those light, mocking eyes, those finely chiseled features. But how she could get on his nerves sometimes! When it came to selecting furniture or clothes or flowers, Françoise had exquisite taste. In dealing with people, she lacked tact. Antoine suffered when Françoise hurt the feelings of one of their friends. He felt both responsible and helpless. For a long time, he used to reproach her for the way she behaved; she either took his criticism in poor part or paid scarcely any attention, confident that she would be forgiven come evening, when he would desire her. Finally, he had come to accept her for what she was. After ten years of marriage, he knew she would never change.

"Mowgli! Come here!"

He went into the post office. On the way home, his meditation on Françoise became more somber. Was she even faithful to him? He thought so, but that on several occasions she might have been flirtatious and even imprudent—that was only too certain. Would he have been happier with Sabine Lambert-Leclerc? He pictured again the garden in Pont-de-l'Eure where Sabine used to receive him when he was a young man. The whole town considered them engaged, and they, without ever having spoken of it, were convinced that someday they would marry.

She was a fiery creature, he thought, remembering how her body would press clingingly against his as they danced.

She was the first girl he had dared be bold with, perhaps because he had sensed that she would be acquiescent. He had wanted her very much. Then Françoise had appeared and suddenly all other girls had ceased to exist for him. . . . He was bound to Françoise now. Ten years of life together. Three children. The race was run.

When he came in to find her in the living room, fresh in a brightly flowered mousseline dress, he forgot his bitterness. It was Françoise who had created this house, this garden, that presently their visitors would be admiring. It was Françoise who had made him leave Pont-de-l'Eure and the factory only a few years before the '29 crash. All things considered, she'd been good for him.

"Are Micheline and Bacot eating at table with us?" he asked.

"No," she said. "I thought it would be nicer with just the four of us. . . . Straighten your tie, Antoine."

Nice . . . Another word he detested. "No, it is not going to be nice," he said to himself as he stood before the mirror re-knotting his tie. Sabine would be captious; Françoise would flirt with Lambert-Leclerc, who would be at his dogmatic, authoritative ministerial best; and he, Antoine, would be glum and taciturn.

"Nice!"

There was the sound of a car's tires grinding to a stop in the graveled driveway. The Quesnays assumed a casually busy air. A moment later, a couple came in. Sabine had black, slightly frizzled hair, heavy shoulders, and beautiful eyes. Lambert-Leclerc was becoming very bald; three strands of hair were plastered across his skull like a three-bar hurdle in an obstacle race; he looked in a bad humor. Very likely this dinner had been forced on him, too.

"Darling, good evening!" Françoise said, embracing Sabine. "Good evening, M. le Ministre—"

"Darling, no!" Sabine said. "You are not going to 'minister' my husband. . . . You call me Sabine; call him Alfred. Antoine, good evening."

The evening was so mild and crystalline that Françoise had coffee served out on the terrace. Conversation during dinner had not been easy. The women were bored. Antoine, mulish, and annoyed with himself for being so, kept imprudently contradicting Lambert-Leclerc, who, being better informed, scored all the points.

"You are optimistic because you are in power," Antoine said, "but actually the situation of France is tragic."

"Not at all, my dear fellow, not at all. Questions of money are never tragic. French budgets have been showing deficits for six hundred years, and that's all to the good. . . . People who live on their incomes have to be ruined now and then. Otherwise, what would we be headed for? Imagine if private fortunes had been earning compound interest since the days of Richelieu—"

"The British budget is balanced," Antoine grumbled. "It even shows a surplus, and the English, as far as I know, are none the worse off for that."

"My dear friend," said Lambert-Leclerc, "I've never been able to understand this mania for comparing two countries that do not have the same histories or the same customs or the same needs. If France really wanted a balanced budget, we would give her one tomorrow. She doesn't want it. Or if you'd rather, I'll put it this way: she doesn't want it badly enough to want also to take the steps necessary to get it. The preparation of the budget is not a fiscal problem; it's a political problem. Tell me how big a majority you want in order to stay in power, and I will tell you what kind of a budget you can chart. The people in the Ministry of Finance stand ready to work up a socialist budget for you, or a radical or a reactionary budget.

. . . Just speak up. It's all so much more simple than outsiders believe."

"Is it all that simple? Would you dare talk like that to the voters?"

Françoise could recognize by imperceptible signs, by a sudden hardening of the eyes, that her husband's temper was rising. She intervened.

"Antoine," she said, "you should take Sabine down to the cloister and show her the view."

"Let's all four go," Antoine said.

"No, no," Sabine said. "Françoise is right. You have to break up couples. It's more amusing that way."

She rose. Antoine could do no less, and he followed her, but not without a furious glance at Françoise, which she declined to notice.

Just what I was afraid of! he thought. Here I am, alone with this woman for a half hour. Is she going to take advantage of it, and demand the explanation she's been waiting ten years for? . . . Won't that be fun! . . . And Françoise hoping, I suppose, that that bigwig minister who's so pleased with himself will flirt with her . . .

"What is that divine fragrance?" Sabine Lambert-Leclerc asked.

"Orange trees. The arbor we were sitting under combines orange trees, lemon trees, wisteria, and climbing roses. Our roses are running wild, though; they need pruning. . . . Follow this little path that goes down—here. . . ."

"Aren't you running wild, too, Antoine, living in all this solitude?"

"Me? I've always been wild. . . . It's pretty dark, but you can see a little something, I hope. On both sides of the tile pool there are clumps of cineraria. . . . The garden is planned on a theme of opposites. Dark flowers—blue or violet—contrasted with lively yellow tones . . . At least, that was Françoise's idea. . . . Here on this slope she's tried to create a kind of maquis—genista, mastic trees, laburnum, asphodel—"

"I'm glad to see you again alone, Antoine. I'm devoted to your wife but, after all, we were such great friends, you and I, before you met her. . . . Do you still remember?"

He prudently slowed his step so as not to walk too near her.

"Of course, Sabine. How could I not remember? . . . No, straight ahead, across the little bridge—and here is the cloister. . . . The flowers between the flagstones? Just pansies . . ."

"Do you remember the dance at the club, my very first dance? And how you drove me home in your grandfather's car? . . . My parents had gone to bed, and we went into the little sitting room and, without saying a word, you caught me in your arms and we began—very gravely—to dance again."

"Didn't I kiss you a little that night?"

"A little! . . . We kissed for an hour! It was delightful. . . . You were my hero."

"Then I must have disappointed you."

"And when the war—Oh, no, no, just the opposite! You dazzled me. You were so marvelous. . . . I knew all your citations by heart. I still know them; I could recite them to you now. . . . Then, when you were wounded and when you got engaged to Françoise Pascal-Bouchet during your convalescence, then, yes, very frankly, then I was disappointed. I used to admire you *so much*. . . . When I saw you marry a girl I knew so well, who'd been a schoolmate of mine at St. Jean's, who was charming but a little stu—well, stupid—oh, Antoine, do forgive me, but I was surprised. Saddened. . . . And not only I. The whole town—"

"Why? We belonged to the same world, Françoise and I, and we were perfectly suited for each other. . . . Look, Sabine. That wall that looks as if it had been planted with lights, that's the Monte Carlo rock. Don't lean over too far; the terrace drops straight down to the sea. Sabine, be careful!"

Involuntarily, he seized her by the waist; with astonishing speed, she turned and kissed him full on the lips.

"Sorry, Antoine. I wanted to too much. . . . It's harder to hold yourself at arm's length from a body you've known. . . . Do you remember how we used to kiss at the tennis club? Oh, I know I'm shocking you. You're still very, very Quesnay. . . . I'm sure you've been a faithful husband."

"Prodigiously faithful. Immaculate."

"For ten years! Poor Antoine . . . You've been happy?"

"Very happy."

"Then it's all for the best, my sweet. But the curious thing is, you know, you don't look happy."

"Where do you see that?"

"I don't know. Some impatience in you, some irritability, some aimlessness . . . After all, Antoine, you were a Quesnay of Pont-de-l'Eure—a man of action, a leader. And here you are, living far away from your work, your friends. . . . I realize you sacrificed everything to please your wife. But can it be you don't regret it?"

"Perhaps at first I minded leaving. But I've found other ways to be busy here. I've always loved history. I work at that. I've even had several books published that have had some success."

"Some success! Why, they've had great success, Antoine. They're remarkable. Especially your *Louis XI*."

"You've read them?"

"Have I read them? A dozen times! First of all, because I also adore, just adore history. . . . And because I was looking for you in your books. I've never stopped being very much interested in you, Antoine. And I consider you an excellent writer. . . . No, I am not exaggerating. And I was ever so slightly surprised—to you I'll admit this—that all through dinner Françoise never said a word about this side of your life. Two or three times my husband tried to talk to you about your books, and each time Françoise cut in. . . . She should—or so it seems to me—be very proud."

"Oh, there's nothing to be proud of. But it is true that Françoise doesn't care about my kind of book at all. She prefers novels. And above all, she is an artist in her own right. She's an artist about her clothes and in her management of her garden. Can you imagine, she's decided where the smallest sprig of a plant should go. . . . And when the depression hit Pont-de-l'Eure, our income dropped, and ever since Françoise's done everything herself."

" 'Françoise does everything! Françoise has such taste!' And the funny part of it is, the dear man believes it! . . . But, my dear Antoine, you are too modest. I knew Françoise when she was a girl. She had a great deal less taste then, I assure you. Or what she did have was that excessive Pascal-Bouchet hankering for bibelots, for ornaments—fussy things. It's you who have formed her, taught her the beauty of simple lines and of order. . . . Above all, it is you who have provided her with the means to maintain this style of living. The dress she's wearing tonight is pretty, it's a perfect choice, but don't forget my dear, that it is also a Schiaparelli. Being able to afford that kind of thing makes good taste a fairly simple matter."

"Don't be misled, Sabine. Françoise made that dress with the maid's help."

"Oh, Antoine, really! Don't go around telling women things like that. There's a whole technique to the bias, a perfection in the seam. . . . And furthermore, Schiaparelli's prints are exclusive with her. That combination of gold rosebuds and periwinkles is to be had only from her. . . . But it doesn't matter, after all."

"It matters, unfortunately, more than you think. I told you we don't have the same income as before. Far from it! Pont-de-l'Eure provides nothing for me, and Bernard writes that it may go on like that for several years. . . . My books sell pretty well. . . . I write a few articles. . . . All the same, poor Françoise would scarcely have the means to dress out of the big couturier houses."

"Then it's a miracle, my dear Antoine, unbelievable but a miracle. What can I do? I bow. . . . Anyhow, I've always had a soft spot in my heart for Françoise. And I've never understood why people don't like her."

"Don't people like her?"

"They detest her. You didn't know that? . . . I've been struck to find the same opinion about her here in Nice as in Pont-de-l'Eure."

"What do they criticize her for?"

"Oh, it's always the same . . . For her egotism, for flirting with the men, for being a tiny bit disloyal toward women. Very insincere, in fact. And then, that tactlessness! . . . I've always stood up for her. As long ago as when we were boarders together at St. Jean's, I used to say, 'Françoise Pascal-Bouchet is a much more worthwhile person than she seems. It's just that affected tone and that disagreeable voice that put you off!' "

"You find her voice disagreeable?"

"Antoine! . . . Well, it's true, after ten years you probably don't even hear it any more. And in any case, it isn't her fault. I don't blame her for it. No, what I find harder to forgive is that she has a husband like you and . . ."

"And what?"

"No, nothing . . ."

"You have no right, Sabine, to start a sentence that is quite evidently loaded with double meanings and then to stop. . . . Do your informants also say that Françoise has had lovers?"

"Are you serious, Antoine?"

"Terribly serious. Yes, I am."

"But you know perfectly well, my dear, people say that about every pretty woman. . . . Still, who knows? Where there's smoke, as the saying goes . . . And Françoise is so imprudent. When I think that in Pont-de-l'Eure, people went so far as to accuse her of being your brother's mistress!"

"Bernard's?"

"Yes, Bernard's."

"That's absolutely idiotic. Bernard is loyalty itself."

"That's what I've never stopped saying. Françoise has no idea what a good lawyer she's got in me. What is this little white cluster that shines so in the moonlight?"

"Convolvulus."

"Charming. They are the lilies of the field in the Bible, aren't they?"

"No, I think not. . . . Would you like us to rejoin the others?"

"You're in a frightful hurry, Antoine. I could stay out here in the garden with you the whole night long."

"I'm a bit chilly."

"Give me your hand. . . . Why, it is, it's ice cold! Would you like half of my wrap? . . . To think that we just missed living our whole life like this, pressed close to each other. . . . You've never regretted it, Antoine?"

"What do you want me to answer to that, Sabine? What about you? Are you happy?"

"Very happy . . . Like you, my poor dear Antoine, my happiness is built on despair. I make the best of things. You know? . . . But I want to be frank with you. For a long time, I

wished I were dead. It's better now. I'm more at peace. . . .
And you are, too."

"You understand me so well, Sabine."

"Don't forget that I loved you once, Antoine. That makes us
see another person very clearly. . . . Hold me, will you, the
path is very steep here. . . . Tell me, Antoine, when did you
discover what Françoise is really like? When did you see her as
she really is? . . . Because when you married her, you were
mad about her."

"I'm afraid there's a misunderstanding between us, Sabine.
I'd like you to understand. . . . I have, even today, a great
affection for Françoise. . . . Affection is a silly, weak word. I
love Françoise. But, as you were saying, the first two years of
our marriage were years of absolute adoration and of love that
I've every reason to believe was mutual."

"Really!"

"What do you mean, 'really'? No, no, Sabine, you're going
too far. . . . You won't take away my memories. Françoise has
given me proofs of love that the blindest of men could not
mistake. We lived for each other. We were happy only when we
were alone. . . . You don't believe me? But, Sabine, I know
what I'm saying. I was there. And you were not."

"I was there before you, my poor friend. I've known your
wife since she was a child. She and her sister Hélène were
brought up with me. I can still see Françoise in the courtyard
at St. Jean's—she was carrying a tennis racket—saying, 'I must
marry the older Quesnay boy, and I will.' "

"That isn't possible, Sabine. The Pascal-Bouchets and my
family had always been at odds. Françoise didn't even know
me. We met by chance, in 1917, when I'd been invalided out
and was on furlough."

"By chance? I suppose that's actually what you must have
believed. But I can still hear Hélène explaining the situation to
me. The truth of it is that when war broke out, their father, M.
Pascal-Bouchet, was ruined. He was both a libertine and a collector, and those are expensive hobbies. . . . His daughters
used to call him 'the Pasha,' and he deserved the name in more
ways than one. . . . Restoring the Château de Fleure had finished him. 'My dears,' he used to say to Françoise and Hélène,

'there are only two marriages around here that can save us: with the Thianges and with the Quesnays.' "

"Who told you that story?"

"I told you, the sisters themselves."

"And you didn't warn me?"

"I couldn't give a friend away. . . . And then, I didn't want to spoil her only chance. . . . Because Françoise—well, no one in Louviers or in Pont-de-l'Eure, unless he was a simple Don Juan like you, would have married her. . . . Norman families don't like bankruptcies."

"But M. Pascal-Bouchet never went bankrupt."

"That's true, and why didn't he? Because during the war, the government supported him, thanks to his other son-in-law, Maurice de Thianges, who was a deputy. . . . After the war, as you know better than anyone else, your grandfather finally helped him out. Which was exactly what he'd hoped for. . . . Oh, there is that divine scent again. We must be getting near the terrace. . . . Stop a moment, Antoine, I'm all out of breath."

"That's because you've been talking while you were climbing the cliff."

"Feel my heart, Antoine. It's pounding as if it would burst. . . . Wait. Wipe your mouth with my handkerchief. Women are so dreadful; they detect the slightest trace of lipstick. . . . No, not *your* handkerchief, after all! That would be—Really, if you were less of a model husband, you would have known that much long before this. . . . And brush your left shoulder; I may have left a touch of powder. . . . There . . . Now we're presentable again and can show our faces in public."

A few moments later, the visitors took their leave, the two women bidding each other the most tender good-bye.

Lord of the Shadows

IT IS A VERY CONVENIENT thing for an intelligent
woman who has known how to gather around her a circle of
distinguished friends whom she enjoys entertaining, also to
possess an immensely wealthy banker-husband who enables her
to furnish and maintain a great country house. Denise Holmann was such a woman. She had a delightful house in Normandy, at Saint-Arnoult, and every week during the summer,
from Saturday until Monday, she would invite friends to visit. I
used to meet the Bertrand Schmitts there, and the Christian
Ménétriers; occasionally Jenny, the novelist, and the actor Léon
Laurent, when he was not in a play; politicos like Monteix
or Lambert-Leclerc; and Dr. Bias. To this stable of "regulars"
Denise sometimes added less intimate guests, and so it happened that one Saturday I found there Fabert, the playwright,
whose *Carnaval* had been running for two years, and a less well-
known couple, whom I nevertheless very much liked, the Antoine Quesnays.

Fabert I knew very well. We'd both gone to the Lycée Jan-
son. His reputation as a Don Juan used to get a bit on my
nerves. Not that it was undeserved; he had had various of the
most gracious and remarkable women of our time, but what I
objected to was his talking about them, even naming names, in
what was the most fatuous poor taste. His successes were not
easy to account for. He was anything but handsome, but his tall,
broad-shouldered frame and rather brutal face created an impression of power that I think surprised and fascinated women.
His prestige as a man of the theater had procured him actresses,
and his prestige as a lover of actresses, still other triumphs. The
charm of his conversation did the rest. Fabert did know how to
tell a story. He talked like a dramatist; he knew how to build
up an effect and hit on the clever curtain line. Women were
never bored with him, which is rare. But most of all, he was
very attentive. Being lucky enough to work fast, he was able to
devote much of his time to women. And the truth of it is,
women belong to men who want them, who want them more
than anything else. Also, in the case of some women, money
does no harm, and Fabert was the most widely produced playwright in Paris.

His wife, Odette, was spending this particular weekend
with him at Saint-Arnoult. They weren't often seen together.
His thousand and one adventures took up a great deal of Fabert's time. At first, Odette had suffered. She had married for
love, and she had brought her husband a not inconsiderable
dowry at a time when he needed it. Little by little she became
resigned, and I even know that on occasion she would indulge
in a flight of her own, but on this score she was as discreet as
her husband was not. Her attitude toward Fabert was still one
of rather overawed admiration; she enjoyed all the privileges of
being the wife of a famous author; she took some odd satisfaction in observing the rapid succession of Robert's mistresses,
for, after all, she herself endured. That was her victory. Generally, Robert lived in a bachelor apartment, with whatever current favorite. Odette kept the handsome apartment on Rue de
la Muette, and Fabert would come there, on formal occasions,
to sit opposite her and preside over dinner. The silverware

shuttled back and forth between bachelor apartment and conjugal domicile.

Fabert dabbled now and then in the stock market, and dropped some of his author's royalties there. "Robert should never play the market," Odette said to me, with her calm shrewdness. "He's much too nervous." On the Saturday on which this story begins, I had taken a walk with him along the little byways of Saint-Arnoult, and he had extolled the middle-class competencies of his wife. "Ah, if I'd followed Odette's advice and invested in an apartment building, I'd have saved my capital. . . . Poor little Odette, I may ruin her yet. She'd be satisfied with a one-room fifth-floor walkup, provided I came to see her now and then. . . . She keeps that big apartment on de la Muette so people can't say that when I left her, I asked her to reduce her scale of living. . . . Really, she does live only for me. You know, it's touching."

Actually, Odette had put considerable sums of money into her apartment to have walls knocked down and Robert's former study transformed into a boudoir-sitting room for herself. But Robert, who spent fortunes on women, was fond of saying, appreciatively, how disinterested they were. He wanted to believe he was loved for himself; he managed to persuade himself that this was true, and it was true in part. But only in part. When he invested a million francs in a couturier's house, the head of which happened to have a very pretty wife, he took pains to proclaim, "It's no gift, it's an investment." Odette, seemingly ingenuous but utterly practical, had her clothes made by the designer for nothing. Fabert's only regret with regard to his wife was that, in her difficult situation, she exhibited a little too much serenity. At the outset of their marriage, when she had wept without remission, she had inspired more pride, therefore more interest, in him. For all his praise now, he seemed to me a bit irritated that she should be looking so well.

"But after all," he said to me, "Odette can't be really unhappy, since she's putting on weight. . . . What do you think?"

I actually did think that she was no longer unhappy, but I refrained from saying so. Anyhow, he was already taken up by a fresh idea. "Who are the Quesnays?" he asked. "She's delicious, that girl."

"Françoise Quesnay is no 'girl.' She must be thirty."

"The best age," he said, with relish. "The body is still young, the mind has matured. The age when infidelities allow for a bravura performance . . . What kind of man is the *marito*? I tried to talk to him at tea. A mute! Is he intelligent?"

"Intelligent? Yes, Antoine is intelligent, but terribly shy. He wouldn't dare say a word in front of you."

"Funny," Fabert said absently. "I haven't met such a pretty woman in a long time."

"They've never lived in Paris. He was in business, not very far from here, in Pont-de-l'Eure. They're childhood friends of our hostess. Antoine left his factory after the war to write, and since then they've been living in the Midi."

"What? That mute writes? What on earth can he write?"

"Books on history. With emphasis on the economic and social aspects. Not bad at all."

Fabert began to laugh his very special laugh, a kind of triumphant neigh.

"Mute, shy, and a historian. She will deceive him."

He loved to make incisive diagnoses of emotional situations in the style of a great doctor.

"That's not likely," I told him. "Denise has told me about their marriage. It's a Montague-Capulet story, so there's a strong bond."

"A matter of technique . . . Well, my weekend work's cut out for me."

Whereupon his quick mind leaped to a different subject:

"By the way, do you have a friend in America whom you could wire for a tip on wheat futures? Last month, in New York, I met some financial wizard who made me speculate on wheat's going up, since when it has been steadily going down. I'm losing eight hundred dollars a point."

I confessed to knowing few grain brokers, and we turned back to Saint-Arnoult.

Evenings on the terrace at Saint-Arnoult combined charm and a kind of grandeur. In the foreground, to the left, a meadow planted with apple trees sloped toward the valley floor; on the right, another meadow, bare of trees, fell away in a symmetrical curve flanked by a border of pines. These two lovely lines crossed near the center of the scene, and the simplicity, the sweep of the earth, and the deep country silence gave the landscape a singular tranquillity. The air was fragrant with honeysuckle and mint. Overhead, the stars invited the dreamer to metaphysical reveries.

Fabert, his powerful mug incongruously lighted by a moonbeam, was recounting some escapades, all very flattering to him, for the benefit of Denise, Françoise Quesnay, and Isabelle Schmitt; whether they were listening with admiration or amusement I couldn't tell. Odette was talking in a low voice with Bertrand Schmitt. My armchair was in the shadow and a little to one side, next to Antoine Quesnay, who seemed emboldened by the darkness.

"That Fabert and his women," he said to me. "To hear him, you'd think he was the only . . . Why, even I—and I stay clear of that kind of thing—even I sometimes have the chance or the impulse. . . . The other day, the wife of a friend of mine practically threw herself in my arms. . . . Yes, the other night, a night like this one but even more beautiful, because it happened at home, in the Midi . . . I pushed her away. Oh, gently. But she was furious. I said to her, 'Look, you're a friend of Françoise. There's such a thing as loyalty.' And she answered, 'You don't know anything about life. You'll make women, even your own wife, hate you.' Maybe she was right. I'm still a child about some things. . . . And yet it's so different from what Françoise tells me. . . . Will she someday— For me it's hard to imagine all these men and women running after each other, betraying each other, accepting the fact of being betrayed. I can't be happy that way. I have to be clear in spirit, at peace with myself, direct."

"Because you're a social animal. But that kind of equilibrium is becoming rare. In almost everyone, the physical and the moral animal are in conflict. It makes for problems, but that's the way it is. You're not going to change men—or women, either."

"Especially not women," he said. "They're terrible."

I looked at his wife leaning toward Fabert. Three things shone in the moonlight: her bracelet, her black-and-white necklace, her eyes. Dressed for the sacrifice, I thought, and a ravishing victim.

Now Fabert was talking about death. We moved nearer to the group.

"If," Fabert was saying, "if I had good reason for being dissatisfied with life—say I had a succession of flops, or I lost all my money—then I would kill myself. The only thing about suicide that makes me hesitate is how, is the method. I'd rather fancy walking out into the sea, walking out and out until I was submerged. That would take guts, wouldn't it?"

"Only the moment would come when you would stop walking," Dr. Bias said. "Let me suggest a more practical method. Lie down on the beach when the tide is out, take a heavy dose of sleeping pills, and the sea will cover you."

"That's very ingenious," I said. "That wouldn't even be suicide. The sea would have killed you."

"One cannot fool God," Christian Ménétrier said soberly.

Fabert laughed his satanic laugh.

"I like that idea!" he said. "Doctor, thank you. But I'll take a rug along. Wet sand? Not for me!"

After a moment's reflection, he added:

"A beautiful rug . . . Chinese or Persian . . . And I'll take Odette along."

Half humorously, half seriously, Odette said:

"Thank you, no. Count me out this time, please. Robert changes his mind so easily that he'd make me swallow his Gardénal, and suddenly decide to go on living himself. How would that make me look? Furthermore, I'm a believer. I'm afraid of the consequences."

Whereupon everyone began to tell stories about death. Christian Ménétrier described a children's party. A magician had performed, and after the usual card and juggling tricks, he had announced he was going to make himself disappear. He threw a blanket over his head that covered him entirely; then he said, "Presto! I vanish!" The blanket was seen to collapse; people sensed a man's body lying on the ground. For a minute or two there was a surprised silence, and then the head of the house said, "We see you. This isn't very funny, and it certainly isn't fun for the children." Nothing moved. The magician was dead.

"What an act!" Françoise said, laughing.

Fabert took it amiss that another man should capture the attention of a woman he had singled out for himself. It grated on him that a story told by Christian should have amused Françoise, and he immediately began another tale.

"A couple of friends of mine," he said, "used to play chamber music every week. The husband played the violin, the wife the piano, and two professional musicians rounded out the group. One evening, their usual cellist was sick, so he sent a substitute, who suddenly collapsed while they were playing a quartet. They bent over him. He had stopped breathing. My friends were terribly upset. They called a doctor, who came, confirmed the death, and advised them to notify the family. What family? They scarcely knew the dead man's name. They went through his pockets to find a name or address. Nothing. They phoned the police, and the officer on duty said that it was too late, that someone would come by next morning. What to do? They stretched the corpse out on a couch and respectfully played a Beethoven trio. Around midnight, the second violin had to leave, and the head of the house said to him, 'Listen, with the best will in the world, I can't keep him here. Tomorrow the children have to come into this room, and it will be a very unhealthy shock for them. . . . Take him to the morgue.' The other man protested, but finally gave in. The two of them carried the body downstairs and went in search of a taxi. When the driver saw that one of his fares was dead, he refused to take him. 'I don't want any trouble,' he said. They took the body back into the house, stashed it in a corner formed by the elevator shaft, and left a note on the concierge's doormat: 'Be careful tomorrow morning when you sweep the hall. There's a corpse under the stairway.' "

"How funny!" Denise said. "And yet, why funny? It's more lugubrious."

"People laugh only at what they fear," Bertrand said. "Death is comic because we fear it."

Fabert, wanting to hold the floor at any price, launched

quickly into a series of stories about sudden or bizarre deaths. "Let's admit it," he said, "to die in a stranger's house is simply bad manners. Yet I knew a boy who was exquisitely polite but who—quite involuntarily, of course—was guilty of such a breach. After lunch at the Rothschilds', as coffee was being served, he pressed his hand to his heart, said, 'I do beg your pardon most awfully,' and dropped dead."

Fabert passed, with mounting verve, from funereal stories to tales of gambling and love affairs. Around one, Bertrand, who did not like to stay up late, suggested it might be time to go to bed. Fabert, who was terrified of being alone at night, had a moment's anguish, and then proposed reciting his new play, which he did brilliantly, acting out the scenes, imitating the different voices, and laughing at his own inventions. He managed in this way to keep us there until two. The men yawned and exchanged impatient glances, shaking their heads in despair; the women listened, captivated and submissive.

The next day I learned that Antoine Quesnay would be leaving in the afternoon. He had to be in Paris for a dinner engagement, and the Bertrand Schmitts had offered to bring Françoise with them on Monday morning. I took Denise aside:

"Frankly, Denise, I don't like it. . . . You know Fabert. He talked to me about Françoise with that special fever of excitement that in him bodes no good. If he gets her alone one evening, he is going to make a play for her."

"We'll all be here."

"Denise! We've all had experience with his tricks. He'll find a dozen ways to get this poor woman out into the garden, in the moonlight—"

"There's Odette."

"You know as well as I that Odette never interferes. Have you put the Faberts up in the same bedroom, at least?"

"No, he hates that. . . . She is in the loggia, on the second floor, and he has the blue room on the ground floor."

"So?"

"But, my dear, what concern is it of yours? Are you Françoise's guardian?"

"Up to a point, yes. And I like her husband, who's a very good fellow. He's more than that—"

"A little boring, a bit of a noodle—"

"I don't find him so, unless you call a noodle a man who has the flaw of adoring his own wife. That would surprise me in you, with your love of 'great spirits.' "

" 'Noodle,' " she said, "in my vocabulary has a nuance of affection. . . . Seriously, what do you want me to do? I didn't advise Antoine to leave, and out of courtesy I had to invite Françoise to stay on."

"You could have put her on her guard against Fabert, whom she doesn't know at all. You still could."

"Fabert is my guest, as you are. I don't see that I have the right either to disparage him or to play him a bad turn. Furthermore, I quite like him, despite his faults—or maybe because of them. He is outsized, morally as well as physically. That isn't usual."

"There's nothing for it, you know. All women, even the most intelligent, fall for his humbug."

"I will quote your favorite author," Denise said. " 'Women are no more duped by the games men play than they are by their own.' "

"No more duped, but duped as much . . . Oh, all right. Since you don't want to or you can't warn Françoise, I'll take care of it."

"Do your noble best, my dear. It won't change a thing, but you'll have a clear conscience. Careful! Here comes her husband."

Antoine Quesnay was walking across the lawn toward us. I looked at him attentively. "He's worth a hundred of Fabert," I said to myself. He made his excuses again to our hostess: "A dinner with some old friends from the war . . . I'd accepted months ago. I can't say no now."

Denise went off to give some instructions to the servants, and I sat down in an armchair by Antoine. He was in a mood for confidences, and I must say I liked him very much. I asked what had made him give up his business. "For a long time," he said, "I thought that the active life would be a healthy opium for me. Then I stopped believing in what I was doing, and I grew careless. I tried the writing as a solution, but I often get tired of that, too. The truth is, the only thing that takes me out of myself is love. That brings a few perfect moments—brief moments, it's true—but they and the waiting for them are enough to give some value to life. That's why I chose to live in the Midi with Françoise. I really want nothing but her. But often I'm afraid that she's bored. Ah, life is such trouble."

"You don't have enough confidence in yourself," I said to him. "Other people, when they judge us, never go above our own evaluation of ourselves."

"That I know. I don't think very much of myself, it's true. . . . Or rather, for me to be happy I have to be attached to something bigger than I am. During the war, I wasn't unhappy in the Army when I had the kind of superior I could respect. . . . Nor at the plant, in the days when my grandfather ruled things with an iron hand. At bottom, most men feel this need. The people who join choral groups or football teams all feel this need of a faith. But I believed that love for a woman could take the place of faith. Now I sometimes ask myself whether only the love for God . . . I don't know. The trouble is, one would have to be sure."

He left after lunch. We all walked out with him to his car, and he held Françoise in a long embrace. I was watching Fabert. As the car pulled away, he laughed his triumphant whinny.

I had promised myself to have a talk with Françoise. Chance, with perhaps an assist from her, stood me in good stead. There was one spot at Saint-Arnoult that I had picked out where I could read in peace. A fairly comfortable bench, painted the ritual green, invited the passerby to sit down before a fine view of genista-covered slopes. A clump of lindens shaded it. The branches were drowsily alive with the humming of bees. I had brought with me a volume of Balzac and was rereading for perhaps the hundredth time the *Secrets de la Princesse de Cadignan* when I vaguely sensed that someone was coming. I looked up and saw Françoise, fresh and smiling, walking toward me.

"So!" she said. "You've discovered this retreat, too."

"I discovered it long before you. . . . I've been coming to

Saint-Arnoult for ten years. You aren't taking a siesta like the others?"

"No, I felt full of energy and very much pleased with the world, so I decided to take a walk. . . . May I sit down? Is this paint a threat to my dress?"

"A pity if it were; the dress is too becoming. But there's no danger. This bench hasn't been painted in years."

"It's true," she said, sitting down, "that you've become well acquainted with the house, and I can understand why. It's very pleasant, and Denise, I find, is a divine hostess. If you want to be alone, she leaves you alone. If you feel like conversation, the house is full of interesting people. How amusing that Fabert is! Last night I felt as if I were watching one of his plays being performed by a full cast of wonderful actors."

Far away, in the valley, the clock in the church tower slowly rang the hour.

"Yes," I said, "Fabert is witty and talented, but he is a very dangerous man."

She laughed.

"You men, you do amuse me. You're the third person since this morning to warn me about Fabert."

"Who were the other two?"

"Bertrand and Christian, of course."

"And not your husband."

"Poor Antoine. No, he knows how to suffer in silence."

"Do you know I am devoted to your husband? I talked with him a bit this morning. He has a quality, a depth of feeling, that is surprising."

"He's very nice, I know."

"He is more than nice."

"I know that also. . . . But you started to say something about Fabert. Why do you think he's dangerous? And for whom? For me, I suppose?"

"For you as for all other women. Picture to yourself, Françoise, a man who is utterly without scruple in love. I use the word 'love' for lack of a better, for he scarcely 'loves' a woman. . . . He chases them, the way other men hunt pheasant or deer. A good game bag gives him a statistical pleasure . . . And the briefer pleasure also, no doubt. But once the prey has been downed and recorded, it no longer interests him. He moves on to the next. I've known him since we were both boys, and I could scarcely tell you how many women I've seen whose lives have been ruined by him. They've lost husband, children, self-respect. . . . Several have tried to kill themselves. That sends his pride skyrocketing."

"All this is most romantic. Fabert, in a word, is Satan himself."

"Exactly. Yes, he is Satan, who rebels against God's will and who loves evil."

"A very attractive Satan . . ."

"Satan is a gentleman. Everyone knows that."

"Do you believe in the Devil?"

"I believe in him when I see him. Look at his eyes. . . . Listen to me, Françoise. Don't you find a man diabolic if, without any feeling of love whatever, he sets about seducing a woman who's been virtuous all her life? A man who has set rules for this little war—or tested recipes, if you like—and who coolly chooses the weapon best suited to bring his victim down?"

"How do you know that he chooses 'coolly' and not for love?"

"Because he's told me so, because he boasts about it! . . . Listen, would you like me to tell you what's going to happen between him and you?"

She looked at me, laughing.

"Nothing is going to happen. Why do you pretend that a poor little country housewife will interest a man who has heaps of more flattering—and more brilliant—women?"

"Fishing for compliments? You interest him, one, because you are beautiful—'by all accounts beautiful,' as Christian says. Second, precisely because you are not from the big city. He's skimmed the cream of the Paris crop long since. Now, to restock his harem, he's reduced to debutantes, but they're not always easily come by. The small-town woman—she's new, she's not been tried yet. If, by way of a bonus, she is also virtuous, she becomes the most desirable prey of all. The Devil needs good souls; they're the only ones he genuinely enjoys tempting."

She leaned down, picked a blade of grass, and flicked off an ant that had ventured onto her skirt.

"A good soul," she said. "What does that mean? . . . Oh, I'm confused . . . unsure. . . . We're poor things, we women. We need someone who is strong to support, to steady us. You speak very warmly about my husband, and you're right. Antoine is a very good man. But a support? No. That isn't to say, by any means, that I don't love him, but—"

"That's all I was afraid of. You are available."

"I've said nothing of the kind."

"You have, without knowing it. So you fit Fabert's classification."

"What do you mean, 'Fabert's classification'?"

"That's his word for it. With his men friends, he is very free in explaining that in the game of love, as in the game of chess, there is a small number of openings, the classic gambits one must know by heart, each of which is adapted to a specific type of woman. I don't exactly remember his list, but more or less it amounts to this. Available women or, if you prefer, accessible women, can be divided into sensual women, maternal women, and intellectual women. Each of these classes must be attacked differently—"

"Who are the inaccessible women?"

"Women in love, women strongly attached to another man, and the brood mares, the ones who care only about their children. But that's another story. Coming back to the vulnerable women: for each type, Fabert has a ploy that is always the same and, he says, works perfectly."

"For example?"

"I don't know them by heart. To the maternal ones, he complains of being, appearances to the contrary, a man who is very much alone, ill, unhappy, a man who needs to be consoled. They cannot deny their vocation; they fly to the help of every adult male who claims he's a child. That was the case with George Sand, who was incapable of refusing herself to an invalid. . . . To the sensual ones, Fabert says, 'You don't know what pleasure is. . . . Oh, yes, I know, you have a husband, a lover—and he's not bad, I grant you. But I've talked with him about love, and he knows nothing about it. Nothing! Real love

is not an instinct, not even a sentiment. It's an art and a technique. I could make you feel, give you a happiness that you've
never dreamed of. . . .' That's the general idea. Only he devel-
ops it much better . . . and at greater length . . . and with
more passion."

"An art? And why not? After all, he's got so much experience—"

"Françoise! You've been snared! So soon?"

"Not at all. I'm playing with you. And what does he say to
the intellectual ones?"

"The truth is, I've forgotten, but I imagine it runs like this:
'You are too good for the world you live in. You're not appre-
ciated. You need a man who, instead of smothering you, en-
courages your gifts and abilities.' At which point, he volunteers.
In all three cases, of course, you must add one more ingredient
—the confession of an admiration such as he's never experienced before. Your hair, your eyes, your body, your grace, and
whatnot whatnot . . . Season with moonlight and serve hot.
Those are Fabert's recipes."

"I don't see anything very new about them," she said, "or
very dangerous. We've all heard them before."

"Perhaps, but not said with such drive, with such drama.
The Devil has his own devices. If I ask you to be careful, it's
because I know all his tricks. Tonight, for example, he will
surely ask you to take a walk with him. I hope you'll refuse."

"And if I accepted," she said, "which class do you think he'd
put me in?"

"He hasn't confided in me. But an expert has an instinct,
and his choices aren't often wrong."

"Which class would you put me in?"

"An expert doesn't talk, either. But you'll see what his game
is going to be from the way he moves his first pawns. Or rather
I hope you won't see and that you'll be prudent enough never
to be alone with him."

She stood up.

"Would you like to walk a bit? This is a light dress, and I'm
not too warm."

We walked in the direction of the village, along a road bordered by high banks covered with blackberry bushes. I looked

at Françoise out of the corner of my eye—the curly blond hair, the profile at once firm and soft, the fine carriage of the head— and I thought to myself: This charming woman simply must not be allowed to throw herself away on a man who'll have forgotten her in six months.

"Do you know the story of Silvia Noiretelle?"

"No. Don't forget I'm a small-town woman. The story has some connection with Fabert?"

"More than a connection. It's a story in which Fabert was the hero. Or the villain, rather. Silvia was a ravishing woman, very serious, who had married Hubert Noiretelle, the big engineer and bridge builder. The ideal marriage. Two children. The husband away from home a little too often because some of his projects were abroad. But she was sensible, prudent, like some of Giraudoux's women, busy with her children, surrounded by a pleasant family. In a word, an idyllic situation—"

"Until one day the big bad wolf—"

"Right. It happened, unfortunately, that Fabert met Silvia at the home of friends. Immediately the same avalanche of questions rolled over them that I had to endure in connection with you. Where is her husband? Why haven't I met her before?"

"He asked you such things about me?"

"What do you think? Those and a lot more. But to come back to Silvia. Fabert went over and sat beside her and played up to her, and she was flattered. The next day he laid siege in earnest. Telephone calls, flowers, theater tickets—nets, mines, and countermines. The husband was in Turkey. Silvia was free, too free, but for a while she put up a heroic defense, until one day she made the mistake of going to Fabert's house, and she became his mistress. It was too bad, the way it is always too bad to see something fine tarnished and spoiled. However, with another man, the affair could have been kept secret. But for Fabert, it's an even greater pleasure to broadcast a conquest than to make it. When Noiretelle got back, all Paris knew and was talking about the affair. Silvia herself, levelheaded Silvia, was behaving in the wildest way. If her husband hadn't discovered the truth, I believe she would have shouted it at him herself."

"She was in love, that's all."

"One of Fabert's plays was about to be produced in London.

He proposed that she go over with him. She hesitated a long time. She knew it would mean a break with her husband and with her family. Fabert was ferocious, the way he insisted on this proof of passion, and she gave in."

"And her husband rejected her?"

"No. Her husband was a generous man. He wanted to give her a chance to come back to their children, so he covered up for her absence at first. But a long series of catastrophes bedeviled them. . . . Fabert spells trouble. . . . An auto accident while she was with him, which created a scandal and left her disfigured . . . Exasperated in-laws demanding a separation . . . Then Jacques, her little boy, got meningitis and died while she was in the States. When the situation became too absurd and intolerable, they divorced. And presently Silvia was completely abandoned by Fabert, who had found a younger woman."

Françoise, who was bantering no longer, sighed and leaned down to pick a four-leaf clover.

"What a tragic affair," she said. "What became of Silvia?"

"She became one of those bitter, lonely women, like so many others you see in Paris. . . . The end of the story is quite horrible. One evening I went to the Comédie-Française and during intermission was standing in the corridor, talking with Fabert. She walked by us—ravaged, her face graven with deep wrinkles. He saw her, and he let out that devilish neigh of his. 'Jezebel!' he said. 'I call her Jezebel because she is always "as on the day of her death pompously bedecked." She hates me. But she's a whore, that's what she is.' That's how Don Juan treats his victims."

Françoise was silent for a long time. A car passed us, leaving behind a trail of dust and fumes.

"Let's turn back," Françoise said. "I'm tired."

The evening out on the terrace was more beautiful than ever. The leaves were motionless. Now and then one heard some sound—the call of a night bird, a dog barking down in the village, the whistle of a train in the valley. The Saint-Arnoult guests had broken up into little groups and were talking in low voices. I had stayed apart, lying back in my chair and watching the stars, and the immensity of the sky reminded me that our earthly troubles are quite futile. Fabert had sat down by Françoise and was talking to her animatedly. I was sorry to notice how attentively she was listening.

Everything around us is great except ourselves, I thought. What can one more conquest matter to Fabert in comparison to this infinite, mysterious universe? But he's spinning his nets as carefully as a spider; he wheels around women like a bat chasing insects at night. But after all, what does it matter if every species has its instincts?

Then I thought:

It matters a lot when it's a question of the human species. Poor Françoise . . . I hoped I'd saved her.

Denise called out to me:

"Why the splendid isolation? Are you dreaming?"

"Yes," I said, "a nightmare."

Later, as the group separated, Françoise and Fabert bid each other good night so ostentatiously that my fears were confirmed. When I got to my room, I went over to the window and saw two shadows, one gigantic, moving toward the woods. I promised myself to watch for their return, but I fell asleep.

The next morning I didn't see them. They had gone off together in Fabert's car. Françoise had left a note for the Schmitts: "Don't be worried about me. I had to leave suddenly for Paris, and M. Fabert has been kind enough to take me. He asks, will you please let his wife know; she is still sleeping."

The outcome is only too easily imagined: the harvest of miseries that Fabert has sowed in the life of every woman who's had the fatal distinction of pleasing him. In the case of Françoise Quesnay, however, the worst was avoided thanks to the extreme goodness of her husband, who was able, with dignity, to save his home if not his love. A long time went by without my seeing them. Then, some three years after that night at Saint-Arnoult, I went down to Nice during the winter, and Françoise was staying at the same hotel. At first I didn't recognize her; she had changed so. She came up to me with perfect naturalness and almost at once talked about our last meeting.

"That star-filled night," she said. "I'll never forget it. You were too good a prophet."

"Unfortunately, yes. I saw you go out together in the moonlight. And naturally he told you—"

"What you had foretold, word for word."

"And yet you listened to him."

"Ah!" she said. "It was so well played."

Ariane, My Sister . . .

Evreux, October 7, 1932

THÉRÈSE TO JÉRÔME

I've read your book. . . . Yes, read it as I've read all the
others. And don't worry; I thought it was fine. I think that if I
were you, I would ask myself, "Did she find it rang true? Did it
make her suffer to read it?" But you don't ask yourself such
questions. You're sure, are you not, that you've been more than
just, more than magnanimous. Yet what tone do you choose to
take in talking about our marriage?

"In my eagerness to pursue an imaginary woman who would
be a companion in work as well as a lover, I had neglected to
observe the real Thérèse. The early days of our life together
were to reveal to me a being who was at once foreseeable and
surprising. I was a man of the people and an artist; in Thérèse
I encountered an authentically upper-class woman. She had all
the virtues and failings of her class. My wife was faithful, unas-

suming, even intelligent in her way. But, alas, one could not imagine a person less fashioned to share a life of struggle and spiritual searching. . . ."

Are you sure about this, Jérôme? And was it a life of "spiritual searching" that you bound me to when I finally gave in to your pleading and, against my parents' advice, agreed to marry you? However that may be, Jérôme, what I did then took some courage. As far as the public went, you were an unknown. Your political ideas infuriated and frightened my family. I left a rich home and a closely knit family to lead a hard life with you. Did I object when you declared after a year that you couldn't work in Paris and dragged me off to your house in the provinces, to that lonely, harsh countryside, with one terrified little maid— the only human being I met in those days who was more of an outcast than I? I put up with everything, accepted everything. For a long time I even pretended to be happy.

But what woman could be happy with you? Sometimes I laugh—bitterly, yes—when the newspapers talk about your strength, your moral courage. Your strength! . . . I have never, Jérôme, met a weaker person than you. Never. Not one. I write this without any hostility. The time for rancor is past, and since I no longer see you, my nerves have steadied again. But it's good that you should know. The perpetual anxiety, the nervous fear of people, the morbid need of praise, the childish terror of sickness—no, these have nothing to do with strength, although the response these miseries provoke in you (your novels, I mean) give your disciples the illusion of strength.

Strong? How could you be, when you're so vulnerable that if a book fails it makes you literally sick? So vain that the slightest word of praise from any fool makes you immediately doubt his foolishness? It's true that two or three times in your life you have fought for ideas. But that was only after patient calculation, and because you were sure by then that those ideas would prevail. In one of the rare moments when you ever confided in me, you made a confession that you, with your caution, must have instantly regretted but that I, in my bitterness, carefully preserved.

"The older a writer grows," you told me, "the more advanced his opinions must be. It's the only way he can keep the young people with him."

Poor young people! When they've got so naïvely, passionately drunk on your *Messages,* little did they imagine with what contrived fervor and meticulous Machiavellianism you wrote them.

Not strong, then. Nor manly . . . Yes, that also must be said, no matter how cruel it may seem. You were never a lover, my dear Jérôme. After our divorce, I discovered physical love; I learned to enjoy its fullness, its peace, and to know the beauty of night, when a woman, fulfilled, sleeps in the arms of a vigorous man. So long as I lived with you, what I knew of love was bleak imitations, pitiful parodies. I didn't suspect how poorly off I was; I was young and quite unaware. When you told me that an artist must husband his physical ardor, I believed you, but I would have liked at least to sleep beside you. I wanted the warmth of another body, a little tenderness, a little understanding. But you fled from my arms, my bed—my room, even. And you had no idea how miserable I was.

You lived only for yourself, for the clamor around your name, for that strange emotion your personality aroused in women readers—you knowing all the while that that personality was not the real you. A half-dozen unfriendly lines in a paper worried you more than the unhappiness of a woman who loved you. If ever I saw you concerned about me, it was when some politicians or writers whose opinions mattered to you had promised to come dine with us. Then you wanted me to shine. The evening before these visits, you would talk to me for hours; there was no question of work's being sacred at such times. You explained exactly what I should and what I should not say, and what were the venerable crotchets of this powerful critic and the greedy appetite of that popular leader. You wanted our house to look poor at such times, because that fitted in with your preachments, but the food and drink had to be delicious because great men are still men.

Do you remember, Jérôme, when you began to make money, lots of money? You were both very happy and a little uncomfortable. Happy because at heart you're a little French peasant craving one more acre of land, and uneasy because your ideas didn't square with wealth. Oh, how amused I used to be by the transparent devices your greed conjured up to quiet your conscience. "I give practically everything away," you would say. But it was I who managed the accounts, and I knew what you kept back. Sometimes I would remark, very innocently, "You know, Jérôme, you're becoming very rich."

You would sigh:

"The system—I hate it. But what can one do? As long as it exists, one has to learn to live with it."

How unfortunate that the fashionable thing was to oppose the system, so that the more you attacked it, the richer you became. What a cruel, cruel fate! Poor Jérôme! However, it must be admitted that your orthodoxy was impeccable where I was concerned. Like all women who are deprived of love, when I saw you were a millionaire I began to want luxuries—furs, jewelry. I freely admit that your resistance to this was of the most high-minded order.

"A mink coat!" you would say. "A pearl necklace! You! What are you thinking of? Can't you see what my enemies would say if my wife were to become like all those middle-class women whom I've become famous by satirizing?"

Yes, I could see. I understood that the wife of Jérôme Vence had to be above suspicion. I took the full measure of my indecent, greedy appetites. It was true, of course, that you had your own toys—your stocks and bonds and properties. But bank accounts are invisible, whereas diamonds glitter for everyone to see. You were right, Jérôme, as always.

Once again, I accepted everything, everything, just as I accept this last book. I hear people around me exclaim admiringly over your daring opinions, your goodness (you are one of the most truly evil people I've known), and your generosity to me. I say nothing. Or sometimes I agree. "Yes," I say, "he treated me very well. I have nothing to complain of." Am I right to let you off so easily? Is it wise to let this legend of which you are the hero grow and spread? Must one tolerate the fact that young people accept as their mentor a man I know is not a man? Sometimes I ask myself this. But I don't do anything. I will not even write a memoir of my own to set the facts right. You have filled me with a disgust for words. Good-bye, Jérôme.

II

JÉRÔME TO THÉRÈSE

You wanted to hurt me the way you used to when you lived with me. . . . Be happy in the thought that you have succeeded. You do not know yourself, Thérèse. You think of yourself as the victim, but you're the torturer. It took me a long time to understand you. I accepted you for what you pretended to be, a gentle woman, the eternal sacrificial lamb. Only little by little I discovered your insatiable thirst for scenes, and your cruelty and deviousness. Because you were humiliated as a child by your clumsy parents, you wanted your revenge from life. And you took your revenge on the people who were unlucky enough to love you. When I met you I believed in myself. You wanted to strip me of that self-confidence; you attacked my mind, my ideas, my body. You made me ridiculous in my own eyes. Even today, now that I'm quit of you, I am ashamed when I remember how your bluntness secretly hurt me.

How you used to look at me out of those eyes, those implacable eyes of yours! "You're so small," you would say, "so very small." That was true. I was short and, like most sedentary people, I had more fat than muscle. Was that a crime? Or even a defect? I could see so clearly that in your eyes it was, at the very least, ridiculous. Love calls for a giving of one's self, for trust. Two people drop, together with their clothes, their fears, their vulnerabilities, their shame. Lying beside you, I felt I was being judged by an enemy who never lost control of his senses, who was always observing me with cold lucidity. How could I have been a good lover for a woman I was afraid of? How could I have become for you what a man in love should be—a being of instinct and audacity—when in my partner I found only constraint and prudery? You reproach me with having fled from your bed. Are you sure you did not drive me from it?

"However that may be," you write, "what I did in marrying you took some courage." But didn't you always know that I would quickly win a place for myself? You chose me, Thérèse, because you had found in me something real, something alive, which in your family was not exactly usual. And perhaps also because you sensed that I was vulnerable, and because to wound another person is your keenest, your only pleasure. It's hard for me, now, to remember the man I was when I met you. . . . A fairly exceptional man, it seems to me, a man who had faith in his own ideas and in his own genius. That man you did everything to kill. When I thought I was happy, you murdered me with pity. How strange! You married me for my strength, yet it was that strength that you set on so furiously. But one mustn't look for any self-awareness or logic in your actions. You are miserable, like so many women, the slave of your organs and your nerves, warped by some adolescent drama, and enraged by its failure. So long as you lived with your parents, they bore the brunt of the diffused hate that is in you; from the day I became your only companion, I was the one you persecuted.

"A brand-new tirade," you'll say. "An indictment improvised to answer my letter."

And you will triumphantly show my book around, especially the passage that you so carefully underscored: "My wife was faithful, unassuming, intelligent. . . ." Take care, Thérèse, not to believe too unreservedly in a comment that was too indulgent. Since you force me back to my last line of defense, since you oblige me to use all my weapons, I will admit that that phrase is a lie. A conscious lie. I wanted to seem to be generous. I was wrong. Any hypocrisy spoils a work of art. I should have described with pitiless harshness the monster that you are, and the harm you have done me.

"Faithful? . . ." I knew long before I left you that you had stopped being that. But why should I write as much in a public document? Why should I bestow on you the prestige of unfaithfulness at my own expense? "Unassuming? . . ." You have a demonic pride, and the urge to dominate, to obliterate, explains most of your behavior. "Intelligent? . . ." Yes, a great many people now think that you are intelligent. Indeed, that's what you have become. But do you know why? Because I formed you. Because for twenty years you got from me everything you lacked—ideas, cultivated interests, language. Even today, after this long separation, you live on the breath you sucked from me, and your letter, which you thought would finish me off, owes whatever vigor it has—to whom? To me.

Vanity? No, pride. I need to repeat to myself that I believe in myself in order to be delivered of your evil spell. I don't want to take up your letter point by point. That would mean playing your game, and inflicting useless pain on myself into the bargain. But one word more. "Sometimes I laugh bitterly," you say, "when the papers talk about your strength. . . . I've never met a weaker person than you." You know perfectly well, Thérèse, that there you are attacking me on two different levels, pretending they are only one. You have no right to do this. Whatever kind of man I was in my relations with you concerns only us. I now believe, as you do, that in that battle I was too weak. It was out of pity, but pity is not always innocent of cowardice. Only you also pretend not to know that a man can be weak in his personal life and still create a strong work of art. And very often it is because he was weak in life that his work is robust. What young people see in my work—rest assured, Thérèse—is there. And thinking more carefully now, if you did make me suffer so much, perhaps now that I have been freed of it I should thank you for it. An immense part of what I can be I owe to your faithful hatred.

You are, above all else, a destroyer. This is the form your spite has taken in you. Because you have not been happy, you hate happiness. Because you are not a sensual woman, you despise pleasure. But spite makes you a penetrating, passionate observer. Like rays that can reveal a flaw in a huge block of steel, the one flaw that threatens its solidity, you go straight to a man's weak point. It's a remarkable gift, Thérèse, but it is also an accursed gift. Because you forget that virtues are realities, that iron girders do resist the weather. The weaknesses in me that you point out so cruelly do exist, I know. You've seen clear and true, with singular sharpness. But they exist buried in a mass so heavy and so resistant that no human force can shatter it. You yourself failed, and my work and my spirit both survived your baleful reign.

"What woman," you write, "could be happy with you?" I

want you to know that since our divorce I also have found love. With a simple, good wife I have finally known peace. I can guess your smile: "Yes, but what about her?" If you saw Nadine for a single moment you would not question her happiness. Not all women need, as do you, to kill in order to live. Whom will you destroy now?

III

Paris, February 2, 1936

NADINE TO THÉRÈSE

You will perhaps be surprised, Madame, to receive a letter from me. Legend has it that we must be enemies. I do not know how you may feel about this. As for me, not only do I not hate you but rather I feel a kind of involuntary sympathy. If once, at the time of your divorce, you were for a few months the Adversary, the adversary that had at all costs to be driven from the heart of the man I had chosen, very soon after my marriage you became an invisible companion. No doubt the wives of Bluebeard meet, in a semilife, in the memory of the spouse they have shared. In spite of himself, Jérôme used to talk to me about you. I would try to imagine what your attitude had been toward that strange, difficult man, and often I thought that your hardness had been more adroit than my patience.

Since Jérôme's death I have had to put his papers in order. Among them I found many letters from you. One in particular moved me. It is the letter you wrote him five years ago, after the publication of his *Journal*. I had often said to him that chapter would offend you. I had begged him to leave it out. But weak as he was, he was also of an obstinacy and a quite remarkable courage when it was a question of his work. Your response was brutal. Perhaps you will be surprised by my saying that I find it quite fair.

Do not think I would betray Jérôme now that he is dead. I loved him, and I am faithful to him, but I judge him and I cannot lie. The writer in him was admirable both for his talent and his conscience. But what you have said about the man is the truth. No, Jérôme was not an apostle, and if he could seem so to his disciples, at least he never deceived us, his wives. He had to surround his actions, the choice of his political opinions —everything, really—with a halo of sanctity, but the motives that made him act were, as we both know, quite small. He made a virtue out of his hatred of the world, but the underlying cause of that hatred was his sick timidity. Toward women he behaved like an attentive, respectful friend, but, as you wrote him, that was because of a lack of vigor rather than out of true tenderness. He shunned official honors, but that was out of pride and calculation much more than from humility. In a word, he never made a sacrifice that did not turn to his own advantage, and we had to play at being the dupes of this adroit clumsiness.

Truthfully, I believe that he himself did not know his real nature and that this man who was so penetrating and so severe when analyzing the hearts of others died believing that he was a sage.

Was I happy with him? Yes, in spite of many disappointments, because he was a perpetually new spectacle, a prodigiously interesting human being. Even the duplicity I have just described made him a living enigma. I never tired of listening to him, questioning him, observing him. His weakness touched me above all else. In the last years, my feelings for him were more those of an indulgent mother than those of a loving wife. But what does it matter how one loves so long as one does love? When I was alone, I cursed him; the moment he appeared, I was conquered again. For that matter, he never knew about my distress. What would have been the point? I thought that if a woman had unmasked him, had forced him to see himself in a true mirror, she would simply have made him hate her but would never have convinced him. You yourself did not dare speak out until you knew you would never see him again.

And yet what a mark you left on him! From the moment you separated, Jérôme did nothing but write and rewrite every year, with me at his side, the story of this rupture. You were his one heroine, the central character in all his books. In every one of them I found, under different names, your Florentine-pageboy hair, the dignity of your carriage, your aggressive ardor, your disdainful purity, and the hard brightness of your

eyes. He was never able to depict me, either my feelings or my
appearance. Several times he tried, to please me. Oh, if you
knew how it hurt to see this character that he was modeling in
front of me evolve every time, in spite of the sculptor, into a
woman who resembled you. One of his stories has my name—
Nadine—as its title, but the prudent, inaccessible virgin who is
the heroine—who can help but see that she is still you? How
often I wept as I was copying out chapters where you play out
your many roles—the mysterious fiancée; the unfaithful, adored
wife; the hateful, unjust, yet desired adversary.

Yes, after you left him, he lived on memories, on the bad
memories you had bequeathed him. I tried to make a quiet life
for him, wholesome and entirely given over to work. I wonder
now if I was right. Perhaps a great artist needs to suffer. Perhaps for him monotony is an evil worse than jealousy, than
hate, than grief. It is a fact that during the time you were his
wife, Jérôme wrote his most human books; and it is a fact that,
deprived of you, he chewed and rechewed the last months of
your life together like a cud. Even the cruelty of the letter lying
in front of me now did not cure him. He spent his last years
trying to reply to it, in his heart and in his books. His last—un-
finished—manuscript is a kind of implacable confession in
which he tears himself apart trying to excuse himself. How I
envied you the frightful power to torment him that your coldness gave you.

Why am I saying these things to you now? Because for a long
time I've needed to say them. Because you are, it seems to me,
the only person who can understand them, and also because
this sincerity will, I hope, help me in obtaining a favor from
you. You know that since Jérôme's death, a great deal has been
written about him. I do not find that what has been written
about his work is very exact or very profound, but on this
score I shall take care not to intervene. Critics have the right
to be wrong; posterity will judge, and I believe that Jérôme's
books belong among those that will endure. But I cannot preserve the same composure when biographers deform his figure
and my life. The details of Jérôme's life, the intimate traits of
character, only you and I have known well. After long hesita-

tion, I have decided that it is my duty, before I, too, disappear, to put these memories down.

I am, therefore, going to write a book about Jérôme. Oh, I know very well I have no talent. But here it is the material, not the form, that matters. At least I shall be leaving testimony that perhaps someday some writer of genius will make use of for a definitive biography. For several months I have been hard at work, gathering together all the documents I will need. However, I have very little material for one period, which is the period of your engagement and marriage. I felt that it would be a bold thing, unconventional but honest and loyal, to come directly to you and to ask for your support. I would probably not have dared, if I had not felt this strange but genuine sympathy I spoke of earlier. It seems to me that, without ever having seen you, I know you better than anyone. Instinct tells me that I am right to deal with you on the basis of this almost audacious trust. May I ask you please to write me when and where I can meet you to explain my plans. I imagine that you will need a little time to find old papers (if you've kept them!) and to put them in order, but in any case I would like as soon as possible to have a talk with you. I should like to tell you how I envisage this book. Then you will see that you have nothing to fear from me—no severe or even prejudiced treatment. On the contrary, I will use all my friendly guile to do you justice. Naturally, I know that you have remade your life, and I will be most careful not to quote anything or to relate anything that might embarrass you today. I thank you in advance for what you will, I am sure, do to make my task easier.

NADINE JÉRÔME-VENCE

P.S. This summer I am going to Uriage, where Jérôme was introduced to you, so that I can better describe, from firsthand impressions, the background of his meeting you on the terrace of the Hôtel Stendhal. It would also be helpful for me to visit your family's estate.

P.P.S. I am poorly informed on Jérôme's liaison with Mme de Verniez. Do you know more about that than I? He used to talk continually about you, but about this youthful adventure

he was always discreet, closed, reticent. Is it true that Mme de
V. rejoined him in Modena in 1907 and traveled with him all
over Italy?

Was the paternal grandmother of Jérôme called Hortense or
Mélanie?

IV

Evreux, February 4, 1936

THÉRÈSE TO NADINE

MADAME,

To my great regret, I can be of no help to you at all. I have
decided, actually, to publish a biography of Jérôme Vence myself. Unquestionably, you are his widow, you bear his name,
and for this reason a small volume of memoirs signed by you
will be well received. But between us frankness is essential: let
us face the fact, Madame, that you knew very, very little about
Jérôme. You married him when he was already famous and
when his public life infringed on his private life. I, however,
was witness to the formation of the writer and the birth of the
legend, and as you yourself are willing to admit, the best of his
work was composed near me or in memory of me.

Add to this the fact that no serious biography of Jérôme can
be written without the documents that I have. I have two thousand letters from him, two thousand letters of love and of hate,
without counting my replies, of which I kept the first drafts.
For twenty years, I clipped all the articles that appeared about
him or his books, and filed the letters from his friends and
from his unknown admirers. I have in my possession all his
speeches, lectures, and articles. The Director of the National
Library, who has just made an inventory of these treasures, said
to me, "It is an incomparable collection." One example: you
ask me the first name of one of his Bordelais forebears. I have
at hand an entire dossier on this Hortense-Pauline-Mélanie
Vence, as I have on each and every one of the forebears of
Jérôme.

He liked to call himself "a man of the people." This is not
true. At the end of the nineteenth century, the Vences owned a
small estate in Périgord, and were very well off; the maternal

grandparents of Jérôme had gradually acquired a property of some hundred hectares toward Mérignac. Under Louis-Philippe, his grandfather had been mayor of his village, and one of his great uncles was a Jesuit. Everyone in the vicinity considered the Vences well-to-do, middle-class people. I intend to bring out these facts. Not that I want to underline the reverse snobbism that was one of poor Jérôme's failings. I intend to take an impartial, even understanding, position. But I am resolved also to be exact. That, Madame, was where the great man whom we both loved and whom we have both judged showed himself most deficient.

Insofar as you are concerned, I will certainly be no less generous than you wish to be toward me. Why should we tear each other apart? You were Jérôme's mistress before your marriage, as the letters I have prove; I will refrain from quoting them. I detest scandal for others as much as for myself. Furthermore, whatever my grievances against Jérôme, I am still a faithful admirer of his work, and I will serve it to the best of my ability, with total self-abnegation. Perhaps it would be desirable, since our two books will appear at about the same time, for us to exchange proofs. In this way, we will avoid contradictions that might seem suspect to the critics.

Of Jérôme's old age and his declining health after the first heart attack you know more than I. That is an aspect of his life that I leave entirely to you. I plan to end my book with our separation. (What point is there in bringing up the quarreling that followed?) But in an epilogue, I will speak briefly about your marriage, also my own, and relate how I learned of Jérôme's death while I was in America with my second husband. All of a sudden, in a newsreel theater, I saw shots of the official funeral, late photographs of Jérôme, and a shot of you, Madame, stepping down from the dais on the arm of the President of the Council. This can make a most effective ending.

But you will also write, I have no doubt, a charming little book.

V

Paris, February 7, 1937

MME JÉRÔME VENCE TO ÉDITIONS DU LYS

I have just learned that Mme Thérèse Berger (who, as you know, was my husband's first wife) is preparing a volume of memoirs. To anticipate her book, we shall have to come out with ours immediately after the summer holidays. You will have my manuscript by July 15th. I am happy to learn that options have been asked for in the United States and Brazil.

VI

Evreux, December 9, 1938

THÉRÈSE TO NADINE

MADAME,

Following the success of my book in America (it was a Book-of-the-Month Club selection), I have just received two long cables from Hollywood, about which it is my duty to consult with you. One agent, acting for one of America's biggest producers, proposes to film a *Life of Jérôme Vence*. You are aware, I daresay, that Jérôme was very popular in the United States among liberal intellectuals, and that *Messages* is considered a classic there. This popularity, together with the almost apostolic stature that our husband achieved in America, has convinced the producer that he should think in terms of a stirring, uplifting film. Some of his requests at first startled me indeed. On second thought, it seemed to me that no sacrifice would be too great if we could assure Jérôme that universal consecration in the eyes of the masses that today only the cinema can confer. Both of us knew him well enough to be confident that this is what his own reaction would have been, and that absolute historical truth was the least of his concerns where his reputation was involved.

These are the three thorniest points:

1. Hollywood is anxious to have Jérôme be a man of the people, wretchedly poor, and wants to present his early struggles against poverty in a tragic light. That, as we know, is not true, but after all that is the version that Jérôme himself liked,

and we have no cause to be more scrupulous on this point than the hero was.

2. Hollywood insists that during the Dreyfus affair, Jérôme should have been a violent activist in the case and thereby jeopardized his whole career. This is historically inexact and chronologically impossible, but it can in no way damage his memory. Quite the contrary.

3. Lastly, and this is the most troublesome point, Hollywood finds it very awkward to put two women in Jérôme's life. His first marriage having been a love marriage (and all the more romantic because of the conflict with my family), the special aesthetic of the films requires that this be a happy marriage. The producer asks my permission to "blend" the two women— that is, you and me—in one. For the conclusion of the film, he would use the details provided by your book but would attribute to me your attitude during the period of Jérôme's illness and death.

I can readily imagine your distaste and, on this last point, I first replied with a flat refusal. But the agent has cabled a second time, and he advances an unanswerable argument. The role of Mme Vence must be played, naturally, by a star. However, no famous actress would agree to appear in a film if she had to disappear in the middle. He gives me an example. In *Marie Stuart,* in order to persuade a prominent actor to take on the role of Bothwell, they had to involve Bothwell in the Queen's youth through a purely imaginary love affair. You will admit that if history, in its best-known aspects, can be adapted in this way to the exigencies of the screen, it would be quite ungracious of you and me to display a pedantry that is even a bit ridiculous, since only our humble lives are concerned.

Let me add this: (a) this "blended" woman would not look like you or me, since the actress who would play us would be a person who is under contract at this moment with the producer and who does not resemble either of us; (b) the fee offered is very substantial (sixty thousand dollars, which at the current rate of exchange amounts to more than a million francs); and (c) naturally, if you were to agree to the stipulated changes, I would reimburse you very generously for what your book will have contributed to the collaboration.

I must ask you to answer by wire, for I must, in turn, cable Hollywood.

VII

NADINE TO THÉRÈSE

DEC 12 1938 SUBJECT TOO IMPORTANT TO BE HANDLED BY WIRE STOP TAKING PARIS TRAIN 2:23 PM ARRIVING AROUND 6 STOP BEST WISHES. NADINE

VIII

Evreux, August 1, 1939

DEAR NADINE,

Here I am again in this country house that you know and are good enough to love as much as I do. I am alone, for my husband is away for three weeks. I would be so happy if you were to come for a visit, to stay as long as you can and would like. If you want to read, write, work, I am myself very busy with my new book, and I will leave you quite at peace. If you prefer to visit the countryside, which is delightful, my car is yours. In the evenings, if you have time to rest in the garden with me, we will be able to talk of our memories—our "unhappy memories"—and our various business matters.

With my affectionate greetings,

THÉRÈSE BERGER

Home Port

"The strangest story of my life?" she said. "You embarrass me. There've been a great many stories in my life."

"There still are, I imagine."

"Oh, no. I'm growing old—and wise. Which is another way of saying that I need quiet. Now I'm quite happy when I can be alone for an evening and read old letters or listen to records."

"It can't be that men don't pursue you anymore. Your face is as lovely as ever, and there is a—I don't know—a suggestion of experience, of suffering, perhaps, that makes it moving, irresistible. . . ."

"You're very sweet. Yes, I have some admirers still. The trouble is, I don't believe them anymore. I know men so well—unfortunately—know all their heat so long as they've not got what they want, and then the cooling off—or the jealousy. I say to myself, Why go see a play when you know the ending so well? . . . When I was young, it was different. Each time it seemed to me that I'd met the perfect person, the man who would rescue me forever from all my doubts and insecurities. And I played the game for all it was worth. Why, five years ago, when I met Renaud—my husband—I felt as if I were living a second springtime. He was strong, he was almost brutal. He swept all my doubts away, laughed at my fears and scruples. I thought I'd found a savior. Not that he was perfect. He wasn't a cultivated man, and even his manners weren't exactly polished. But he brought me something I had never had—stability. A life buoy. At least that's what I thought then."

"You don't think so any longer?"

"You know perfectly well I don't. Renaud has had some terrible setbacks. I've had to console and reassure and encourage— I've had to defend the Defender. Genuinely strong men are very rare."

"Have you known one, at least?"

"Yes, I've known one. Oh, not for very long, and in the strangest circumstances. . . . Look, you were asking what was the strangest adventure of my life. That was!"

"Tell me about it."

"Heavens! Do you know what you're asking? I'll have to go way back—it's a long story and you're always in such a hurry. Can you give me a little time?"

"Indeed, yes, I'm all attention."

"So be it. . . . This happened twenty years ago. I was a young widow. Do you remember my first marriage? To please my parents I had married a man much older than I, and I was devoted to him, yes, but like a daughter, really. To love him seemed to me rather like a duty, a debt of gratitude, not a pleasure. Then, after three years, he died. He left me rather well off, so that I, who had lived under a family's and then a husband's wing, suddenly found myself free. I was mistress of my own actions, of my whole future. I may say, without being vain, that I was quite pretty—"

"Far more than pretty."

"If you insist . . . However that may be, I was attractive to men, and soon I had practically a regiment of men at my heels, all of them terribly attentive. My favorite was a young American, a man by the name of Jack Parker. Several of the Frenchmen who considered themselves his rivals I found more compatible. They shared my tastes, they knew how to be charming and complimentary. Jack read almost nothing; he didn't really like any music except jazz and blues, and when it came to painting, he was perfectly happy to follow whatever the current fashion was. And he hadn't the slightest idea how to talk about love. Well, let me be more exact: he never spoke of it at all. His way of paying court to me consisted in his seizing my hands at a movie or theater or in the garden by moonlight and saying to me, 'You are just wonderful.'

"I should have found him a great bore, but I enjoyed going out with him. He seemed to me so restful, so open. He gave me the same feeling of security that later, at the beginning of our relationship, my present husband did. My other men friends were slow to make their intentions clear: Did they hope to become lovers or husbands? They never quite declared themselves. But none of that with Jack. He thought the idea of an affair was scandalous. He wanted to marry me and take me to America, where I would present him with beautiful children who would have his curly hair, and the same straight short nose, the same slow, nasal speech, the same naïveté. He was vice-president of his bank. One day, perhaps, he would be president of it. In any case, we would never lack for anything, and we would have a most expensive car. That was his view of the world.

"I admit I was tempted. . . . You're surprised? But it's in my nature, you know. Because I am a rather complicated person, simple people attract me. I got along badly with my family. To go live in the United States was one way of getting away from them. Jack had gone back to New York, after a stint of several months in the Paris branch. When he left, I had promised to join him there and to marry him. You'll notice that I had not been his mistress. That was not my fault. I would have lived with him, if he had asked. But he would never have done any such thing. Jack was an American Catholic, with very strict standards, and he wanted a proper marriage at St. Patrick's, in New York, with lots of ushers in morning coats, all wearing white carnations in their buttonholes, and bridesmaids in organdy— Well, that wouldn't have upset me, either.

"We had agreed that I would arrive in April. Jack was to

make the plane reservation. Instinctively, I'd thought of traveling Air France; it seemed so natural that I hadn't even mentioned it to him. At the last moment, I received a ticket for
Paris-London, London-New York; it was delivered by an American line that at the time was not authorized to pick up or
leave passengers here at the Paris airport. It annoyed me a bit,
but, as you know, I'm a pretty easy person to get along with,
and rather than start all over again, I accepted the situation. I
was to reach London around seven in the evening, have dinner
at the airport, and take off at nine for New York.

"Do you like airports? I don't know why, but I love them.
They are cleaner, more modern than railway stations. And
they're as functional as an operating room. Strange voices so
distorted that you can scarcely understand them keep talking
over the loudspeakers, calling passengers to far-off, exotic
places. You stand by great plate-glass windows and watch giant
planes land and take off. It's all unreal, but it's not unbeauti-
ful. I had had my dinner and had sat down quietly to wait in
one of those moss-green leather armchairs when the loudspeaker garbled a long announcement that I couldn't understand, but I did catch the words 'New York' and the number
of my flight. I was a bit upset, and looked around me. Other
passengers were getting up from their chairs.

"I'd noticed in the chair next to me a man in his forties, an
interesting-looking man. He had a rather emaciated face, wild
hair, and his collar was open—all very much in the style of the
English Romantic poets, Shelley especially. Looking at him, I'd
thought: Writer or musician, and I hoped I'd have him as a
seat companion on the plane. He noticed my confusion, and he
said to me, in English:

" 'Excuse me, are you a passenger on Flight 632?'

" 'Yes. What did they just say?'

" 'That there's some technical difficulty, and the plane will
not leave until six tomorrow morning. For passengers who
want to sleep over in a hotel, the company will be furnishing a
limousine in a few minutes to take them back into town.'

" 'What a nuisance! Go to a hotel to get up at five o'clock in
the morning . . . Such a bore! What are you going to do?'

" 'Oh, by luck I've a friend who works, actually lives, here at the airport. I left my car in his garage. I'll pick it up and go back home.'

"There was a moment's pause, and then he said:

" 'Or rather, no . . . I'm going to take advantage of the delay to make a little tour. I'm an organ maker and I have instruments in various London churches that I have to inspect from time to time. This is an unexpected chance for me to check up on two or three of them.'

" 'You can get into churches at night?'

"He laughed, and pulled an enormous ring of keys from his pocket.

" 'Of course! Generally I do inspect my keyboards and pipes at night so that I won't disturb anyone.'

" 'Do you play the organ yourself?'

" 'As well as I can.'

" 'It must be very beautiful—organ concerts at night, all alone and in the dark.'

" 'Beautiful? I don't know. I love church music, but I'm not a great organist. I do tremendously enjoy playing, though.'

"He hesitated a moment, and then he said:

" 'Madame, I am going to make a strange proposal. . . . You don't know me, and you may not want to put yourself in my hands. But if you would enjoy coming with me, I could take you along and then bring you back here. . . . You must be a musician?'

" 'That's true. How did you know?'

" 'Because you are beautiful, the way an artist's dream is beautiful. That never misleads one.'

"I was touched by the compliment, I admit. The man had a strange authority. I knew that to run about London in the middle of the night with a total stranger was risky. I foresaw the possible dangers. It never occurred to me to refuse.

" 'Let's go,' I said. 'What shall I do with this bag?'

" 'We'll put it with mine in the luggage compartment.'

"I could never tell you which three churches we visited that night, or what my mysterious companion played. I remember spiral staircases that I climbed with his help, moonlight filtering through stained-glass windows, and music—sublime music. Bach, Fauré, Handel I recognized, but I think that most of the time my guide was improvising. It was overwhelming. At times the music was like the torrential confessions of a soul in torment. Then came limpid, heavenly passages, and others like the softest caress. I was quite literally drunk. I asked the name of this great artist. His name was Peter Dunne.

" 'You must be very famous,' I said. 'You're a genius.'

" 'Don't believe that. It's the night, the hour, that gives you this illusion. Actually, I am a mediocre player. But faith inspires me—and tonight, you.'

"This kind of declaration neither surprised nor shocked me. Peter Dunne was one of those human beings with whom you achieve an extraordinary intimacy within minutes. . . . He was not of this world. When the visit to the three churches was over, he said quite simply:

" 'It's not quite midnight. Do you want to spend the three or four hours you have still to wait at my house? I'll make you some scrambled eggs. And there's some fruit, too. The maid was to come tomorrow morning to pick up any food.'

"I felt very happy and, since I'm telling you everything, let us admit that I was hoping vaguely that this evening would be the beginning of love. Women depend more than you men do on the motions of their senses and on their need to admire. The divine music, the night filled with song, the gentle, firm hand that had guided me in the dark—all these things had aroused confused desires in me. If my companion had wanted me, I would have been his—that's the way I am.

"I liked his little apartment. It was overflowing with books, and the walls were painted eggshell white with a black border. I felt at home at once. I took off my hat and coat by myself. I offered to help him prepare our supper in the minute kitchen. He refused.

" 'No, I'm used to it. Go find something to read. I'll be with you in a few minutes.'

"I chose Shakespeare's Sonnets, and I'd had time to read three that marvelously matched the exalted state I was in. Then Peter came in, set a little table in front of me, and served my supper.

" 'Everything is delicious,' I said. 'I'm enjoying it. I was hungry. What an amazing man you are! You do everything well. It's a happy woman who shares your life.'

" 'No woman shares my life. . . . But I'd much rather hear you talk about yourself. You're French, that goes without saying. And you're leaving for America?'

" 'Yes, I'm going to marry an American.'

"He seemed neither surprised nor displeased.

" 'Do you love him?'

" 'I must love him, since I've decided to take him as a companion for life.'

" 'That's not always a reason,' he said. 'There are some marriages that one lets oneself slip into slowly, insensibly, without really wanting to. Suddenly we are confronted with the fact of an engagement. We don't have the courage to pull back. One more unfulfilled destiny . . . But I'm wrong to be saying these pessimistic things to you, when I know nothing about your own choice. It's not likely that a woman like you will have made a mistake. The only thing that surprises me . . .'

"He stopped.

" 'Tell me. Don't be afraid of offending me. I'm a very clear-minded person—I mean, very capable of looking at my actions from outside, observing and judging them.'

" 'Well!' he said. 'The only thing that surprises me is not that you have chosen an American—there are some very remarkable, even very attractive American men—but that you have wanted to spend all your life with him in his country. You're going to find that it really is a "new world" and that its values are not your values. . . . Perhaps these are the prejudices of an Englishman. And perhaps your fiancé is perfect enough in himself so that you need not attach any importance to the society that will surround the two of you.'

"I thought for a moment. It seemed to me, I didn't know why, that everything I was saying to Peter Dunne was extraordinarily important and that it was my duty to translate for him, exactly, the slightest nuance of my thoughts.

" 'Don't think that,' I said. 'Jack—my husband to be—is not a perfect man, and I am sure that he could never, of himself, make up for the absence of a world that I value and will miss. . . . No, Jack is a charming boy, a good man, who will be a good husband in this sense: he won't be unfaithful, and he will give me healthy children. But aside from the children, his business, politics, and small talk about our friends, we'll have very few interests in common. . . . Understand, Jack is not at all unintelligent. He is a very able businessman. He has a certain feeling for beautiful things, a fairly sure taste. . . . Only, poetry, painting, music—in his eyes, these are not important. He never gives them a thought. . . . Is that so bad? After all, art is only one of many human activities.'

" 'Of course,' Peter Dunne said. 'One can be a very sensitive man without loving the arts, or rather without knowing them. And I even prefer a frank indifference to noisy, aggressive snobbism. But to be the husband of a woman like you . . . Has he at least that sensitivity of the heart that lets us divine the inner feelings of the person we live beside?'

" 'He doesn't look that far. . . . I please him. He doesn't know why, he doesn't ask himself why. He doesn't doubt that he can make me happy. Won't I have a hardworking husband, an apartment on Park Avenue, an expensive car, and excellent Negro servants chosen by his mother, who comes from Virginia? What woman could ask for more?'

" 'Don't be sarcastic,' he said. 'Scarcasm is always the sign of a bad conscience. And when we aim it at people we should love, it kills all affection. . . . Oh, yes, yes. And it's very serious. The only salvation is to feel genuine tenderness and compassion for people. Almost all of them are so unhappy—'

" 'I don't think Jack is unhappy. He is an American, well adjusted to his own society, which he honestly believes is the best in the whole world. What would he have to fear?'

" 'You, in time. You will teach him to suffer. . . .'

"I don't know whether I've been able to make you understand the state of mind I was in that evening, but I was ready to accept everything. It was fairly extraordinary that I should be alone, at one o'clock in the morning, in the apartment of an Englishman whom I had met only a few hours earlier at an airport. It was more amazing still that I should have confided in him about my personal life and plans for the future. And it was incredible that he should be giving me advice and that I should be listening to it with what amounted to real respect.

"But that's how it was. There was a kindness, a dignity, that emanated from Peter and that made the situation quite natural. Not that he put on airs as a prophet or preacher. Far from it. He was a man without affectation. He laughed heartily if I said something amusing. Only, one sensed in him a direct seriousness, which is the rarest thing in the world. . . . Yes, that's it, a direct seriousness. . . . Do you know what I mean? Most people don't say what they think. Behind all their words, there is always some hidden thought. The idea they express masks another that they want to keep well concealed. . . . Or else they say no matter what, without thinking. Peter acted like some of Tolstoi's characters. He went straight to the heart of things. That struck me so that I asked him:

" 'Are you part Russian?'

" 'Why? How amazing that you ask me that! Yes, my mother was Russian, my father English.'

"I was so proud of my little discovery that I asked him more questions:

" 'You're not married? You never have been?'

" 'No . . . because . . . This will seem very arrogant to you. I am keeping myself for something bigger.'

" 'For a great love?'

" 'For a great love, but not the love of a woman. I have the feeling that, beyond the miserable appearances of this world, there is something very beautiful that one must live for.'

" 'Do you find this "something" in religious music?'

" 'Yes, and in the poets. And also in the New Testament. I would like to make something very pure of my life. You must forgive my talking to you like this about my life, and in such—such an emphatic, such an un-British way. . . . But you seem to understand so well, so quickly. . . .'

"I got up and went to sit at his feet. . . . Why? I wouldn't know how to tell you. It was all I could do.

" 'Yes, I understand that,' I said. 'I feel as you do that it is madness to throw life away—it's the only thing we really possess —in meaningless snatches, futile responsibilities, and petty quarrels. I wish every hour of my life could be like the one I am spending with you now. And yet I know that this can't be. I haven't the strength. I'll give in and float with the current, because that's the easier thing to do. I am going to be Mrs. Jack D. Parker; I will play canasta; I will improve my golf score; I will go to Florida in the winter; and that is how the years will pass until one day I will be dead. . . . You'll tell me, perhaps, that this is a pity, and you'll be right. But what can I do?'

"I leaned against his knee, and at that moment I belonged to him. . . . Yes, I think possession doesn't mean anything. The giving of oneself is everything.

" 'What can you do?' he said. 'Keep your own command-ment. Why drift with the current? You know how to swim. I mean you are capable of action, of rising to real stature. . . . Yes, you are! . . . And furthermore, it doesn't require a long struggle to master our own destinies. In the course of a human life, a few rare moments are given us in which everything is decided for a long time to come. These are the moments when we must have the courage to say yes—or no.'

" 'And you think that I'm in one of those moments when I must have the courage to say no?'

"He stroked my hair, then quickly withdrew his hand, and seemed to be reflecting.

" 'You're asking me a very hard question,' he said finally. 'What right have I, who scarcely know you, who know nothing about you or your family or your future husband, what right have I to give you advice? I risk being so grievously wrong. It isn't I who must answer, but you yourself. Only you know what you hope to get out of this marriage. You're the only one who has all the elements in hand and can foresee the consequences. All that I can do is draw your attention to what, in my opinion —and to what I think you also believe—is essential, and ask you: "Are you sure you will not be killing the best part of you?" '

"It was my turn to think for a moment.

" 'Oh, Peter, I'm not sure. The best part of me . . . is a hope for I don't know what kind of exaltation, it's a thirst to give, to sacrifice myself. When I was little, I used to dream of being a saint or a great heroine. Now I dream of devoting myself to an admirable man and, if I am able, helping him carry out his work, fulfill his mission. . . . There . . . What

I've just said to you I've never told anyone. Why you? I wonder. Something in you invites confidences—and confidence.'

" 'That something,' he said, 'is renunciation. The man who is no longer looking for what people call happiness for himself becomes capable, perhaps, of loving others as they should be loved, and in that way he finds another kind of happiness.'

"What I did then was bold and perhaps a little mad. I caught both his hands and I said:

" 'And why, Peter Dunne, why shouldn't you have your share of real happiness? I also scarcely know you, and yet it seems to me that you are the man I have unconsciously always been looking for.'

" 'Don't believe that. . . . I seem to you very different from what I really am. I would not be a desirable husband or lover for any woman. I live too much in myself. I would not be able to endure having around me, from morning to night, night to morning, a human being who would demand—and who would have the right to demand—attention every living minute—'

" 'The attention would be mutual.'

" 'Very likely, but I don't need attention.'

" 'You feel strong enough to face life alone. Is that it?'

" 'Putting it more exactly, I feel strong enough to face life together with all men of goodwill . . . to work with them to make a wiser, happier world . . . or at least to try to do that.'

" 'Would it be less difficult if you had a companion beside you? Of course, she would have to share your faith. But if she loves you—'

" 'That isn't enough. I've known more than one woman who has been in love and who has followed the man she loves like a sleepwalker. One day, she wakes up and sees with terror that she's teetering on the edge of a precipice. She has only one idea: to get down, to get down to the solid ground of everyday life. . . . The man, if he has any pity in him, follows her and he, too, climbs back down. And then, as we say, they raise a family. . . . One more fighter disarmed.'

" 'You want to fight alone.'

"He lifted me to my feet, not ungently.

" 'It has never cost me more to say so, but that is true. I want to fight alone.'

"I drew a long, slow breath:

" 'A pity. I was ready to sacrifice Jack to you.'

" 'Better you sacrifice Jack *and* me.'

" 'To whom?'

" 'To yourself.'

"I picked up my hat and went to the mirror to put it on. Peter held my coat.

" 'You're right,' he said. 'We should be leaving. The airport is a long way away, and it would be a good idea to get there before the others.'

"He went to turn off the kitchen light. Before we left, he took me in his arms—I felt that he hadn't been able to resist it—and held me closely. Like a brother . . . I didn't resist. I gave in to a strength that I wanted to give in to, but he quickly dropped his arms, opened the door, and motioned me to go before him. Down in the street we found his little car, and I got in beside him without a word.

"It was raining and the London streets were dismally depressing. After a moment, Peter began to talk. He described the people who lived in those little houses, each identical to its neighbor, and their monotonous lives, their meager pleasures, their hopes. He evoked them with astonishing power. He could have been a fine novelist.

"Presently, on the outskirts of town we came to the factory area. My companion had fallen silent. I was taken up with my own thoughts. I was visualizing tomorrow and my arrival in New York and Jack, who after this moving experience would admittedly seem a little ridiculous. Suddenly I said:

" 'Peter, stop!'

"He braked hard, and asked:

" 'What's the matter? Don't you feel well? . . . Or did you forget something at the house?'

" 'No . . . But I don't want to go to New York. I don't want to get married again.'

" 'What?'

" 'I've thought it over. It's you, you opened my eyes. You said there are moments in life when everything is decided for a long time to come. . . . This is one. And I've decided. I won't marry Jack Parker.'

" 'This is a terrible responsibility for me. I think I gave you good advice. But I could be wrong.'

" 'You couldn't be wrong. But above all, I can't be wrong. I see so clearly now that I was about to do something utterly mad. I shan't leave.'

" 'Thank God,' he said. 'You've saved yourself, because you were heading for disaster. But aren't you afraid to go back to Paris, to explain—'

" 'Why? My family and my friends didn't want me to leave. They said I was acting too much on impulse. They'll be glad to see me come back.'

" 'And Mr. Parker?'

" 'Jack will be upset for a few days, or a few hours. His vanity will be hurt, but then he'll tell himself what troubles he would have had with such a flighty woman, and he'll be relieved that the break took place before, not after, the marriage. . . . Only, I must send him a cable, so that he doesn't go to meet me for no reason.'

"Peter started up the car again.

" 'What shall we do?' he asked.

" 'Let's go on to the airport. Your plane is waiting for you. I'll catch another one, back to France. The dream is over.'

" 'It was a beautiful dream.'

" 'A waking dream.'

"When we reached the airport, I went to the cable desk and wrote out a message for Jack: 'HAVE COME TO CONCLUSION MARRIAGE ILL-ADVISED STOP TERRIBLY SORRY BECAUSE LOVE YOU VERY MUCH BUT COULDNT SPEND REST OF LIFE ABROAD STOP HAVE THOUGHT BEST BE FRANK STOP SENDING CHECK TO REIMBURSE TICKET STOP DEVOTEDLY MARCELLE.' I reread it and crossed out 'spend rest of life abroad' and substituted 'live abroad.' That was still clear and three words less.

"While I was sending the cable, Peter had gone to find out about the departure of his plane. When he came back:

" 'Everything's all right,' he said. 'Or rather everything's all wrong. The engine's been repaired. I'm leaving in twenty minutes. But you have to wait here until seven. I don't like to leave you alone. Do you want me to buy you a book?'

" 'No,' I said. 'I've a lot to think about.'

" 'You're sure you're not sorry about any part of it? There's still time, but once you've sent the cable, it will be too late to change your mind.'

"I didn't answer, and handed the wire to the clerk.

" 'Deferred?' he asked.

" 'No, straight.'

Then I slipped my arm under Peter's.

" 'My dear Peter, I feel as if I were seeing off my oldest friend.'

"I could never tell you all that he said to me in the twenty minutes left to us. Rules about how to live, really. At times you've said to me that in some ways I am like a man, that I'm a steady friend, that I don't lie. If all these pleasant things are true, I owe them to Peter. Finally, the loudspeaker called: 'Passengers for New York, Flight 632.' I went as far as the gate with Peter. I reached up and kissed him on the mouth, like any wife. I never saw him again."

"You never saw him again! Why not? Hadn't you given him an address?"

"Yes, but he never wrote. I think he liked to enter into the lives of people, set them on the right track, and then disappear."

"And all the times you've been in London you've never tried to find him again?"

"What for? He'd given me, as he said, the best of himself. We would never have recaptured the fantastic feeling of that night. . . . No, it was right the way it was. It's a mistake to try to revive a moment that has been perfect, too perfect. . . . But wasn't I right to say to you that this was the strangest adventure of my life? That a man who changed my whole destiny, who made me live in France and not in America, and who has had the most lasting influence on me was a stranger, an Englishman, whom I met by chance at an airport. Don't you find it remarkable?"

"It's like the old tales in which a god disguises himself as a beggar or a foreigner so that he can approach mortals," I said. "But, frankly, Marcelle, this unknown man didn't transform you so very much, since in the end you married Renaud. And Renaud, under a different name, is the same man as Jack."

"Of course," she said. "You don't change a person's nature. You retouch it."

Myrrhine

THE BEST WRITERS of our generation admired Christian Ménétrier. He also had enemies; success always produces a few, especially when, as with Ménétrier, success comes late. Colleagues and critics had got accustomed to thinking of him as a hermetic poet who deserved to win respect but not a public, so that to esteem his work had been both honorable and offensive to no one. However, his wife, Claire Ménétrier, was an ambitious, ardent, and active woman. It was she, really, who launched him around 1927, when she persuaded the musician Jean-François Montel to base a lyric opera on her husband's *Merlin et Vivian*. But it is to the actor Léon Laurent that we owe the transformation of Christian into a highly performable and widely performed dramatist. The story is not very well known, and it strikes me as interesting and worth recalling for the light it throws on little-studied aspects of the creative imagination.

Léon Laurent, who played such a constructive part in the

renaissance of the theater in France between the two world wars, seemed on first meeting the antithesis of the temperamental theatrical figure. He was free of any self-importance and utterly disinterested in his readiness to support a great play; in a word, he practiced the religion of the theater. He was also a remarkably cultivated man—cultivated not only in the sense that what he valued deserved to be valued but that he could recognize and appreciate the most difficult, unusual works. As soon as he had established a company of his own, he had the courage to produce Aeschylus' *Prometheus*, Euripides' *Bacchae,* and Shakespeare's *Tempest*. For many of us, his Prospero and Hélène Messière's Ariel will remain among our finest theater memories. He rejuvenated Molière, Musset, and Marivaux by his fresh interpretations and staging at a time when the sleep-logged Comédie-Française was still waiting to be awakened by Bourdet. And not least, he had the knack of finding among contemporary writers men who were capable of carrying on the great tradition of French verse drama. French dramatic literature owes him both a school and a company.

As I said, on first meeting you would not take him for an actor at all. His way of speaking, his style, even his language suggested more a young professor or maybe a doctor. But this impression did not last long. Five minutes of watching him play was enough to convince you that here was a great actor with an incredible range, as able to create with dignity Augustus in *Cinna* as to project the agreeable Abbot in *Il ne faut jurer de rien* or Basil, the tragic clown, in *Le Barbier de Séville*.

Christian Ménétrier admired him, and used to go see everything he did, but would probably never have had any direct contact with him, for both men were shy, if Claire Ménétrier had not busied herself to see to it that they met. Claire shared her husband's enthusiasm for Laurent's acting; also, she was eager for Christian to work in the theater, and she rightly believed that only a really cultivated actor could convince him to try his hand at it. So, very deliberately, she set about bringing Léon Laurent into their circle. She succeeded. With her pale complexion and intensely blue eyes, Claire was still exceedingly beautiful, and Léon Laurent was exceedingly responsive to beauty in women. What's more, when the two men got to know each other, they discovered an abiding pleasure in "talking theater" together. Christian had many lively ideas about the stage, and most of them coincided with those of the actor-director.

"The realists have made a big mistake," Christian said once. "They try to imitate everyday speech on the stage. That's precisely what the public is *not* looking for in the theater. We should never forget that originally the drama was a ceremony. Processions, entrances, choruses all had an important place in it. . . . Even in comedy . . . They tell us that Molière used to study the language of the porters of the Pont-au-Change. That's possible—actually, it is a fact—but he studied it in order to stylize it."

"I agree," Léon Laurent replied. "I absolutely agree. And that's why, Ménétrier, I'd like to see *you* do something for the theater. Your verse patterns and your imagery are exceptional, you know. And appearances to the contrary, that makes excellent stuff for an actor. Sculpt some statues for us. We'll breathe life into them."

Habitually, Léon Laurent spoke in short phrases, his fine voice lending them a sustained resonance.

"But I *do* write theater," Christian said.

"No, old man, you don't. . . . No, no. You write poems in dialogue, or you write armchair theater, but you don't confront the public."

"Because nobody produces me."

"Put it this way—you've never tried to be produced. To this point, you've never paid any attention to what the stage demands, what it needs. But that's what makes it theater. Write a play for me. . . . Yes, for me, for the specific actor I am. Then you'll see what rehearsals are. A school in themselves! Look, there's just one thing—in my opinion, it's your only flaw—and it's that you still affect a kind of symbolism. Well, the moment your lines are spoken aloud, you'll hear the dissonances yourself. The stage is for the author what the record is for the public speaker. He hears his own voice projected. He catches his own mistakes and corrects them.

"That's what I keep saying to Christian from morning to night," Claire said. "He's born for the theater."

"I don't know," Christian said.

"Try. Try at least once. . . . And let me say again: write the play for me."

"But what kind of plot?"

"Oh, you've got dozens," Léon Laurent said. "What do you mean? Every time I see you, you spin out a whole first act, and usually it's first-rate. A plot? Just sit down at your desk and write what you've already told me. . . . It's simple, really. And I guarantee that, sight unseen, whatever you bring me I will play."

Christian sat for a moment, looking thoughtful.

"Yes, maybe I do have an idea," he said. "You know how I feel about the threat of a war. I've tried hard—and with no success whatever, I may say—to make people recognize the perfectly obvious intentions of the lunatics who are running Germany—"

"I've read your articles in *Figaro*," Laurent said. "I find them sound and helpful—but, you know, current events in the theater . . ."

"Oh, I'm not proposing a play based on what's happening now. No, no, I'm thinking in terms of a transposition. You remember the attitude of the Athenians when Philip of Macedonia was staking out claims to his *Lebensraum* and was occupying the little cities of Greece one by one. 'Watch out,' Demosthenes told the Athenians. 'Watch out. If you don't go to the help of Czechoslovakia, you will be gobbled up in your turn.' But the Athenians were self-complacent, frivolous—and Philip had his fifth column. Demosthenes failed, and one day it was Athens' turn. . . . That would be the second act."

"Fine!" Léon Laurent said enthusiastically. "Well, there's our plot. Now get down to work. Right away!"

"Not so fast, not so fast," Christian said. "I have a little bit of reading to do. But I can see you as Demosthenes haranguing his fellow citizens. . . . You would play Demosthenes, wouldn't you?"

"Of course."

Claire, who was delighted, sat listening as the two men discussed the play until five in the morning. When they broke up, the major scenes had been plotted. Christian had even hit on the final curtain line. After many vicissitudes, suddenly it seems that Philip's death may, by a miracle, save Athens. But Demosthenes does not believe in miracles or that Athens can be saved except by the will, courage, and steadfastness of the Athenians. "Yes," he says, "I know, I know. Philip is dead. . . . But what is the name of Philip's son?" And someone replies, "Alexander."

"Perfect!" Léon Laurent shouted. "Perfect! I can see how I will say the line. Ménétrier, if you haven't finished this play within a month, you don't deserve to belong to the theater."

A month later the play was finished. Today we know that it justified all of Claire and Léon Laurent's hopes. However, after a triumphant first reading, when Laurent came to see Ménétrier to discuss casting and rehearsal schedules, he seemed preoccupied and reticent. Christian had the impression—he was extremely sensitive, like all artists when it is a matter of their work—that the actor was no longer entirely satisfied.

"No," he said to Claire, after Laurent had gone. "No, he's not happy. . . . Why not? He didn't tell me why not. In fact, he didn't tell me anything. . . . It's one of those imponderables. But it isn't that he doesn't like the play. He talked to me again about his role and the scene before the Assembly, and there was no mistaking his enthusiasm. But something's on his mind. . . . What? I can't figure it out."

Claire smiled.

"Christian," she said, "you are a genius and I admire you with all my heart. But you are still delightfully naïve when it comes to elementary relationships between human beings. I didn't even see Laurent today, but I can tell you what's wrong with him."

"And what is wrong?"

"What isn't wrong? Or better, what's missing? What's missing in your play, dear, is a part for Hélène Messière. . . . Now be fair. Admit it. I did warn you."

Claire was impatient.

"How could there be a part for Messière? She's a charming

actress. She's perfect for Musset or Marivaux, but what would she be doing in a political drama?"

"Oh, my darling, you do ask all the wrong questions! It isn't at all a matter of knowing what Hélène could do in a political tragedy, but much more simply of how Léon Laurent will be able to live in peace with his mistress."

"Hélène Messière is Léon Laurent's mistress?"

"Where have you been, dear? They've been living together for four years."

"How would I know that? And what connection has that got with my play? Do you believe that Léon Laurent would want—"

"I don't *believe*, Christian. I am *sure* that Laurent wants and, if necessary, will insist on a part for Messière. And may I say, it doesn't seem to me too hard to give him what he wants. If you were to add a character that—"

"Never in this world! It would destroy the whole balance of the play!"

"All right, Christian. We'll talk about it another time."

They did indeed talk about it another time, after Laurent had become more and more somber and reticent, and had begun to raise difficulties about interpretations, previous commitments, tours, and so forth. Christian, his play written, was burning to see it produced; he became anxious and irritable in his turn.

"Listen, dear," Claire said to him. "Will you leave me alone with Laurent someday? He'll dare tell me what's troubling him, and I promise you that I will fix everything—but on one condition, naturally. That you will write in a new part."

"How, how? I can't juggle a play that purports to be a work of art just because—"

"Oh, Christian! It's so easy, and you have so much imagination. . . . In the second act, for example, where you have the Macedonians organizing a fifth column in Athens, why wouldn't it be utterly plausible for them to make use of an intelligent courtesan, the friend of powerful Athenians, bankers and politicians? . . . There's your character, and a completely credible one."

"Well, maybe. One could even— Yes, you're right. It would

be interesting to show certain clandestine propaganda methods, all of them as old as human society. . . ."

Claire knew that any seed dropped in Christian's mind always bore fruit. She saw Laurent, and their conversation went very smoothly.

"What a splendid idea," he said, with relief. "You know, I didn't dare mention it to your husband. He is intransigent about his work. But it's terribly hard to win the public over to a play without women. Even Shakespeare. Take *Julius Caesar*. And Corneille added the character of Sabine to his *Horace,* and Racine put Aricie into the Phèdre myth. Also—I'm going to tell you the whole story—I wouldn't like to put on a play that Hélène wasn't in. . . . No. She's very young, and she's devoted to me, but she loves to dance and she hates to be alone. If I were to leave her alone evening after evening, she'd go out with other men, and I confess that would be—would be worrisome, shall I say. But if your husband can write in a bit part for her, that will change everything. . . . The play will be in rehearsal a week later."

Thus the character Myrrhine was born. When he created her, Christian was mindful of some of Aristophanes' cynical, witty women and of the romantic Marivaux women Hélène Messière had played with such brilliant success at the start of her career. The product of this paradoxical mixture was, to the author's great surprise, an original and beguiling character. "A jewel of a part," said Laurent. Hélène Messière was invited to dinner by Claire so that Ménétrier could read the new version to her. She was a ravishing creature, tiny, with long, low eyebrows, and a graceful, catlike wariness, who spoke seldom but never said anything stupid.

"Yes," Christian said later. "This little ingenue who is so little ingenuous is going to make a dangerous, believable fifth column."

"You don't like her *too* much, do you, Christian?"

"Oh, no, and furthermore, she's in love with Laurent, isn't she? He's not only her lover, he's her creator. He made her. She'd be nothing without him."

"Do you believe, Christian, that if she is aware of such a debt, it would inspire any great tenderness in her? I—I'm something of a misogynist. I'd be inclined to expect the opposite, a kind of unconscious resentment. . . . But what does it matter! Messière likes the part. Everything is going smoothly."

Indeed, for a week everything did go well. Then Laurent turned taciturn again.

"Now what's the matter with him?" Christian wanted to know.

"This time I've no idea," Claire said. "But I'll find out."

Laurent did not have to be pressed to explain the new difficulty.

"It's simply this. The part is charming, and Hélène is in seventh heaven. Only . . . well, we do live together, you know, and we take the same taxi to the theater. It would be silly not to. . . . But if Hélène is only in the second act, what is she supposed to do in her dressing room for a whole hour? . . . Either she'll get bored—and she won't put up with that for long—or she'll invite people in, and I know me. . . . It will hurt my performance, not to mention my feelings. My feelings don't matter to Ménétrier, but my performance . . ."

"In a word," Claire said, "you would like Myrrhine onstage in the first act."

"Madame, it is impossible to hide anything from you."

When she transmitted this new request to her husband, he exploded. "Never has a writer been forced to work in such a way!" he shouted. Claire, knowing how her husband's mind worked, understood that it was necessary, above all, to reassure his conscience.

"But, Christian, all playwrights have worked this way. You know perfectly well that Shakespeare always kept the physical appearance of his actors in mind. Racine wrote for Champmeslé. Mme de Sévigné says so herself."

"She detested Racine."

"But she knew him very well."

So Myrrhine was in the first act. Need it be said, however, that the problem of getting the couple to the theater in the same taxi was no more important than the matter of getting them home in one taxi, and that in the final version of the play Myrrhine had to be in the last act, too. Here again, Claire had had to intervene.

"Well, Christian, why wouldn't Myrrhine, after the defeat, become a virtuous, patriotic woman again? Put her in with the guerrillas. Make her Demosthenes' mistress."

"Claire, really! If I listened to you, I'd become pure Hollywood. . . . No! I've had enough. Not one more line! I will not add one . . . more . . . line."

"Why do you insist it's so banal or implausible for a woman of easy virtue to be a patriot, too? It's happened often enough in real life. Take Castiglione, who conquered Napoleon III out of love for Italian unity. . . . It's simply a question of preparing for Myrrhine's conversion in a subtle, unexpected way. No one could do that better than you. The idea of making her Demosthenes' mistress was just a joke, of course."

"Why a joke? Look at some of the men in the French Revolution. . . ."

With her own mind at rest, Claire was able to pacify Laurent, and the role of Myrrhine, inflated and enriched, became a major part in the play. Came opening night. It was a triumph. All Paris saw Messière with Laurent's eyes. The public, which shared Ménétrier's political preoccupations without being able to express them, and which longed, without knowing it, for a national theater on the order of Aeschylus' *Persians,* gave the author a standing ovation. The professionals praised the skill with which a classic subject had been modernized without ever lapsing into parody. Even Fabert, who was always very severe toward his colleagues, had a kind word for Claire, as they were standing together later on the stage.

"You must have had a finger in that Myrrhine business, you lovely conspirator," he said, with his brusque charm. "There are no two ways about it. She's a woman, a real woman, but that austere spouse of yours, left to himself, would never have conceived her that way. . . . Be honest, your Christian doesn't know much about women!"

"I'm glad you like the character," Claire said, "but I had no part in it."

The next day, in his column Robert Kemp wrote only about Myrrhine. "Henceforth," he said, "people will speak of a Myrrhine the way they speak of an Agnès or a Célimène. . . ." Claire, reading with infinite satisfaction over her husband's shoulder, could not keep from murmuring, "And to think that if it hadn't been for that taxi problem, Myrrhine would never have existed."

The rest belongs to history. As everyone knows, *Philippe* was translated into all major European languages, and in France it ushered in a whole new development in French theater. What is not generally known is that last year—Hélène Messière having left Laurent to marry a Hollywood director—Laurent suggested to Claire that the part of Myrrhine be cut; since her husband's death, Claire was looking after his literary interests.

"After all," Laurent said, "it isn't essential to the play. It didn't even appear in the first version, as you and I know. Why not go back to that? It would give the Demosthenes an ascetic hardness that personally I like much better. It would dispense with my having to find a new Myrrhine. And it would be an economy; we'd have one less young star, one less salary, to pay."

But Claire, with her gentle obstinacy, held firm.

"Listen, Laurent, you will create a new Myrrhine with no trouble at all. You're so extraordinary about that kind of thing. As far as I am concerned, I will never agree to anyone's touching my husband's play. What Christian has joined, no one will sunder."

And so Myrrhine, child of genius and necessity, has continued her triumphant existence.

Biography

THE LARGE DINING ROOM was lighted only by shaded lamps. It was the fashion in London, that season, to dine in semidarkness. When Hervé Marcenat found his place, he saw that he had been seated beside a very elderly woman, her head garlanded with pearls—Lady Hampton. He was not displeased. Old women are indulgent, and sometimes they tell very good stories. This one, to judge from her oblique, mocking glance, seemed to possess a lively sense of humor as well.

"What language do you want to speak, M. Marcenat? French or English?"

"If it is the same to you, Lady Hampton, I prefer French."

"And yet you write on English subjects. I've read your life of Joseph Chamberlain. It amused me immensely, because I knew all those people. What are you going to do now?"

The young Frenchman sighed.

"I'd like to do a study of Byron, but so much has already been written about him. New things have turned up, I know.

Today we have the Mary Shelley letters, and the papers of Countess Guiccioli, but they've all been published. I would have to offer some unpublished material, but I find hardly any."

The old woman smiled.

"What if I were to supply you with a completely unknown adventure of Byron's?" she said.

Hervé Marcenat gave the abrupt, involuntary start of the hunter who, suddenly, through the brush glimpses a deer or a wild boar, or of the businessman who is tipped off about a stock about to soar.

"A completely unknown adventure of Byron's? That would be extraordinary, Lady Hampton, after all the research that's been done."

"Perhaps I am wrong to say 'absolutely unknown.' The name has been mentioned before. Lady Spenser-Swift."

Hervé grimaced.

"Ah . . . her . . . Yes, I know. But there's nothing precise, nothing sure."

"Dear M. Marcenat, how often are you sure about these things?"

"Very often, Lady Hampton. In many cases, there are letters or other evidence in existence. Letters can lie, of course, and evidence can be suspect, but there the critical sense must operate."

Lady Hampton turned toward her neighbor and surveyed him through her lorgnette, a very fine old piece.

"And what would you say if I brought you the diary Lady Spenser-Swift—her name was Pandora—kept during her affair with Byron? Together with the letters she received from him?"

The young Frenchman flushed with pleasure.

"Lady Hampton, like the Hindus I would say that you are my father and my mother. You would be making my book possible. But do you really have these papers? Forgive the question, but it seems so amazing. . . ."

"No," she said. "I know that these papers exist. I do not own them. They belong to the present Lady Spenser-Swift, who is a friend of mine. Victoria and I were in boarding school together. To this point, she has not shown them to anyone."

"Why would she give them to me?"

"Because I shall ask her to. You don't know this country well enough yet, M. Marcenat. It is mysterious and unpredictable. Our country houses hold treasures in their cellars and attics. The owners care very little about such things. The family must be ruined and the house sold for such records to see the light of day. It took an enterprising, persistent American to get the famous Boswell papers out of their croquet case."

"Do you believe that an enterprising, persistent Frenchman can have the same success without the fortune that was paid for the Boswell papers?"

"Vic Spenser-Swift doesn't care about money. Like me, she's over eighty. Her income is quite enough. No, what would decide it would be whether you can make her like you, and also whether you can lead her to hope that you will draw a flattering portrait of her husband's great-grandmother."

"Lord Spenser-Swift is dead?"

"He was a baronet, not a lord. Sir Alexander Spenser-Swift. The title died with him. Victoria still lives in the house where Byron visited. It's in Gloucestershire, a charming Elizabethan manor house. Do you want to try your luck and go down?"

"I'd be overjoyed—if I'm invited."

"That I will see to. I shall write Vic this very evening. She is sure to invite you. . . . And do not be put off if the tone of her letter is brusque. Victoria considers it the privilege of our advanced years that one may say exactly what one thinks. Whom should one treat tactfully? And why?"

A few days later, Hervé Marcenat was driving his little car through the delicious Gloucestershire countryside. The summer had been rainy, as always. Trees and flowers had thrived. Windows of the meanest cottages displayed lavish bouquets. The houses, all built of the lovely golden stone of the area, remained as they had been in the time of Shakespeare. Hervé, who was very sensitive to the fairy-like aspects of England, was enchanted by the park at Windhurst, Lady Spenser-Swift's house. He drove along a driveway winding through well-clipped, luxurious lawns over which giant oak trees reigned. Masses of fern and horsetail surrounded a small lake. Then he glimpsed the manor house, covered with Virginia creeper, and when he stopped in front of the door, his heart was pounding. He rang. No answer. After waiting five minutes, he noticed that the doorknob turned easily, and he went in. In the dark hallway, no one; chairs, however, were piled high with coats and scarves. From a nearby room issued a monotonous voice that sounded as if someone were declaiming a prepared speech. Hervé walked over and discovered a long room, its walls hung with large portraits. A group of tourists was clustered around a butler dressed in tails, dark-gray waistcoat, and striped pants.

"This," the butler was saying as he gestured toward one portrait, "is Sir William Spenser-Swift, 1775-1835. He fought at Waterloo; he was a personal friend of Wellington. The portrait is by Sir Thomas Lawrence, as is also this one of his wife, Lady Spenser-Swift."

Among the visitors there was a murmur:

"The one who . . ."

The butler made an imperceptible sign of acquiescence and complicity, but his demeanor remained grave and dignified.

"Yes," he said, in a very low voice. "The one who was the mistress of Lord Byron. It was for her that he wrote the famous sonnet 'To Pandora.' "

One couple in the group recited the first two lines. With a noble nod of the head, the butler approved.

"Exactly," he said. "Now we come to Sir Robert Spenser-Swift, the son of Sir William, 1808-1872. The portrait is by Sir John Millais."

Bending over his flock, he added confidentially:

"Sir Robert was born four years after Lord Byron's visit to Windhurst."

One young woman asked:

"Why did Byron come here?"

"Because he was a friend of Sir William."

"I see," she said.

Hervé Marcenat lingered behind the group to study the two portraits longer. The husband had a broad face, reddened by the open air and good wine. He looked irritable and pompous. The wife had an airy, grave, and chaste beauty. Looking more closely, however, one sensed behind the candid glance a secret sensuality, and perhaps even cruel mischievousness. The young man was still dreaming when the group passed by him again. The butler leaned down and murmured discreetly:

"Excuse me, sir, but do you have your ticket? You came after the others. They had all paid. So if you will be so good—"

"I'm not a tourist. Lady Spenser-Swift has been kind enough to invite me to spend the weekend to see some papers that interest me."

"Excuse me, sir. You are the young Frenchman recommended by Lady Hampton? One moment, sir. I will show these people out, and then I will inform Her Ladyship. Your room is ready, sir. The luggage is in the car?"

"I have only one bag."

On days when Lady Spenser-Swift opened her house to strangers because this gave her certain tax exemptions, she herself took refuge in a sitting room on the second floor. Hervé Marcenat was fetched there. He found the old lady imposing but not terrifying. A cheerful briskness tempered her haughtiness.

"I don't know how to thank you," he said. "To receive a stranger . . ."

"Nonsense," she said. "You are not a stranger. You have been presented by my best friend. And I have read your books. I have been looking for a long time for someone who might be capable of telling this story with tact. I believe you are the man."

"I hope so, Madame, but it is the greatest stroke of luck for me, after so many good English biographies, to find your unpublished papers."

"What happened," she said, "is that so long as my husband was alive, he was not willing to have anyone see his great-grandmother's diary. Poor Alexander had some quite archaic prejudices."

"Do these papers contain such—such dreadful things?"

"I have no idea," she said. "I've not read them. . . . No, I have not. They're written in a minute script that kills my eyes, and, in any event, we all know what to expect from the diary of a twenty-year-old woman who is in love."

"But it is possible, Lady Spenser-Swift, that I will find in these documents the proof of a liaison between Byron and your husband's great-grandmother. In that case, do I understand that I am authorized to tell everything?"

She looked at him, her surprise mixed with a touch of disdain.

"Obviously. Otherwise, I should not have invited you."

"You are generosity itself, really. . . . There are so many families that try, despite all evidence to the contrary, to defend the virtue of their ancestors for generations on end."

"Nonsense!" she said again. "Sir William was a dolt who did not understand his young wife and who, furthermore, was unfaithful to her with every girl in the vicinity. She met Lord Byron, who was not only a great poet but a man with the face of an angel and the wit of a demon. She chose the better man. Who can blame her?"

Hervé sensed that it would be better not to insist. But he could not keep from saying:

"Excuse me, Lady Spenser-Swift, but since you have not read the papers, how do you know that Lord Byron was here as anything more than the husband's guest?"

"It is a family tradition," she said sternly. "My husband had it from his father, who had had it in turn from his father. Furthermore, you will not lack for proof, since the papers, I repeat, are yours. I am going to show them to you, and you will tell me how you want to work."

She called the admirable butler.

"Miller, you will open the red vault, fetch some candles, and give me the keys to the chest. I am going to go down with M. Marcenat."

The scene was quite impressive. The vault, situated below ground level and hung with red damask, was not lighted, like the other rooms in the manor, by electricity. The glow from the candles cast trembling shadows. Against one of the walls stood an enormous strongbox disguised as a medieval cabinet. Opposite it stood a wide divan. The old woman, who had majestically descended the stairs on the Frenchman's arm, took the keys and turned them rapidly in three safety locks to form a secret number. Upon which, Miller opened the big doors wide.

Marcenat could see the gleam of silver dishes and leather jewel cases. But his hostess went directly to a thick album bound in white morocco leather.

"Here," she said. "Pandora's diary. And here are the letters that she fastened together herself with this pink ribbon."

She glanced around her.

"Let's see. . . . Where are we going to set you up? Would this big oak table do? Yes? Good. Miller, you will put two candlesticks on either side of M. Marcenat. Then you will close the safe and we will leave this young man to his work."

"May I stay here the greater part of the night? I have very little time, and I want to read everything."

"My dear sir," she said, "one should never be hurried, but you do as you like. Your dinner can be brought down to you on a tray, and you can be completely by yourself. Tomorrow morning, your breakfast will be served in your room and you will be able to work all morning. At one, you will lunch with me. Does this program suit you?"

"Admirably, Lady Spenser-Swift. I can't tell you how much—"

"Then don't try. Good night."

Hervé was alone in the vault. He took pen and paper from his briefcase, sat down at the big table, and, with a shiver of anticipation, opened the album. The writing was, as the old woman had said, small and hard to read. Very likely Pandora had deliberately made it unreadable. Her husband might find this diary. Wiser to take a few precautions. Marcenat was accustomed to coping with elliptical handwriting. He easily deciphered Pandora's scribbles. The tone of them at once amused him. It was the tone of a very young woman, almost a child. She underlined many words, in token of vehemence or impatience. The journal began in 1811, a few weeks after her marriage.

October 25, 1811

I am weary this morning, positively *ill* and quite unable to ride. William is out hunting. I have nothing to do, so I shall begin my journal. This album was given me by *dear, dear* Papa, whom I so very much mind having left. I fear that my husband will *never* understand me. William is not a bad man, but he does *not* know that a woman needs *tenderness.* Is he even interested in me, I wonder? He talks more about political things and his horses and his farmers than about his wife. I do believe that he has not *once* uttered the word *love* since our marriage. Ah, yes! The other day, he said to Bridget, "My wife's love for me is deuced touching." I did not move an eyelash. . . .

Hervé scanned numerous pages filled with complaints and mockeries. Pandora was pregnant and was joylessly awaiting her child. It would bind her more closely still to a man who had been unable to arouse any feeling of affection in her. From these ingenuous jottings, little by little a very harsh portrait of Sir William emerged. His egoism, his vanity, his vulgarity had been pitilessly recorded by a witness who nourished a ferocious bitterness toward him. Another face was lightly sketched—that of a neighbor, Lord Peterson, as charming as Sir William was odious.

December 26, 1811

Yesterday, Christmas Day, Lord Peterson brought me as a gift an *adorable* little dog. I was, as always, alone, but I received Lord P., since he is so much older than I. He talked to me about literature and art. I longed to write down all the *brilliant* things he said. It was *delicious* to listen to him. He has such a *marvelous* memory. He recited poems by Sir Walter Scott and Lord Byron to me. It did me *endless* good. I feel that if I lived with a man like Lord Peterson, I would make *immense* progress. But he is old and, furthermore, I am married for life. Alas, poor Pandora. . . .

Later, the journal revealed that she had been greatly struck by a poem of Lord Byron's, *Childe Harold's Pilgrimage.* She had even spoken of it to her husband, who had replied:

"Byron? Know him very well. Met him while I was making—as was he—the Grand Tour. Eh, we spent some jolly nights together in Italy. When we got back, he invited me down to Newstead Abbey. That's where he keeps a troupe of nymphs I could tell quite a few little stories about, only they're not made for the chaste ears of my wife, ha, ha!"

The white album then bore witness to Pandora's remarkably adroit maneuvers to get Sir William to invite Byron down to Windhurst. The husband objected: "What'll we do with him?" he said. "He'll be bored. His bad leg won't let him walk with me. He doesn't hunt." The wife insisted: "I can keep him company." At that Sir William was indignant: "You entertain that skirt-chaser, that Don Juan! . . . D'you suppose I'd leave my wife alone with a man like Byron? I've not the slightest wish to allow that rascal to poach on my land."

But as Byron's London success turned into a triumph, the country gentleman seemed to grow more proud of this friendship. He would speak of it to neighbors. The birth of her child furnished Lady Spenser-Swift with an excellent pretext. Why not ask Lord Byron to be godfather to the little girl? Such a great name would be very flattering. Sir William let himself be swayed: "I'll write him, but he'll never accept. He's weighed down by too many women and too much work." But Byron did accept. He loved contrasts and dissonances. The very idea of making a godparent out of a diabolic poet—the godfather, what's more, of a little girl—amused and tickled him no end.

Hervé Marcenat was so absorbed in his reading that he was impervious to hunger, thirst, and weariness. However, the admirable Miller came to visit him, accompanied by a footman carrying a tray.

·"Lady Spenser-Swift sends her compliments, sir, and asks if you need anything."

"Nothing. Tell her it's so interesting that I am going to work through the night."

The butler looked at him with a vaguely disapproving air.

"All night, sir? Really, sir? Then I will send down some fresh candles."

Hervé did not so much eat as nibble at a terribly English supper, then went back to the album. The arrival of Byron elicited a feverish description, the tiny script becoming even more illegible.

> . . . This morning, at eleven, the arrival of Lord B. How handsome he is! And how *pale!* He looks unhappy. His bad leg humiliates him. One can tell, because he *runs* instead of walking, so that people shouldn't notice. His infirmity only makes him *much more* interesting. One *strange* thing is that William had warned me about him, and had told me that he is *unendurably* bold with women. But he's scarcely spoken to me. Now and again, he looked at me from the corner of his eye, and once I *surprised* him watching me in a mirror. But in conversation he addresses himself to William or to Lord Peterson, and *never* to me. *Why?* . . .

Through the long night, Hervé Marcenat followed the slow spell cast day after day over Pandora by the poet. It seemed obvious that the ingenuous, inexperienced young woman had not understood the reason for the visitor's most un-Byronic attitude. Byron had come to Windhurst resolved to behave, first because he was at that moment desperately in love with another woman, and then because he held it a small part of honor to seduce the wife of his host, and, finally, because he found Pandora naïve, very young, and very fragile, and he did not want to make her suffer. At bottom, he was a sentimentalist who masked his tenderness behind cynicism.

For all these reasons, he had made no gesture toward her. Then the scene became more lively. Sir William had recalled Newstead Abbey and the more than accessible nymphs who lived there. One of them had pleased our country gentleman, and he expressed the wish to see her again. "Come now, Byron, won't you invite me? . . . Without my wife, naturally." Byron had chided him: "Aren't you ashamed, and you so newly married? What if your wife were to take it into her head to make reprisals?" Sir William had burst out laughing. "My wife! Ha, ha! My wife is a saint, and, furthermore, she adores me."

Pandora, ears well cocked, had caught this exchange from a distance, and she had recorded it in her diary with indignant comments: " 'She adores me!' What a fool! Am I condemned to spend my life with this dolt? And *why* no reprisals, pray? After this scene, I was in such a rage that had Lord Byron tried this evening to lure me into the park to *kiss* me, I do believe I should have let him do so."

It was past midnight. Writing as fast as he could, Hervé was covering whole pages with notes. In that dark vault, where the nearly burned-out candles were flickering more and more feebly, he felt as if he were surrounded by living ghosts. He heard the gross "Ha, ha" of the ruddy-faced host; he watched the mounting tenderness betrayed in Pandora's delicate face; he thought he could glimpse Byron, in a dark corner, observing this poorly matched couple with a mocking air.

He had to stop to replace the candles, which were guttering out, and then went back to his reading. Now he was following the various devices Pandora tried—and for so young a woman, she showed unexpected daring and artfulness—to rouse Byron from his abstraction. Piqued by his indifference, she led him on. On the pretext of playing a game of billiards with him, she contrived to see him alone.

. . . This evening I said to him, "Lord Byron, when a woman *loves* a man, and when this man pays her no attention, what should she do?" He replied, "This," and caught me in his arms with the most astonishing strength and—

Here a phrase had been crossed out, but Hervé could decipher the words "kissed me." He drew a long breath. He could scarcely believe his good luck. "Can I be dreaming?" he said to himself. "This is typical of the accomplishment dream, when what you most hope for comes true in your dream." He got up and went over to touch the big cabinet, the divan, the walls, to assure himself that his surroundings were real. No doubt about it; everything around him was solid and the album authentic. He went back to his chair.

. . . I was frightened, and I said, "Lord Byron, I *love* you, but I have just had a child. That binds me to its father forever. I could never be more to you than friend. And yet I need you. Help me." He was *amazingly* kind and understanding. From that moment on, when he is with me all his bitterness seems to melt away. I believe that I do him *good*. . . .

The young Frenchman could not suppress a smile. He knew his Byron, and he could not imagine him long pursuing platonic dalliance with a delicate young woman. He could virtually hear him: "If she imagines I'm a man to sit holding her hand for hours on end while I recite poetry to her, ah! how wrong she is. We've reached the point where we must come to terms."

Then Hervé bethought himself that he would doubtless find a true indication of Byron's state of mind in the packet of letters that Lady Spenser-Swift had also entrusted to him. He hurriedly undid the ribbon. Yes, the letters were from Byron. Hervé was familiar with that impetuous hand. But there were other papers in the bundle in which he recognized the handwriting of the diary. He skimmed several. They were drafts of Pandora's letters that she had kept.

Reading this correspondence, he saw with amusement that he had not been mistaken. Byron had quickly tired of the platonic. He asked whether he could not meet Pandora at night, when the house would be asleep. She demurred, but not energetically. Hervé thought: If the letter of which this is the draft was sent to him, Byron must have felt that victory was very near. And indeed, the candid young woman had written simply: "It's impossible, because I don't know where to see you without attracting the attention of everyone."

He went back to the diary. She had recorded that in order to deliver and receive letters, she was pretending to lend Byron books from her library. In this way, she could, in front of the *marito,* hand the *cavaliere servente* books that contained letters. "And all this at twenty!" Hervé exclaimed to himself.

. . . Today William out hunting, and I *alone* with Lord B. the entire day, but under the eye of the servants. He was *charming*. Someone had told him about the vault, and he asked to see it. I did not dare go down with him, but I asked Mrs. D., the nurse, to show it to him. When he came back, he said to me with such a *strange* air, "This vault will one day be for me the place in all the world that I shall remember with the greatest emotion." What did he mean? I *fear* that not only do I understand but accept without the slightest qualm the idea that this emotion will be bound to his memory of *me*. . . .

Together, the letters and diary made it possible to reconstruct the course of the adventure. One night, Pandora had consented to meet Byron in the vault, at an hour when her husband would be snoring and the servants would have withdrawn to the upper floor. He had pressed her urgently. She had begged him to spare her. "Lord Byron," she had said to him, "I am at your mercy. You can do with me what you will. No one is spying on us, no one can hear us, and I have no strength to oppose you. I have tried, and love has brought me here against my wish. My salvation can come only from your hands. If you use your power over me, I shall submit, but I shall die of shame and grief."

She had wept abundantly. Touched by the young woman's tears, Byron had had a moment of pity. "What you ask of me," he had told her, "is very nearly beyond human strength, but I love you enough to give you up." They had remained a long time on the couch, wrapped in each other's arms, and then Pandora had gone back to her bedroom. The next day, Byron had said that he was called back to London by Murray, his publisher, and he had left Windhurst. Pandora's entry for that day amused the young Frenchman greatly.

"Oh, fool! fool!" she had written. "Everything is finished. Everything is lost, and here am I, condemned never to know love. Why did he not understand that I could not, after all, throw myself at his head! A woman brought up as I have been, and as young as I am, could not have the cynicism of those corrupt, libertine women he has known until now. I *had* to cry in front of him. It was up to him, a man of experience, to reassure me, calm me, and win my consent to a love that I felt so strongly. Now, by going off he has ruined all our chances. I shall never forgive him."

Two more letters had been exchanged after this episode. Byron's was prudent; one sensed that in writing it he had thought of the husband who would perhaps open it. Pandora's draft betrayed the young woman's intimate feelings and her secret rage. Later on in the journal, there was occasional mention of Byron in connection with a new poem or a new scandal; ironic allusions, in which one could read a deep resentment. Then, after 1815, the poet seemed to have disappeared entirely from Pandora's thoughts.

Through the air vent a pale light filtered into the vault. It was dawn. As if he were coming out of a trance, Hervé looked around him and slowly put foot again in the twentieth century. What a strange and remarkable story he had lived during that night. And what pleasure he was going to have in writing it. But now that the work was finished, the fatigue from a sleepless night swept over him. He stretched, yawned, blew out the candles, and went up to his room.

The clock chimed, announcing lunch. Out in the hall, Hervé found the grave Miller, who conducted him to a salon where Lady Spenser-Swift was waiting for him.

"Good day, M. Marcenat," she said, in her strong, mannish voice. "I'm told that you did not sleep very much. Did you at least work well?"

"Wonderfully. I read everything and took twenty pages of notes. It's an unbelievable story. I can't say enough—"

She interrupted him.

"Exactly," she said. "I told you so. That little Pandora always seemed to me to have the face of a passionate woman."

"She *was* a passionate woman. But the great thing about the story is that she *never* was Lord Byron's mistress."

Lady Spenser-Swift turned purple.

"What?" she said.

The young man, who had brought his notes with him, related the whole story and, for the edification of his hostess, attempted to analyze the two characters as they confronted each other.

"And that is why," he concluded, "Lord Byron, for the first and last time in his life, surrendered to the demon of tenderness and why your husband's great-grandmother never forgave him for his gentleness."

Lady Spenser-Swift had listened to the recital without interrupting, but at this point she burst forth.

"Nonsense!" she said. "You've misread it or misunderstood it. Not the mistress of Lord Byron! But the whole world knows she was. There isn't a family in this county that hasn't handed the story down through the years. . . . Not the mistress of Lord Byron! . . . I am extremely sorry, M. Marcenat, but if that is your last word, I cannot permit you to use these documents. . . . Why not? Because you would go around telling all over France and this country that that great love never existed! Why, Pandora would turn over in her grave!"

"Why? Pandora knew the truth better than anyone else. She herself says in her diary that nothing that was not innocent ever happened."

"That diary," said Lady Spenser-Swift, "will go back into that cabinet and will not come out again. Where did you leave it?"

"On the table in the vault, Lady Spenser-Swift. I didn't have the key, so I couldn't put it back in the cabinet."

"We are going down there immediately after lunch and put everything back as it was. I should never have shown you those family papers. Poor Alexander did not wish it, and he was right—for once. . . . And as for you, sir, I am obliged to ask that you maintain absolute silence about this—this so-called . . . discovery."

"It is obvious that I cannot publish anything without your authorization, Lady Spenser-Swift. And, furthermore, I would not want to do anything in the world to be in any way disagreeable. I must confess to you, however, that I don't understand—"

"It is not necessary," she said, "that you should understand. What I am asking you to do is to forget."

He sighed.

"As you wish. I give up this memory . . . and my book."

"That's very good of you, and very loyal. I expected no less from a Frenchman. Now let us talk of something else. Tell me, M. Marcenat, how do you find the English climate?"

After lunch, they went down to the vault, accompanied by Miller. The heavy doors of the cabinet were opened. The old lady herself replaced the white album and the packet of yellowed letters tied by the pink ribbon, among the leather jewel cases and the silver coffeepots. Miller locked the cabinet.

"There!" she said gaily. "Safe for eternity!"

When they went back upstairs, a first group of tourists, brought by car, was coming into the hall and buying tickets and postcards. Miller was ready to play his portrait scene.

"Let us go in for a moment," Lady Spenser-Swift said to Hervé.

She stood in a corner, a good distance from the group, but she listened attentively.

"This," said the butler, "is Sir William Spenser-Swift, 1775-1835. He fought at Waterloo; he was a personal friend of Wellington. The portrait is by Sir Thomas Lawrence, as is also this one of his wife, Lady Spenser-Swift."

A young woman stepped quickly forward to see better, and she murmured:

"The one who . . ."

"Yes," Miller said, in a very low voice, "the one who was the mistress of Lord Byron."

The old lady threw a triumphant glance at the young Frenchman.

"You see?" she said.

Thanatos Palace Hotel

"How's AmSteel doing?" Jean Monnier asked.

"Fifty-nine and a quarter," one of the typists in the pool answered.

The clattering typewriters were beating out a syncopated jazz rhythm. Through the windows one glimpsed the concrete giants of Manhattan. Telephones shrilled, ribbons of ticker tape unfurled and, at incredible speed, littered the office floor with sinister streamers speckled with letters and figures.

"AmSteel?" Jean Monnier asked again.

"Fifty-nine," Gertrude Owen answered.

She stopped a moment to glance at the young Frenchman. Sunk in a chair, his head in his hands, he looked utterly devastated.

One more who's played the market, she thought. Too bad for him! . . . And too bad for Fanny . . .

For Jean Monnier, assigned to the New York branch of the

Holmann Bank, had married his American secretary two years before.

"Kennecott?" Jean Monnier asked.

"Twenty-eight," Gertrude Owen answered.

A voice shouted outside the door. Harry Cooper came in. Jean Monnier stood up.

"What a day downtown!" Harry Cooper said. "A twenty-percent drop across the board. And still there are some fools saying this isn't a crisis!"

"It's a crisis," Jean Monnier said, and he went out.

"That one's been hit," Harry Cooper said.

"Yes," Gertrude Owen said. "He risked his shirt. Fanny told me. She's leaving him tonight."

"There's nothing for it," Harry Cooper said. "It's the crisis."

The handsome bronze doors of the elevator slid open.

"Down," Jean Monnier said.

"How's AmSteel doing?" the elevator boy asked.

"Fifty-nine," Jean Monnier said.

He had bought it at a hundred and twelve. Loss: fifty-three dollars a share. And his other investments faring no better. The little fortune amassed earlier in Arizona had been poured into buying on margin. Fanny had never had a cent. He was finished. Out in the street, hurrying for his train, he tried to visualize the future. Begin again? If Fanny would have the courage for it, it might be possible. He remembered his early struggles, the period of tending sheep in the desert, his rapid rise. After all, he was barely thirty. But he knew Fanny would be merciless.

She was.

The next morning, when Jean Monnier awoke alone, he felt drained of all courage. He had loved Fanny, despite her flinty coldness. The Negro maid served his slice of melon and bowl of cereal, and asked for money.

"Where's Mrs. Monnier?"

"Away on a trip."

He gave the woman fifteen dollars and figured out his bank balance. He had a little less than six hundred dollars left. Enough to live on two months, maybe three . . . And then?

He looked out the window. Almost every day for a week, the papers had carried accounts of suicides. Bankers, brokers, speculators preferred death to a battle already lost. A twenty-story fall? How many seconds? Three? Four? And then the crushing. thud . . . But suppose the force of it didn't kill you? He imagined the hideous pain, the broken limbs and shattered bodies. He sighed and then, tucking a newspaper under his arm, he went out to a restaurant, where he was surprised to discover that he still had an appetite for waffles drowned in maple syrup.

" 'Thanatos Palace Hotel, New Mexico' . . . Who's writing me from that queer address?"

He also had a letter from Harry Cooper, which he read first. The boss was asking why he had not shown up at the office. His account was short eight hundred and ninety-three dollars. What did he intend to do about it? The question was either cruel or naïve. But naïveté was not one of Harry Cooper's vices.

The other letter. Under an engraved design of three cypresses appeared the letterhead: THANATOS PALACE HOTEL. *Director: Henry Boerstecher.*

DEAR MR. MONNIER:

The fact of our writing you today is not a matter of chance but is the result of our having certain information about you, which leads us to hope that our services can be useful to you.

You have not failed to notice, certainly, how in the life of the most courageous of men, such completely adverse circumstances can arise that further struggle becomes impossible, and death assumes the aspect of deliverance.

To close our eyes, to fall asleep, never to wake again, to hear no more questions, no more reproaches . . . Many of us have had this dream or actually formulated such a wish. However, except in very rare cases, men do not dare break free of their troubles, which is understandable when one observes those among us who have tried to do so. For the majority of suicides are ghastly failures. The man who wants to put a bullet through his head manages only to sever the optic nerve and blind himself. Another, who thinks that some barbiturate will put him permanently to sleep, mistakes the dosage and comes to three days later, his brain liquefied, his memory destroyed, and his body paralyzed. Suicide is an art that allows for neither mediocrity nor amateurism and yet, because of its nature, does not allow one to acquire experience.

This experience, dear Mr. Monnier, we are prepared to supply if, as we believe, the problem interests you. As founders of a hotel situated on the U.S.-Mexican border, removed from all inconvenient control thanks to the desert-like character of the region, we have considered it our duty to offer those of our human brothers who, for serious and irrefutable reasons, might want to quit this life, the means of doing so without pain and, if we may put it so, without danger.

At Thanatos Palace Hotel, death will await you in your sleep, and in the most gentle form. Our technical skill, acquired over fifteen years of uninterrupted success (we welcomed last year more than two thousand guests), allows us to guarantee a minimal dosage and immediate results. May we add that for visitors who would be troubled by legitimate religious scruples, we do, by an ingenious method, eliminate all moral responsibility.

We realize quite well that the majority of our clients have limited funds at their disposal, and that the frequency of suicides is inversely proportional to a credit balance in the bank. Therefore we have tried, with no sacrifice of comfort, to bring the rates at the Thanatos down to the lowest possible figure. It will be sufficient for you to deposit, on arrival, three hundred dollars. This amount will cover all your expenses for the duration of your stay with us, the extent of which must remain unknown to you, and it will defray the costs of the operation, funeral, and interment. For obvious reasons, service charges are included in this down payment and no gratuities will be asked of you.

It is important to add that the Thanatos is situated in a region of great natural beauty, that it provides four tennis courts, an eighteen-hole golf course, and a fine swimming pool. Its clientele includes both men and women, almost all of whom come from cultivated backgrounds; as a result, the social pleasures of one's stay, quickened as they are by the unusual situation, are incomparable. Travelers are requested to get off the train at the station in Deeming, where the hotel bus will meet them. They are also requested to announce their arrival, by letter or wire, two days in advance. The telegraph address is Thanatos, Coronado, New Mexico.

Jean Monnier took a pack of cards and laid out a game of patience that Fanny had taught him.

The trip was very long. For hours on end, the train passed through fields of cotton where the dark heads of Negro workers bobbed above the white foam. Snatches of sleep and reading filled two days and two nights. Finally, the landscape turned rocky, titanic, dreamlike. The train ran through a deep ravine, between rock walls of prodigious height. Immense horizontal bands of violet, yellow, and red swathed the mountains. Halfway up floated a long scarf of cloud. In the little stations where the train paused, the traveler saw Mexicans in broad-brimmed sombreros and embroidered leather vests.

"Next station Deeming," the Pullman porter said to Jean Monnier. "Shine your shoes, suh?"

The Frenchman collected his books and closed his valises. The simplicity of his last trip astonished him. He heard the sound of rushing water. The brakes screeched. The train ground to a halt.

"Thanatos, sir?" asked the Indian porter running alongside the train.

This man had already piled on his cart the luggage of two blond young women who were following him.

Can it be, Jean Monnier thought, that those charming girls have come here to die?

They were looking at him, too, very seriously, and murmuring something he could not hear.

The Thanatos bus did not, as one might have feared, look like a hearse. Painted a bright blue, its seats upholstered in blue and orange, it gleamed in the sun among the broken-down cars that made the station yard, swarming with swearing Indians and Mexicans, look like a junk yard. The rocks lining the road were covered with lichen that enfolded the stone in a blue-gray film. Higher up, metallic multicolored rocks glinted in the sun. The chauffeur, wearing a gray uniform, was a heavyset man with bulging eyes. Jean Monnier, out of discretion and also so as to allow his companions some privacy, took the place beside him; presently, as the car undertook the assault of the mountain along a series of hairpin curves, the Frenchman tried to draw his neighbor out.

"Have you been driving for the Thanatos a long time?"

"Three years," the man muttered.

"It must be a strange sort of job."

"Strange?" the man said. "Why strange? I drive my bus. What's strange about that?"

"Do the passengers you take up ever come down again?"

"Not often," the man said, with a trace of constraint. "Not often . . . but it does happen. I'm one, for example."

"You! Really? . . . You came originally as a—a client?"

"Look, sir," the chauffeur said, "I took this job on so I wouldn't have to talk about myself, and these curves are rough going. You wouldn't want me to kill you, you and these young ladies, now would you?"

"Obviously not," Jean Monnier said.

Then his answer struck him as rather droll, and he smiled.

Two hours later, without a word, the chauffeur pointed to where on the high plateau rose the silhouette of the Thanatos.

The hotel was built in Indo-Spanish style, very low, with terraced roofs and red walls of cement that roughly approximated the native clay. The rooms faced south, across sunny balconies. An Italian doorman welcomed the visitors. His shaved face suddenly evoked for Jean Monnier another world— the streets, the flowering boulevards of a great city.

"Where in the devil have I seen you before?" he asked the doorman, as a bellhop picked up his bag.

"At the Ritz in Barcelona, sir. My name is Sarconi. . . . I left when the Civil War broke out."

"From Barcelona to New Mexico! Quite a change!"

"Oh, a doorman's job is the same everywhere, sir. Only the papers that I must ask you to fill out are a little more complicated here than anywhere else. I'm sorry, sir. . . ."

The printed forms presented to the three arrivals were indeed crammed full of questions, spaces for answers, and explanatory notes. One was requested to indicate with great exactness the date and place of one's birth, the names and addresses of those who should be notified in case of accident:

> Please give at least two addresses of relatives or friends, and copy out by hand and in your native language the following Statement A: "I the undersigned ————————————, being of sound mind and body, certify that I renounce life of my own free will and, in case of accident, discharge the management and staff of the Thanatos Palace Hotel of all responsibility."

Seated facing each other at the table, the two young women were carefully filling out Statement A; Jean Monnier observed that they were writing in German.

Henry B. Boerstecher, the manager, was a quiet, gold-bespectacled man, very proud of his establishment.

"Does the hotel belong to you?" Jean Monnier asked.

"No, sir, the hotel belongs to a corporation, but it was my idea, and I am manager here for life."

"How is it that you don't have the worst kind of difficulties with the local authorities?"

"Difficulties?" Mr. Boerstecher sounded surprised and shocked. "But we do nothing here, sir, that is out of line with our duties as hotelkeepers. We provide our clients with what they want, all that they want, and nothing more. Furthermore, sir, there are no local authorities here. Boundaries in this area have been so vaguely defined that no one knows for sure whether it belongs to Mexico or to the United States. For a long time, this particular plateau was considered inaccessible. A legend hereabouts has it that a group of Indians gathered here—this was two or three hundred years ago—to die together and escape the European settlers. People here used to claim that the spirits of the dead forbade access to the mountain. That's why we were able to acquire the land for a very reasonable price and to live a perfectly independent existence."

"The families of your clients never get after you?"

"Get after us!" Mr. Boerstecher cried indignantly. "And merciful.God, why? What courts would they go to? The families of our clients, sir, are only too happy to have such delicate and almost always painful matters taken care of without publicity. . . . No, no, M. Monnier, everything here goes along pleasantly, correctly, and to us our clients are like friends. . . . Would you like to see your room? It is, if you have no objections, No. 113. You're not superstitious?"

"Not at all," Jean Monnier said. "But I was brought up in the Church, and I must tell you that the idea of suicide—"

"But there is, and there will be, no question of suicide, sir!" Mr. Boerstecher said in such a peremptory tone that the other man did not press the matter. "Sarconi, show No. 113 to the gentleman. And the three hundred dollars, sir—will you be kind enough to deposit them on your way with the cashier, whose office is next to mine."

In room No. 113, illuminated by a splendid sunset, Jean Monnier searched in vain for some trace of a lethal machine.

"What time is dinner?"

"Eight-thirty, sir," the valet said.

"Does one have to dress?"

"Most of the gentlemen do, sir."

"Well, then, so will I. . . . Will you lay out a white shirt and black tie."

When he came down into the lobby, he saw that the women were indeed in evening dresses and the men in tuxedos. Mr. Boerstecher came up to him, officious and deferential.

"Ah, M. Monnier, I was looking for you. Since you are alone,

I thought it might be pleasant for you to share your table with one of our guests, Mrs. Kirby-Shaw."

Monnier shook his head wearily.

"I haven't come here," he said, "to lead a social life. But . . . could you show me the lady without introducing me?"

"Of course, M. Monnier. Mrs. Kirby-Shaw is the young lady in the white satin-crepe dress sitting near the piano and leafing through a magazine. I don't think her appearance could be displeasing. Far from it . . . And she is a very pleasant woman, well-bred, intelligent. . . . An artist."

Definitely Mrs. Kirby-Shaw was a very pretty woman. Soft brown curls were pulled back, revealing a high, strong forehead, and gathered together in a chignon low on the neck. Her eyes were warm and full of humor. Now why in the devil would such an attractive creature want to die?

"Is this Mrs. Kirby-Shaw—well, is this lady one of your clients on the same basis and for the same reason as I?"

"Cer-tain-ly," Mr. Boerstecher said, and he seemed to invest the word with profound meaning. "Cer-tain-ly."

"Then introduce me."

By the time dinner—simple but excellent and well served— was over, Jean Monnier already knew at least the essential outline of Clara Kirby-Shaw's life. She had been married to a rich man, who was very good to her, but whom she had never loved and whom she had left six months before to follow a young writer to Europe, an attractive, cynical fellow she'd met in New York. She had supposed he was ready to marry her as soon as she had got a divorce, but no sooner had they arrived in England than he indicated very definitely that he intended to get rid of her as fast as possible. Surprised and hurt by his harshness, she had tried to make him understand how much she had given up for him, and the dreadful situation she was now in. He had laughed heartily.

"Clara, really!" he had said to her. "You are a woman from another age. If I'd known you were Victorian to this degree, I'd have left you with your husband and your children. . . . You must go back to them, my dear. You are made to bring up a big and proper family."

She had then conceived one final hope—to persuade her husband, Norman Kirby-Shaw, to take her back. She was sure that if she had been able to see him again alone, she would easily have won him back. But surrounded by family and associates who exerted a constant pressure on him that was hostile to Clara, he had proved inflexible. After several humiliating, futile attempts, one morning in her mail she had found the Thanatos prospectus and had understood that here was the one immediate and easy solution to her painful problem.

"And you're not afraid of death?" Jean Monnier asked.

"Yes, of course . . . But less afraid than I am of life."

"A good answer," Jean Monnier said.

"I didn't mean it that way," Clara said. "And now tell me why *you* are here."

When she had heard Jean Monnier's story, she reproached him warmly.

"It's almost beyond belief!" she said. "What do you mean? You want to die because your stocks have gone down! Don't you see that in a year, or in two or three or more years, if you have the courage to live you will have forgotten, and perhaps even made up, your losses?"

"My losses are only an excuse. They'd be nothing, it's true, if I still had some reason to live. But I told you, too, that my wife has left me. I have no close family back in France, and I left no woman friend behind. . . . To be completely honest, I left France after a love affair had broken up. . . . Whom would I be fighting for now?"

"For yourself! For people who will come to love you later, and whom you're sure, sure to meet. Because several painful experiences have shown you how despicable some women can be, you mustn't judge all the others unfairly—"

"Do you really believe that there are women in this world— women whom I could love, I mean—who would be capable of accepting, at least for a few years, a life of struggle and poverty?"

"I am sure of it," she said. "There are women who love a struggle and who find some kind of romantic attraction in poverty. I do, for example."

"You?"

"Oh, I only meant . . ."

She stopped, hesitated, then went on:

"I think we should go back to the lobby. We're the last people in the dining room, and the headwaiter is prowling around us in positive despair."

"You don't suppose," he said, as he placed an ermine cape around Clara Kirby-Shaw's shoulders, "you don't suppose that —that tonight . . ."

"Oh, no," she said. "You just arrived."

"And you?"

"I've been here two days."

When they left each other, it was agreed that next morning they would meet and take a walk up the mountain.

The morning sun was bathing the balcony with a slanting sheen of light and warmth. Jean Monnier, who had just taken an ice-cold shower, was surprised to find himself thinking: How great to be alive! Then he reminded himself that he had only a few dollars and a few days ahead of him. He sighed.

"Ten o'clock! Clara will be waiting for me."

He dressed quickly, and felt very buoyant in his white linen suit. When he rejoined Clara Kirby-Shaw near the tennis courts, she, too, was dressed in white and was walking up and down, flanked by the two Austrian girls, who fled at the sight of the Frenchman.

"Did I frighten them?"

"You startled them. . . . They were telling me their stories."

"Interesting? . . . Tell me about them later. Were you able to get a little sleep?"

"I slept wonderfully well. I suspect the ominous Boerstecher of slipping a little chloral hydrate in our drinks."

"I don't believe it," he said. "I slept like a log, but it was a natural sleep, and this morning I feel perfectly clearheaded."

After a moment, he added:

"And perfectly happy."

She looked at him, smiling, and said nothing.

"Let's take this path," he said, "and now tell me about the little Austrian girls. You are going to be my Scheherazade here."

"But our nights will not be a thousand and one."

"Unfortunately . . . *Our* nights?"

She interrupted him:

"Those infants are sisters, twins. They were brought up together, first in Vienna, then in Budapest, and they have never had any other close friends. When they were eighteen, they met a Hungarian from an old and noble family, handsome as a demigod, musical as a gypsy, and they both, the same day, fell madly in love with him. After a few months, he asked one of the sisters to marry him. The other sister, in despair, tried to drown herself but failed. Then the one who had been chosen resolved to renounce Count Nicky, and they worked out a plan to die together. . . . That's when—like you, like me—they received the Thanatos prospectus."

"They're mad!" Jean Monnier said. "They're young, they're ravishing. . . . Let them live in America, and some other men will fall in love with them. A few weeks of patience . . ."

"It is always," she said sadly, "for lack of patience that one is here. . . . Each of us is wise about the others. Who was it who said that we always have the courage to bear other people's troubles?"

All day long, the guests of the Thanatos saw a couple dressed in white wandering along the paths of the hotel park, skirting the rocks and strolling the length of the ravine. The man and woman were talking passionately. When night fell, they turned back to the hotel and the Mexican gardener, seeing them locked in each other's arms, turned his head away.

After dinner, Jean Monnier spent the rest of the evening in the small, deserted salon, whispering to Clara Kirby-Shaw, who seemed moved by whatever he was saying. Then, before going up to his room, he sought out Mr. Boerstecher. He found the manager seated before a great black ledger. Mr. Boerstecher was checking figures and, from time to time, he drew a red line through an entry.

"Good evening, M. Monnier. Can I do something for you?"

"Yes, Mr. Boerstecher. At least, I hope so. . . . What I have to say will surprise you. . . . The change is so sudden. . . . But life is like that. . . . In a word, I've come to tell you that I've changed my mind. I don't want to die anymore."

Mr. Boerstecher looked up in surprise.

"Are you serious, M. Monnier?"

"I know," the Frenchman said, "that I'm going to seem incoherent, indecisive to you. But isn't it natural that when circumstances change, our intentions change, too? A week ago, when I got your letter, I felt absolutely hopeless and all alone in the world. I didn't believe that the battle was worth the effort. . . . Today everything is changed. And at bottom that is thanks to you, Mr. Boerstecher."

"Thanks to me, M. Monnier?"

"Yes, because that young woman you sat me down opposite at table is the one who has brought this miracle about. . . . Mrs. Kirby-Shaw is a delicious woman, Mr. Boerstecher."

"I told you so, M. Monnier."

"Delicious and heroic. . . . When she learned about my difficult situation, she agreed—she is willing to share it with me. Does that surprise you?"

"Not at all. We are familiar here with these dramatic reversals. And I am delighted for it, M. Monnier. You are young, very young—"

"So, if you see nothing in the way, we will leave tomorrow, Mrs. Kirby-Shaw and I, for Deeming."

"Am I to understand that Mrs. Kirby-Shaw, like you, is renouncing—"

"Yes, naturally. Furthermore, she will confirm it herself presently. There is just one rather delicate matter to settle. The three hundred dollars that I deposited with you, which was about all I had to my name—does that money belong irrevocably to the Thanatos, or could I get a part of it back to pay for our tickets?"

"We are honest people, M. Monnier. We never insist on payment for services that have not been rendered. Tomorrow morning, the cashier will make out your bill on the basis of twenty dollars a day for room and meals, plus service, and the balance will be returned to you."

"That is very courteous and generous of you. Ah, Mr. Boerstecher, how much I owe you! Happiness rediscovered . . . A new life . . ."

"At your service," Mr. Boerstecher said.

He watched Jean Monnier go out and walk down the corridor. Then he pressed a button and said:

"Send Sarconi in."

In a few minutes, the doorman appeared.

"Did you call for me, Signore?"

"Yes, Sarconi. It will be necessary to supply the gas to Number 113 this evening. Around 2 A.M."

"Should we give the Somnial before the Lethal, Signore?"

"I don't think it will be necessary. He's going to sleep very well. . . . That's all for this evening, Sarconi. And tomorrow, the two sisters in No. 17, as scheduled."

As the doorman was leaving, Mrs. Kirby-Shaw appeared at the office door.

"Come on in," Mr. Boerstecher said. "I was just going to send for you. Your client's been in to announce his departure."

"It seems to me," she said, "that compliments are in order. That was a job well done."

"Well and quickly done. I shan't forget it."

"Then it's for tonight?"

"It's for tonight."

"Poor boy," she said. "He was sweet, and so romantic. . . ."

"They are all romantic," Mr. Boerstecher said.

"You're cruel, all the same," she said. "The very moment they find a new taste for life, you make them disappear."

"Cruel? On the contrary, all the humanity of our method lies here. . . . This fellow had religious scruples. I've quieted them for him."

He consulted his ledger.

"Tomorrow, a day off . . . But the next day, I have another new arrival for you. A banker again, but a Swede this time . . . and no longer young."

"I liked that young Frenchman," she said dreamily.

"We do not choose our work," the manager said severely. "Here is your ten dollars, plus a ten-dollar bonus."

"Thanks," said Clara Kirby-Shaw.

As she slipped the banknotes in her purse, she sighed.

When she had gone out, Mr. Boerstecher reached for his red pencil and, using a small steel ruler as a guide, he carefully crossed a name from his ledger.

Friends

HOW STUPID MEN ARE, Solange Villier reflected, looking at Juliette. The young woman's eyes were filled with tears, her delicate head was lifted like some timid forest creature's, and she was utterly bewitching to contemplate. Fools, really fools, Solange was thinking. Francis has a kind of talent, no doubt about it, and a margin of success, but he should thank heaven daily that he has a wife as gracious, sweet-natured, and worshipful as Juliette. And whom does this idiot choose to run after like some clumsy adolescent boy? Chantal! Chantal, who is older than Juliette, far less pretty, and who lives quite openly with Managua! No wonder the child's in tears. . . .

She smiled at Juliette. Suddenly she felt immensely kind and filled with a desire to be helpful.

"My dear," she said, "do see this for the banal little incident it is, and take it with a bit more humor. It's not serious, and I'll help you get out of it. The truth is, my dear, that charming as you may be, you do not know how to hold onto a man. I'll teach you. . . . Why does your husband chase after Chantal, who has neither your figure nor your face nor your wit? After Chantal, who's been going to beauty clinics and face-lifting surgeons for years! . . . Because she makes him feel that other men love her. Because she tells him, 'I can't tonight. I'm seeing So-and-so. . . . Tomorrow? Ah, tomorrow no, I'm going out with So-and-so. . . .' Listen to me, little one. I like you. And every young woman should have someone she can trust and confide in. It so happens I am available. Be like my own sister. We'll do things, go places together, and I'll show you how one has to be with husbands. Look at mine. He's well trained."

"But I don't want to train Francis. I love him. I just want him to love me."

"Of course you do. That is the objective, but still you must think about the means. And, the world being what it is, the means are coquetry, knowing how to make him jealous, and, in homeopathic doses, flattery. Francis is a writer. He must attach boundless importance to his work. Do you know how to talk to him about it?"

Juliette sighed forlornly, and looked around her with tear-filled eyes, her lips parted in pretty helplessness.

"I hope so. But I admire him so much that often I don't feel—don't feel worthy, don't dare judge him."

"How very modest!" Solange said.

"You can never understand," Juliette said passionately. "No one, no one knows what kind of man Francis is. First of all, he knows everything. He has a facility that is near genius. Like Balzac, he writes a novel in a month. But that's nothing. In everyday life, he's sensitive, generous, tender. He senses what a woman wants before she is aware of it herself. Living with him is an enchantment."

"Really?" Solange said, and she lifted her head like the battle horse hearing a bugle. "Really. I'd never seen that aspect of him."

"You scarcely know him," Juliette said. "Until this dreadful meeting with Chantal, he hardly ever went out—and never without me. But for the past six weeks, he's been avoiding me. He finds excuses to travel, so that he can meet her. This sum-

mer he left me alone in the country to run off to Dalmatia and
Apulia."

"Apulia?" Solange was amused, because Chantal had been
talking to her only the evening before about Bari and the heel
of the Italian boot.

"Now he tells me he wants to spend a weekend with you at
Marly, but that you haven't invited me. Will Chantal be
there?"

Solange glanced away from that ardent little face for an instant; then, seizing on her role, she looked Juliette full in the
face.

"She *was* to have been there," she said. "I didn't know. Francis had told me that you have a horror of weekends, which is
why I didn't invite you. But now I will arrange things differently. I'll put Chantal off on some excuse or other, until Easter
or later, and keep only the guests who don't matter, which will
leave me time to have a serious talk with your husband. I
promise to send him back to you repentant and disabused."

"Disabused?"

"Yes, disabused of his illusions about Chantal. I am going to
show him the *real* Chantal. She's very far from being what he
thinks. What's the matter, my dear? You look as miserable as a
captured bird. I can feel your little wings fluttering desperately
in my hand."

Juliette hesitated.

"It's that . . . I thought you were Chantal's best friend."

"Little one," Solange said severely, "we must know what it is
we want. You've come to see me. That proves, it would seem,
that you trust me. Yes? Then don't split hairs. I do not consider myself Chantal's friend at all. We are allies. We both
have pleasant homes and we throw them open to each other.
That is all. Sometimes I've thought that I was drawn to her,
but I've always been put off by the way she handles friendships
—she's so self-seeking. Mind you, so long as she attaches herself
to men of Managua's type, I find that perfectly legitimate and
I'm only too glad to help her. But if she's making you unhappy,
then no. There I draw the line. She'll find out she's got me to
deal with. Anything else?"

"Well, no . . . Only, you had invited her with Francis, and then—"

"Look, my dear. I had invited her with Francis at a time when I was far from supposing that Francis was so much interested in her—or that you had such a passion for Francis."

"You knew perfectly well that Francis was my husband."

Solange laughed.

"You do say some irresistible things, Juliette. Now run along, little one, and sleep in peace. I will get rid of Chantal for you, I promise. . . . All right? Feel better now? Kiss me good-bye, dear."

A few days later, Francis Bertier, arriving at Marly, was surprised not to find Chantal. The very first evening, while Villier was having coffee with the American guests out on the terrace under the stars, Solange, with the excuse of a sore throat, kept Francis behind in the drawing room and had him sit down near her.

"Let me look at this Don Juan," she said. "I've lost track of the number of women who come telling me how unhappy you make them. . . . Starting with your wife."

"Juliette? I hope she hasn't allowed herself—"

"Dear Francis! You want the right to be unfaithful to that adorable girl but find it scandalous that she should dare complain about it. . . . And with whom, I ask you. With a woman like Chantal! Mark you, I am a friend of Chantal's, and I would cut out my tongue before saying anything against her. But all the same, Bertier, she is a hundred times less beautiful than your Juliette."

"Perhaps. However, 'beauty is not that which governs love.' I know Juliette's good points better than anyone, only . . ."

"Only?"

"Only the other woman amuses me, she inspires me. Juliette looks at me beatifically, without saying a word, as if I were some wonderful landscape. Chantal excites me, she makes me come alive."

Solange opened her eyes wide and burst out laughing.

"Chantal *inspires* you? Forgive me, Francis, but I've never heard anything so funny in my life. If someone had asked me,

'Which of your friends is least likely to interest a writer?' I would have answered, 'Chantal.' "

"Why?"

"Because, first of all, she is an egoist, and cares only about her own affairs, which are monumentally unimportant. Then, because she has nothing to say, and says that badly. . . . No, don't protest. Have you ever really listened to her? . . . No, my dear, no man, even when he is in love, ever listens. . . . But above all, because she is absolutely unappreciative of your talent. After all, Francis, you *do* have talent. Everybody agrees about that. Chantal is the *only* woman I've ever heard say she sees nothing in your books. Nothing at all."

He shook his head with a touch of irony.

"Solange, don't imagine that I'm going to believe that."

"Shake your head as much as you like, my dear. I have witnesses. Only last evening, we were talking about you here with the Bertrand Schmitts. She said, and I quote her, 'Poor boy, he is so sweet, but that last book of his passes the limits of banality.' "

"You heard her yourself?"

"With my own ears, and I hope you believe that I jumped down her throat. Bertrand, too. But then, everyone knows why she says such things. You know, too, or you can guess. . . ."

"I don't guess anything." Francis Bertier had turned very red, and he spoke with some difficulty.

"Quite simply because they are dictated to her by Managua, who is a snob, and who swears only by Christian Ménétrier and that whole closed, boring circle of his. . . . Chantal has never had an opinion of her own in her entire life. She depends for her opinions on the men she's loved."

"And you believe she loves Managua?"

Solange placed her hand—it was a very beautiful hand—on Francis' clenched fist.

"Are you trying to fool me, Francis? You're not going to tell me you didn't know what the whole world knows. . . . You didn't? Why, he's turned all pale! Really, my poor dear, I am so very sorry. But you must admit I could scarcely think that a novelist, an expert in human foibles, could have come near such an open affair and not even see it. Well, that's all very well, it's rather touching, actually. . . . *Contento lui, contenti tutti.* . . . Come, Francis dear, don't look like that. As if your whole world had just turned upside down. All because you discover that Chantal is a trollop. As if that were news! Well, don't imagine I'm sorry that I've set you straight. On the contrary. I am proud to think that, thanks to me, a man of your stature will no longer be the dupe of a woman who is not worthy of him. Mark you, I perfectly well understand that an artist cannot accept the middle-class code of marital morality. Your little Juliette is delicious—"

"Solange, you're not going to tell me that Juliette—"

"Oh, good heavens, no! Poor child, she adores you. But just because of this adoration, she can't give you what your art needs—the spice, the restlessness—oh, the comedy of life, which is your theme. Now, I *adore* Juliette, but looking at it impartially, I can see that she alone cannot fill your life. Only, why choose a Chantal? I know more than one woman who would be happy and proud to become your confidante and, if she had the rare luck to be capable of it, your inspiration. . . . Oh, I remember what I meant to poor Robert when he was just beginning. . . . It was I who gave him the idea for *Prière aux Oudaias.* . . . Oh, Francis! You can't imagine how intoxicating it is for a woman to see her dream transformed into a masterpiece, into a *masterpiece,* by the man she loves. It is *marvelous! . . .* But ever since Robert was killed, that is a happiness I've not known."

She brushed her hand over her eyes, as if to wipe away a tear. At that moment, Villier came into the drawing room and abruptly switched on the lights.

"The bats have begun their evening dance," he said, "and the air is a bit chilly. I think that Mrs. Loganberry will be more comfortable indoors. I've told the girl to close the shutters."

"You are quite right, dear," Solange said, blinking in the sudden light.

Three days later, Solange telephoned Francis.

"*Dear* Francis, I hope I'm not disturbing you in the middle of your work. . . . I am? I'm so sorry. Or rather, no, I am not sorry. I *needed* to hear your voice. . . . Yes, really. Our conversation the other night upset me more than you know, Francis. . . . What did you say?"

"Nothing," said Francis.

"You can't imagine what you mean to me, Francis. An idea, a teacher, a confessor, a guide . . . My husband is a good friend, of course, and he is utterly devoted to me, but everyone knows that women don't matter to him. But a great writer like you understands them, and that is so *mar*velous! It's set me to dreaming a little dream, and now you must tell me whether it can come true. Jacques is spending the weekend of the twelfth in Belgium, and I'd love to have you at Marly, just the two of us. . . . We could, if you like, talk the whole night through and really get to the root of our problems. . . . What are you saying, dear?"

"Nothing," said Francis.

"I know, there's Juliette. . . . Poor little dear! I love her with all my heart. . . . But actually, I would like to talk to you about her, and I'm sure she'd understand perfectly."

"Perfectly," said Francis.

"What is the matter, dear? Your voice sounds so hard, so ironic. . . . What have I done? What have I said wrong? . . . You make me so unhappy, Francis. I feel guilty, and I don't know about what."

"Really?" said Francis.

"Really . . . If I've displeased you in any way at all, explain to me, dear. I will try to do better. . . . I want to be completely soft, completely yielding in your hands. . . . You'll come to Marly?"

"No," said Francis.

"No? But why not? I will give you two *mar*velous days. Aren't you tempted? . . . Really, Francis, what is the matter? You seem so absent, so distant."

"I will tell you face to face," Francis said. "If I may, I will come to see you this afternoon. Will you be at home around six?"

"I will, since you say you are coming. No engagement can stand in the way of that. . . . Francis? Hello! Hello!"

He had hung up.

He found her alone, in a mauve dressing gown with a plunging neckline that revealed a still firm throat and bosom. She received him wordlessly, with a meek, questioning, subdued glance. With almost aggressive deliberation, he sat down and looked at her for a few moments in silence. Her inquiring eyes never left his face as she offered him a cigarette and took one herself.

"Well, Francis? Are you finally going to inform me of the charges against me? I can't imagine what dreadful things someone must have said about me. . . ."

"No one, Solange, has said anything about you. I will reproach you only for what I have observed myself. Here are the facts, as I know them. Then you tell me honestly if you approve of your own conduct. . . . Two weeks ago, I gave you to understand that I should like to meet Chantal at Marly. You immediately invited her and me for the weekend. . . . Disloyalty to Juliette—"

"You forget, Francis, that I scarcely knew Juliette at the time and that Chantal is my best friend."

"Just a minute! Juliette comes to see you; she confesses her fears to you; you promise her your support; you disinvite Chantal; and three days later, you demolish—with the most efficacious ferocity—you demolish the image I had of her. . . . Disloyalty toward Chantal."

"This is going a little far, Francis. One would say—"

"Just a minute! When you saw I was utterly thrown by this, you set about hitching me to your chariot. Second disloyalty to Juliette."

She laughed uncertainly.

"This is too absurd, Francis! Who, in this story, was the first to be disloyal, if not you? . . . What? You ask me to oblige you and then reproach me for doing it. You are unfaithful to your wife—stupidly—but it is I who have wronged her. I try to rescue you from a tramp, and I am blamed. You go pretty far, my dear."

"I am not trying in the slightest, Solange, to absolve myself at your expense. Yes, I have wronged Juliette—seriously—and I am going to try to make up for that by going back to her, and being faithful this time. But admit that dragging me off to

Marly to be alone with you was not the way you would have kept the promise you made her."

She exhaled a long, slow thread of smoke through her nose, reflected a moment, and then smiled, once more all amiability.

"Perhaps you're right. I didn't see it that way. I promise you that the day I had Juliette here I wanted with all my heart to be kind to her. I sacrificed Chantal to her, and, after all, Chantal is much more useful to me in life than Juliette. . . . Yes, because your little wife made me feel sorry for her. Only Juliette has been *too* clumsy. She told me things about you that made me want to know you better. Then I talked with you a whole evening in the dark. What do you expect, my dear? I am a woman, very much so. I am not made of wood."

She laid her hand on his, and Francis quickly withdrew.

"How afraid he is of me!" Her little laugh was slightly nervous. "Take heart, O neophyte of fidelity. I am not Mme Potiphar. You've nothing to be afraid of."

For an hour they talked frankly, like old friends. As he was leaving, Francis said casually:

"Tell me, Solange, what you told me the other day Chantal had said about my book—was that true? Or was that more of your mischief?"

"There's an author for you," she said. "That's the one thing that touched him to the quick. Well, I am very sorry, my dear, but it is true."

A few days later, Juliette came to thank Solange.

"You've been so good! And clever! I would never have believed it was possible. Francis has become just as he was before that escapade. The whole Chantal thing is finished."

"Didn't I promise you, dear?" Solange said triumphantly. "You'll see, I am a *very* good friend."

They kissed fondly on the cheek.

Dinner
Under the Chestnut Trees

"Do you care for more soup, M. Ménétrier?" the waiter asked.

"No, thank you," Christian said.

"Please feel free, sir. Ask for anything you like."

"I will, I will, thank you," Christian said. "Bring the *pâté* and leave us alone."

"And M. Laurent?" the waiter said. "Another touch of Gruyère on your soup, sir?"

"M. Laurent does not want a thing—except to be left in peace," Christian said.

The waiter moved off, hurt and downcast.

"Don't bully him, Christian," Claire Ménétrier said. "He means well."

"Maybe," Christian said, "but does he have to keep interrupting the conversation?"

What Christian loved above all other pleasures was a small dinner in Paris, with a few good friends, two or three brilliant storytellers, and a constant cascade of anecdotes, ideas, and paradoxes. He preferred the free play of quick minds to political or literary discussions, which he considered a waste of time. On this particular evening, he had managed to combine the actor Léon Laurent with Jenny, the novelist, and he was expecting great things from these two virtuosos. Jenny, at seventy, had lost none of the dazzling verve of her youth. Léon Laurent, an excellent actor, had a lively curiosity about life and literature, and he was a prodigious mimic.

"What were we talking about?" Claire asked.

"Victor Hugo," Laurent said. "About Hugo and his pride. 'They accuse me of being proud,' he said, 'and it's true. My pride is my strength.' He believed in the transmigration of souls, you know, and claimed that he himself had been Isaiah, Aeschylus, and Juvenal. 'I found a line of mine in Juvenal,' he announced once. 'The exact translation of my French verse into Latin!' Which is pretty funny, if you stop to think of it."

"Of course," Christian said, "but what a genius! I don't say 'Victor Hugo, alas,' but 'Victor Hugo, thank God.' And a genius not only as a poet. There are marvelous passages in *Les Misérables*."

"Together with some amazing bits of foolishness," Laurent said. " ' "Iron," ' he once wrote, 'is English for *"fer,"* hence the word "irony." ' Imagine that! Hugo knew Latin very well, but he didn't know a word of Greek."

The waiter brought the *pâté de foie gras* and the *pommes sarladaises*.

"Wouldn't you like some more truffles, M. Ménétrier? You have only to ask. . . ."

Christian brushed him aside, and then came back to the word "irony" and asked Jenny whether she had read Thomas Hardy's *Life's Little Ironies*.

"No," she said, "but I love Hardy. He was tough and universal. *Tess* is very fine. . . . What did he mean by 'life's little ironies'?"

"A given experience or action produces consequences that are the precise opposite of what one might have expected, or faults are rewarded and virtue punished, or people invest facts with a meaning they never had."

"I see," Jenny said. "Like Helena's hair."

Three faces turned toward her inquiringly.

"What?" she said. "Have I never told you about that?"

"No," Christian said, "and yet you know how very much interested in Helena I am. There's another person who had genius."

"She's the only great French woman poet since Marceline," Laurent said. "Much superior to Marceline. But what a strange woman! She always rather frightened me."

"Me, too," Christian said. "She didn't like me. For that matter, she didn't like men. She loved fame—and love, too, but only as a theme in poetry. Above all, she loved herself."

"That isn't quite so," Jenny said. "She would have liked to love herself, only she never quite managed it. That was her tragedy. She didn't need lovers, only admirers. Which is where Robert Walter comes in, and the story of Helena's hair."

"Come, now," Claire said, "don't keep us in suspense. Tell us the story of Helena's hair."

"Mme Ménétrier, a bit more *pâté?*" the waiter said. "Don't hesitate."

"A very little bit," Claire said, with a sigh. "Don't swear, Christian. He's going."

I

"Perhaps you remember," Jenny took up her story, "how attentive Robert Walter was to Helena. . . . Yes, the banker. All Paris was talking about it twenty years ago. What was there between them? An affair? Not very likely. At the time, Helena passed for being in love—to the extent that she was capable of love—with our friend Claude. And I know for a fact that Walter had a mistress—that fairly well-known actress, Liliane Fontaine, who had married Lucien Munès. But Walter fancied himself—and with reason—a literary connoisseur. He loved poetry, and Helena's friendship flattered him. Rich people are always bored, and she was immensely witty. As for Helena, why wouldn't she have welcomed an admirer who talked to her

about herself the way she needed to hear herself talked about?
With positive idolatry, that is, but also with sincerity. He
meant it when he ranked her above all other poets. Don't forget that in those days Valéry's star was rising, and his reputation was beginning to eclipse Helena's. She was vulnerable
enough to mind, and called on the faithful to rally round.
Now, Walter owned several newspapers. He was in a position,
and he knew how, to take care of a friend's reputation. Add to
this the fact that he entertained a great deal, and entertained
brilliantly. At his house, Helena met everybody who was anybody in the literary and political world. Last but not least, he
was an excellent financial adviser for her. Money, however, was
a subject he did not like to go into outside his bank, and I
always found him much more eager to discuss Racine than the
Royal Dutch Oil Company, although he was far more competent in Royal Dutch matters than in Racine. Thanks to discreet tips from Walter, Helena used to make substantial
amounts on the stock market, which allowed her to lead that
nonchalantly luxurious life you all knew."

"But Helena had money," Christian said. "Didn't she come
from a long line of Romanian financiers? She had property in
the Carpathian Mountains, where oil flowed like water."

"For a long time," Jenny said, "the Romanian leu had been
worth very little, and those oil deposits had been opened up
only in the field of the imagination, and all those volumes of
poetry, beautiful as they were, sold scarcely at all. The days
when *Childe Harold* could pay all Byron's debts are gone forever. In a word, Robert Walter's financial advice was very welcome, and for him it was a graceful way of giving money to a
friend without seeming to. Robert was like that. I know for a
fact how much he did for older writers who had fallen on evil
days, but he hated to mix money matters with friendship or
love. He wanted to be sure he was sought after for his qualities
of mind and heart—and in him it was a legitimate pride, after
all, because he had both. Christian, you must remember his
visits to Rue Spontini. He was always to be found there between six and seven, when Helena used to take her beauty rest.
She would lie on a black divan, with her eyes closed, and Walter would read aloud to her. Now and then some phrase would

excite Helena. She was propelled into a sitting position as if by some invisible spring, and she would launch into one of those Shakespearean-fool monologues she had such a knack for. Robert would listen to her as if he were drunk. He was very intelligent but absolutely tongue-tied, and her facility simply enchanted him. He would sit there until the time came for Helena to dress for some dinner or other. She used to advise him with what seemed like frankness about his private life, but at bottom she was convinced that he loved her."

"Which wasn't entirely untrue," Claire said.

"I don't agree with you, Claire. Or at least it depends on what you mean by 'love.' Robert didn't desire Helena. He often talked to me about that androgynous body of hers, and spoke with quite evident distaste. What he admired most in her, next to her poetry, was her magnificent black hair. She used to wear it—remember?—in great braids around her very tiny head. Sometimes she would take it down for him, and one day I saw him bury his face in that cascade of hair, but he did it with devotion. When he arrived and when he left, Helena kissed him on both cheeks, but you know she used to treat all her friends like that, men and women, and her kisses meant nothing but friendship. She could have loved Robert, you know. He was good-looking and he dressed extremely well; he had perhaps a little too careful but a pleasant voice; and he treated women with the kind of courtesy that is quite rare today. Yes, definitely, without any risk of ridicule or regrets, Helena could have become his mistress, but he didn't want that. He was a very sensual man, and he knew—in Paris everyone knows these things about a woman after she's been in circulation awhile—he would find her a withdrawn, inept partner. And he had Liliane, who had none of Helena's genius but who was much more of a lover."

"A mercenary lover," Laurent said.

"No!" Jenny said. "No, Laurent. I've seen that couple from close at hand. Liliane truly loved Robert, all question of money aside, and furthermore, for the reasons I mentioned, he gave her very little. Only there was Munès, the husband, who was aware of the situation. He hadn't lived with Liliane for a long time but, being of a practical turn of mind, he was willing to be deceived provided he could reap some profit from it. You remember Munès, Christian?"

"Indeed I do. . . . A tall, languid fellow, getting along in years, with dyed hair. He looked like a rug merchant. He used to direct a little avant-garde theater."

"The theater where Liliane used to play, and that was the nub of the complicated connections between them. Lucien Munès hung on to his theater, but he lost money on it and was always in need of backers. Liliane, on the other hand, needed Munès in order to get the parts she wanted."

"Liliane had a lot of talent," Laurent said.

"A great deal, yes, but you know as well as I that to have talent *and* to be the wife of a director is double security. I used to see a lot of this particular ménage, and I've heard some odd conversations there. Munès, who was a cynical fellow, said once to Liliane, 'That's all very well, darling, but your friend Walter has promised me ten thousand new financing, and I don't see it forthcoming. . . .' Those were the days when ten thousand could still make a big difference in a theater budget. Liliane called me as witness: 'Jenny, what can I do? I've told Walter a dozen times that my husband would be needing an angel, but he pays no attention, and I know why. He wants to be loved for himself. And the funny part of that is, he *is*.' Lucien shrugged. 'That may be, but he can't believe that *I* can love him for himself. Now listen, Liliane. So far I've been patient and understanding, and I've put up with everything, but enough is enough. Here's a contract that I've had my lawyer draw up, and it covers all the terms of the Walter subsidy. I'm putting it in your hands. Either your Robert signs it within a week or he will have to give you up. Is that clear?' Liliane tried to brazen it out: 'That depends on me!' He laughed sneeringly. 'Oh, no, my dear, it depends on *me*. If I put you out, your Robert is not going to marry you, or give you new roles, or even receive you in his house. He has his precious little life as bachelor and man about town, and he has his beloved poet lady.' 'Who is nothing more than a friend,' Liliane said. 'So they say, so they say. . . . He's proud of you so long as you are a leading lady, a star. Will he still be proud when you have to run after engagements?' It was true, and Liliane knew it only too well. She took the contract her husband was holding out to her, pretended to glance through it, folded it, and put it in her handbag."

"Did she make Walter sign it?"

"Don't be impatient. You're going straight to the point, Claire. Let me have the pleasure of spinning out my story. . . . The following Saturday—yes, I remember it was a Saturday, and you'll see that this is an important detail—I lunched with the Munès, and Lucien seemed completely satisfied. 'Liliane's a good girl,' he told me. 'The contract will be signed Monday.' As we were leaving the table, I managed to be alone with Liliane. 'It wasn't too difficult?' I asked. 'Pretty hard,' she said. 'Poor Robert didn't want to understand. Because, first of all, he himself could never be so cynical as Lucien. And then because he's proud and he doesn't like to give in. But I put on a tremendous scene. Oh, the best performance of my career! I described my home life to him, how harsh Lucien is, the impossible demands he makes. . . . And I showed him how he, Robert, was egotistical, asking everything of me, although he's incapable of making the smallest sacrifice for me. I told him that I love him, which is true, and that I want nothing more than to go away with him, to live with him, which is equally true, but that since he doesn't want that, I am forced to put up with, to endure Lucien. . . . And finally I broke down his resistance.' "

"Why didn't Walter sign right away?" Claire asked.

"Because he wanted to have the contract looked over by an expert, too, and find out exactly what he would be committing himself to. That's natural enough."

"I can see Fontaine in that scene from here," Laurent said. "She must have been superb. I played with her in *Wedding March*. Do you know that she made me cry."

"That day she made Robert Walter cry, but the next day it was her turn. I told you, the next day was a Sunday. Robert had been invited to spend the weekend with the Thianges, who own a handsome hunting lodge near Rambouillet. And there he had the most banal and the most dangerous accident in the world. He tried to jump across a little ditch, slipped, the gun he was carrying went off, and Walter was hit in the abdomen."

"A real accident?"

"No one questioned that. . . . You're thinking of a disguised suicide? But why would that happy man kill himself? No, it was a simple, stupid, irreparable accident. They carried him back, dying, to the house. Between groans of pain, he kept insisting, 'A notary, I want a notary.' Thianges telephoned to a notary in Rambouillet, but the man was in Paris and his office was closed. The doctor, seeing that Robert had only a few minutes to live, asked him, 'Do you want to make a will?' 'Yes,' Robert answered, 'I want to leave my entire fortune to . . .' But no one was able to catch the name. He fell into a coma and died the same day."

"And you think he wanted to make Liliane his heir, to set her free?"

"I'm sure of it, Claire. She had moved him, she had made him feel remorseful, and he had no near relatives. It was the natural thing to do. But that was not how Helena saw it. After all, she lived in almost another world, she scarcely knew Liliane existed, and knew nothing at all about Walter's relationship with her. For Helena, Robert's last words could only end one way: 'I bequeath my entire fortune to Helena. . . .' She was deeply moved. That same evening she wrote a poem, a very fine one; it's called 'On the Death of a Friend.' Then she let down the long hair he had loved and, shaking with sobs, she cut it off.

"Two days later, she attended the funeral, with her head swathed in black crepe. The Munès couple, who were present, watched her in surprise. As she passed beside the grave, with a romantic gesture she threw her hair onto the casket, and as it fell, the long braids unwound. It created a tremendous sensation. 'Poor boy,' she said, as we left the cemetery together, she leaning on my arm. 'Poor boy! I always knew that he loved me, but he never had the courage to tell me so nor I to make him speak. I owed this sacrifice to his spirit. . . .' And that is the story of Helena's hair."

II

"It grew out again," Claire said.

"Obviously," Jenny said, "and the new raven fleece has since gone to join her imaginary lover. Life is very simple, at bottom, even when it is ironic."

"Very simple and very hard," Christian said. "Papa Hugo was not wrong. Irony does come from iron."

"M. Ménétrier," the waiter said, "what will you have for dessert? A soufflé? *Profiteroles?* Crepes suzette? Whatever you wish."

"For me, fruit," Jenny said.

"Strawberries and cream?" Christian asked.

"Strawberries and no cream," Laurent said. "I have to watch my weight."

"Chilled fruit," Claire said, "with ice cream—vanilla or strawberry."

"As you like, Madame," the waiter said. "At your service, Madame."

"Strawberries with powdered sugar for everyone," Christian said. "You can serve them."

"I also have a story, a very recent one," Claire said, "that seems to me one of the little ironies of Paris life. Were you at the Museum of Modern Art yesterday, Jenny, for the opening of the Komaroff Collection?"

"Yes, I saw you across the room, but I couldn't battle my way over to you. What a crowd! And those paintings, what gems! Bonnard, Seurat, Matisse, and a dozen more are better represented there than in the best American collections. That little Sisley is the finest thing of his I've ever seen. I'd no idea that this Komaroff owned such treasures. Who is he, exactly? Russian? English? I saw from the catalogue that he has a British title—Sir Ivan Komaroff."

"He's of Russian origin, and a British subject," Christian said. "He is the copper king."

"And by a miracle the king of copper has made a very happy choice of some of the best French painting? Did he bring an innate taste for good painting with him from Russia?"

"Now it's my turn, Jenny, to say 'Don't be impatient. . . .' First of all, had you ever met Lady Komaroff?"

"No. Why 'had'? Is she dead?"

"Three years ago. We knew her, Christian and I. She was an American from Baltimore, a very pretty woman, and she loved France, and Paris especially, with a passion that very few French people can even conceive of. The rest of us love Paris and we are really happy only in France, but that's natural. France is our country, we are among our own people, and Paris is the background in which we've been brought up. But think of those foreigners who have dreamed of Paris since they were children. They study the street maps of Paris so well that when they come here for the first time, they feel at home and never have to ask their way of anyone. Our monuments are so famil- iar to them that they don't even feel they're seeing them for the first time. And yet the light, the air, the ease, the wit—all this surpasses anything they have imagined. For them, Paris be- comes one of those magic potions that produce such a sense of well-being that once a person has tried them, he can no longer do without them."

"That's true," Laurent said. "I was sitting at table the other day next to a young Chilean woman, and this is what she told me: 'Back home in Santiago, the shutters were always drawn. In the middle of the day, we lived with electric light. Mother insisted on it, and I never understood why. When I grew up, I got up enough courage to ask her. And then she explained to me that at the time Papa was Secretary at the Embassy in Paris, they lived in an apartment from which she used to see the Arc de Triomphe and the Champs Élysées. "I loved that view so much," she told me, "that I have never been able to bear an- other. That's why I live never looking outside, and will, until the day comes when we can all go back to Paris.' "

"Your little Chilean friend was going a bit far," Claire said, "but there are thousands of women in the world who suffocate the moment they are deprived of this oxygen. This was the case with Lady Komaroff. She had started out in life as a young American girl with no money, the daughter of a Baptist minis- ter in Maryland, but she was remarkably beautiful. Her father, at very great sacrifice, managed to send her to college, where she studied literature and fine arts. She wrote poetry and she painted, both quite badly. She suffered from that flaw that ruins so much American talent—striving to keep up with the latest fashion. The college where she was studying had the excellent policy of sending some of its students to Paris for their third, their junior, year. For her it was a revelation. Suddenly she discovered Beauty."

"And was discovered by Komaroff."

"Wait, Christian! Don't spoil my effects. . . . Before her marriage, this little Zelda—yes, she was called Zelda, like Scott Fitzgerald's wife—lived a life of enchantment in Paris. She was staying with a French family, and the oldest son was courting her."

"With any success?"

"With a little success—evenings at the films, a kiss now and then . . . She was trying to paint portraits, and through this family, which knew the Holmanns, she got a commission to paint a portrait of Denise. Dear Denise has always remained a student at heart. In her view, any chance to be in touch with penniless youth was a good thing. She became Zelda's friend, gave her clothes, invited her to the house. And it was there that one day Komaroff, who had business dealings with Holmann, and who was already very rich—but not yet the king of copper —met this ravishing girl. He was thirty years older than she, and had been a widower for two years. It was a classic case of love at first sight. She teased him, she was rude to him, and it only made him all the more attached to her. After squiring her around through a whole winter, he offered to marry her. She consulted Denise Holmann, who heartily advised against the marriage. 'Look at my case,' she said. 'When Edmond and I married, I cared much more about him than you care for Komaroff, but we had all this damnable money between us, and our marriage has been a failure. I tell you this because all the world knows it. Oh, we've patched together the pieces of happiness as best we could, and they'll last as long as we do. . . . However, I hope that you want more than that.' But Zelda loved success, comfort, security. Komaroff offered all those things, and he was persistent. She gave in. For her it was the beginning of a prodigious climb. Ten years later, she had one country house in England, another in Sologne, a private home on Rue de Varenne, a villa in Antibes, a yacht, and a private plane; she was Lady Komaroff, one of the three best-dressed women in the world, and she was bored to extinction."

"Why? Didn't he love her?"

"Oh, yes! He never loved another woman, but he had scarcely any time for her, added to which he was a fearful bore. One of those men who come alive only to talk about the profits from this or that deal, the returns from his stock holdings, or the production of a factory. And since he surrounded himself with friends who were just like him, Zelda had been looking for a long time, but with no luck, for a Consoler."

"Was she looking consciously?"

"I don't believe she said to herself, 'I am looking for a lover.' More likely she thought: I am looking for a friend. Despite all her travels, she kept her old love for France, for French art, and for the charm of Paris. Her husband tried to surround her with beautiful things, but he had very little taste. In a word, she became one of those spoiled, discontented women who spend half the day in bed perpetually threatened by migraines, and she was well on her way to a sanitarium when chance suddenly offered her the companion of her heart's desire. It was the young curator of a museum in the provinces, Berger-Corot —descended from the painter on the mother's side—who had won a quick and brilliant reputation for himself in the art world because of what he had been able to do with a hitherto obscure museum. Working with a very small budget, by some kind of sixth sense, of divination, he had managed to gather together the best painters of the coming generation. Denise and a half-dozen other people had said to Lady Komaroff, 'Since you're driving south, make a detour and visit the museum at Annecy. It's quite extraordinary.' So Zelda decided to stop over at Annecy, and Berger-Corot did the honors of the municipal collection. He was an aesthetic-looking man, with a long chestnut mustache that made him appear older than he was—even this pleased Zelda—very modern in his tastes, but not prepared to slight tradition. 'One must never forget,' he said, 'that in the days when Renoir and Degas were passing as revolutionaries, they venerated the Old Masters.' With anyone else, and ten years earlier, Zelda would have hotly debated this point the whole night through. However, Berger-Corot's calm

authority and the courteous scorn he did not trouble to hide
for the aesthetic judgments of the laity had immediately fascinated Lady Komaroff. To the great surprise of Sir Ivan, who
was in Bolivia at the time, she spent two weeks in Annecy. She
had taken a suite in the one good hotel in town and, guided by
the young curator, she explored the countryside. It is a region
of mountains, forests, and waterfalls—Courbet had worked with
that landscape, and so had Cézanne. Zelda was burning to
learn, and Berger-Corot to teach."

"So he taught her many things."

"Just so," Claire said, "and things that she must have found
pleasant, because when she left him she could no longer do
without him. She did have to go on to Antibes, however, for
she had announced that she would be arriving there two weeks
earlier. Finally, she made up her mind to go, but the moment
Sir Ivan had come back from Latin America, she asked him to
invite Berger-Corot to join them on the Riviera. She didn't lack
for good arguments. 'We've been buying paintings in a blunder-
ing way for ten years,' she said to him. 'In spite of all the help
we've had from the biggest dealers—or maybe because of it—
we're spending millions to no purpose. We've built a collection
that basically doesn't interest us or anyone else, because it is
pedestrian. . . . Yes, I know, we have a Rembrandt and a Rubens and an El Greco and two Goyas, like everybody else, but
it's a mediocre Rembrandt, a run-of-the-mill Rubens, the Goyas
are late ones, painted in Bordeaux. On this basis, we will never
match a Richard Wallace, a Mellon, a Frick, a Camondo. . . .
But here is a man who has spent a hundredth, a thousandth,
of what you have put into our boring paintings, but who has
built a collection that people come from literally every corner
of the earth to see. The day I was there, I met the curator of
the Providence Museum, in Rhode Island, and the director of
the Oslo Museum. . . . Why? My dear, because this man has
something that we do not have, neither you nor I. He *knows*.' "

"Wait . . . I've met this Berger-Corot," Léon Laurent said.
"He came to Paris to live. It was he who took me, around 1935,
to see the Komaroff Collection."

"Naturally," Claire said. "He created it. And this is how it all
came about. Sir Ivan, being a husband who wanted to give his

wife pleasure, invited Berger-Corot to Antibes; and, being a simple husband, he took an immediate liking to the young expert. To succeed with Komaroff, Berger-Corot held two aces: in the matter of art, he offered him competence, and in the matter of his household, he assured him peace. From the moment of his arrival, the weeping fits, the migraines, the complaints ceased. Zelda's behavior became reasonable, even sweet. Then, when it came time for their guest to leave, she said to her husband the evening before: 'I've had an idea, Ivan. You've always intended to build yourself a gallery of paintings at Motte-Beuvron. Why not put this boy in charge of it? You tell me you like him. We'll never find anyone more competent. His demands would be very modest. They told me at Annecy how much he makes there. It's less than three thousand dollars a year, and, for that matter, we could easily arrange for him to live in the château. . . . Do this, Ivan, and you will see that in ten years people will be talking about the Komaroff Collection the way they talk now of the Groult Collection.' "

"In other words," Jenny said, "we owe this admirable art treasure to Lady Komaroff's desire to lodge her lover under the conjugal roof without her husband's being able to say a word against it."

"Even better," Claire said. "She had him installed there by the husband himself, and paid a salary in the bargain. Let's concede that Berger-Corot earned his pay. He worked to build this collection the way he had worked formerly for the museum, and out of it he made for Post-Impressionism what the Jeu de Paume is for Impressionism. And since he was a friend of Matisse, Vuillard, Marquet, Friesz, and the others, negotiations and purchases were much easier for him than for poor Sir Ivan."

"And the affair?" Jenny wanted to know. "What happened with the affair? That is the important point, Claire."

"The affair was a success. Berger-Corot's one fault was his immense self-satisfaction. Living with Zelda, who thought he was God, he was perfectly content. You can imagine how intoxicating it must be, when one is a young man mad about painting, to have at one's disposal almost unlimited funds to buy paintings one loves, to create a museum in perfect freedom, without hostile superiors and incompetent public officials to interfere—and then to live in this 'house of miracles' with a charming woman who loves and adores you. Never was there a happier man, but no doubt he deserved his happiness, for she kept the same admiration for him to the day of her death."

"What became of him?" Laurent asked.

"Well, you know that Zelda died of cancer three years ago. Her lover survived her only a short while. Whether it was grief or accident I don't know, but the following winter he caught a severe grippe, and then came a heart attack, and suddenly he was gone. . . . Sir Ivan was left alone with this wonderful collection, but he didn't want to keep it. He had debated a long time whether to present it to France or to England. But this powerful man who has had everything has one nagging weakness—he loves decorations. A clever minister who remembered that France had lost the Wallace Collection for lack of a red ribbon had the wit to offer one this time. Hence yesterday's splendid ceremony, where, as you saw, Sir Ivan was decorated with the Légion d'Honneur in the midst of his paintings and praised to the skies by the Minister of National Education in the august presence of the President of the Republic."

"And all that," Christian said, "because for ten years his wife had a lover who was a great walrus-mustached art expert."

"M. Ménétrier," the waiter said, "a drop of kirsch on your strawberries?"

III

For some moments, Léon Laurent had been sitting with the abstracted air of a man who while he is listening to one story is also thinking of the story he will have presently to tell himself. In any conversation, Jenny was consummately skillful in playing orchestra conductor. She had noticed Laurent and was biding her time until she could have the theme picked up again by this fresh instrument.

"In your theater, Laurent," she said now, "you must have seen more than one of life's little ironies."

"With your permission," he said, "I will tell you a strange

story from the theater world. I have it from a prominent lawyer whom I saw last week in connection with a detective film—"

"That's so, you seem to love detective roles, Laurent," Claire said. "Might one ask why?"

"My dear friend," Laurent said, "the role of detective provides a man of my age with the same intoxication that a Don Juan part gives a younger actor. The omniscient detective feels he is all-powerful."

"So you, shall we say, procure your pleasure from the triumphs of the character you play?"

"Of course," Laurent said. "The actor, like the writer, 'reimburses himself as best he can for the injustices of fate.' You were talking about Liliane Fontaine a while ago. She insists that she can only play a love scene perfectly when she is not in love. . . . But I don't want to go on tonight about the actor's paradox. It's getting late. The waiters are beginning to hover around and would clearly like to chase us away, but I would still like to tell you my gangster story."

"Good!" Jenny said. "I adore gangster stories."

"So, I heard from my lawyer," Laurent said, "that for the last three years, two notorious gang leaders have been living in Paris, with no love lost between them. One of the bosses, Mario le Fou, was a young fellow from the Midi, a daredevil—an excellent technician in bank robberies, but too reckless and too quick on the trigger. A large number of robberies had been attributed to him, plus a few murders, but the police could never put the finger on him. The other man—his name was Salvèdre, but he was known to the trade as 'the Professor'—was kingpin in the network of car thieves. He had perfected this job to a point where it had become a kind of assembly-line operation, in which several shifts or crews worked for him. He himself was never implicated. His role was to divide the city into sectors and to assign them among his lieutenants, and then to organize the collection, rapid repainting, and resale of the cars they picked up. He passed for being a distinguished, cultivated man—hence the nickname of 'Professor.' He had a college degree and a licence to practice law, and was, so my lawyer told me, an extremely pleasant person to meet. In fact, he moved in circles in Paris where no one suspected his identity or his criminal activities. His daughter, Marcelle Salvèdre, went to one of the best of the fashionable schools in town, and married a man whom I know well and who works in a perfectly honorable profession. Salvèdre had a mistress, an extremely pretty little woman called Marian Carstair—English of origin who, through the course of a very movemented youth, had preserved the delicate, tender face of a Reynolds angel. Salvèdre worshiped this girl. He was a bit sentimental, apparently, and, for that matter, he never showed any brutality in his professional activities. He insisted that his men work unarmed, and he always urged them to take on only a sure thing, where no violence would be necessary. So, although the police knew that he was at the center of a whole web of thefts, they had never been able to get any conclusive evidence against him. They kept him under surveillance, but where did they find him? Not in shady bars but dining at the Ritz or at Larue, with people who were above reproach."

"A good character for Conan Doyle," Christian said.

"A good character for me," Laurent said. "It's a role I'd love to play."

"That need to be all-powerful," Jenny said.

"Exactly," Laurent said. "Nevertheless, this man who was so completely master of himself began to show a touch of impatience when Mario le Fou and his gang suddenly seemed to be encroaching on his territory. Strictly speaking, it wasn't that there was any treaty between the two men that marked out their zones of influence, but up to this point there had been a tacit, friendly understanding. Mario and his friends had the exclusive on housebreaking; Salvèdre ruled over the streets and the immense outdoor garage otherwise known as the Paris curb. Suddenly last May, without warning, Mario's men began rounding up cars. At first, Salvèdre, who was a reasonable, easygoing man, thought that very likely they needed a few for their own work, and he shut his eyes. But soon the rhythm of operations built up until he could no longer doubt that they were deliberately defying him. Under the pressure of complaints from his own men, he decided to see Mario, although he found it distasteful to be in contact with a kind of gangster he didn't approve of. Naturally, he could not meet Mario in a public place. It was decided that the two bosses would meet in Marian Carstair's little apartment, in Neuilly."

"But weren't they both shadowed?"

"Yes, but skillful in eluding their shadowers . . . And, in fact, they met without being disturbed. Mario gave some highly implausible explanations and promised to pass on very firm orders to his crews. Salvèdre had impressed him by his correct dress and polished language, but at the same time had irritated him with his air of superiority. On the other hand, Mario had found Marian Carstair charming. That evening she was wearing a very low-cut dressing gown that allowed the glimpse of a gently swelling, perfect bosom. She was mildly flirtatious because Mario was younger and more handsome than Salvèdre. And perhaps also because the scent of blood hovered around him, whereas Salvèdre's hands were clean."

"Right back to Papa Hugo," Jenny said. " '*Les belles ont le goût des héros et le mufle/ Hagard d'un scélérat, superbe sous le buffle,/ Fair bâiller tendrement l'hiatus des fichus. . . .*' "

"I know," Christian said. "The last lines go: '*Et c'est la volupté de toutes ces colombes/ D'ouvrir leurs lits à ceux qui font ouvrir les tombes.*' "

"And so it was that this dove was tempted to open her bed to the black-haired bandit, and that Mario and Marian did meet again, for presently one of Salvèdre's men reported to him that Miss Carstair was receiving his rival on evenings when he, Salvèdre, was going to Lyons or to Marseilles, where he had just opened branch operations. Whatever horror a man may have of blood, some offenses are intolerable. The Mario gang, flouting any promises, were continuing to poach on Salvèdre's territory; furthermore, Mario was stealing his mistress, whom he loved dearly. He had to put an end to both. One evening, after announcing *urbi et orbi* that he was leaving for Lyons, he took a Browning and went straight to Marian Carstair's apartment. It was on the fifth floor of a building near the Pont de Neuilly. Naturally, he had a key. He found his mistress and his rival together and naked in bed. Without a moment's hesitation—a second's hesitation with a man like Mario would have been fatal—he killed the man with one bullet through the forehead. He could have killed Marian, too, who had leaped from bed and thrown herself at his feet, with her long blond hair streaming over the rug. But he loved the girl, and her great beauty touched him, so he simply brushed her aside without any brutality. He replaced the revolver in his pocket and left."

"A great scene," Jenny said. "The movie is made."

"Wait! As he walked down the four flights, Salvèdre, who was a methodical man, had time to reflect. He who had such a horror of violent crime had just put himself in a very bad spot. The murder of a rival is rather readily absolved by French juries when it is a matter of a crime of passion, but he had killed the gang leader who was his professional competitor without simultaneously striking down their shared mistress. The public prosecutor would argue, would he not, that the motive for the crime had not been jealousy but gang warfare. Perhaps he would even be suspected of having used Marian to entice the other gangster into a trap. All this would strike a very unpalatable note. At the foot of the stairs, he stopped and thought for a long time. Then he turned and climbed up again, stopping at every landing and breathing heavily, like a deeply disturbed man. When he reached the apartment, he went in and found Marian kneeling beside the corpse with its punctured forehead. She looked up at him with a grief-stricken, questioning expression. He did not say a word, drew the Browning from his pocket, and killed her with a ball under the left breast."

In the restaurant, around the four diners the lights were beginning to go out. The waiters were discreetly signaling their wish to go home.

"I've almost finished," Laurent said. "Salvèdre went directly to his lawyer, who is a friend of mine and the man to whom I owe the story. With his usual coolness and sobriety, he related what he had done. 'You understand me,' he said. 'I hated to kill her. The poor child. She hadn't done anything so very wrong, and, in any case, she didn't deserve death, but you see my situation. . . . If I had spared her, there would be no crime of passion. If I executed her together with her accomplice, it seemed to me that I was making your defense case easier. Am I right?' 'No doubt about it,' the lawyer said. 'Considering it from the point of view of morality and charity only, you were doubly guilty. But it is a fact that, while there's no possible defense for your first murder, your second will surely win you an acquittal."

"A slow thinker!" Christian said.

The last lamp went out and there remained above the table only two lighted brackets. Christian called for the check.

"Don't feel hurried, M. Ménétier," the waiter said. "By all means, take your time."

Bodies and Souls

"No. I don't believe you Englishwomen have the zest for emotion that our Frenchwomen have."

"What right have you to say such a thing? What do you know about it?"

"Why shouldn't I know? You treat love as if it were a sport. A great passion is boring, you think—or in bad taste."

"That's a very odd way to describe the country of Shakespeare. What seems to us in bad taste is to flaunt passion, but not the experience itself. As a people, we are more reserved, that is true. But I am positive that one would find more great love affairs among us than with you. Some of our women who strike you as being frigid would do anything for love. And that is precisely what they do do. Did you ever know the Duchess of Stafford? The late Duchess, I mean—Sybil."

"I was invited down to Warfield several times when I was a young man. But that was before the First World War. She must have died around 1920?"

"She died later than that, but toward the end she didn't see anyone. How do you remember her?"

"A face so beautifully modeled that it could never grow old . . . A birdlike woman who was at her best in light or private conversation . . . She used to run that immense house admirably. A weekend at Warfield unfolded like a perfectly rehearsed show, and yet every Saturday a veritable army of guests would descend on the house. The Duke amused me. He had such self-confidence, such an instinctive sense of authority, and such contempt for anyone else's opinion that he achieved a kind of unflawed wholeness. He used to dress like his farmers—you remember?—only his clothes were even more worn than theirs, full of holes, even. He spoke very little, and badly at that, stammering and yawning. And yet his prestige was so great that one word from him in the House of Lords always carried the day for his party. . . . I love these granite-like men."

"That's all very true, but I was talking to you about the Duchess."

"The bird that nested in the hollow of that mountain."

"Don't believe it. Sybil had numerous lovers, always with the most perfect discretion—which is to say that all London knew but that neither she nor the Duke would have countenanced anyone's speaking to them about it. The Duke approved of his wife's lovers' being invited to Warfield. They assured the even tenor of his life. Also, most of them belonged to his party. It was at Warfield, among the smooth shoulders of women and the glitter of crystal chandeliers, that the really important public issues were dealt with. All the men had known each other at Eton or Harrow, or at Oxford or Cambridge. In those days, British politics was essentially a weekend business, and the affairs of the women made it easier for their husbands to meet."

"May I point out that you are adding fuel to my fire? I don't see much passion in the cynical attitude that good form alone—"

"Wait. My story hasn't even begun. Passion appeared on the scene around 1890, when a man five years younger than she, Harold Wicks, converted the Duchess to the strictest fidelity."

"Harold Wicks? I never knew that."

"But you have heard of him."

"A great deal. As a highly gifted political man and, as you English say so freely, a future prime minister."

"He was indeed a future prime minister."

"Who never became one."

"No, and presently you will know why. Like the prince in the fairy tale, Harold seemed to have been granted every charm while still in his cradle. He had golden red hair and a face as perfectly chiseled as Byron's, but his expression was never somber or moody. On the contrary, one sensed a wit and an airy grace that had made a Shelley and later a Rupert Brooke. While he was still at Oxford, his friends realized that he was destined for a brilliant career. When he was twenty-five, the party found a constituency for him. He was handsome, eloquent, fond of sports—a combination that won him overwhelming victories in elections. Before he was thirty, he had got a minor but promising post in the Cabinet that was presided over then by the great Charles Brooks, who was more familiarly known as C.B."

"I met C.B. when he was an old man. He was frail, courteous, courageous, and distinguished. But a little distant . . ."

"One had to grasp the nuances of his nature. With his friends, he was exquisite. You should have seen him at Warfield, lying on the rug at Sybil's feet like the family cat, or in the park watching a sunset. 'Very tasteful this evening,' he would say, giving a plus mark to Nature. . . . Do you remember how, around the turn of the century, the country's elite was divided into two coteries—and by 'elite' I mean the two or three thousand people who used to visit noble houses in the country every weekend, and therefore believed they were the leaders of England? There was the Prince of Wales's clique, which was made up of the *bons vivants*, the connoisseurs of wine, cigars, horses, and women, and the expert financiers and cosmopolitan diplomats. Then there was C.B.'s group—people used to call them 'the Souls'—which included a few very cultivated statesmen who read the classics in the original Greek and Latin, a few of the more aesthetic writers, and also women, young and old, who were of a philosophic or poetic turn of mind. In the

Prince's coterie, which was sometimes called 'the Bodies,' love affairs were brief and carnal; in C.B.'s group, they were platonic, mystical, and enduring. Sybil—and her husband, the Duke, even more—belonged by temperament to the Prince's circle. Harold Wicks, because his gifts were so varied, oscillated on the frontier between the two domains. His cultivation and a kind of spiritual unrest brought him close to the Souls, but his very lively taste for women drew him toward the world where they were more easily approachable. His liaison with the Duchess finally threw him into the carnal camp, which would have saddened his chief—imperceptibly—if C.B. hadn't considered regret unworthy of a philosopher."

"But if I remember correctly, the Souls exasperated the Duchess. I've heard her say, 'It's so restful to find someone who talks about nothing but the weather and horses.' Or, 'I love stupid people and generally they love me.'"

"Your memory doesn't trick you. Only, when Sybil was with the Souls she could split a hair with the best of them, just like a professional Soul. And it's a fact that she kept Harold Wicks for herself for several years. . . . How? I remember finding myself one day in a three-way conversation with C.B. and Cynthia, Lady Romfrey—Lady Romfrey was a Soul, indeed one of the highest-ranking members of the fraternity. This was at Warfield, one spring day, in the shelter of a boxwood arbor. 'Nothing could be more natural,' Cynthia was saying, 'than that Sybil should have wanted Harold. What's most surprising is that she caught him. Other men could have been seduced by the title, or by the remains—and they're not to be slighted—of great beauty, or by the pastoral, ducal charm of Warfield. Or they would have been glad to be supported in their career by a man of Lord Stafford's weight. But Harold has been force-fed with duchesses from the cradle. And he has talent enough to take care of himself.' 'My dear,' C.B. answered, stretching out his long legs, 'the more you study human behavior, the more complex you find it. Sybil is infinitely less profound than our Harold, but she is amusing. Who knows if our friend may not need to be amused if he is to endure himself? I know this young man very well. He is full of conflicts. Politics has killed the poet in him, but that poet is taking a long time to die. Philosophy has cast doubt into the heart of an Anglo-Catholic. Sybil's chatter covers this dangerous dialogue. And never forget that she makes life extremely easy for him. Why did she insist so that I come this weekend? Because Harold needed a long talk with me. . . . He's had it. Why is Cambon expected tomorrow? Because Harold is preparing a speech on Africa, and he wants to know the French position. . . . All these things are admirably contrived for him. He knows that very well.' 'Excellent reasons, C.B.,' Cynthia said, 'but reason does not rule love. Let a young woman appear tomorrow—' 'But a great many young women have appeared over the last six years.' 'And by the same token, Sybil is six years older. . . . The other evening, at my house, Harold talked for a long time with Celia Norton. Now there, if he wanted to marry, is the wife he should have. And Harold *must* get married. If ever a man was singled out by Destiny, he is. But a minister, and above all a prime minister, needs a household, a wife. . . . *You* aren't married, C.B., I'm not forgetting that, but you are a saint. Harold is too vulnerable to stand alone. Sybil might hold him for another four or five years at the outside, and then . . . It's not pleasant to see an aging woman cling to a man, not pleasant for her or for him. I know that—' "

' But the Duchess was not old at that point. What could she have been? Forty?"

"A little older. And you're judging her as a man of today. In the last century, people aged more quickly."

"I was very young myself then, and I found her very beautiful. But tell me about Celia Norton. I imagine she plays a role in your story."

"How perspicacious of you! . . . Yes, a big role, but not so big as you suppose."

"Come, dispense with all the mysteries and get on with your story. Who was Celia Norton?"

"You've met her several times."

"I don't think so."

"Yes, you have, but then she was called Lady Brennan."

"What! The marvelous Lady Brennan? That serious, touching creature?"

"The same, and she was even more marvelous as a young

woman. . . . Divine . . . Oh, that's a worn-out word, but she
did have the carriage of a goddess. A complexion like magnolia
blossoms. Gray eyes that were flecked with dark lilac. Her
charm was gentle and subtle at once, and she was prodigiously
intelligent but utterly unpedantic. She was my age, and I saw
her debut in society. All the men were mad about her, but she
didn't seem to notice. She kept her air of a Diana who had in
her something of a Minerva."

"And she won Harold Wicks?"

"The way she won them all—just by her presence. But the
extraordinary part was that Harold—"

"Won her?"

"How you do rush things! . . . She simply let it be clear
that it did not displease her to be sought out by him. Thinking
back, it was quite natural. He was the most remarkable man of
his generation, and she the most perfect woman. They had
been created for one another by a nominating decree of Providence. . . . It was a Frenchman who said that, wasn't it?"

"Yes, Renan . . . What! You've read Renan? I must
admit—"

"I told you Englishwomen are reserved. . . . In a word,
Celia and Harold saw each other again several times, always
with the same delight, and in Soul circles people began to talk
of a possible marriage, all very favorably. As I told you, up to
that point Harold had stayed on the frontiers of the Bodies
and Souls. Celia drew him into our camp. Several times he
refused invitations to Warfield in order to go to Bramley, to Sir
Edward Norton's, Celia's father. Naturally, his attentiveness in
this quarter, plus a change in his attitude, plus the remarks of a
few women friends only too happy to bear sad tidings, alerted
the Duchess to the great danger."

"She must always have known that someday Harold would
marry."

"No doubt, but there are marriages and marriages. A woman
who wants to keep her lover for herself can choose for him a
wife so mediocre that the wife will enhance the value of what
he's just left and to which he will quickly return. But Celia
Norton, on the contrary, was one of those women who make a
man forget everyone who's gone before, and this the Duchess

very well knew. The marriage had to be prevented at any cost. However, Sybil could not offer any violent opposition—first, because she hated scandal as much as she loved sin, but especially because her opposition would only have hastened what she dreaded. For all his exquisite manners, Harold Wicks could be brutal if he was provoked. When he did not come to Warfield for several weeks, thus signifying that their liaison was finished, she wrote him a meek, resigned letter, begging him only to come once more, the following weekend. The Duke, she said, needed to see him and also had noticed his absence, which was creating a bad impression."

"That last detail would be worthy of the most Parisian of Becque's Parisians."

"My dear, I am weary of explaining to you that we English-women have nothing to learn from your Parisians. . . . At this point in my story, I must introduce a new female character."

"As beguiling as Celia Norton?"

"In her way, yes, but quite different. At that time, there was a Russian living in London, a Count Ananiev, who had had to leave Russia after some quarrel or other with the Czar. He had been received in London by the best society and in particular by the intimates of Edward VII, one of whom was the Duke of Stafford. This Count Ananiev had a daughter, Natalie—"

"I see what's coming."

"You see nothing of the sort. Natalie Mikhailovna had neither the pure beauty nor the serenity of Celia Norton. Exile meant for her that life would be precarious, and she was a fighting animal. Her emerald-green eyes were always on the lookout for an unknown enemy. And what a figure! She dressed rather too daringly—she enjoyed exciting men, and she succeeded. Sybil had seen something of her own youthful self in this young foreigner, and had taken her up. Natalie was to be seen at Warfield every weekend—"

"Where the Duke—"

"No, my dear, no! The Duke did not bother himself about young women. When he was not talking politics or horses, he stayed clear of his guests. No, Natalie was the friend of the Duchess. Sybil even had a studio set up for her in one of the pavilions in the park, for the girl was a talented sculptor."

"And you're going to tell me she didn't have the Duke pose for her?"

"No artist in the world could have managed to persuade the Duke to pose. But Sybil did have Harold Wicks pose for several weekends in a row."

"Rash Duchess."

"Less rash than you think. She was present at all the sittings. But it was soon obvious that Natalie had fallen in love with her model. How could it have been otherwise? Harold was handsome, virile, brilliant. He was interested in Russian fiction, and talked about it competently, as he did about everything. And he had charm. All this was quite enough."

"And he, for his part—"

"He, for his part, could not be indifferent to such glowing admiration and to such fresh, provocative sensuality, but he carried in his heart the face of Celia Norton, and that lovely profile superimposed itself on any other image, and blurred it. Sybil had quickly seen that the sittings were in no way dangerous."

"Dangerous not for the model but for the sculptor."

"Of course. Sybil was aware of that, too, which explains why, in her extreme distress over the rumor of her lover's imminent engagement, she decided to appeal to Natalie."

"That was falling from Charybdis into—"

"Not at all. If Harold married Celia, he would have henceforth, for his whole life, a wife after his own heart—a woman able to share his life in every area, cultivated as women no longer are, and one who was, despite her youth, even then the friend and confidante of the Prime Minister. No hope, therefore, of ever seeing him come back to the Duchess. Sybil could admit—and even approve—of Harold's marrying, as I told you, if she was sure of dominating the couple. With Celia, who would have been an associate as well as a companion, and who shared Harold's slightly utopian ideas about the future of the party as well as his tastes in art, the marriage would have been marvelous and indissoluble. 'Anything, even Natalie, rather than that!' the Duchess said to herself."

"But your portrait of Natalie—"

"Natalie was fantastically beautiful, it's true, and she had a certain aggressiveness, but she lacked all the rest. And the rest is everything. She was a foreigner, and you know how little a foreigner really counts in English society. Celia had known since childhood the great families that are so necessary to a young, ambitious statesman. She had an instinct for political life. Her tact had already impressed C.B. and the other party leaders. Natalie . . . Natalie amused Society, she was not a part of it. Or belonged only as a guest—"

"So the Duchess thought that if Harold Wicks married the little Countess Ananiev, he would soon come back to her. Is that it? But just how does one persuade a man to sacrifice the woman he loves to a woman he doesn't love?"

"You'll find out. I admit it involved a diabolic, bold, shameless plan, but whoever wants to win his point . . . You must remember, before passing judgment on her, that Sybil herself had had a very movemented life and had developed a personal morality that was very free. Think back to your Frenchwomen of the eighteenth century; they will help you understand her. In the end, Sybil had a frank and even cynical talk with Natalie. 'I know,' she said to her, 'that you love Harold. Am I wrong?' Natalie admitted that she was not wrong. 'Well,' Sybil went on, 'if you want to marry him—' Natalie interrupted to say that, alas, she had no such idea. 'I know that, too,' the Duchess said, 'and if you want to bring him around to such an idea, you will have to follow exactly and without question the tactic I'm going to sketch out for you. It will surprise you, shock you, but follow it. . . . Saturday next, Harold is coming to Warfield. You will occupy the bedroom next to his. Between the two rooms there is a connecting door. Under some pretext or other, during the night you will mistake your way and you will enter Harold's room. . . .' I leave the rest to your imagination."

"Diabolic for sure—and not very prudent. It wasn't at all sure that such light conduct would lead to marriage. After all, a man can, without too great scruples, take a girl who throws herself in his arms and not feel that he has to marry her."

"Can't you wait, and let me go on? Natalie was terrified by this scheme. Once again you must go back to the eighteenth century. Young girls were virgins; adventures were reserved for married women. I don't know what the Duchess, her wits sharpened by passion, was inspired to suggest to her. The fact remains, she convinced Natalie. Before every weekend, with the help of her secretary, the elderly Miss Ford, Sybil used to assign her guests their rooms. It was a very simple operation, after all, since it involved enabling people to meet again the people they wanted to meet again—or so the Duchess believed—or to meet for the first time, but it was slightly complicated by the fact that Miss Ford was not supposed to know or understand the rules of the game. Naturally, Miss Ford knew perfectly well what the purpose of this little chore was, and Sybil knew that Miss Ford knew, but both proprieties and private purposes were served by silence. A very British solution, I hasten to add to spare you the temptation of saying it."

"I wouldn't have said it. Only thought it."

"Thank you."

"Miss Ford must have been very much surprised when she was instructed to give to a person so tempting as Natalie Ana- niev a neighbor who was the customary partner of the lady of the manor."

"Why so? Miss Ford had been around for a long time, and I'm sure she saw the drift of it all quite clearly. At this point, if I were a novelist I could offer you a voluptuous account of Natalie's first night of love, but I would have to invent all the episodes, because no one was ever given any details about it."

"Not even the Duchess?"

"She simply knew when she saw Natalie's languid face the next morning that everything had gone according to plan."

"Harold Wicks offered to marry her?"

"What do you take him for? I repeat, he loved Celia Norton. He gave in to a temptation that had been too strong, but he tried not to attach too much importance to his brief encounter with Natalie. After all, it was she who had initiated hostilities. He even had the courage—and if you had known Natalie at that time, you would understand it called for a great deal—to refuse an invitation to Warfield for the following weekend. From there on, it was the Duchess' move."

"Without Miss Ford this time?"

"Miss Ford had nothing more to do with it. The Staffords had come back to London, to their Mayfair house, and Sybil sent young Countess Ananiev an urgent message. This was a few weeks after the crucial night. She found a disturbed, deeply unhappy young woman, who even dared upbraid her sharply. 'On your advice, I've given him every reason to despise me. I love him more than ever, and I can't ever hope to be married to him. Celia Norton is talking openly about her engagement, and the announcement of their wedding plans is to be made any day.' "

"Perfectly legitimate reproaches. The poor child . . ."

"The Duchess answered all the reproaches and laments with utter serenity. 'Before passing judgment on my plan,' she said, 'wait for it to be fully carried out. What I am going to ask you now will seem even more cynical to you than my first advice. But if you do as I say, you'll win your game—and Harold. If you don't, you will lose—and lose beyond repair. What you must do now is go to him and tell him—or ask me to tell him for you—that you are pregnant.' Natalie cried out in honest horror. 'But that's not true!' Sybil went on: 'It isn't true, apparently, and I am sorry for that. However, it is plausible and it would make the marriage necessary. Then it would be up to you, obviously, to win your husband's affection and also his forgiveness. Being the person you are, that should not be difficult.' "

"Your Duchess was a monster of duplicity."

"No, she was a woman in love defending her love."

"At the expense of three other people, and by the most dreadful methods."

"She would have defended it against a hundred enemies. . . . As would I, in her place. You still don't know very much about women, my dear. We can be tigresses, if need be, to keep what we love. Your Balzac understood that."

"And Natalie agreed?"

"She let things take their course. The Duchess undertook to inform Harold, pretending to be surprised and reproaching him bitterly for having offended the canons of decency and hospitality by taking advantage of a young girl in a house that should have been doubly sacred to him. He was appalled, but when she added that there remained for him only one solution —marriage as soon as possible, followed by a trip abroad—he became furious. He loved Celia, he said, and he had made commitments to her that he intended to keep. 'Don't you see,' she said, 'that you have nothing more to offer her? In a few weeks, this whole story will be out. The Duke knows already, and blames you for it. You know very well that with us a man in politics is finished if his honor can be challenged. This little adventure, I am sorry to say, is far from being honorable. Will Celia Norton still want you after a scandal? Will she be able to accept the fact that while you were talking to her about your love—' "

"What a horrible woman!"

"I've told you already, I don't find her so. Up to the day of her death I felt a great deal of friendship for her. . . . Furthermore, I am telling you a true story, so passing judgment is not involved—"

"She really had told her husband?"

"Certainly. He was one of her strongest trumps. His great influence in the party made him indispensable to a young Undersecretary of State. After a few agonizing days, Harold realized that he was in a frightful situation and he requested an interview with the man he esteemed most highly in the whole world—the Prime Minister. Notice that he approached C.B. not so much as his political chief but rather as a philosopher and a mentor in matters of conscience. C.B. listened to him with surprise and chagrin, but spared him any censure. When Harold had finished his confession, the Chief stretched out his long legs, leaned his head against the back of his chair, and sat for a long time deep in thought. Then, wearily and sadly, he said, 'This distresses me, Harold. You know what hopes I put in you. I considered you the best man of the younger generation. . . . Your marriage to Celia, who is also one of my spiritual children, was the crowning point of all my hopes. But after what you have just told me, hesitation is out of the question. You have to marry Natalie Ananiev. You must out of loyalty, but also out of prudence. If this story were to become known, it would ruin you, and I don't want you to be ruined.' Harold's trust in C.B. was absolute. Although he was in despair, he obeyed. He hadn't the courage to see Celia again, and in any case, such a meeting would have been both painful and useless. He wrote a long letter, frank and tender, in which in a veiled way he confessed both his lapse and his love, and in which, while he gave her back her freedom, he insisted that he could never forget or replace her."

"Here I don't find your shining young knight loyal to Natalie. To marry one young woman while allowing it to be understood that you love someone else is to insinuate that you're acting under pressure, and that immediately arouses suspicions, quite natural suspicions. Since he had decided to make her his wife—"

"You're being very severe today. I would like to have seen you in his place. You would have been painfully upset, as he was, and undecided and unhappy. . . . And what would you have done? I knew Harold very well, and I tell you he was an honorable man, and he wanted to do the honorable thing. . . . He had consulted his chief, he had received advice that was tantamount to an order, and he followed it."

"At least, did he put a good face on things for Natalie's sake, during their pseudo-engagement?"

"I scarcely ever saw them together, but I knew from Sybil that everything went off as well as possible. Harold had perfect manners, Natalie loved him, and she was young and beautiful."

"That potion, Goethe said, could make a man see a Helen in every woman."

"I don't know if he saw Helen in Natalie. Most assuredly, he didn't find in her Celia's wonderful intelligence. The ceremony was quite private, but not too private, since it couldn't appear clandestine. Sybil seemed to be resigned. In fact, she was jubilant, but she didn't want that to be apparent too soon. Then the Parliamentary recess began, and the young couple left for France."

"Natalie continued not to be pregnant?"

"Unfortunately, yes. And naturally, she had very soon to confess this to her husband."

"She could have said she'd been mistaken."

"She could have, yes, but she was endowed with that fearful Slavic frankness, and she told everything except the part played by the Duchess, whom she didn't want to betray. To justify the subterfuge, she pleaded love. But to no point. The fury of that well-bred man went beyond anything one could imagine."

"He struck her?"

"For her it would have been better if he had. No, he didn't strike her, but he swore that he would never speak another word to her. From that day on, he lived with her—in the same house, I mean. He continued to go out with her into society, although as little as possible. At home, he sat opposite her at table. But he stopped being her husband, and even her companion."

"It's hardly believable."

"This story happened in England, my dear, and whatever you may think, English passions and English ways of expressing these passions are violent. Presently, two foreseeable developments resulted from this situation—"

"Harold Wicks went back to the Duchess, all according to plan."

"That was, yes, the first consequence, and I should add that Natalie refused to accompany him to Warfield, which made Miss Ford's task easier. . . . The second consequence was that Celia Norton married."

"One could imagine her choosing an eternal celibacy dedicated to the life of the mind. She was a Soul."

"One can imagine everything, but facts are facts. She married Lord Brennan, who was fifteen years older than she."

"But such an intelligent, good man. I remember how much I admired him when I was young."

"Celia must have felt the same way about him. I wouldn't go so far as to say that she loved him, but she was a devoted, tender wife. I don't believe that without her he would have succeeded C.B. as party leader—"

"The party was no longer in power."

"That's true, but presently it did return, and if her husband had not died, Celia would have had the opportunity to prove herself the ideal wife of a prime minister. You know that she had two sons by him?"

"Of course. The older was killed in the First World War, and the other is the present Lord Brennan."

"Right . . . Yes, in 1916, the older boy was eighteen and he volunteered immediately, and so did Harold Wicks. Wicks was a colonel, and by chance—only by chance—Lady Brennan's son was assigned to his regiment as a second lieutenant. That gave our friend Harold an opportunity to begin a correspondence with Lady Brennan—"

"Who was by then a widow."

"Yes, she had been since 1913. . . . I should say that his leaving for the war had been an opportunity for a reconciliation between Harold and his wife, which was a great happiness for Natalie. A great and a short happiness, since, as you know, Harold was killed in the battle of Loos, at the side of his commanding officer—and of Rupert Brennan. I like to think that Celia Brennan united them in her grief. She didn't survive them very long, however, and my story would end here if there were not an astonishing development on quite another side."

"On the side of the Duchess, you mean."

"The Duchess and Natalie, who had been reconciled at the time of Harold's death. The two women became inseparable. Both of them virtually withdrew from society. They set to reading and classifying the papers Harold had left. Natalie—you remember I told you she was a sculptor—undertook to do a monument in honor of the husband she had found again only to lose him soon after. She worked in a big studio, and the Dowager Duchess of Stafford, Sybil, often came to keep her company. They would talk abut Harold. They had stopped competing for him, and now took a melancholy pleasure in enjoying the memory of him together. These meetings were so pleasant that when the monument was finished, Natalie declared she was not satisfied with it, and she destroyed it so that she could begin another."

"There's something rather fine about this dual old age consecrated to eternal adoration."

"You see that Englishwomen do know how to love."

"I see . . . but one of these two was a Russian."

"You are insufferable!"

The Curse of Gold

THE MOMENT I WALKED into the restaurant in New York where I was a regular customer, I noticed the little old man seated at the table by the door, eating a thick, very rare steak. The red meat had caught my eye first, because it was so very rare, but then also the sad, delicate face of the man. I felt sure I'd known him before, in Paris or somewhere. When I had sat down at my own table, I called the owner, an energetic, clever man from Périgord, who had managed to turn a narrow little cellar into a haunt for gourmets.

"M. Robert, that customer sitting to the right of the door—he's French, isn't he?"

"Which one? Oh, the man sitting alone? . . . That's M. Bordacq. He's here every day."

"Bordacq? Bordacq the industrialist? Why, of course, I recognize him now. I've never seen him here before."

"Because usually he comes before anyone else. He's a man who likes to be alone."

The *patron* leaned over my table, and said under his breath:

"They're a queer pair, you know, he and his wife. . . . Very queer. You see him alone at lunch. Well, if you were to come in this evening, at seven, you would find his wife alone at dinner. You'd think they didn't want to see each other. And yet they're on the best of terms. They live together at the Hotel Delmonico. It's a mystery to me, that ménage."

"*Patron,*" a waiter said, "check for No. 15."

M. Robert left me, but I kept thinking of this couple. Bordacq . . . Of course. I'd known him in Paris. Between the two wars, one often used to see him at the house of Fabert, the playwright, who had a surprising liking for him, probably because they shared the same hobby—safe investments—and the same terror of losing all their money. Bordacq . . . He must be nearly eighty. I remembered that he had retired from business around 1923, with a very respectable number of millions. At that time, he was panicked by the decline of the franc.

"It's insane!" he used to say. "I will have worked forty years, to end my life in the poorhouse. It's not just that my annuities and bonds aren't worth anything anymore, but industrial stocks aren't going up. Our money is melting away between our fingers. What will we do in our old age?"

"Do like me," Fabert said to him once. "I've put everything I own in sterling. There's a perfectly safe currency for you."

When I saw the couple again, three or four years later, they were both downcast. Bordacq had followed Fabert's advice, whereupon the franc had gone up and the pound had gone sharply down. Bordacq's then current obsession was how to escape the income tax, because the rates were rising.

"Don't be such an innocent," Fabert kept telling him. "Do like me. There is one stable asset, only one. It's gold. If in 1918 you had bought gold bullion, your profits would not be simply on paper, you would never have paid any income tax, and you would be far richer today than you are. Convert everything you own into gold and sleep like a baby."

The Bordacqs had obeyed. They had bought gold, rented a safe-deposit box, and now and then sampled the lively delights of going to half open the door of the sanctuary and pay homage to their god. Then I had lost sight of them for ten years.

One day in 1937 I had met them—he distinguished and mournful, she naïve and animated, a little old lady, very neat in her black silk dress with lace jabot—at an art dealer's in the Faubourg Saint-Honoré. Rather timidly, Bordacq had consulted me:

"You are an artist, sir. Do you think there's any chance that the Impressionists will go any higher? . . . You don't know? People tell me they will, but they've already gone up such a lot. One should have got into this market thirty years ago. Obviously, the ideal thing would be to know which school will follow them, and one could be picking things up today for nothing. But that's the trouble—nobody can guarantee me a thing. What times we live in! Even the experts don't know anything. It's unbelievable, you must admit. I ask them, 'What's going to go up next?' They hesitate, they hem and haw. One says Utrillo, another says Picasso. . . . But that's no help. Everyone knows that much."

"What about your gold bullion?" I asked him.

"I still have it, I still have it. And considerably more besides . . . But now the government's talking about requisitioning gold, opening people's safe deposits! . . . It's frightful. You'll tell me, 'The better part of wisdom would be to invest everything abroad.' But where? The British government is as bad as our own. Holland and Switzerland are too much exposed in case of war. . . . There's the United States, of course, but since Roosevelt, even the dollar . . . And then we'd have to go there to live, or risk having our line of retreat cut off someday."

I no longer know what answer I made. The Bordacqs were beginning to irritate me, clutching their hoard while around them a whole civilization was crumbling. When we left the gallery, I said good-bye, and watched them walk away with prudent little steps, both dressed in black, both utterly correct and lugubrious. And now here I found them again, on Lexington Avenue, at the Serpent d'Or. What had happened to them during the war? How had they come to land in New York? I was curious to know, and when Bordacq got up, I went over and introduced myself.

"Oh, I remember very well," he said. "I'm delighted to see you again. I hope you will give us the pleasure of coming to

tea. We are at the Hotel Delmonico. My wife will be very
pleased. . . . Life is monotonous for us here. Neither one of us
knows English."

"Are you living in America permanently?"

"We must," he said. "I'll explain. Come tomorrow at five."

I accepted and I kept the appointment. Mme Bordacq was
wearing the same black silk dress with lace jabot as in 1937,
and, around her throat, her beautiful pearls. She seemed to me
in very low spirits.

"I am so bored!" she said. "We have only these two rooms,
and not a single friend. . . . Oh, I would never have believed
I'd end my life in exile like this."

"But whatever forced you to take such a step, Madame?" I
said. "As far as I know, you had no special reason to fear the
Germans. Naturally, I understand that you might not have
wished to live near them, but that is very different from exiling
yourselves to a country where you do not speak the language."

"Oh," she said, "the Germans had nothing to do with it. We
came here well before the war."

Her husband got up, went to open the hall door to make
sure no one was listening, closed and locked it, and then, sitting down beside me, he said in a low voice:

"I'm going to explain everything to you. We know you're discreet and we would be only too glad to have your advice. I do
have an American lawyer, but you'll understand me better.
. . . This is the way it is. . . . I don't know whether you remember, but after the Popular Front came to power, we felt it
was dangerous to keep our gold bullion in a French bank. So
we found a way, clandestine but quite safe, to have it taken to
the United States. Naturally, we had decided to live here ourselves. There was no question of our being separated from our
gold. That goes without saying. Here in New York, early in
1938, we had it converted into dollars because we did not believe
—and we were right—that America would make a further deval-
uation, and because people who we knew were well informed
told us that Russia, with her new prospecting operations,
would be lowering the value of gold. But the problem was, how
to keep our dollars? In a bank account? In currency? Stocks? If
we had bought American securities, we would have had to pay

income tax, which is terribly high here. So we kept it all in currency."

I could not keep from interrupting:

"In other words, to avoid a tax of fifty percent, you voluntarily levied a tax of a hundred percent on yourselves?"

"There was another reason," he said, more and more mysteriously. "We saw the war coming, and we thought bank accounts might be frozen and safe-deposit boxes opened, especially since we are not American citizens. . . . So we decided to keep our money with us all the time."

"With you!" I cried. "What do you mean? Here in the hotel?"

Both of them nodded, with the shadow of a smile, and they exchanged a look compounded of pride and cunning.

"Yes," he went on, in a scarcely audible voice, "yes, here at the hotel. We put everything, a little gold and all the bills, in a big trunk. It's there, in our bedroom."

He got up, opened the connecting door, and, taking me by the arm, showed me a black, very ordinary-looking trunk.

"That's it," he murmured, and he closed the door with something akin to a genuflection.

"Aren't you afraid," I asked, "that this story of the treasure trunk will get around? What a temptation for thieves!"

"No," he said. "first of all, no one in the world knows except our lawyer—and now you, and I trust you completely. Everything's been carefully worked out, I assure you. A trunk does not attract attention, the way a chest would. No one would dream there's a fortune in it. And above all, we stand guard in this room night and day."

"You never go out?"

"Never together. We have a revolver, which is in the drawer nearest the trunk, and one of us is always in the apartment. I go to lunch in that French restaurant where you met me. My wife takes her dinner there. So the trunk is never alone. Do you understand?"

"No, my dear M. Bordacq, I do not understand. Why should you condemn yourselves to such a miserable, prison-like life? . . . Taxes? What do you care? You have ample means for everything you will need as long as you live, haven't you?"

"That isn't the issue," he said. "I don't want to give them money that I worked so hard to earn."

I tried to change the subject. Bordacq was a cultivated man; he was well read in history, and I tried to persuade him to talk about the collection of autographs he had formerly owned, but his wife, who was even more obsessed than he, kept bringing us back to the one topic that interested her.

"There is one man I am afraid of," she said, in a low voice. "It's the German waiter who brings our breakfast. Sometimes he glances in the direction of this door in a way I don't like at all. But at that hour we are both here. I don't think there can be any real danger."

Another problem was the dog. They had a poodle, an amazingly intelligent creature, which was lying in one corner of the room, and he had to be walked three times a day. Here again they took turns. When I left them, I was both exasperated by such maniacal folly and fascinated by two such extraordinary characters.

After that visit, I often tried to get away from my work early and go to the Serpent d'Or for dinner at seven o'clock precisely. In this way, I could sit at Mme Bordacq's table. She was more communicative than he, and more naïve in telling me about their worries and their plans.

"Eugène," she said to me one evening, "is really a most intelligent man. He thinks of everything. This evening he suddenly had the idea that *they* might call in all paper currency and exchange it for new bills, to prevent hoarding. In that case, we would be forced to declare ours."

"Yes," I said, "but what harm would there be in that?"

"It would be very serious," she said. "We didn't declare anything when the U.S. Treasury Department, in 1943, took a census of property belonging to refugees. We would be in dreadful difficulties. . . . But Eugène has a new plan. It seems that in certain South American republics there is no income tax. If we could transfer our capital—"

"How could you transfer it without making a customs declaration?"

"Eugène thinks," she said, "that we would first have to become citizens of whatever country we would choose. If we were Uruguayans, for example, the transfer would be authorized."

This struck me as so splendid that the next day I went to lunch with Bordacq. He always welcomed me very cordially.

"Ah," he said, "I'm particularly glad to see you, because I want to ask you for some information. Do you know what the formalities are for becoming a Venezuelan?"

"Heavens, no," I told him.

"Colombian?"

"Nor that, either. You should ask the Venezuelan or Colombian consuls a question like that."

"Ask the consuls!" he said. "Are you out of your mind? And attract attention to ourselves!"

He pushed his plate of roast chicken aside disgustedly, and sighed.

"What a period to live in! To think that we could have been born in 1830 and have spent our whole life free of this financial inquisition, this fear of being literally plundered. Today every country in the world has turned into nothing but a highway robber. . . . Even England. I'd stored some paintings and rugs there that I wanted to bring over to America. Do you know what they insisted on? For the export permit, a duty of one hundred percent! Confiscation pure and simple. We are at the mercy of thieves, my dear sir, exactly as if we were set upon in the middle of a forest."

Soon after that, my business took me to California and I did not know if the Bordacqs became Uruguayans, Venezuelans, or Colombians. When I came back to New York a year later, I asked M. Robert, the owner of the Serpent d'Or, about them.

"And the Bordacqs? Do you still see them?"

"Why, no," he told me. "Don't you know? She died last month—of a heart ailment, I believe—and from that day to this I have not seen the husband. It must have been a great blow to him and I think he's sick."

I thought to myself that the explanation was quite different. I wrote a note of sympathy to M. Bordacq and asked if I might call on him. The next morning he telephoned to me to come. I found him pale and very much thinner; his lips were bloodless, and his voice had faded to a whisper.

"I learned of your loss only yesterday," I said to him, "and I wanted to offer to help you in any way I can, because aside from the pain of your loss I imagine that your life must have become impossible."

"No," he said, "no. One gets used to it. From my window, I can see the passersby and the automobiles. And then, I must tell you that this way of life gives me finally a wonderful feeling of security. Before, when I used to go out for lunch, I always spent a painful hour. I kept wondering what was happening while I was away. My poor wife was here, I know, but I could hardly see her handling a revolver, especially with her heart in that condition. . . . Now, by leaving that door open, I can always keep my eye on the trunk. Everything I care about is near me. That makes up for much grief. The only problem is poor Ferdinand."

The poodle, hearing his name, got up and came to sit at his master's feet, looking up at him inquiringly.

"Yes, of course, I can no longer walk him myself, but I have found one of the—the bellboys, as they call them here. Now really, why couldn't they say *chasseurs* like everyone else? Oh, they make me laugh with their English. Well, I found a young boy who is willing, for a token fee, to take Ferdinand out and attend to his little needs. So that there is really no serious problem that needs solving. You are very kind, sir, to offer to help, but things are going along all right, I assure you, quite all right."

"You no longer want to go live in South America?"

"No, no. What would I do that for? Washington has stopped talking about replacing its paper currency, and at my age . . ."

He did indeed look very old, and the regime he had imposed on himself did not seem to agree with him. He had lost his pink complexion and he had difficulty in speaking.

Can one even say, I thought, that he is still alive?

Seeing that I could do nothing for him, I left. I intended to go visit him occasionally, but a few days later, as I opened the *New York Times,* my eye was immediately caught by a headline: "FRENCH REFUGEE DIES, LEAVING TRUNKFUL OF CURRENCY." I read the short news item. The man was, in fact, my Bordacq. He had been found dead, in the morning, wrapped in a blanket and lying on his black trunk. It was a natural death, and his treasure was intact. I stopped by the Delmonico to find out when and where the funeral would be. I also asked the desk clerk for news of Ferdinand.

"What's going to become of M. Bordacq's dog?"

"Nobody claimed him," he said. "We sent him to the pound."

"And the money?"

"If there are no heirs, it will end up the property of the American government."

"What better end," I said.

But I was thinking only of the end to the story.

For Piano Alone

EVERY EUROPEAN ARTIST who has traveled to the United States knows that in every American city of any importance there lives a woman who is rich, quite pretty, and mad about music and modern painting. She is the wife of an industrialist, unless she happens to be the wife of a banker or a prominent lawyer. Her husband's interest in the arts is purely a matter of courtesy, but he is proud of his wife, he gives her as much money as is needed for her patronage of concerts and exhibits, and with time he even acquires a rudimentary stock of small talk that allows him to take cautious part in conversations about Picasso and Erik Satie. Such couples are the salt of the earth. It is thanks to them that the aesthetic education of Americans has made such remarkable progress in fifty years and that the country's museums are among the finest in the world. In all periods of history, merchant princes have been the artists' good angel. What once was true in Florence is true today in Denver or in Chicago, but in the case of the Medicis, the prestige went to the men; in the Florences of the New World, the wife rules, the man pays, and he enjoys only a reflected glory.

Before the last war, in Philadelphia, the useful and honorable role of female Maecenas was played by Mrs. Grover P. Robinson. She was a gracious woman who, in 1938, was around forty, and was courageously allowing her hair to turn gray, a decision for which she was censured by her contemporaries. She could do this at no risk, for her charm was based not on her youthful features but on her supple, long-limbed body and her vivacious expression. Although she was from the South and kept her aristocratic Southern manners, her activity was in sharp contrast to the indolence of the ladies of Virginia. No hostess has ever made so many phone calls, written so many letters, or presided over so many committees. She had a genius for organization, which would have made her a remarkable businesswoman. In a completely disinterested way, she put this gift at the service of the fine arts or, more exactly, of the several modern artists who had become her favorites. She was surrounded by a little court, comprising famous virtuosos, illustrious composers, avant-garde painters, and assorted writers that she had plucked at random during their lecture tours and added to her coterie the way a florist adds a few sprigs of green to a bouquet of brilliant flowers. Mrs. Robinson's name was Katherine, and all her friends called her Kitty.

Every year, before the war, Kitty went to Paris to get her bearings afresh and harvest the annual crop of knowledgeable opinion. She had several advisers there, art dealers and critics, whose judgment she relied on. Not that she lacked taste. Proof of that was to see her house and garden in Philadelphia, which were done with an art worthy of the English aesthetes. But in relation to Europe, and France especially, she had a strange inferiority complex, a neurotic fear of making a mistake, of admiring the wrong thing. She believed, in good faith, that there are fashions in art as in clothes. Provided she had the experts' approval, the most recent, the newest school gave her a genuine pleasure that she could already no longer find in the one before the last. She did preserve a soft spot for the Impressionists, because they had enlightened her youth and because her art counselors still tolerated them, but around 1936 her enthusiasm was reserved for the Cubists, the Expressionists, and, above all, the Abstract Expressionists. In music matters, she found life difficult, for here her qualified friends were no longer able to agree among themselves. Some swore only by Stravinsky, others by Prokofiev. The French talked to her about the Six, but added that as a group they had nothing in common, and from time to time one of the Six, come to Philadelphia for a recital, would deliver a passionate eulogy of Gounod, whom she, trusting the covenants, had long believed negligible and hopelessly dated.

Fortunately, her role was not so much to judge as to welcome, and on this terrain she knew her own strength. No one entertained better than she. Every man of talent who stopped over in Philadelphia was invited to stay with the Robinsons. There he found waiting for him a room embellished with wallpaper of an abstract design, with windows looking out on pools strewn with water lilies and bordered by iris; the bathroom was finished in pink tile and supplied with multicolored bath salts and Turkish towels with designs à la Rouault. The cuisine was French, the cook Belgian, the chambermaid Danish, the butler English, the chauffeur Italian. Kitty would come every night to make sure that her guest had everything he needed and sometimes, after a triumphant concert, would accord him a sisterly kiss on the cheek. She cared very little for men but she cared passionately about success. Several affairs were attributed to her: one with a Czech artist who had painted her portrait and modernized her Gibson Girl face, dividing it in two by a broad, oblique black line along which he had made the right side slip toward the bottom of the canvas by some few centimeters; and one with a Finnish poet. But all that belonged to a dimly known, possibly legendary past. The one lasting romance of which she was assuredly the heroine was her liaison with Rosenkranz.

Need one describe Boris Rosenkranz? Every cultivated reader knows this admirable pianist, the greatest of our generation, who, having taken Europe by storm as a young prodigy, had made his place in America on his very first tour. What accounts for Rosenkranz' unique prestige is not his virtuosity, which is matched by others, or the delicacy of his expression, for in this respect Robert Casadesus is his superior; his forte is a mixture of intelligence and vitality. "Dynamism" is a rather disagreeable word, but it aptly denotes the superabundance of vigor that makes a Rosenkranz recital a kind of sonorous, tonic, mental massage, and puts his listeners, his female listeners especially, in an amazing state of exaltation. He excels in the martial Chopin, Tchaikovsky and the modern Spanish repertoire; in the United States, he does not hesitate to conclude a concert with a Souza march arranged for piano. Some purists say he makes too many concessions to public taste, but that is not very fair, for in these pyrotechnics he preserves an exact sense of proportion. Vitality is one factor in aesthetic emotion; the figures on the Sistine Chapel ceiling are not vulgar for being more than human size.

Rosenkranz the man resembles Rosenkranz the artist. He has the same brilliant energy, together with an engaging manner and a sense of humor. None of the virtuoso's vanity. His gifts are so natural that he himself thinks of them that way, and takes no particular pride in them. In a group of friends, he wants simply to be an amusing companion. Accounts of his tours, descriptions of the unbelievable people who entertain him, imitations of his rivals, pastiches of other great musicians, improvised musical analyses of personalities—such things make for an animated, high-spirited evening whenever he is present. Women in every country throw themselves at his head, attracted both by the music and by the man. He has had some clamorous affairs with some of the loveliest women of the day. Kitty had conquered him thanks to a crossing she had made with him on the *Île de France*—a crossing she had deliberately planned. She had not won an exclusive (like many performers, he had a girl in every music port), but he showed a special regard for her; she was both a flattering mistress and an inspired impresario mindful of their double fame. He allowed her to join him secretly several times a year, in New York or at some beach or in some mountain resort. Every winter he gave a concert in Philadelphia, and at that time he would spend several days with the Robinsons.

I had happened to meet him, and, like everyone else, I had

enjoyed the pleasure of his company. The Rosenkranz cult was, with the Robinsons, a religion that had its own rites. Kitty would take a group of eight or ten to Boris' concert. One communed via Beethoven or Ravel; one exchanged enraptured glances; one rejoiced for Kitty's happiness. After the concert, one went backstage to congratulate Boris, and Kitty would embrace him. Then one went back to the Robinsons' house. After changing his shirt, which would be soaking wet, Boris would rejoin the company, and then one spent two perfect hours with him that were pretty inflexibly programmed. Every year one had to ask Rosenkranz to tell a certain story about an Italian conductor, to give an imitation of a certain German pianist, to do an improvisation à la Beethoven, modulating into Chopin' and then into Debussy. Toward midnight, he would do some card tricks, one of which was so infallible that it enchanted Grover P. Robinson.

"It's out of this world!" he would exclaim each time. "Out of this world! You've seen for yourselves. Boris was in the next room when I picked a card. He didn't communicate with a single one of us when he came back. And yet he went straight for the nine of spades! . . . Out of this world!"

Grover was as full of admiration for, and as attached to, Boris as was Kitty. He was proud of the preference shown them by a man whom the whole city applauded and whom twenty Main Line families invited in vain. Actually, Robinson was a very good man, exceptionally generous, and, appearances notwithstanding, he had genuine finesse. If he lacked a little polish in matters of music or painting—being more competent in his business, which was the manufacture of artificial silk—he was nonetheless possessed of a good sense and good nature that saved him in every situation. And in the one situation that might have made him seem ridiculous—for all his guests knew that Kitty was in love with Rosenkranz—he appeared as the wise man who is above and beyond such adventures. Brought up as a Puritan—or, more exactly, as a Quaker—he was so far from thinking that his wife and his friend could betray him that he became lovable and touching by virtue of its being a fact. His greatest audacity was to tease Kitty about her favorite painters.

"Well, after all, Boris," he would say, "I call you as witness. Is Kitty's left eye an inch higher than her right? . . . Well, the way she sees it, it is. And when Beiking told her there was no reason why her hair and the color of her hair should be in the same place on the canvas, she was beside herself, she was so pleased. And that was that. And so I have to live in the midst of bits and pieces of my wife, who's been chopped up by barbarians."

Kitty, rather awkwardly, would come to the defense of modern painting. Grover would glance at us conspiratorially; Boris would side with Grover and help play the game. It used to remind me of the studied play of the Duc and Duchesse de Guermantes: "Come, come, Oriane . . ." "Basin, you know very well . . ." I used to feel slightly uneasy when I thought how secure the unfortunate Grover felt in his happiness and how vulnerable his real position was. Although I was very fond of Kitty and quite responsive to her charm, I held it against her that she deceived a husband who made life so easy for her, who gave her complete freedom and all the weapons she needed to make her conquests. She didn't treat him unkindly, often praised him, in passing would blow him a quick kiss, and she busied herself solicitously with the assorted medicines he had to take, but mixed in with this routine domestic affection there was a condescension that irritated me a bit. She seemed to be saying to us: "You are my witnesses. . . . It is a pity, after all, that with my great gifts I should be tied for life to this poor man. But I will play the game to the end."

Above all, she exasperated me when she seemed to imply, by an imperceptible shrug of the shoulders, that her husband understood nothing of the more noble sentiments and the great works of art. My own impression was quite the opposite. Grover had not been exposed to a vestige of culture in his youth, but he had read a great deal, and his taste seemed to me surer than his wife's. The odd thing was that Boris seemed to share my feeling and that he, too, often seemed put off by Kitty. I remember one day, after a concert, his saying to me under his breath:

"My dear fellow, when Kitty enters the sacristy crying 'It was divine!' I get worried. But when Grover takes me by the arm and whispers in my ear, 'It went all right tonight, Boris,' then I know I haven't been too bad."

During the war, Boris continued his tours across the United States with as great success as ever. I was teaching in a college in the West, but during a reception given him as he was passing through San Francisco, I scarcely saw him. Then came the Allied landing in North Africa; I spent one year in the service and did not come back to the United States until after I was demobilized. While I was in New York, Boris gave a concert at Carnegie Hall. I went to hear him, afterward went backstage to shake hands, and asked what word of Kitty. He answered in a distant, detached way:

"I haven't had any for a long time."

"What? You haven't been to Philadelphia this year?"

"Not yet," he said. "I should be going next month, but you know . . ."

Behind me, the crowd of admirers was pressing forward. I had to move on, and I did not see him again that evening. A few weeks later, an association of Philadelphia lawyers and judges invited me to come speak on the role of the French Army in Africa and Italy. I immediately wrote Kitty to say I would be coming, and she replied with an invitation for me to stay with her, which I accepted with the greatest pleasure. When I arrived, I found Judge Clarke at the station; it was he who had organized the meeting, and he had volunteered to take me to the Robinsons', since he knew them and their house was outside the city proper.

"I asked you to come a day sooner," he said to me, "because Boris Rosenkranz is giving a concert of Russian music tomorrow. If our meeting had taken place the same night, there would have been a terrific conflict. All the ladies would have abandoned us, I'm afraid."

"I don't doubt that," I said. "And in any event, I am delighted to have the chance of hearing Boris. Probably I'll find him at the Robinsons' and I'll stay over for the concert."

The Judge smiled.

"I would be surprised," he said, "if you found Rosenkranz staying with your hostess."

"Why? Have they had a falling out?"

"I don't know anything about it. . . . And I haven't said a word. But you will find, I think, that Kitty has become very domestic this past year."

"Now, Judge Clarke, you do know something."

"No, or at least what I know is not what a court would consider admissible evidence. But you'll see for yourself."

Kitty received me with her customary hospitality, which was at once warm and impersonal. She showed me to my room, and I noticed that it was the larger of the two guest rooms, the Picasso bedroom, which she had always given to Rosenkranz when we were both staying there. She said:

"I hope you will stay a long time."

"A long time? Worse luck, I can't. I've got to lecture in Washington day after tomorrow, but I will stay through tomorrow evening, if I may, for Rosenkranz' concert."

She did not answer except to ask what I would like for breakfast.

"Am I mistaken?" I insisted. "Isn't Boris giving a concert here tomorrow?"

"Possibly . . . I think so. . . . But I scarcely go out at all, you know. I am not very well."

I saw that I must ask after her health. At that moment, Grover appeared at the bedroom door; he had just got home from the plant. He smiled his usual friendly smile and put both hands on my shoulders.

"Finally," he said. "We've missed you. Aren't you ashamed of yourself, going off at your age to play soldier in Africa! And Kitty tells me that we have to listen to you lecture this evening! As if I didn't work hard enough all day long! Why in the devil do we have so many friends who are dying to perform in public?"

I laughed and said that they were not under the slightest obligation to go to the lecture, and that indeed I would be grateful if they did not, because nothing intimidated me more than talking in front of friends, and since Kitty wasn't well—

"Kitty not well! She's in better shape than you or me! I've had every doctor in Philadelphia called in, and they all say that organically there's nothing wrong. It's all psychological. . . . The war, that's what ails Kitty. She's been deprived of her

174 : THE COLLECTED STORIES OF ANDRÉ MAUROIS

trips to Europe. But she's also a little to blame herself. Instead
of enjoying at least what distractions are available here, she
doesn't want to see people anymore. . . . For example, tomorrow Boris is giving a concert—"

"Grover!" Kitty said, shuddering. "I have *begged* you not to
talk to him about that!"

He tried to take her affectionately by the waist, but she
avoided him.

"Well," he said, "I want to talk to him about it. He'll tell
you the same thing I have, that you're not being sensible. Imagine, she didn't want to invite Boris to stay with us! A boy
whom we've loved as if he were our own son, who got his start
in this country thanks to her! That alone was too much to
believe. But now here she is, telling me she doesn't even want
to go to the concert. Tell her, will you, that we can't do a thing
like that."

"The two of you go," she said dryly. "These days, music gives
me a headache."

"You went to the Horowitz concert."

"Exactly. And it turned out to be a bad idea. Excuse me,"
she said, "I must take an aspirin."

I was left alone with Grover, and I felt a little ill at ease. He
sat down in one of the armchairs in my bedroom. His kindly,
austere face and his black suit struck a discordant note in that
white room and in the midst of those particolored canvases.

"Poor Kitty," he said. "You must find her very much
changed."

"A little . . . I admit I didn't expect—"

"Oh, this's been going on for a year," he said. "I try to be
patient. The doctors tell me it will work itself out. But this last
bit beats the limit. We can't treat Boris like this. He's just not
going to understand. If Kitty won't do it, I'm going to telephone him myself tomorrow morning and invite him to supper
after the concert."

I sensed an imminent disaster.

"I don't think," I said to him, "that that's a very wise move.
Would you like me to go to his hotel and see what his state of
mind is?"

"I'd be very grateful to you," he said.

He sighed, took off his glasses, and wiped his eyes. I felt sorry for him and said to myself I would speak to Kitty, but I was never alone with her that evening. Before the lecture, I had to go to an official dinner; when we got back to the house, we were all tired and the Robinsons did not insist as usual on my having a nightcap.

Breakfast at their house is a genuine meal that people take together on the terrace, which in winter is glassed in and well heated. Kitty, an early riser, arrived at nine, all massaged, coiffured, and dressed for the day. Grover came in with a bundle of papers, ready to leave for the plant. I had preserved a pleasant memory of these morning meetings filled with projects and news, when everyone, confronting his fruit and cereal, felt as fresh as the day was young. This time I sat down at table with a little trepidation. I was going to have to speak of Rosenkranz and of my plan to call on him. How would Kitty react? I was expecting a vehement objection, but she said coldly:

"Do as you like. All I ask is that you be here at one for lunch."

"But, Kitty, may I tell Boris that you will come to the concert, and ask him to come here afterward for supper?"

She closed her eyes wearily, and then made an evident effort to control herself.

"You are at home here," she said. "You have the right to invite your friends here."

She took a swallow of coffee, and added, as if speaking to herself:

"Anyhow, he won't come. . . ."

I had the desired authorization, and I went on quickly to talk about other things. Grover read us an article on some pending labor legislation and talked to me about his relations with the unions, which were not bad. Then, having eaten an apple, he got up from table.

"Do you want me to drop you in town?"

"Yes, thanks. I'll go see Boris. Judge Clarke told me he's staying at the Palace. And what are you doing this morning, Kitty?"

"I'm waiting for my secretary," she said. "There's a stack of letters on my desk that I haven't answered. Don't worry about me."

A half hour later I was at the hotel and I called Boris' room from the lobby. His cadenced, lilting voice with its Slavic accent answered:

"Why! You here! . . . By all means, come up. You'll find me in pajamas. I came in on the night train."

When he came to open the door, he was, in fact, naked under a broad-striped Japanese robe.

"What a *joy* to see you again!" he said, with heavy emphasis on the "joy." "But tell me this instant, are you staying with the Robinsons? Do they know you've come to see me?"

I put the case to him as exactly as I could, and said frankly that I didn't understand her, and that she made me feel sorry for her.

"My dear friend," he said, "she makes me feel sorry, too. *Enormously* sorry. But what can I do? Listen—you are a man of discretion. I am going to tell you the whole story. Only perhaps I shouldn't. . . . No, of course I shouldn't. But if one can't speak the truth, what is the point of conversation? Now I ask you . . ."

He was striding up and down the room in his samurai robe, as animated as if he were playing the "Grande Polonaise," and his Russian accent gave his words their own very special character.

"I think," he went on, "that you'd known for a long time there was something between me and Kitty. My dear, I *swear* to you that would *never* have happened if I had known Grover first. . . . But when I met her on the boat, for me she was simply a pleasant companion for the voyage—pretty, agreeably complimentary, very well dressed. You would have done exactly what I did, I'm sure. There are very few saints. And even *saints* . . . Later, when I became a friend of the husband's, I tried to put an end to all that. I didn't manage to. You know Kitty. She is possessive, jealous, and very much her own mistress. Since Grover allows her to travel alone and she can go off on the most absurd excuses, she pursued me everywhere. . . . Mind you, at first I was rather pleased. She was charming, in her way, when she wasn't talking about music. But after all, she isn't the only woman in the world, and that was something she was unwilling to understand. Little by little, I felt the leash pulling on my neck, and I wanted to be free. . . . Everything blew up last summer, when without warning me she came to join me in Mexico. There I felt at a safe distance, and I had a woman with me. Ah, my *dear,* what a woman! . . . A Russian . . . Such eyelashes! Compared to a Russian, my *dear,* other women— Well, Kitty came down with some semiofficial support from the State Department on the pretext of arranging for artistic exchanges. Artistic exchanges! Now I ask you! . . . Artistic exchanges with me! One morning she turned up at my hotel. They told her that Señor and Señora Rosenkranz were still sleeping. You can imagine the scene. Allegro furioso! . . . My *dear,* in the end I told her I never wanted to see her again. You would have done the same thing, I'm sure. . . . You understand?"

"I understand perfectly. And if it concerned only you and Kitty, I'd think it would be best to leave things as they are. But there is Grover, unfortunately. He doesn't understand. He has no idea, even, that such things could happen to him, he's doing his best to take care of a neurotic Kitty, and he wants passionately for you to come to their house this evening. 'After all,' the poor fellow says, 'you're not going to break a tradition of ten years!' You've talked frankly to me, Boris, and by that token you authorize me to be frank with you. I think that you should accept Grover's invitation, even if you come only for a few minutes. Will it be painful for you and Kitty? Maybe, but it will save a very decent man from a grief he doesn't deserve."

"My dear, not another word. I will come," Boris Rosenkranz said. "I had made other engagements, but I will come."

We all three went that evening to his concert. He had included in the program some Scriabin that I wasn't familiar with, Moussorgsky's "Pictures at an Exhibition," Borodin's "Petite Suite," Balakirev's "Islamey," and Rimski-Korsakov's Concerto Opus 30. He played well, but not very well. Often, when I had heard him before, I had admired the rapport he established between himself and the public. One would have said that he held the whole hall in his hands, that he lifted his listeners' minds and hearts. That evening, the contact was intermittent. On the surface, the public's enthusiasm was not lacking. There are names toward which the public recognizes a debt of tumultuous appreciation. And so there were the usual calls for encores. He played "The Fire Dance" and an improvisation on a theme by Gershwin. It was all very much as it should have been. But we all knew that we were not really swept off our feet.

"Shall we go back to congratulate Boris?" I asked, as the applause died down.

"What's the point?" Kitty said coldly. "He's coming out to the house."

"What's that got to do with it?" Grover asked, quite put out. "Other years we always used to go, and then he was even staying with us."

"You go if you want to," she said. "I'm too tired to get caught in all that crowd."

Since it was hard to separate on account of the car, none of us went back. We drove home in silence and waited for Boris, his manager, and the few local music buffs who had been invited at the last minute. My memory of this evening is dismal indeed. First there was the agony of waiting. "So long as he comes!" I said to myself. "He promised, but maybe he was annoyed not to see us after the concert. He did say he had another engagement. . . ." Every time conversation lagged, it was only Grover's good humor that picked it up. Old Mrs. Cornelius Vanheyden said to Katz, the conductor:

"Since I'm on your committee, Mr. Katz, I want you to play at the first concert after my death the whole of the Verdi *Requiem* in memory of me."

"Never," Katz said dryly. "It's too long."

Whereupon a fresh chill fell on the room. Finally, Rosenkranz' ring restored us all. Since the war—I'd forgotten this—he always rang four times, for the V for Victory, and the Fifth Symphony. He came in, jovial, natural, completely at ease.

"Good evening, Kitty," he said, with a Russian emphasis on the "good."

He held out both hands and before she had time to react, kissed her on both cheeks. She remained her icy self and formally presented him to old Mrs. Vanheyden, who cried out with irritation:

"Introduce Boris to me! To me! Why, I knew him before you did!"

Then Grover said to Judge Clarke:

"You know our friend Boris, Judge? Yes, you know him as a great virtuoso, but do you also know that he is a great presti- digitator. After supper you must do your card trick for the judge, Boris. . . . You'll see, Judge, he's tremendous. If he de- cided to be a thief, you would never be able to convict him."

Poor Grover wanted at all costs for this evening to be as successful as those of earlier years, and when people sat down at table, he insisted that Boris perform his repertoire.

"Boris, tell the Judge the story of when you arrived in Cleve- land. . . ."

But one hostile listener is enough to kill a story. Joy is a sign of collective understanding, and the pretext for it does not matter when friendly feeling reigns. Kitty's sighs of boredom, although civil and contained, and her impassive face at the end of the story smothered the laughter.

Grover himself noticed.

"What is it this evening?" he asked. "What's wrong? What's the matter with you, Boris?"

"The matter with me, Grover? Nothing. I'm delighted to be here with you again. Really delighted . . ."

"Of course. And we're delighted to have you. But you didn't tell the Cleveland story the way you used to."

"Maybe it's getting a little old."

"Most likely it's that we are all getting a little old," Kitty said bitterly.

That evening she was like the bad fairy who with one wave of her wand destroys men's best efforts. She knew it, and she took satisfaction in playing the part. She killed every one of Boris' stories, and all those of the Judge, who was an excellent raconteur himself. After dinner, she killed the music, when Boris sat down at the piano and played snatches from Liszt and Wagner. She talked in a whisper during a Chopin Nocturne.

"Boris," Grover said, "play us a musical portrait of Kitty."

Rosenkranz improvised a kind of prelude that I liked, but at the end of it Kitty declared:

"I don't recognize myself."

"I don't recognize you either, anymore," I said to her softly. She turned away.

Grover watched in dismay as the evening collapsed. He looked like the mayor of a little town who has organized a fireworks display to amuse his staff and who watches his rockets fizzle out one after another. What was going on? Even the pinwheels did not glow. The powder was all damp. Finally, the Judge, who was feeling very sorry for him, said:

"What about that card trick?"

Grover's face cleared. The card trick could not fail.

"You're going to see, Judge! Notice that he goes into the next room while you choose your card. Now slip it back into the pack. Boris!"

Boris reappeared, picked up the pack, pronounced some weird formulas, then fanned out the cards and handed one to the Judge.

"It was the nine of clubs?" he asked.

"It was indeed, Mr. Rosenkranz," the Judge said.

But he didn't say it quite naturally. Kitty and old Mrs. Vanheyden were talking together in low voices and were not even looking. Poor Grover, who was glancing around the group to seize the admiring looks, encountered only strained or absent faces.

"All the same," he said, "it's out of this world."

And looking at Boris, who was still holding his cards in his hand with a jovial, guilty air, he said again:

"Out of this world."

The Departure

I COULD NO LONGER MOVE OR SPEAK. My arms and legs, my tongue, my eyelids no longer obeyed my will, and although my eyes were open, I saw only a luminous fog in which brilliant droplets danced like particles of dust in a sunbeam. I sensed that I was dying. I could still hear, however. The veiled sound of words reached me, more like whispering than conversation, and I recognized voices. I knew that our family physician, Dr. Galtier, was standing by my bed, his gravelly voice muffled as if by a soft pedal. There was also another doctor, whose authoritarian tone grated on my taut nerves, and Donatienne, my wife, whose voice I could hear alternating between choked sobs and breathless questions.

"Is he conscious?" she asked.

"No, Madame," the strange doctor said. "Definitely not. He is not even delirious anymore. This is a coma. It's a question of hours, perhaps minutes."

"Don't you think," Galtier said timidly, in his hoarse voice, "don't you think that an injection—"

"Why torment the poor man?" his colleague interrupted. "At his age, a man doesn't survive such a shock. The penicillin was our last chance. It didn't have the effect we were hoping for. There's nothing, unfortunately nothing, more to be done."

"Don't you think," Galtier said respectfully, "that the patient's constitution is as important a factor as his age? I examined him a month ago, just before this attack of pneumonia. His heart and blood pressure were those of a young man."

"It seemed that way," the specialist said, "it seemed that way. And people believe it. But age is age."

"Really, Doctor," Donatienne said emphatically, "my husband was young, very young."

"He believed he was young, Madame, and there is no more dangerous illusion. . . . You should get some rest. He can no longer see you, I assure you. The nurse will call you if—"

Donatienne's ´sob, almost a scream, ripped the veil, and I thought I saw her eyes—far away, like fires along a fog-shrouded coast. But that lasted only an instant, and then the voices faded away. I was alone, in a silence one could have cut with a knife. How long? I don't know, but it was when anxiety had become too intolerable that I suddenly had the crazy idea of getting up. I wanted to call the nurse. I tried to several times, but she didn't come. Then I called, or I believed that I called "Donatienne!"

My wife did not answer.

I'm going to look for her, I thought.

How did I know I would be able to lift my emaciated legs, put my feet down on the carpet, and walk? I remember only that I was sure I could, and I was right, because, despite the heavy fog that still filled my bedroom, I moved with no effort from my bed to the closet where my clothes were hanging. However, just as I was nearing the closet, my hand touched my body and, to my surprise, my fingers told me that I was already dressed. I recognized the rough texture of the overcoat I'd bought in London for traveling in bad weather. Looking down, I saw that I was wearing shoes, that I was indeed standing on my own two feet, only I was standing not on a floor but on uneven

paving stones. In what sleepwalking state had I performed the
motions that had got me up out of bed, into my clothes, and
out of the house? I was too excited to think about it. What
seemed certain and wonderful was that I was no longer dying
or even sick. What city was this? Paris? . . . The mustard fog
seemed more like London. I shielded my face with both hands
outstretched against invisible obstacles and took a few steps,
trying to find a wall. In the distance, I heard the majestic,
regularly spaced moaning of foghorns. The wind seemed to me
brisk and salty, like ocean air. What port was this?

"Hey, you there! Look where you're going!"
"Excuse me," I said. "I can't see a thing. Where am I?"
The man was carrying a powerful flashlight. He turned it on
me, then on himself, and I saw that he was in uniform, but it
was not the uniform of a French policeman or English bobby;
it looked more like an American pilot's jacket. He seized me by
the shoulder, not roughly, and wheeled me around to the left.
"Go straight ahead in this direction," he said, "and you'll
come to the field."
I understood that he was talking about an airfield. The
strange thing was that he didn't seem to question my wish to
get there and that, for my part, I didn't ask myself why I
should be taking a plane trip when I was scarcely up after the
worst illness of my life. I simply said, "Thank you, Captain,"
and followed the path he had shown me.
Was the fog lifting or were my eyes getting used to it? I
couldn't tell, but I did begin to distinguish human shapes.
They were all going in the same direction as I. Gradually, the
crowd grew more dense and soon we formed a kind of proces-
sion. We tried to walk quickly, because, without being able to
explain why, we sensed—if I may judge from my own feelings
—that it was urgent to arrive. But it became more and more
difficult to move ahead, and the road, it seemed to me, was
growing more narrow.
"Don't push," a woman said to me.
She had the voice of an elderly woman.
"I'm not pushing," I said. "People are pushing me."
"Do like everybody else and take your turn."

184 : THE COLLECTED STORIES OF ANDRÉ MAUROIS

I stopped in my tracks, which made my valise (for I was, I noticed at that moment, carrying a valise) bump against the legs of the man behind me. I turned around. The fog was thinning out, and I saw very clearly the irritated face of a Negro, young and handsome, who was wearing a red shirt open at the neck.

"Excuse me, sir," he said, in a bitter, sarcastic voice, and he made an exaggerated bow. "Excuse my black legs for bumping into your white valise."

"You can see I didn't do it on purpose," I said.

"I am so sorry, sir," he said, with a series of mocking bows, "I am so sorry. It won't happen again, sir."

Ahead of us I now made out a long column of perhaps several thousand travelers. Still farther ahead, there was the dim outline of a gate, buildings, a control tower, and hangars. A few motors were revving up in the distance, and the sirens continued to sound their warnings. A stronger wind was sweeping away the low, dramatic clouds, now and again ripping them apart.

From that moment on, we moved forward very slowly. The woman who was in front of me turned around, and I could see that her hair was braided and gray, and that she had beautiful, gentle Irish eyes. She wasn't angry any longer, and she smiled at me. "It's hard going," she seemed to be saying to me, "but you and I have courage, and we'll go through with it without complaining." After another hour of slogging ahead, she swayed.

"I got up so early," she said. "I'm worn out."

"Sit down on my bag," I said.

But as I set the bag down, I was struck by how light it was.

"My God," I cried. "I haven't got my pen or my slippers!"

And I rushed off toward the city. Why was I running? Who was waiting for me? Where was I going? I didn't know.

How did I find my way about this strange city? And how did I come to be living in a room in this little hotel near the harbor? Electric signs flashed rhythmically on and off. My pen lay on the table and my slippers were under the bed. I threw them into my bag, together with some books and papers, a razor, a bathrobe, and I left, still running. A monstrous bus was coming down the street toward the wharf, which was patrolled by port and military police, with revolvers thrust in their white leather belts. I jumped onto the bus. After ten minutes, it set me down not far from the rose-gray column outside the airfield gate.

Once again I had to endure the agony of moving forward step by step. When, after two hours, I drew near the gate, I understood why our advance had been so slow. The airfield could be entered only by a narrow wicket, beside which stood a guard, so that the last hundred yards, the column had to shrink to single file. There were only six people ahead of me! Now I could see the face of the guard, one of those incorruptible bulls that every power establishment needs. Three . . . two . . . one . . . It was my turn. I stood alone before the bull.

"Which line?" he asked.

"Is there more than one?" I asked.

"Obviously," he said, without impatience. "Catholic Line, Anglican Line, Presbyterian, Baptist, Mormon . . ."

"Your lines are set up by church affiliation?"

"Hurry up," he said. "Which line?"

"What if the passenger has no religion?" I asked. "Isn't there an Agnostic Line?"

"Sure," he said, surprised, "but I don't recommend it. It's a small one, new and not too well organized yet. You'd have nothing but headaches. If you want to hold the confessional aspect down to the minimum, take the Unitarian Line. It's very clean, well run, and up to date."

Behind me the column was growing impatient.

"There are some people," a little old man behind me said, "who must have their little chat in front of a ticket window, and the rest of the world can just stand around and wait."

I flushed and said to the guard:

"I'll go Unitarian."

"Central hangar. Wing S. Next!"

As the gatekeeper had said, the Unitarian Line seemed comfortable and well run. An air of efficiency enveloped the polished wood counters, the card files classified by staggered multicolored tabs, the maps dotted with tiny airplane models, the Cubist posters proclaiming "Fly Unitarian," and the pretty uniformed young women who received the passengers. One of them came up to me and asked:

"Have you your exit permit?"

"No. What permit? I didn't know—"

She sighed, then politely:

"See Mr. Frazer," she said.

Mr. Frazer, a robust young fellow dressed in black, reminded me of the athletic chaplains in American universities. His cordiality, although professional, seemed to me genuine.

"We are happy, very happy, to have you with us," he said. "Our clients are our friends. More and more, intelligent people are flying Unitarian."

"That's what I should like to do," I said, "but this young lady is asking about an exit permit."

"That's right," he said, "it's required, it's required. You get your exit permit and we take care of the rest."

"But where do I go to ask for it?" I said. "What steps must I take?"

At that moment, a little light flashed on his desk.

"One moment, please," he said, and picked up the telephone to his right.

"Yes, Doctor," he said. "Yes, Doctor . . . Ten more . . . Well, well, sir, you keep us busy. But the ten will be taken care of. . . . Yes, Doctor, I promise."

He hung up the phone to his right and picked up the one to his left, which had begun to flash.

"Fifty?" he said. "Very good, Colonel . . . Right . . . What ranks? . . . All enlisted men . . . Right . . . We'll try to keep them together. Thank you for thinking of us, Colonel. Always glad to be of service, sir."

Thereupon he spoke into both phones at once, and I thought I heard my name.

"You couldn't interview him this afternoon?" he asked. "Yes, he's in a hurry. . . . Why? Look, Franck, you know perfectly well why. It's the usual story. . . . About four? Good. Thanks, Franck. I'll do as much for you someday."

He turned to me, with an amiable expression.

"Go to Building B, Wing I, Room 3454, and ask for Mr. Franck, who will examine you. You'll have to wait, naturally, but you'll get through this afternoon. He promised me. Please, not at all. We're very glad to have you with us."

The young woman in the black uniform came over and he arose, signifying that I was dismissed.

I had a great deal of trouble finding Building B. To reach it, one had to follow a narrow path across muddy fields, and the yellow fog had invaded the field once more. Hordes of distracted travelers milled around me.

Building B was a skyscraper, and an automatic elevator took me to the thirty-fourth floor. Before Room 3454 a file of men and women stood waiting. Resignedly, I took my place in line. This time the torment was in two parts. In the darkness of the corridor you had to stand. When finally you entered Mr. Franck's waiting room, you discovered twenty or so armchairs. A frosted-glass partition separated them from the Inspector, who from time to time called out "Next!" Then the person nearest rose, and all the others moved one chair nearer. The woman ahead of me was young. She was wearing a beaver coat and kept wiping away her tears. Finally she was called, and she stayed only a few seconds. When she came out, she seemed to me less downcast. Behind the frosted glass, the voice said:

"Next!"

I went in. Behind a white wooden table sat a man in shirt sleeves, with a fat, intelligent face. He inspired confidence at once, and spontaneously I set my bag down on the table and started to open it. He smiled.

"No," he said. "I'm not interested in your luggage. My job is to evaluate what you are taking with you in the way of memories, attachments, passions."

"About which the law—"

"Just so, the law allows you only a specified quantity of memories, which should be cheerful. How old are you?"

"Sixty-five."

He consulted a ready reckoner and jotted down a figure.

"At your age," he said, "the maximum allowed is less. You can have one ounce, so to speak, of sensuality, some interest in the arts, a few family ties tempered by a strong egotism, and that's about all. Will you glance through this list of forbidden feelings and tell me whether you have anything to declare."

" 'Burning ambition?' No, I have no ambition. Once upon a time, I wanted recognition—and honor, perhaps. I won them. And I discovered that they bring no happiness. So that's finished."

"Good," the Inspector said. "Any desire for power?"

"On the contrary, a horror of it. I believe that the man who governs is in fact governed, that he's the prisoner of his public service and of his party. I have no desire to be responsible for actions not of my own choosing."

"Very good. No excessive love for your profession? You are, according to the form you've filled out, a playwright. Don't you think you could and should write one more play—your best play?"

"No. Unfortunately, I know I'm no longer able to write. I tried last year. I still believed in myself then. And I produced a monster. . . . That was the end of that."

"You're quite sure?"

"Yes, I've done what I've done, and my work is worth what it's worth. I'm content to be judged by it as it stands."

"Very good. Excellent. Money? Wealth?"

"I've never cared about money, and the day of great fortunes is gone."

"No mistresses?"

"None in the last fifteen years, since my wife, Donatienne—I married very late."

"You love her."

"With all my heart."

"Ho! Not so fast! 'With all my heart' is an expression that is not permitted here. . . . Let's see. . . . You love her physically? Intellectually? With affection?"

"In every way."

"As much as ever?"

"More than ever."

Inspector Franck's face darkened.

"I am very sorry," he said, "but in these circumstances I cannot grant you a permit."

"But I want to leave!"

"You say you want to leave, but who would really want to leave a world if it meant leaving behind someone so precious?"

"You don't understand me," I said angrily. "It's for her sake that I want to leave. For three months I have been a burden to her. I could do nothing but ruin her life from now on. I have to leave!"

Franck shook his head.

"I am truly sorry," he said, "but we have never granted a visa to men who still feel such strong passion. . . . We know them. We reserve a place for them—at the expense, naturally, of others—and at the last moment they leave us in the lurch, and the place is lost to everyone."

I had visions of myself thrown back into that choking fog, among that aggressive, milling mob, in the clanging streets of that strange city. I saw myself wandering about it, lugging a bag, dead tired, with neither purpose nor hope nor strength. I was afraid, and I threw myself on his mercy.

"Please," I said. "Give me a chance. You seem to be an understanding man. You can imagine how, after so much suffering, I desperately need to escape into a new world. I am tired. Let me rest. If I still have one passion that is too much alive, let me rid myself of it through absence, with time—but don't throw me back into the shadows outside."

Mr. Franck was looking at me compassionately from out of his heavy-lidded, soft-pouched eyes. He pressed his lower lip with his pencil, in an odd, upward movement.

"What you need," he said finally, in a tone of professional authority, "is a transit visa for iimbo."

"If that's a solution to my problem, yes, certainly."

"That would be a solution to your problem, but it doesn't depend on me, unfortunately."

"It depends on whom?"

"On the C.C.C. The Commission of Comas and Catalepsies."

"God! And where is this Commission?"

"In a small building set off by itself in the southeast corner of the field."

He looked at his watch.

"But you don't have time to get there before closing."

"Then what should I do?"

"Go back to town. And come back tomorrow."

"I'll never have the strength to make it."

"Oh, yes, you will," he said. "Yes, you will. You all believe that. But this can go on ten, twenty days. . . . Next!"

And so once more I found myself out in that gloomy, swampy field, invaded now by both the night and the fog. Among shadowy, wandering shapes, I searched, almost on tiptoe, through the misty darkness for the exit gate. A screeching streetcar carried me back again to an overheated room, where the flashing signs and rumbling trains kept me from sleeping. It was humid and suffocating, and the hours passed like a nightmare. At dawn, I took my bag and set off again for the airfield. I hoped that by arriving at this inhuman hour I would be among the first to go through the gate, but other travelers had had the same idea, and the line had never been longer. When, finally, after three hours, I reached the gate, I said to the guard, as if I were an habitué:

"You've seen me before."

"What line?"

"Unitarian."

He let me through. Now I had to find the offices of the C.C.C. "Southeast corner of the field," Franck had said. I took my bearings as best I could. The sun was hidden, but a vague, dim glow revealed its probable position. I crossed spongy fields covered with miserable clumps of reeds and scraggly little bushes swarming with some kind of viscous creature. At last I saw an isolated building of red brick, on one wall of which the letters C.C.C. stood out in white. It was one of those small, nondescript administrative buildings that bureaucracy spawns everywhere. With despair, I saw that even in this forsaken corner a large number of applicants were waiting before the door. Many of them were children; some were crying.

I will not describe this new wait. I was so tired that I hadn't the strength to complain; I was even too numb to suffer. When my turn came, I found myself seated across the table from a young woman in a gray-blue uniform. She was neither pretty nor ugly, her hair was plainly dressed, but I had noticed, while she was attending to the man ahead of me, that she was quick and businesslike. Clearly she did not belong to that class of official who delights in making one's situation more difficult than it is.

"You say you've seen Mr. Franck? Did he give you a note for us?"

"Yes, here it is."

"Good. I see. . . . What you're asking for is a temporary entry visa. How long do you think you will need to . . . well, let's not say to forget, but to weaken, this attachment? Twenty years? Thirty?"

"I don't know," I said. "At my age—"

"You no longer have any age," she said. "Ten years?"

She rapidly filled in the blanks on the form, had me sign it, and then led me over to an old man sitting in the middle of the room.

"Mr. Commissioner," she said, "a temporary for Mr. Franck. Everything's in order."

The old man signed the form without looking at it, and then stamped his signature with the date.

"Now hurry back to Mr. Franck," the young woman said to me kindly. "It's three-thirty already, and the office closes at four."

"Hurry," she had said, but I could barely move my aching body. Outside, I saw that the fog was denser than ever. Presently I lost my way, stumbled into a clump of reeds, and fell. Covered with mud, I struggled to my feet, shivering and so nervous that it took me several hours to find Building B. It was closed.

"You'll have to go back to town," the janitor said, "and come back tomorrow."

I was so weary that I took advantage of the dark and the fog to slip around the back of the building, where I spent the night in a ditch, under a cart. I woke up shaking with cold and aching all over so that I could hardly walk. For the first time since I had begun this dismal trek from office to office, the sun was shining brilliantly. It seemed very high in the sky, and I looked at my watch. It was past noon. Very likely I had fallen asleep just before dawn and had slept late. I hurried around to the front of the building, and saw a line of men and women so long that the guards had had to divide it into sections.

Waiting . . . One step forward . . . Another . . . The agony of hearing the hours strike . . . One . . . Two . . . Waiting now in front of the elevator . . . Three . . . Four . . . No more hope. Back to the city. Another hellish night. The morning rush. The waiting before the gate. The wait outside Building B. The wait in front of the elevator. Inching down the corridor on the thirty-fourth floor. Room 3451 . . . 3452 . . . 3453 . . . 3454 . . . The slow advance, one chair at a time . . . "Next!" I walked into Mr. Franck's office at last.

"Ah, it's you," he said. "Have you the visa?"

"Yes," I said, collapsing in a chair. "Yes . . . Here it is."

He looked at it with benevolent satisfaction at first, then more closely and with displeasure.

"Why didn't you come yesterday?" he demanded. "This visa is no longer valid."

"No longer valid? What do you mean? Why not?"

"The C.C.C. visas are valid only for twenty-four hours. . . . Why? I have no idea, sir, but that's the regulation. Hurry over and ask them to extend it. They'll do it immediately. Next!"

At this I became wild with anger. I could see the swamps, the mud, the endless tramping back and forth, the useless waiting. With no thought for those austere surroundings or for the twenty people outside who could hear me, I shouted frantically:

"I've had enough! Yes, I've had enough of being sent from one office to another, from one clerk to another, from one visa to another visa. I've been bullied enough, I've suffered enough. Enough, you hear! Enough! Enough! If it's this hard to leave, I don't want to leave!"

I was pounding on Mr. Franck's desk. He looked frightened, as well he might, for I was beside myself with rage.

"I don't want to leave anymore! I don't want to leave anymore!"

Franck called his secretary and together they seized me by the shoulders and pushed me out of his office. Two guards who had been alerted by the noise came running up, and they took me in charge and threw me out of the building. I was free, and I began to run across the airfield, shouting:

"I don't want to leave! I don't want to leave!"

Some other passengers gathered round and a few of them tried to reason with me. But I did not hear one word they said.

"I don't want to leave!"

I rushed toward a sudden lightening of the sky. The wind became brisker and saltier. Two beams of light pierced the fog. What coast did they mark? I could hear the sea roaring in the distance.

"I don't want to leave anymore!"

The two beacons drew nearer. . . . Beacons? Or eyes? They were eyes—the gentle, anguished gray eyes of my wife, of Donatienne.

"I don't want to leave anymore," I told her, weakly.

"Doctor!" she cried. "He just spoke!"

"Then he is saved," the hoarse voice of Dr. Galtier replied.

The last shreds of fog clung to the curtains. The familiar forms of chairs and tables were taking shape in the newly recovered light. On the walls, paintings were restored to their bright colors, and near me, very near me, the eyes of Donatienne—tearful, proud, tender, oh, so tender—were glowing.

The Fault of M. Balzac

Life imitates art much more than art imitates life. — OSCAR WILDE

THE EVENING had been spent smoking cigarettes and passing judgment on men and their works, the opinions expressed being as bereft of charity as they were of substance. Then, toward midnight, the conversation was suddenly rekindled, the way a fire one had believed dead rouses the surprised sleeper to a brightly illuminated room.

After some comment about one of our friends—a seemingly rather frivolous woman who had astonished us all by entering the Carmelites—the talk had turned to how inconstant human character is, and how difficult for even an intelligent observer to foresee the simplest actions of the people with whom he lives.

"But I ask myself: How could one possibly foresee," I had

said, "when every possible contradiction is to be found in each one of us. An accident sparks one set of feelings rather than another, we find ourselves classified and judged accordingly, and that social armature fixes us for the rest of our lives in a given stance, heroic or despicable as the case may be. But the tag on the mannequin does not often correspond to a true classification. Indecent thoughts cross the minds of men who live like saints. They brush such thoughts aside, because the kind of life they've accepted allows no room for them. But suppose circumstances had placed those same individuals in another shop window. Their reactions to the very same ideas would have been different. This works both ways. Charming impulses flit through the hearts of scoundrels, like reflections over water. So it is completely arbitrary to talk about personality. For convenience in our speech and behavior, it's permissible to say 'So-and-so is a profligate and So-and-so is a sober, steady fellow.' But even a mildly honest analyst finds that character is a fluid thing."

Christian had objected to this. "Yes," he had said, "what you are calling 'personality' is actually only a chaos of sensations, memories, and impulses, and this chaos is incapable of organizing itself. But what you seem to forget is that it can be organized from without. Any given set of beliefs can orient the tiny dispersed elements of personality the way a magnet orients iron filings. A great love or a religious faith or one prejudice stronger than all the others—any one of these can supply the invisible armature the spirit lacks, and enable it to achieve the state of equilibrium that is, practically speaking, happiness. The point of support, of attachment, should always be outside the self, and that's why—well, reread *The Imitation*. Remember? 'When Thou abandonest me to myself, I see how I am but weakness and pure nothingness, but in seeking only after Thee and in loving Thee with a pure love, I have found Thee and found myself together with Thee.'"

At that point, Renaud clapped shut the book he had been leafing through, stood up, as he almost always does when he wants to speak, and walked over to stand before the big stove that heated our host's studio.

"Faith?" he said, lighting his pipe. "Yes, faith or passion—either one can create order in the spirit. Yes, of course. But for a man like myself, who has never been fortunate enough to have a faith—or a great love, either—the main force making for equilibrium would, I believe, be fiction. . . . Yes, fiction. What has to happen is something like this. The mind sketches out a character that is to its satisfaction, and then tries to live up to it. In my case, novels and plays help me enormously in fashioning the mask that is necessary to what I am prepared to call, in a nonreligious sense, salvation. When I feel lost, when I am casting about helplessly in that mélange of contradictory desires Christian was just talking about, when I find myself mediocre, or when I dislike myself—that often happens to me—I go back to certain books that I have loved, and I look for the particular tone of some passed emotion. And as I contemplate my model, I see again the ideal portrait that once upon a time I had traced for myself. I recognize the chosen mask. And I am saved. Tolstoi's Prince André, Stendhal's Fabrice, the Goethe of *Dichtung und Wahrheit*—these are the 'organizers of my chaos.' And I don't think mine is such a rare case. In his day, didn't Rousseau modify—even create—the sensibility of millions of Frenchmen? Didn't D'Annunzio do the same for modern Italy? And Wilde, for at least some Englishmen around the turn of the century? What about Châteaubriand, Ruskin, Barrès?"

"Excuse me," one of us interrupted. "Did these men create the sensibility of their day or did they merely record it?"

"Record it? Never, my dear friend. The great writer draws the types that his period aspires to, not the types it produces. The courteous, gallant knight of the *chansons de geste* was conceived in a world of brutish clods, and he then transformed his readers. The philanthropist of the Hollywood film is the hero of a nation of men with money. Art offers the models, men execute them, and in mass-producing them render them useless as works of art. When France was full of live Manfreds and Renés, she lost her taste for Romanticism. Proust is going to produce a generation of analysts who will detest the analytical novel and love only the spare, unembellished tale."

"A good subject for a Hoffmann or a Pirandello," Ramon said. "The novelist's characters come to life and curse him."

"Nothing could be surer, Ramon, and it's true down to the last detail. Even the actions of your characters will one day become the acts performed by flesh-and-blood people. Remember what Gide said? 'How many secret Werthers there were who did not know of each other's existence and waited only for the bullet of Goethe's Werther to kill themselves. . . .' I know a man whose whole life was transformed by one simple act of one of Balzac's heroes."

"Do you know," Ramon said, "that during one whole season in Venice, some French people there played a game in which they took the names of Balzac characters and assumed their personalities? When you went to Florian's, you met no one but Rastignac, Goriot, Nathan, the Duchesse de Maufrigneuse. Several of the actresses made it a point of honor to play their roles out to the end."

"That must have been delightful," Renaud went on, "but even so, it was only a game. In the case of the man I am talking about, it was his real life, his one and only life, that suddenly changed under the influence of something he remembered from his reading. He was at the University with me, a fellow by the name of Lecadieu. . . . Altogether the most remarkable man in a class that was not by any means mediocre."

"Remarkable in what way?"

"Oh, in everything . . . A powerful, strange personality, a penetrating intelligence . . . And an incredible erudition. He had read everything from the Church Fathers to the Nibelung-enlied, from the Byzantine historians to Karl Marx, and behind all the words, he was always able to find something that was human and shared. Whenever he talked about history, we would all go away electrified. I remember particularly his once describing one of the Catiline conspiracies. He was both a great historian and a great storyteller. And he was the most passionate reader of novels I've ever known. Stendhal and Balzac were his gods. He had memorized whole passages from their books, and everything he knew about the world he seemed to have learned from them.

"He resembled them a little, physically. He was sturdily built and ugly—but it was that intelligent ugliness that bears the stamp of quality, that is somehow monumental, and almost always typical of the physique of a great writer. I say 'almost always' because other, less visible flaws—a lack of character, a vice, some frustration—can arouse the need to reincarnate the self which the creative person must experience. As a young man, Tolstoi was hideous, Balzac was a great hulk, Dostoevski looked like a fawn, and the face of young Lecadieu always reminded me of the face of Henri Beyle at the time he left Grenoble.

"One guessed that he was poor. In fact, several times he took me to his brother-in-law's—the man was a mechanic out in Belleville—where we used to eat in the kitchen. Lecadieu used to show him off to the whole school with a kind of ostentation. Very much a Julien Sorel attitude and, for that matter, everything he said or did went to show how the character of Julien haunted him. When he would be talking about the scene in the dark garden—when Julien seizes Mme de Rênal's hand with no feeling of love whatever—he spoke as if he were telling his own life story. His circumstances did not allow him to practice his audacities on anyone but waitresses and models, but we knew that he was chafing for the moment when he would perhaps be able to conquer women who were proud and passionate—and chaste.

" 'To force your way into society by writing a great book is possible, of course,' he used to say to me. 'But that's so slow! And furthermore, how is one supposed to write a good novel without knowing really complete women? But women, Renaud, real women—we've got to resign ourselves to it, for it's true—are to be found only in high society. For such complex, fragile creatures to develop, there must be idleness, wealth, a climate of luxury and boredom. Other women? Other women can be desirable, they can be beautiful, but what do they do for me? Physical love? Marcus Aurelius' "two bellies rubbing one against the other"? Taine's "I have reduced love to a function and that function to a minimum"? Or a flat, monotonous, life-long devotion? . . . Not for me. What I must have is the pride of victory and the romantic setting. . . . Perhaps I'm wrong. . . . No, I'm not. How could one be wrong in stating one's own nature? I am romantic, my friend, hopelessly, consciously romantic. I need to be loved to be happy and since I'm ugly, I have to be powerful to be loved. My whole life plan is based on these premises, and you may say what you like, but for *me* it's the only reasonable one.'

"At the time, I was full of that prudent common sense that is often supplied by poor health, and Lecadieu's 'life plan' seemed utterly absurd to me.

" 'I'm sorry for you,' I told him. 'I'm sorry for you and I don't understand you. You condemn yourself to feeling upset and anxious—you're that already—all your life, and probably to failing before adversaries who aren't worthy of you. What do I care that other people may seem to win success, if I have really won the true success, which is an inner thing? . . . After all, Lecadieu, what do you want? Happiness? Do you really believe that power or even women can give you happiness? What you call real life I call unreal. How can you want things that are by nature imperfect and traitorous when you have the chance to be one of those people who can consecrate their lives to ideas, and thereby achieve an almost intangible happiness?'

"He shrugged. 'I know. I've heard that tune before. And I too have read the Stoics. I tell you again, I'm different from them—and from you. Oh, very likely I could find some kind of provisional happiness in books and art and work. But at thirty, or at forty, I would regret the life I'd missed. And then it would be too late. I've a different concept of how the stages of wisdom are arranged. First, free yourself of the obsession of ambition by the one efficacious cure—satisfy it. Then, but only then, live out your life according to the sound good sense that is all the more sincere for knowing what it despises. That's it. A really distinguished mistress would spare me ten years of set-backs and sordid intrigue.'

"I remember now something which I didn't understand very well at the time, but which now seems to me very revealing. He'd found an Irish waitress in some little restaurant—a plain, dirty creature—and he'd known no peace until he'd gone to bed with this girl. To me it seemed all the more ridiculous because she spoke hardly any French, and the one blank in our omniscient Lecadieu was his total ignorance of English. ·

" 'But what an idea!' I kept saying to him. 'You can't even understand her.'

" 'You're not much of a psychologist,' he answered. 'Don't you see, the whole pleasure is there?'

"The mechanism is easy enough to imagine. He could not find in his habitual mistresses the distinction and the modesty that were necessary to his happiness, so he searched for the illusion in the mystery of a strange language.

"He kept a number of notebooks filled with private jottings, projects, and work plans. One evening he had forgotten one of these notebooks on the table, and we leafed through it. We found some notes that made us roar with laughter. I remember one that was very Lecadieu: 'Failure proves the weakness of desire, not its temerity.'

"At the top of one page he had written:

> *Reference points:*
> *Musset at 20 is a great poet.*　　　　*Out.*
> *Hoche, Napoleon, at 24, are*
> *　　commanders in chief.*　　　　　*Out.*
> *Gambetta at 25 is a famous lawyer.*　*Maybe.*
> *Stendhal publishes* The Red and
> *　　the Black at 48.*　　　　*This leaves*
> *　　　　　　　　some room*
> *　　　　　　　　for hope.*

"This agenda of ambition seemed pretty foolish to us at the time, but the hypothesis 'Lecadieu is a genius' was far from foolish. If someone had asked us, 'Does one of you have a chance of escaping from the herd and achieving real fame?' we would have answered, 'Yes, Lecadieu.' Even so, a bit of luck would have been called for. In the life of every potentially great man, some minute event intervenes that sets the ball rolling. What would Bonaparte have become without Vendémiaire at Saint-Roch? Or Byron, without the tongue-lashings of the Scottish critics? Probably nothing more than very ordinary men. Even though Byron limped, which for an artist is a source of strength, and even though Bonaparte was timid and afraid of women. Our Lecadieu was ugly, he was poor, he had talent— but would he find his Saint-Roch?"

"At the beginning of our third year, the director had several of us called to his office. At that time, the director was Perrot—*The History of Art* Perrot—a wonderful man, who looked like a cross between a wild boar fresh from a swim and a Cyclops, for he was blind in one eye and his manner was fearsome. When a student would ask advice about his future, Perrot would say, 'Oh, the future . . . Well, when you leave here, try to find a good job with good pay that requires as little work as possible.'

"Anyhow, that day, when we were assembled around his desk, he made a little speech that went about like this: 'You know Trélivan, the cabinet minister, by name? Yes? . . . Good. M. Trélivan has just sent his secretary to see me. He's looking for a tutor for his sons, and wants to know whether one of you would be interested in giving them lessons three times a week in history, literature, and Latin. Obviously, I would authorize the necessary arrangements. In my opinion, this is an opportunity for one of you to win important patronage and perhaps, at the end of your university work, to have a nice little sinecure where you can piddle away the rest of your days. In a word, it's worth thinking about. Mull it over, agree among yourselves, and come back this evening and give me a name.'

"We all knew Trélivan, who was a friend of Jules Ferry and of Challemel-Lacour, and the most cultivated, the wittiest statesman of his day. When he was a young man he had astounded the Latin Quarter by standing up on a table and reciting from memory the Catiline and Philippic orations. Father Hase, the old professor of Greek at the Sorbonne, used to say that he had never had a better student. When Trélivan moved into high political office, he lost none of the imaginativeness that so delighted us. During debates in the Chamber of Deputies, he used to quote poetry. When his policies were too rudely challenged—that was the period of the attack on Tonkin and the opposition was ferocious—he would open a copy of Theocritus or Plato and quite simply stop listening. Even his wanting a young tutor for his children rather than one of their usual teachers was very like Trélivan, and we liked the idea.

"I would have been glad to go to his house for several hours a week, but Lecadieu, as 'chief' of the group, had priority, and it was easy to see what his choice would be. Here he found the opportunity he so desperately wanted. He would have an assured, effortless entrée to a powerful man and in time might become his secretary. Trélivan could certainly launch our friend into the mysterious world he proposed one day to dominate. He asked for the position, and he got it. The next day he took up his duties."

"Lecadieu and I had got into the habit of having a long talk every evening on the landing of our dormitory floor. So, from the very first week I knew a thousand and one details about the Trélivan household. Lecadieu had seen the Minister only once, the first day. He had had to wait for him until nine in the evening, for the Chamber had stayed in session until late.

" 'Well,' I said, 'what did the great man have to say?'

" 'To be frank,' Lecadieu told me, 'at first I was disappointed. You want a great man not to be a man. The moment you see his eyes, his nose, his mouth, and you hear him speaking ordinary language, it's as if a mirage dissolved. But Trélivan is pleasant, cordial, intelligent. He talked to me about the University, asked me what books and authors our generation likes, and then took me to meet his wife. He says she has more to do with the children than he does. She received me kindly. She seems afraid of him. He affects a rather ironic tone of voice when he talks to her.'

" 'A good sign, Lecadieu. Is she pretty?'

" 'Very pretty.'

" 'But not so young, since the boys—'

" 'About thirty . . . maybe a little more.' "

"The following Sunday, we were invited to lunch by one of our former professors who has since been elected to Parliament. He was a friend of Gambetta, Bouteillier, and Trélivan, and Lecadieu took advantage of this to pick up some information.

" 'Do you happen to know, sir, who Mme Trélivan was before her marriage?'

" 'Mme Trélivan? I believe she's the daughter of an industrialist from Eure-et-Loir. A good middle-class background, as I remember.'

" 'She's intelligent,' Lecadieu said, in that indefinable tone that implies a question, a statement of fact, and that perhaps really expresses a wish for reassurance.

" 'Why, no,' Father Lefort said, surprised. 'Why should she be? It seems to me people say she's stupid. My associate Jules Lemaître, who often visits the house—'

"Lecadieu, leaning across the table, interrupted him abruptly:

" 'Is she faithful?'

" 'Who? Mme Trélivan? . . . Well, my friend . . . she's said to have had lovers, but how should I know? It seems likely. Trélivan doesn't pay much attention to her. He lives, so they say, with Mlle Marsay, whom he got into the Comédie-Française when he was with the Ministry of Fine Arts. I know that he entertains at Mlle Marsay's home and spends almost every evening there. So . . .'

"The Deputy from Caen threw out his hands, shaking his head, and began to talk of the coming elections."

"From the day following this conversation, Lecadieu's attitude toward Mme Trélivan became more free and easy. A veiled impertinence lurked behind the banalities he exchanged with her when she came in during a lesson. He looked at her now with mounting boldness. She always wore rather low-cut gowns that disclosed the swelling roundness of her breasts under a film of tulle. Her shoulders and arms had that firm fullness that precedes without previewing the fleshiness of maturity. Her face was smooth, or perhaps Lecadieu was too young to detect the imperceptible lines. When she sat down, she revealed very delicate ankles that the fragile screen of her silk dress seemed to remove from the gross realm of the physical. So to Lecadieu she seemed at once divine because of her beauty, and at the same time accessible, since legend had it that this flesh was weak.

"I've said that Lecadieu was a notably original and eloquent speaker. Several times when Mme Trélivan came in while he was indulging in the pleasure of evoking for the astonished children the Rome of the Caesars or the court of Cleopatra or the builders of cathedrals, he allowed himself the slightly insolent coquetry of not interrupting himself. 'Yes, yes,' Lecadieu used to say to himself, for he watched her as he went on talking, 'you're thinking that many famous public speakers are less interesting than this little university chap.' Very likely he was mistaken. Very likely, as she stared at the top of her shoes or at the prismatic fires of her diamond, she was thinking of her bootmaker or some new setting for the ring.

"However, she came back. Lecadieu kept a tally of her appearances with a minute precision that she surely never even dreamed of. If she was faithful three days in a row, he would think: She's nibbling at the bait. He would review one by one the remarks he had made to her and that he believed he had filled with double meanings, and then would try to remember what her reactions had been. At this witticism, Mme Trélivan had smiled; another had left her cold; at this mildly daring sally she had glanced at him with chill surprise. If she abstained from coming for an entire week, he would tell himself, 'It's all over. I bore her.' He had stratagems by the dozen to find out from the children, without surprising them, what had kept their mother away. It was always some simple reason. She was away, or she was ill, or she was presiding over one of her committee meetings.

" 'You see,' Lecadieu would say to me, 'when you discover that your own violent feelings are helpless to arouse an equivalent storm in another human being, you would like— But above all, not knowing is terrible. For us another person's thoughts are a total mystery, and that's the main source of passion. If you could guess what women are thinking—good or bad—you wouldn't suffer so much. You'd put your cards on the table or throw up the game. But that calm of theirs, which may hide curiosity or may hide nothing at all . . .'

"One day she asked him for the titles of several books, and this led to a short conversation. The fifteen-minute chat following the lesson became a habit, and very quickly Lecadieu transformed the tutorial tone into that kind of banter that is both serious and trifling, and that almost always serves as the prelude to love. Have you noticed that in conversations between men and women the tone of pleasantry is there only to mask the intensity of the desire? It's as if both people were aware of the force that is carrying them away and of the danger that is threatening them, so they try to protect their peace of mind by the mock inconsequentiality of their talk. At this stage, every remark is an allusion, every sentence is a probe, every compliment a caress. Words and feelings glide along two superimposed planes, and the higher plane, where words are exchanged, can be interpreted only as a sign and symbol of the other, along which the undefined animal images move.

"This passionate adolescent who longed for the day his genius would dominate France lent himself to chatter about the newest play, current novels, fashions—even the weather. He would come back to me with descriptions of black tulle collars or white toques with a Louis XV bow—this was the era of the gigot sleeve and the high-perched bonnet.

" 'Father Lefort was right,' he told me. 'She's not very intelligent. Or to put it more exactly, she thinks only superficially. But what do I care!'

"As they talked, he would look at the hand that Julien had seized, at the waist that Félix de Vandenesse had caught. 'How,' he said to himself, 'can one pass from this ceremonious tone, from this physical rigidity, to the amazing familiarity of love? With the women I've known so far, the first gestures were nothing but pleasantries that were allowed and even invited, and the rest followed naturally. But here the slightest caress seems unthinkable. . . . Julien? Julien had dark evenings in a garden, the complicity of a beautiful night, a life in common. . . . Whereas I can't even see her alone.'

"The two children were always present, in fact, and Lecadieu spied in vain for some encouragement or sign of awareness in Mme Trélivan's eyes. She looked at him with perfect calm, with a self-possession that left no room for any bold gesture.

"Every time he left the town house where the Trélivans lived, he would wander along the quays deep in thought: I'm not just a coward. This woman has had lovers. She is at least twelve years older than I. She can't be too hard to approach. . . . It's true that her husband is a remarkable man. But do women see such things? He neglects her, and she seems desperately bored. . . .

"And he would say over and over to himself: 'I am just a coward. I am nothing but a coward.'

"He would have been less full of self-contempt if he had known the true state of Mme Trélivan's heart—which I learned about much later from a woman who played at that period of her life a role analogous to the one I filled for Lecadieu. Sometimes, twenty years after the fact chance brings you the cross check that would have interested you so intensely at the time of the adventure.

"Thérèse Trélivan had married for love. She was, as we had been told, the daughter of an industrialist, but of an industrialist who was an admirer of Voltaire and a republican—the type of middle-class Frenchman who is rare nowadays but who was very frequently to be met with in the last years of the Empire. In the course of one of Trélivan's election campaigns, he had been invited to the home of Thérèse's parents, and he had dazzled the young woman. It was she who asked to marry him. She had had to overcome the opposition of her family, who quite rightly brought up Trélivan's reputation as a ladies' man and inveterate gambler. Her father had said, 'The man's a womanchaser and he'll ruin you.' She had replied, 'I will change him.'

"People who knew her at that time say that her beauty, her naïveté, and her need to devote herself to some man made a most attractive combination. By marrying a deputy who was still young but already famous, she had imagined a beautiful life—a devoted couple dedicated to some apostolic mission. She had visualized herself inspiring her husband's public speeches, copying them out for him, applauding them from the Chamber gallery—she the faithful support in moments of crisis, the self-effacing but cherished companion in moments of triumph. She had sublimated her girlish effusions in a seeming passion for politics.

"The marriage turned out as one could expect. Trélivan loved his wife as long as he desired her, which is to say about three months. Then he promptly stopped remembering that she even existed. Of a sarcastic turn of mind, realistic, and extremely chary of enthusiasms, he had been much less seduced than irritated by ardor that he probably found a burden.

"Naïveté, which appeals to contemplative men, annoys men of action. He had rejected, tenderly at first, then politely, then dryly, any domestic collaboration. The first pregnancies and the precautions they impose had been his pretext to escape from his home. He had gone back to women friends who were temperamentally more congenial to him. When his wife complained, he had said that she was free.

"She had decided against a divorce, first because of the children, then because she was still proud of being known as Mme Trélivan, and perhaps above all because she did not want to admit defeat to her family. So she had had to acquire the bleak habit of traveling alone with the children, of enduring the officious sympathy of friends, and of smiling when she was asked if her husband was away. Finally, after six years of semiabandonment, weary of everything, haunted by a confused need of tenderness, and despite her disappointments tormented by her girlhood dream of a pure and perfect love, she had taken a lover. He was a colleague and political friend of Trélivan, a vain, clumsy man who also left her after a few months.

"These two experiences had made her distrustful of all men. She would sigh and smile sadly whenever anyone mentioned marriage in front of her. Although as a young woman she had been vivacious and witty, she had become languid and taciturn. Doctors diagnosed a manageable physical illness and an incurable neurasthenia. She lived in the constant expectation of some grave trouble or of death. Above all, she had completely lost the gracious confidence that had been the source of so much of her youthful charm. She believed she was incapable and unworthy of being loved."

"The Easter holidays arrived to interrupt the children's lessons and gave Lecadieu time for a long meditation, from which he emerged resolved to act. The day following his return to work, at the end of the lesson, he requested a private conversation with Mme Trélivan. She supposed that he had some complaint about one of the children, and she took him into a small sitting room. As he followed her, he was perfectly calm, the way one is before a duel once one's mind has been made up. As soon as she had closed the door, he told her that he could be silent no longer, that he lived only for the moments he spent near her, that her face was before him constantly—in a word, he made a most artificial, literary declaration, at the end of which he went to her and tried to seize her hands.

"She looked at him with annoyance and embarrassment, and kept saying, 'But this is absurd. . . . Do be quiet. . . .' Finally she said, 'This is ridiculous. Stop it, please, and go away,' in a tone of voice at once so imploring and so firm that he felt defeated and ashamed. He stepped back, and as he left the room, he said in a low voice, 'I will ask M. Perrot to find someone to take my place with the children.'

"In the vestibule, he stopped for a moment, his head rather in a whirl, then stumbled about a few seconds looking for his hat, so that one of the servants, hearing him, came from the pantry to show him to the door.

"At that moment, this departure of the dismissed lover and the servant standing at his shoulder suddenly recalled to my friend a story by Balzac that he had recently read, a short but very fine story called 'The Abandoned Woman.'

"Do you remember 'The Abandoned Woman'? Ah, none of you are Balzac buffs, then. So I must tell you, for you to understand what happened next, that in this story a young man gets himself admitted on some false pretext to a woman's house, and without preamble declares the most extravagant love for her. She glances at him with the utmost disdain, rings for the footman, and says, 'Jacques—or Jean or whatever—show the gentleman out.' To this point, this is the story of Lecadieu.

"But in the Balzac, as the young man is walking through the vestibule, he thinks to himself: If I leave the house, this woman will think me a fool forever after. At this very moment, she may be regretting having dismissed me so abruptly. It's for me to understand her. To the footman he says, 'I've forgotten something,' and he goes back, finds Mme de Beauséant still in the sitting room, and becomes her lover.

"Yes, Lecadieu thought, awkwardly feeling around for the sleeve of his coat, that's my situation. Exactly my situation. And not only will I be a fool in her eyes forever after, but

she'll relate this adventure to her husband. Then what troubles!
But if I see her again . . .

"He said to the servant, 'I've forgotten my gloves,' crossed
the vestibule almost at a run, and opened the door of the sitting room.

Mme Trélivan was sitting, lost in thought, on a little chair
near the fireplace. She looked at him with surprise, but with
great gentleness.

" 'What?' she said. 'You're back? I thought—'

" 'I told the butler I'd forgotten my gloves. I beg you, listen
to me for five minutes.'

"She did not protest, and it seems certain that in the few
minutes she had had to reflect after my friend had gone out,
she had regretted her virtuous impulse. This feeling, which is
so human, of scorning what is offered and of clutching what
escapes from one, had no doubt worked so that, having dismissed him in good faith, on hearing him leave she had wanted
to see him again.

"Thérèse Trélivan was thirty-nine. One more, perhaps one
last time, life could become for her a terrible and delicious
mélange of pain and joy. One more time she would know the
secret appointments, the hidden letters, the endless arguments
of jealousy. Her lover would be an adolescent; the dream of
maternal protectiveness that her husband had so coldly dis-
rupted she might be able to revive with a man who would owe
her everything.

"Did she love him? I've no idea, but I am inclined to believe
that until that moment she'd never thought of him except as
the brilliant tutor of her children, and this not out of scorn for
him but out of her own modesty. When, after a longish speech
not a word of which she had heard, he went to her, she held
out her hand to him and lowered her eyes with infinite grace.
The gesture was in the tradition of Lecadieu's heroines, and it
so enchanted him that he kissed that hand with sincere passion."

"He made an honest effort that evening to hide his good
fortune from me. Discretion was one characteristic of the lover,
as novels had taught him to conceive of the role. He held out

through dinner and part of the evening. I remember there being a lively discussion of Anatole France's first book and that Lecadieu made an ingenious analysis of what he called its "too self-conscious poetry.' Around ten o'clock, he dragged me away from our friends, and told me the story of his day.

" 'I shouldn't be telling you all this, but I would burst if I couldn't confide in at least one person. I put everything on one card, played it coldly, and I won. So it's true that with women boldness, pure and simple, is enough. My ideas about love amused you so because they came from books, but they turn out to be true in action. Balzac was a great man.'

"Whereupon he began a long recital, at the end of which he laughed, seized me by the shoulders, and concluded:

" 'Life is wonderful, Renaud!'

" 'It seems to me,' I said, shaking off his hand, 'that you're crying victory a little soon. She's forgiven you for being so bold, that's all her behavior means. The same difficulties are still there.'

" 'Ah,' Lecadieu said, 'you didn't see how she looked at me. All of a sudden, she became ravishingly lovely. No, my friend, you don't mistake a woman's feelings. For a long time, I felt she was indifferent. When I tell you that she loves me, I know what I'm saying.'

"I listened to him with that ironic, almost embarrassed amazement that other people's love affairs usually arouse in us. But he was right in thinking that the game was won. One week later, Mme Trélivan was his mistress. He had carried out the decisive maneuvers with great skill, preparing himself for every meeting, planning his moves and his words in advance. His success was the triumph of an almost scientific love strategy.

"Popular theory insists that possession marks the end of the passion of love. Lecadieu's case proves, on the contrary, that it can release the mechanism. True, this woman was bringing him almost everything that from early adolescence had constituted his picture of a happy love. Several points in his idea of pleasure had always astonished me, because I myself did not associate them with pleasure. For example, he needed to feel that his mistress, who in some way had to be superior to him, was sacrificing something—social position, wealth—to come to him. Secondly, he wanted her to be chaste, and to approach love with a reserve that he, Lecadieu, would have to overcome. All of which means, I think, that at bottom he was proud rather than sensual.

"Thérèse Trélivan represented almost perfectly the type of woman he had so often described to me. He was grateful to her for her fine house, for the elegant room where, with the complicity of a woman friend, she received him, and for her gowns and her carriages. Above all, he felt a surge of joy that bound him firmly to her when she confessed to him that for a long time he had intimidated her.

" 'Don't you find that extraordinary!' he said to me. 'A man feels that he is looked down on, or at the very least ignored, and he finds a dozen reasons, each better than the last, to explain a woman's disdain. And suddenly he is transported behind the scenes and discovers that she has been going through the same fears as he, and at the same time. Do you remember? I said to you, "She hasn't come for three lessons. I'm sure I bore her." At that very moment, she was thinking—she's told me so—"It must irritate him to have me there. I won't go for three lessons." To come to know another's mind, a mind that has been strange and even hostile, or so one felt—this for me is perhaps the highest pleasure of love. It's a perfect appeasement, a delicious refreshment, of one's self-love. And, Renaud, I do believe I am going to love her.'

"I was not so carried away, naturally, and I'd not forgotten our conversation with Father Lefort.

" 'But is she intelligent?' I asked.

" 'Intelligent!' he said animatedly. 'What does that mean, intelligent? You meet mathematicians at the university—Lefèvre, for example—who are considered wonderfully intelligent by their fellow-specialists but whom you and I call savages. If I try to explain Spinoza to Thérèse—I've tried—obviously I'm going to bore her, even if she does listen to me with all the attention and patience in the world, but, on the other hand, about many things she amazes me and knows more than I. She knows more about the real life of a certain class of French society in the late nineteenth century than you or I or M. Renan. If we're talking about political personalities or high society or the influence of women, I can listen to her for hours on end without being bored.'

"In the months that followed, Mme Trélivan was endlessly obliging in satisfying my young friend's curiosity about such matters. Lecadieu had only to tell her, 'I'd like just once to see Jules Ferry,' or 'Constant must be a strange fellow' or 'Do you know Maurice Barrès?' for her to promise to arrange a meeting immediately. She was discovering the value of Trélivan's unlimited acquaintance, which until then had seemed to her so tedious and burdensome. She took the liveliest pleasure in paying homage to her young lover on the strength of her husband's social credit.

" 'But what about Trélivan?' I would ask sometimes, when Lecadieu came back full of marvelous stories about his evening. 'How is it he doesn't notice the change in your situation in his own home?'

"Lecadieu became thoughtful.

" 'Yes,' he would say, 'that is rather strange.'

" 'After all, she does receive you sometimes at home?'

" 'Very seldom, because of the children and also because of the servants, but as far as Trélivan is concerned, it would be unheard of for him to be home between three and seven. What is amazing is that she's asked him dozens of times for invitations for me, permission to attend sessions of the Chamber and Senate, and so on, and he always agrees very politely, even in a friendly way, and never asks for any explanations. When I dine at the house, he treats me with a kind of special regard. He always introduces me as "a young university man of real talent." I believe he's taken a liking to me.'

"One consequence of his new life was that Lecadieu was doing practically no work. Our director, bemused by the powerful name of Trélivan, had given up any control over his comings and goings, but the professors were complaining. He was too brilliant to be in danger of failing the final examinations, but he was losing ground. I told him so, and he laughed. To read thirty or forty difficult authors now seemed to him an absurd way to spend time, and quite beneath him.

" 'The examinations?' he said. 'Oh, I'll pass them, since I'm here, but what a drudgery. Does it amuse you to master the

strings that are needed to manipulate these old university puppets? It interests me a little, because strings of any kind interest
me, but I do find that, weighing one idiocy against another, it
would be much more worthwhile to play on some other stage,
which attracts a bigger public. In the world as it is, power is in
inverse ratio to the work performed. Modern society awards the
happiest life to the least useful man. A good speaker, a witty
man, will win the fashionable drawing rooms, the women, and
even the love of the public. You remember what La Bruyère
said: "Rank first of all puts a man in an advantageous position;
it saves him thirty years." Today rank is obtained through the
goodwill of a few men—ministers, party leaders, highly placed
bureaucrats—who are more powerful than Louis XIV or Napoleon ever was.'

" 'What then? You're going into politics?'

" 'Why? No, I'm not making any definite plans. I'm on the
lookout, I'll seize every opportunity. There are hundreds of
careers outside of politics that have its "miraculous" possibili-
ties without any of its dangers. The politician, after all, has to
please the public, and that's a difficult and mysterious thing.
What I want is to please the politicians, and that's child's play;
it's even fun. Many of them are very cultivated men, you know.
Trélivan talks about Aristophanes far better than our professors, and with a sense of real life that they don't have. You
can't imagine such a pure cynicism, such magnificent
effrontery.'

"After that, my eulogies of a professor's chair in some provincial university, with four hours of teaching and the freedom
to think and to work for oneself, must have seemed very flat
indeed.

"Around this time, I learned from a fellow-student whose
father was a frequent visitor at the Trélivans' that not everyone
liked Lecadieu. He did not manage to conceal his sense of his
own complete equality with the great. And his Machiavellianism was transparent. People were surprised to see the lady of
the house constantly attended by this boy who was too big for
his age, with his Dantonesque face. He gave the impression of
being at once timid and irritated by his own timidity; strong,

but too aware of his strength. 'Who is this Caliban who speaks the language of Prospero?' Lemaître had asked.

"Another disagreeable aspect of this adventure was that now Lecadieu was forever in need of money. Clothes played a role in his new life scheme, and on this score that brilliant brain was positively childish. I had to listen to him talk for three evenings about a white ribbed-silk waistcoat some young department chief had worn. In the street, he would stop in front of shoe shops and study the models in the window for minutes. Then, seeing my silence and disapproval, he would say:

" 'Come on! Empty your pockets. I have enough arguments and to spare that will convince you.' "

"Student rooms at the University were like so many little cubicles that ran the length of a hall and were closed off by curtains. Mine was to the right of Lecadieu's, and to his left was André Klein—he's now deputy from Les Landes.

"A few weeks before examinations, I was awakened by what seemed to me a strange noise, and, sitting up in bed, I distinctly heard sobbing. I got up. Klein was already alerted and was listening outside Lecadieu's room, his ear glued to the curtain. The groans were coming from there.

"I hadn't seen Lecadieu since morning, but we had all become accustomed to his absences and no one had noticed that this time he'd been away longer than usual.

"After an inquiring look at me, Klein pulled back the curtain. Lecadieu, fully dressed, was lying on his bed, in tears. You remember what I told you about his strong personality and our respect for him, so you can imagine our surprise.

" 'What's wrong?' I asked him. 'Lecadieu! Answer me. . . . What's wrong with you?'

" 'Leave me alone. . . . I'm going away.'

" 'Going away? What kind of story is this?'

" 'It's no story. I've got to go.'

" 'Are you crazy? Have they thrown you out?'

" 'No. I've promised to go.'

"He shook his head and fell back on his bed.

" 'You're an ass, Lecadieu,' Klein said.

"The other man bridled.

" 'Look,' I said to him, 'what's happened? . . . Klein, leave us alone, do you mind?'

"We were left alone. Lecadieu had already got hold of himself. He stood up, went over to the mirror, straightened his hair and tie, and came back and sat down beside me.

"Then, when I could see him better, I was struck by the extraordinary change in his face. It was as if his eyes were dead. I had the feeling that some essential part of this fine mechanism had been smashed.

" 'Mme Trélivan?' I asked. I supposed she'd died.

" 'Yes,' he said, with a sigh. 'Don't be impatient. I'll tell you everything. . . . Yes, today at the end of my lesson, Trélivan sent the butler to tell me to come to his study. He was working. He said to me, "Hello, young man," and quietly finished what he was reading and then, without another word, handed me two of my letters. . . . Yes, I've been idiot enough to write letters—not just little love notes but letters that you could never defend. I stammered I don't know what—something incoherent, no doubt. I was completely unprepared. As you know, I've been living with a sense of complete security. He, for his part, was utterly calm. I felt that I was being weighed and judged.

" 'When I stopped talking, he knocked the ash from his cigarette—oh, Renaud, that little pause! In spite of everything, I had time to admire him; he was being the great actor. Then he began to talk to me about "our" situation with the most amazing impartiality, detachment, and clear judgment. I can't give you any idea of that speech. Everything seemed obvious and clear to me. He said to me, "You love my wife; you write her so. And she loves you, with a love that I believe is very deep, very sincere. You know, of course, what our married life has been? Your love and hers are in no way reprehensible. What's more, at the moment I have personal reasons for wanting my own freedom. I won't put any obstacles in the way of your happiness. . . . The children? As you know, I have only the two boys. I am going to put them in boarding school. . . . Vacations? Everything will be arranged pleasantly and civilly. The children won't suffer at all. On the contrary . . . Money? Thérèse has a modest fortune, and you will be earning your livelihood. I see only one obstacle or, rather, one difficulty. I am a man in public life, and my divorce will create something of a stir. To keep the scandal to a minimum, I need you. I am offering you a correct and honorable way out. I don't want to have my wife involuntarily feed talebearers by remaining in Paris during the proceedings. I ask that you leave and that you take her with you. I will inform your director and I will have you appointed professor in some college in the provinces. . . ." "But, sir," I said to him, "I haven't taken my degree." "Well? That's not indispensable. Don't worry. I still have enough influence at the Ministry to have someone appointed as a first-form instructor. Furthermore, nothing prevents your continuing to prepare for your examinations and taking them next year. Then I will have you given a better post. Above all, don't suppose that I intend to persecute you. On the contrary. You're in a difficult, a painful position. I know that, my friend, and I'm sorry for you and I'll keep it in mind. If you accept my conditions, I will help you out of your difficulties. If you refuse, I shall be obliged to use legal weapons." '

" 'Legal weapons? What does that mean? What can he do to you?'

" 'Oh, everything . . . A trial for adultery—'

" 'What nonsense! A sixteen-franc fine? He'd look ridiculous.'

" 'Yes, but a man like that can cut off any chance of a career. It would be insane to fight him. . . . By going along with him, who knows?'

" 'Did you agree?'

" 'I am leaving in a week, with her, for the college in Luxeuil.'

" 'And she agrees?'

" 'Ah,' he said, 'she is wonderful. I've just spent the evening with her. I said to her, "You aren't afraid of living in a small city, afraid of all the mediocrity and boredom?" And she said, "I'm leaving with you. That's all I've heard." '

"Then I understood why Lecadieu was giving in so easily. He was intoxicated by the idea of living freely with his mistress.

"I was very young in those days, as was he, and this theatrical development was so dramatic that I accepted it as a necessary

fatality without ever thinking to discuss it. Later, with somewhat more knowledge of human nature, when I thought things
over, I understood that Trélivan had skillfully taken advantage
of the inexperience of a child to clear up his own situation
without creating any scandal. For a long time, he had been
wanting to get rid of a wife who bored him. We learned later
that when all this happened, he immediately decided to marry
Mlle Marsay. He had known about the first lover, but had hesitated to make a scandal then. Given his connections with the
man, who was a colleague, it would have made his political life
rather difficult. The exercise of power had taught him how to
submit and how to wait, and he had bided his time. He could
scarcely have found a more favorable opportunity: an adolescent overwhelmed by his prestige; his wife away from Paris for
a long time if she were to follow her lover, as she very likely
would, since he was young and she loved him; and public brou-
haha kept to a minimum by the disappearance of the principals.
He had seen a sure thing, played his cards, and won.

"Two weeks later, Lecadieu disappeared from our lives. He
wrote occasionally, but he did not appear for the examinations
that year, or the next. The waves raised by this debacle sub-
sided and disappeared. Eventually, an announcement of his
marriage to Mme Trélivan arrived. From friends I learned that
he did take his degree, and later from an inspector general that
he had been appointed to the *lycée* in B———, a post that was
much in demand and that he got 'thanks to political influence.'
Then I left the University, and I forgot Lecadieu."

"Last year, by chance I happened to be in B———, and I was
curious enough to go to the *lycée,* which is located in an old
abbey, one of the most beautiful in France. I asked the concierge what had become of M. Lecadieu. The concierge was a
zealous, grandiloquent fellow. By dint of carrying roll books
and lists of after-class detentions around in an atmosphere so
charged with scientific learning, he had ended up acquiring a
kind of pedantry himself.

"'M. Lecadieu?' he said to me. 'M. Lecadieu has been a
member of the professorial staff of this *lycée* for more than
twenty years, and it is our hope that he will await his retire-

ment here. If you wish to see him, you have simply to walk through the main courtyard and go down to the younger children's playground—you take the stairway to the left. He is sure to be there, talking with the supervisor.'

" 'Why, isn't the school closed for vacation?'

" 'Yes, but Mlle Septime agreed to keep a few children during the day for several families in town. Our headmaster was willing to authorize it, and M. Lecadieu comes to keep her company.'

" 'So! But Lecadieu is married, isn't he?'

" 'He was, sir,' the concierge said reproachfully, and the tone was suddenly tragic. 'It was just one year ago that we laid Mme Lecadieu to rest, on the eve of St. Charlemagne.'

"After all, I thought, it's true, she must have been very nearly seventy. Life in that household must have been strange.

"Then I asked:

" 'She was much older than he, wasn't she?'

" 'Sir, that is one of the most amazing things I have ever seen in this *lycée*. Mme Lecadieu became old overnight, you might say. When they came here, she was—I am not exaggerating—a young girl, blond, rosy-cheeked, well dressed—and proud. Perhaps you know who she had been?'

" 'Yes, yes, I know.'

" 'Well, naturally, the wife of the President of the Council . . . You can imagine that in a *lycée* in a small city . . . At first, we were very much concerned. We are very close here, sir. Our headmaster has always said, "I want my school to be a family," and when he walks into a classroom he never fails to ask the professor, "M. Lecadieu"—or M. Nabout or M. Lecaplain as the case may be—"how is your wife?" But, as I said to you, at the beginning Mme Lecadieu didn't want to know anyone, she didn't pay calls—in fact, she didn't even return them. Many of the gentlemen here held this against her husband, which is understandable. Fortunately, M. Lecadieu was very gallant, and he set things to rights with the ladies. He's a man who knows how to please. Now, when he gives a lecture in town, all the best people are there—the lawyers, the Prefect, everybody. . . . Everything worked out in the end. His wife came around, too. Toward the end of her life, no one here was

better liked than Mme Lecadieu, or more agreeable. But she
had become very, very old. . . .'

" 'Really?' I said. 'Well, if I may, I'm going to try to find
M. Lecadieu.'

"I walked across the main courtyard. It was a former cloister,
dating back to the fifteenth century, a little spoiled for there
being too many windows now through which you could see
desks and scarred tables. To the left, a vaulted flight of steps
led down to a smaller courtyard surrounded by scraggly trees.
Two people were standing at the bottom of this stairway—a
man whose back was to me, and a tall woman with a bony face
and gray hair who was wearing a checked flannel bodice that
was corseted high and tight, in the old-fashioned style. The
couple seemed to be engaged in lively conversation. The
vaulted passageway made a kind of acoustical tube and brought
me the sound of a voice that suddenly and with amazing sharpness evoked the dormitory landing at the University, and this is
what I heard:

" 'Yes, Corneille is the stronger, perhaps, but Racine is more
tender, more delicate. La Bruyère once said, very wittily, that
the one man portrayed men as they are, while the other . . .'

"To hear such platitudes pronounced to such a listener, and
to think that they were said by a man who had been the closest
person to me, the strongest influence on me as a young man,
seemed so strange and, above all, so painful, that I took too
noisy steps to make him turn around, hoping I had been mistaken. The man did turn his head and presented some unexpected features—a graying beard and a bald head—but it was
Lecadieu, all right. He recognized me, too, immediately. A
vague expression—of what? of discomfort, almost of pain—
flitted across his face, but disappeared at once behind a smile
that was friendly if a little uneasy, a little forced.

"I was rather moved, actually, and I didn't want to talk
about the past in front of that watchful old biddy, so I quickly
invited him to lunch and made an appointment for noon at a
restaurant he suggested.

"In front of the *lycée* in B—— there is a little square planted
with chestnut trees. I sat there for quite a long time. 'What

does the success or failure of a life depend on?' I asked myself. 'Here is Lecadieu, who was born to be a great man, and who year after year translates the same Latin texts with generation after generation of Touraine schoolboys, and spends his vacations being polite to some ridiculous monster, while Klein, who is intelligent but by no means a genius, is making Lecadieu's boyhood dream actually come true. Why?' I must ask Klein, I thought, to get Lecadieu transferred to Paris.

"As I was walking toward Saint-Étienne de B——, which is a fine Romanesque church that I wanted to see again, I tried to imagine what had brought this collapse about. At the outset, Lecadieu could not have changed. He would have been the same man, the same exceptional intelligence. What had happened? Trélivan must have kept them mercilessly exiled in the provinces. He kept his promise and assured the rapid promotion, but he forbade them Paris. . . . Living in the provinces agrees wonderfully with some people. As a boy in Rouen, I had professors whose acceptance of a provincial life gave them a kind of golden serenity and a purity of taste that was quite unflawed by fashions and fads. But a Lecadieu needs Paris. In exile, his appetite for power would have led him to look for mediocre successes. To be an intellectual in B——, after all, would be a formidable trial for a strong, original mind. To be a politician there? Very difficult when one doesn't come from that part of the country. And a long road, what with all the inherited rights, the seniority, and the whole hierarchy bit. A temperament like his must have been quickly discouraged. Also, when a man is alone, he can get away, he can work, but Lecadieu had his wife with him. After the first happy months, she must have missed her old worldly life. One can imagine the slow giving in—one surrender, then another. And then she begins to get old. . . . He is a sensual man. . . . There are young girls, enraptured by his literature courses. . . . Mme Trélivan becomes jealous. . . . Life is nothing but a succession of stupid, exhausting arguments. Then sickness, the wish to forget, habit, and that amazing relativity of ambition whereby a kind of satisfaction could be found in sops to his pride that would have seemed to him absurd at twenty—the Municipal

Council, the conquest of a children's supervisor. And yet my Lecadieu, the adolescent genius, could not have disappeared entirely. Somewhere inside that head there must still be great resources—submerged, perhaps, but recuperable. . . .

"When I arrived at the restaurant, after visiting the cathedral, Lecadieu was already there and was carrying on a bantering, pseudo-erudite conversation with the *patronne,* a fat little woman with black kiss-curls. The few words I overheard made my heart sink. I hurried him off to a table.

"We all know how painfully voluble a man will be if he is afraid that some painful reference will come up in conversation. The moment the talk veers toward whatever is taboo, his false animation betrays his anxiety. Throughout the meal, my Lecadieu never stopped talking with a facile, fluid eloquence that was banal to the point of being ludicrous—all about the city of B——, the school, the climate, the local elections, the intrigues of the women teachers.

" 'There is a little teacher in the tenth who, let me tell you . . .'

"The one thing that would have interested me would have been to know how this enormously ambitious man had been able to renounce ambition, how this strong will had capitulated, what his inner life had been since he left the University. But every time I tried to steer him in these directions, he fairly darkened the air around us with a cloud of empty, rambling talk. I noticed again those 'dead' eyes that had struck me so the evening Trélivan had discovered his affair.

"While the cheese was being served, I suddenly got furious, and, throwing away all restraint, I said to him brutally, holding his eyes with my own: 'What game are you playing, Lecadieu? After all, you used to be intelligent. Why are you talking like an anthology of familiar quotations? Why are you afraid of me? And of yourself?'

"He turned very red. A gleam of vitality, perhaps of anger, flashed through his eyes, and for a few seconds I recovered my Lecadieu, my Julien Sorel, my Rastignac, of university days. But then immediately the official mask was clamped over that great bearded face, and he said, with a smile:

" 'Intelligent? . . . What do you mean? . . . You've always been a little queer.'

"And he began to talk to me about his headmaster. M. de Balzac had finished his man."

Love in Exile

SINCE THE FRENCH AUTHOR Bertrand Schmitt had been living in America, he had published little more than memoirs and several books on history. His wife, Isabelle, kept reproaching him: "Do continue to write creative things, Bertrand. The political situation will change and all these squabbles will be forgotten, but Nausicaä will outlast the Greek warriors and Boule de Suif will survive Napoleon III."

"Of course, of course," he said. "But where in New York in this year 1944 are Nausicaä and Boule de Suif?"

"We meet them every day," Isabelle said. "Look, you should write the story of Solange Villier and her ambassador. Now there's a wonderful plot for a novel."

"Novel?" Bertrand said. "No, I don't agree with you. The subject is too slight. But it would be a first-rate plot for a short story. Somerset Maugham or de Maupassant would have made something really good out of it."

"Why not you, Bertrand?"

"Because I can't. . . . Solange would recognize herself and be angry with me—and with cause. Also, I think that we French who are living here in exile should not cannibalize each other."

"Transpose it. Make the ambassador an army colonel, have the action take place in some other country, turn the American industrialist into an Argentine landowner. All that is so easy for you."

"Not so easy as you think, Isabelle. You've seen me work over some twenty years, and you should know that I draw well only from nature. . . . Place the action in some other country! That's easily said, but then many of the essential details would become implausible. And what do I know about the psychology of an Argentine landowner? About how he talks, his foibles? Absolutely nothing! The character would never come to life."

"So write the story as it really happened, keeping the ambassador and that fellow from Pittsburgh."

"It's impossible, I tell you. Solange would recognize herself and she'd be furious."

"I don't believe it for a minute."

"You do not believe that she would be angry to find in a book written by me, who am a friend of hers, a story that made a public scandal in New York?"

"No, I don't think so."

"Sometimes you are remarkably stubborn, Isabelle."

"Not in the slightest. But I know women, and you, Bertrand, insist on seeing them in the light of a man's illusions. Above all, I know my Solange. What she is afraid of, that dear friend of yours, is not scandal but silence. Suppose someone says something nasty about her. What does it matter to her, so long as people are talking about her? Furthermore, who is forcing you to say anything unpleasant about her? Make her a sympathetic heroine."

"The facts don't exactly lend themselves to that. The whole interest lies in the contrast between the candor of the ambassador, who still believes in true love, and the bold cynicism of our Solange."

"Certainly, but cynicism is not necessarily disagreeable. It's much less so than hypocrisy. You can depict Solange as strong, cruel, a little contemptuous, manipulating men like so many pawns on a chessboard. She will be enchanted."

"She'll be furious."

"Try it."

"Isabelle, don't nag."

"Bertrand, don't scare so easily."

"I am not scared. But I do not want to lose a friend. Solange is worth more than a short story. Look, Isabelle, I will offer you a compromise. I will write the story."

"Finally!"

"Wait. I am going to write it, but before publishing it, I will show it to Solange, without telling her that it's about her but just to have her opinion. And I'll see what her reaction is."

"Dear Bertrand."

"What do you mean, *'dear* Bertrand?'"

"Because I adore your little white lies. 'Without telling her that it's about her!' Why do you expect she won't know, since you won't transpose the story?"

"She won't *not* know, but she'll be free to acknowledge a hit or, if she wants, to evade the issue. If she says to me, 'It's not one of your better stories, I don't much care for it,' I'll know where I stand."

"Dear Bertrand!"

"Isabelle, don't push me too far!"

"I'll not say another word. Work away."

Long experience had taught Isabelle Schmitt that it was not easy to persuade her husband to write a novel or short story. Every subject gave rise to objections—moral, sentimental, familial, national. This went on until the moment when the artist, detaching himself from literal reality, superseded the moralist, the friend, the relative, the citizen. Then his craft took possession of him, and nothing existed in the world for him but his characters. From then on, Bertrand seemed to live in a state of happy trance. Perhaps because he had hesitated and waited so long, the subject had matured in his mind, and when the moment of conception came, the story seemed to spring forth, fully fashioned and constructed, with astonishing speed. This was the case with the story of Solange Villier and the ambassador. In three days, the story was written.

"Are you pleased, Bertrand?"

"Not completely pleased. But pleased enough, yes. Six thousand words is a good length. The Pittsburgh fellow worked out pretty well. I didn't think I could do such a believable American. The woman is only sketched in, but the character has charm. I don't know what the American public will think of it. French readers would have loved it."

"Are you still intending to submit the manuscript to Solange?"

"I must. I'll admit that now the story is written I'd be sorry if it weren't published. But I hope Solange won't object. I transposed more than I'd have thought possible."

"Then I'll call the Pierre, Bertrand, and ask Solange to give you an appointment."

"Wait a minute. What's all the hurry?"

"Because I know that if I leave you to your own devices, you'll find dozens of good reasons for putting it off. One must never put off things that are disagreeable but also necessary. Think of this visit as if you were going to see your dentist or have an operation."

"But one that won't hurt."

"Are you so sure?"

That same day, at five o'clock, Bertrand Schmitt walked into the suite of Solange Villier on the thirty-second floor of the Hotel Pierre. He knew that he would find her lying on a divan. Even in exile, she remained faithful to her Paris tactics, always mindful to dissimulate the firmness of her designs by her nonchalant manner. Aware that she had perfect legs, she allowed her skirts to rise well above the knees. On the throw beside her—a mink throw—lay one of Bertrand's books. She held out the softest of hands, with admirably polished nails.

"How delightful, Bertrand! I was enchanted—and a little surprised—when Isabelle phoned. Your wife has never accustomed me to such thoughtfulness. Really, Bertrand, I must have aged, my dear, if Isabelle sends you to call on me! Or . . ."

"Or what, Solange?"

"I know what I mean."

And she smiled, with an imperceptible lift of the eyebrow.

Bertrand, who had brought a leather briefcase with him, sighed and took out the manuscript. Solange's smile widened.

"Do you remember," Bertrand said, "the days when I used to come up to Paris to read you my novels? You were very kind. You used to pretend that those 'openings' amused you. And I was firmly convinced that I was getting the best possible guidance."

"Don't make fun of me, Bertrand. *I* give advice to a novelist of your stature!"

"You're fishing for compliments, Solange. You know very well that you have taught me more about women, about their reactions, the way they think, than all the philosophers in the world. For me you have been all in one what Mme de Berny, Mme de Castries, and the Duchesse d'Abrantès were for Balzac. You have given me—"

"Bertrand! Bertrand! What would Isabelle say?"

"Isabelle would say that I am right. I also owe a lot to Isabelle. But about certain kinds of women Isabelle knows very little, and she realizes it."

"Dear Bertrand! You are insinuating that Isabelle the chaste, Isabelle the pure, cannot even conceive that a creature so profligate as I exists? What you're telling me is scarcely polite, you know. Don't protest, my dear. I'm joking. To get back, you've come to read me a novel?"

"No, just a short story."

"But what a joy, Bertrand! It takes me back to those good old days on Avenue d'Eylau, and to my dear, dear study. It's been years since you've paid me such an honor."

"Because I've been writing nothing but political things."

"Really, Bertrand? And that charming piece in *The Atlantic Monthly*? Isn't that a short story? And that other one—much less good—that you gave to *Textes Européens*. Tell me the truth, now, Bertrand. You're anxious to read me *this* story because I'm the heroine and you want to know whether I'll object. Have I guessed right?"

"No. Actually, I want to read you this story because in certain respects the heroine finds herself in situations that remind —that might be similar, I mean—but the characters have nothing in common with yourself or with—"

"Come, Bertrand, come! You mean to say, with any of my lovers? So say it."

"Let me finish my sentence—nor with any of the men people link you with."

"Isabelle would add that one does not link nonexistent things. Which would be banal but true. But do begin, my dear. No, wait. Give me a cigarette, a match, and an ashtray. Thank you. I'm listening."

Bertrand read his story, pencil in hand, canceling here and there a word that broke the rhythm or struck a false note. He liked to put his writing to the test of being read aloud, because it so infallibly reveals flaws and smudges in the style. From time to time he glanced up at Solange. She was listening dutifully, but with amusement and quite evident interest. The reading lasted forty minutes, during which time Solange did not once interrupt. When Bertrand stopped and stuffed the manuscript back into his briefcase with feigned indifference, she looked at him and laughed, then lapsed into a kind of silent reverie.

"Well?" he said, a little anxious. "Do you find it very bad?"

"I?" she said. "On the contrary. Why do you ask that?"

"Because you don't say anything."

"O man thirsting for praise! I've not said anything, dear Bertrand, because admiration is wordless."

"Don't tease me, Solange. Is it good or bad?"

"It's excellent, Bertrand! . . . Excellent . . . And it is precisely me—as you see me when Isabelle, with that tender generosity she has toward me, retouches my image for your benefit. Only—"

"Only what?"

"Only the difficulty is that your wise virgin isn't very familiar with our technique—the technique, I mean, of all us foolish virgins. Your version of my 'conquests' is a little naïve. You put everything on the basis of feeling. A determined woman resorts, believe me, to much more direct methods."

"For example?"

"For example, finding herself some evening, as if by chance, in a bed that isn't her own . . . Wearing a dress that keeps slipping off her shoulder . . . Pretending to be mildly tipsy

one night on the way home in a taxi . . . Don't be afraid of a
bit more carnal involvement in your love stories, Bertrand. I
quite understand that you are an expert in matters of the
heart. But the heart wouldn't get very far, you know, if some
other organs didn't do their share."

"But look at Stendhal, Solange. There are no finer love stories than his. But sensuality plays its role offstage."

"Maybe that's why Stendhal bores me so! . . . Yes, I know,
I'm being sacrilegious. But I can't help it. Your Stendhal I find
tedious. Do you think he was a bit impotent, perhaps? It seems
to me I've read about some fiascoes of his. . . . But in any case,
in this story you're not presenting a Stendhal heroine. You're
describing me, Solange Villier. You mustn't rob me of my
strongest weapons. Another thing, Bertrand—why have you
turned the ambassador into a colonel? To speak in terms of
status, that diminishes *me*. And from a literary point of view it
is a mistake, because you had noted certain characteristics of
the ambassador that you wanted to make use of, so you end up
producing a soldier who talks like a diplomat. The two things
don't hold together. And the same thing is true of Birch. Why
make him a lawyer when he was a metallurgist? There again,
any intelligent reader will see that the beard is false."

"You are finesse itself, Solange. No professional could have
put his finger more surely on the flaws in the story. But if I
altered the facts, it was only for your sake. You can understand
that if I had drawn the ambassador and the metallurgist too
close to life, all New York would have said that you are the
heroine of the story. That's what I've tried to avoid."

"Why, Bertrand?"

"Why? It seems clear enough to me. Out of friendship. Not
to create difficulties for you."

"What difficulties? Oh, you are a funny boy! Do you suppose
that I am ashamed of what I do? No, Bertrand. The whole
world can know that the ambassador was my lover, and then
Birch, and now Bob Lebreton."

"The whole world does know, Solange."

"Then why not say so, Bertrand? If you absolutely must
make use of me in your books—and the need does seem to be
rather irresistible, since this is the third time, my precious, that

I appear in your work, under different names—then at least show me at my best. Don't take my whole arsenal away from me. Look, Bertrand. When you are in a good mood, you are very sweet and you tell me how I have the art of creating my own background, my own milieu, wherever I go. I think that's quite true. But then why not describe that background? Why do you distort it? What I would like to find in your story, you see, is my mink throw, my lorgnette, the photograph of Proust on my table, your own book with this charming dedication."

"In other words, Solange, you want me to shout from the housetops that this story is a true story and that you are its heroine?"

"Ah, you writers!" she said. "We can't hide a thing from you. You read our most secret thoughts."

When Bertrand got home, Isabelle, who was waiting impatiently for him, asked:

"What did the model say?"

"The model asked for quite a few revisions."

"Really? Such as?"

"You'll see. I don't like to talk about this kind of thing before writing it. It paralyzes me."

He worked for a whole week, adding, cutting, revising, and then dropped off a new manuscript at the Hotel Pierre. Two days later, he was called to the phone, not by Solange Villier but by young Bob Lebreton.

"My dear sir," the young man said, "you scarcely know me, although we have many friends in common, but I would like to talk to you. . . . Yes, as soon as possible. It's something serious that concerns a mutual friend, Mme Villier."

"Mme Villier has asked you to see me?"

"Oh, not at all! Mme Villier doesn't know that I am phoning you. It's I who—well, I'll explain. When could you see me?"

"Whenever you like. Now, if you're free."

"I'll jump in the car and be right over."

Robert Lebreton, rebaptized Bobby by Solange, who was an Anglophile, was a French engineer who, between the two world wars, had hitched his star to Jacques Villier's fortunes and had become second in command in all the older man's affairs. At the time of the armistice in June, 1940, when Villier decided to

come to the United States to exploit various of his patents,
Lebreton had followed him, and together they had set up an
important optical-instrument factory in Rochester. Why and
how the technician Lebreton had become the lover of the wife
and simultaneously the partner of the husband, Bertrand did
not know. Lebreton was not lacking in vigor and he was handsome, but he was beginning to put on weight and he had a
defective tooth that detracted from his appearance. Maybe she
found him convenient, Bertrand thought. He has the advantage of always being on hand. And maybe, too, he keeps her
informed about Villier's business. She does like to know what's
going on. . . . Well, you can never tell.

The bell rang. Bertrand went to open the door.

"You didn't lose any time," he said to Lebreton.

"I have a very full morning. And this afternoon I must go to
Washington. But I absolutely had to see you."

"Please have a chair. . . . Cigarette?"

"No, thank you. . . . M. Schmitt, you're going to think that
I am meddling in matters that are none of my business, but it's
a question of sparing the person I love most in the world real
grief. I mean Jacques Villier."

"*Jacques* Villier?" In his surprise, Bertrand put an involuntary emphasis on the Jacques.

"Yes, Jacques Villier . . . You seem surprised. But I must
tell you that Jacques Villier is more to me than a boss."

Well, he's the husband of your mistress, Bertrand thought.
That is a kind of relationship, at one remove.

The other man went on:

"He's my friend. He's the man who trained me, and to whom
I owe everything. Furthermore, under that rather rough exterior, he is a sensitive and reserved man. A man of immense
delicacy. You have no idea what he does for the workers at the
factory, all with no publicity, no noise. In a word, I'm prepared
to make any sacrifice to spare him the slightest unpleasantness.
Now, it so happens that I spent last evening with Mme Villier.
. . . Yes, Jacques is in Washington for some meetings with
the people at the Pentagon. She had me read a short story of
yours of which you'd given her the manuscript. May I confess
to you that this story shocked me terribly?"

"Really?" Bertrand said. He was both amused and a little uneasy. "Why?"

"Because it's so transparent, so scandalous. Because it's impossible that the reader wouldn't recognize the Villiers. And because if you publish it, you will hurt my best friend, and to no point. Excuse me, please, but don't you find it indecent—the word is not too strong—*indecent* to give the husband of your heroine Villier's own physical appearance, his favorite expressions, his personality? Change at least what can easily be modified. Villier is a giant; make your husband a dumpy little man. Villier is thin; make the fellow a balloon. Villier wears glasses; give him a monocle. Villier is an industrialist; make him a shipowner or a chemist. . . . Solange is blond; make her red-haired or a brunette. . . . Oh, I don't know, I'm not a writer, but it does seem to me that with a little imagination you could put the reader off the track."

"Excuse me," Bertrand said, "but I have to ask you this a second time. Did Solange suggest your making this move?"

"No, no! As I told you on the phone, Mme Villier doesn't know that I'm here."

"So *she* doesn't blame me for describing faithfully what I've observed."

Lebreton hesitated.

"That is . . . well, no, to be completely frank, she doesn't *see* that to publish this story would be dangerous. Which seems to me a very strange aberration in a woman as remarkably intelligent as she is. But women have no tact. They aren't aware. I am acting alone in this. I come to you as Villier's closest friend, as if he were my own brother, to ask not that you give up publishing this story but that you change it. I appeal not only to the writer but to the man of honor and a friend of both the Villiers."

"I'll try," Bertrand said.

Over lunch, he related the visit to Isabelle and added:

"As I was listening to him, I couldn't help thinking how Lebreton's unbounded affection for Villier has, in point of fact, been demonstrated by his having an affair with Solange, and how this man who watches so carefully over his friend's honor hasn't been afraid of compromising that honor by his own actions. . . . But naturally I didn't say that to him."

"Are you going to do what he asked?"

"I'm going to fix a few little things."

"Why? What's Lebreton to you?"

"I don't care at all about Lebreton, but he was right on one point. The portrait of the husband is too photographic. I'll retouch it a bit."

"I bet that Solange will object."

"Solange? Why?"

However, Isabelle Schmitt understood the workings of Solange Villier's mind wonderfully well, for when Bertrand read her the new version, in which the Villier character had been metamorphosed, Solange protested vigorously.

"Why the caution all of a sudden, Bertrand? Why give me such an implausible husband? A man who is fat and potbellied, who wears a monocle and talks like a factory foreman? Why, I would never have married such a person! Whom did you think you would be pleasing by this transformation? Jacques? Jacques couldn't care less what people say about him. Do you suppose he has any illusions about my faithfulness? What's more, do you imagine that he reads your stories? Jacques is interested in his factories, his competitors, and our social position. I am useful to him. I help him play his game well; he's never asked me for anything more. My husband *never* reads a novel. He reads only periodicals about physics and chemistry and books dealing with postwar economic reconstruction. Give me back my husband, Bertrand, or don't publish your story."

Three months later, the story appeared under the title "Love in Exile," in a magazine with a vivid four-color cover showing Eros in chains. Surrendering to Solange's ultimatum, Bertrand had restored all the passages he had modified at the insistence of Lebreton.

The week the story came out, Solange invited Bertrand and Isabelle to a cocktail party. The guests included French and Americans, bankers, army officers, lawyers, and artists. Lebreton passed caviar and smoked-salmon canapés. On a table in the middle of the living room, a copy of the magazine carrying

"Love in Exile" was prominently displayed. From time to time, as Solange passed the table, she pointed out the title to some important guest.

"Have you read 'Love in Exile,' by Bertrand Schmitt? . . . Oh, you *must* read it, my dear, it's *tremendously* good. Bertrand is an old friend and, I don't know why, he can't keep from putting me in all his stories. . . . You've never met him? Look, he's the man sitting on the blue couch across the room, talking with my husband. . . . No, he's not handsome. Why should he be handsome? But you *must* read his story. Since you know me so well, it will amuse you. Would you like me to give you a copy? . . . Oh, not at all. No trouble at all. I ordered fifty."

She stopped her French maid as the woman was passing by.

"Marie, bring Mr. Barnes one of those magazines. You know, from the pile near my bed, on the little Chinese lacquer table. Bring it right away, please."

As they were leaving the Pierre, Isabelle said to her husband:

"Didn't you tell me, Bertrand, that if you were to write that story Solange would be very angry?"

"I?" Bertrand replied. "I never said anything of the kind."

Wednesday's Violets

"OH, JENNY, DO STAY!"

Throughout lunch, Jenny Sorbier had been dazzling. Stories and anecdotes had followed one upon another, told with the polish of an actress, constructed with the art of the born story-teller, and linked together by her inexhaustible verve. Léon Laurent's guests had been charmed, excited, captivated, all feeling that they had lived one enchanted hour beyond the boundaries of time.

"No, it's nearly four and this is Wednesday. You know, Léon, this is the day I take violets to my admirer."

"What a pity!" he said, in the staccato voice that had made him famous on the stage. "But I know how faithful you are. I won't insist."

She embraced the women, the men embraced her, and she left. The moment she had gone, a chorus of praise arose:

"She is really extraordinary! How old is she, Léon?"

"Not much this side of eighty. When I was a child, my

mother used to take me to the Comédie for the matinée per-
formances of the classics, and even then Jenny was a glorious
Célimène. And I'm no longer a young man."

"Genius knows nothing of age," Claire Ménétrier said.
"What's this story about violets?"

"It's a little novel in itself. She told it to me one day, but
she's never written it. However, I am not going to risk telling a
story after Jenny. The comparison would be too formidable."

"Yes, the comparison *is* formidable, but we're your guests.
You have to entertain us, so you must substitute for Jenny,
since she's abandoned us."

"Well, all right, I'll try to tell you the story of Wednesday's
violets. But I'm afraid it's much too sentimental for our taste
today."

"Come now," Bertrand Schmitt said. "Today people are
thirsting for sentiment. They only pretend to be cynical to
hide their nostalgias."

"Do you think so? Well, so be it. I will satisfy this thirst. All
of you here are too young to remember what a sensation Jenny
was. It was so long ago. The stormy hair, which she used to let
cascade over those admirable shoulders; the glancing, almond-
shaped eyes; the mordant, almost hard voice that would suddenly grow hoarse with sensuality—everything about her en-
hanced her exceptional, striking beauty."

"A rousing opener, Léon."

"A little dated, perhaps, but thanks anyway. She won her
first prize at the Conservatoire around 1895, and she was immediately taken into the Comédie-Française. I know only too well
from experience, alas, how hard that great company is. All the
big roles in the repertory are the titular property, as it were, of
the veterans, and they hang onto them for dear life. The most
promising young actress may wait around ten years before she's
assigned the best Marivaux or Molière parts. Jenny was a great
coquette, but she also had to contend with some very powerful
and tenacious women. Anyone else would have become resigned to marking time or after two years have emigrated to the
Boulevard theaters. Not our Jenny. She marched right into
battle, and she gave it everything she had—her gifts as an ac-

tress, her cultivation, her seductiveness, and that intoxicating hair.

"She very quickly won a leading position in the company. The Director swore by her. Playwrights clamored to have her for hard roles they used to claim only she could put across. The critics heaped praise on her with amazing regularity. Even the terrible Sarcey wrote that 'she has certain mannerisms and inflections of voice that would charm a crocodile.'

"My father, who knew her in those days, told me that she adored her work, talked intelligently about it, and was forever searching for fresh, startling effects. At that time, the theater was slipping into a pretty simple-minded realism. But if Jenny had to die of poisoning in some play or other, she would visit hospitals and study the effects of poison. When it came to projecting emotion, she studied herself. The moment her art was involved, she showed the lack of scruple of a Balzac, when he would exploit his own feelings or those of the woman he loved for his novels.

"You can imagine how a girl of twenty-two who was extravagantly beautiful and who had become famous almost overnight would have been courted. Fellow-actors tried their luck, and so did authors, bankers. One of the bankers—Henri Stahl—became her favorite. Not because he was rich. She was living with her family and had very few needs. But because he, too, possessed great charm and, above all, because he offered to marry her. You remember that Stahl's parents opposed the marriage, that it was delayed, that it took place three years later, and didn't last. Jenny's independence did not prove compatible with the conjugal life. But that's another story. Let's get back to the Comédie-Française and our friend's early successes—and the violets.

"Picture to yourselves the greenroom the evening Jenny opened in *Princesse de Bagdad*, by Dumas *fils*. The play has its flaws, and while I admire *Demi-Monde* and *L'Ami des Femmes* and *Francillon* for their solid structure, even I have to smile at the super-Dumas of *L'Étrangère* and *Princesse*. But everyone who saw Jenny in the role wrote that she made it believable. I've often talked about it with her. What's amazing is that she believed in it herself. 'At that age,' she's said to me, 'my ideas were more or less those of a Dumas *fils* heroine, and it seemed bizarre to be playing out on an open stage what was going on inside me, in my most secret self.' Add the fact that in this part she had the chance to undo that marvelous hair and exhibit those bare shoulders. In a word, she was sublime.

"So here she is in the greenroom, between acts, after an ovation. People are crowding around her. Jenny is sitting on a banquette, with Henri Stahl at her side, and chattering with all the euphoria of her triumph.

" 'Ouf! Henri, darling . . . I'm back on my feet, I can breathe again. . . . You saw me three days ago. Wasn't I pretty low? Pouf! Really at the bottom of the well. I was suffocating. . . . And now, tonight—Whee! One hard push and I've surfaced again. . . . What do you think, Henri—was I going to sink in that last act and drown, or was I going to be able to swim through to the end? My lord, my lord!'

"An usher came in and handed her some flowers.

" 'From whom? Ah, Saint-Loup . . . Your rival, Henri. Put them in my dressing room, please.'

" 'There is also a letter, Mademoiselle,' the usher said.

"She opened it and burst into peals of laughter.

" 'It's from a young student. He tells me they've founded a Jenny Club in his *lycée*.'

" 'The Jockey Club's turned into a Jenny Club,' Henri said.

" 'I find students more touching,' Jenny said. 'This one ends his letter with a poem. . . . Listen to this, darling:

> *Forgive me my so humble lines,*
> *For true love's sake scorn not my rhymes,*
> *Above all, not one word, I pray,*
> *To the headmaster of my old lycée.*

Isn't that sweet?'

" 'Are you going to answer him?'

" 'Heavens, no! These come by the dozen every day. If I were to try to answer them all, I'd be lost. . . . But it makes me feel better. These sixteen-year-old admirers I will keep for a long time.'

" 'Not necessarily. By thirty they'll all be notaries.'

" 'Why would notaries stop admiring me?'

" 'And there is also this, Mademoiselle,' the usher said.

"He held out a two-penny's-worth bouquet of violets.

" 'Oh, that is too sweet! . . . Look, Henri. There's no card.'

" 'No, Mademoiselle. The stage doorman told me they were left with him by a young man in the Polytechnique uniform.'

" 'My dear,' Henri Stahl said, 'I do congratulate you. It's not easy to distract those great mathematical brains.'

"She inhaled the fragrance of the flowers slowly.

" 'They smell so good. . . . This is the kind of tribute I care about. I don't like the smug, middle-aged public that comes to see me die at midnight the same way it goes to the Palais Royal at noon to watch the cannon go off.'

" 'The public is sadistic,' Stahl said. 'It always has been. Think of circus acts. What a success the actress would have who could swallow a whole package of needles.'

"She laughed.

" 'And the one who could swallow a whole sewing machine,' she said, 'would be the last word.'

"Someone shouted 'Onstage!' and she stood up.

" 'Well, until later. I'm off to swallow my package of needles.'

"This, according to Jenny, is how the adventure began."

"The following Wednesday, during the last intermission, the usher, with a little smile, came up to Jenny with a tiny bouquet of violets.

" 'Well!' she said. 'My Polytechnique admirer again?'

" 'Yes, Mademoiselle.'

" 'What does he look like?'

" 'I don't know, Mademoiselle. Shall I ask the doorman?'

" 'No, it doesn't matter.'

"The following week, she did not play on Wednesday, but when she arrived on Thursday for a rehearsal, the bouquet of violets, a little faded this time, was in her dressing room. As she was leaving, she stopped to speak to the doorman.

" 'Tell me, Bernard, did my violets come from the same young man?'

" 'Yes, Mademoiselle. This is the third time.'

" 'What does he look like?'

" 'Nice . . . very nice. A little on the thin side. He has hollow cheeks and dark circles under the eyes. A tiny brown mustache. Wears glasses. They look rather funny with his sword. . . . But my word, Mademoiselle, the young man seems very much smitten. He holds out his bouquet of violets and says, "For Mlle Jenny Sorbier," and then he blushes.'

" 'Why does he always come on Wednesday?'

" 'Oh, you don't know, Mademoiselle? The Polytechnique cadets have leave on Wednesdays. Every Wednesday the orchestra and the gallery are full of them. . . . Every one of them with a girl.'

" 'Mine has a girl?'

" 'Yes, Mademoiselle, but she's his sister. They look so much alike, it's amazing.'

" 'Poor boy! If I had a heart, Bernard, I'd have you send him up at least once to the greenroom, so that he could give me his violets himself.'

" 'I really don't advise that, Mademoiselle. So long as one pays no attention to these stagestruck boys, they're harmless. They worship the actresses from a distance, on the stage, and that's enough to keep them happy. But if you pay them the least bit of attention, they hang on like leeches—it's terrible. Give them the tips of your fingers and they want a hand. Give them your hand and they want an arm. . . . Yes, Mademoiselle, you can laugh, but I know from experience. I've been here for twenty years. Whew! How many of them haven't I seen outside this stage door! Young girls with crushes, infatuated boys—old men, too! I always accept their flowers and their notes, but as for letting them go up to the greenroom, nothing doing!'

" 'You're right, Bernard. Let us be unfeeling and prudent and cruel.'

" 'It's not being cruel, Mademoiselle. It's being sensible.'

"Weeks passed. Every Wednesday, Jenny received her tuppence-worth of violets. By now, everyone in the company knew the story. One of the other actresses said to Jenny:

" 'I've seen your cadet. He has a charming, romantic head. A boy who's made to play *Badine* or *Chandelier.*'

" 'How do you know he was mine?'

" 'Because just by chance I was standing beside the doorman

when he brought his flowers, and he said very timidly, "For Mlle Jenny Sorbier, please." It was really touching. One could sense that he is a very intelligent boy and that he is afraid of appearing ridiculous, but yet he can't help being so very much moved. For a moment I was sorry he doesn't come on my account. I'd have thanked him, consoled him. But you notice that he didn't ask for anything, not even to see you. Still, if I were you—'

" 'You would see him?'

" 'Yes, just for a minute. This has been going on for weeks. And summer vacation is coming. You'll be going away. So there's no risk of his attaching himself—'

" 'You're right,' Jenny said. 'It's silly to take one's admirers so lightly when they're young and there are a lot of them, and then thirty years later run after them when they've become few and far between and all bald.'

"That evening, as she was leaving the theater, she said to the doorman:

" 'Bernard, next Wednesday, when the cadet comes with his violets, tell him to bring them up himself after the third act. I'm doing *Le Misanthrope* and I don't have to change. I'll go up to my dressing room and meet him there. . . . No, I'll wait in the corridor, at the foot of the stairs. Or perhaps the greenroom . . .'

" 'Very well, Mademoiselle. You're not afraid—'

" 'What is there to be afraid of? I'm going on tour in ten days, and anyhow, this young man is virtually a prisoner of the Polytechnique.'

" 'Very well, Mademoiselle. What I meant was . . .'

"The next Wednesday, in spite of herself, Jenny played Célimène for the unknown cadet, and with a very lively desire to please him. As she walked through the wings at intermission, she was curious, even anxious. She sat down in the greenroom and waited. A few familiar faces were there. The Director was talking with Blanche Pierson, who was Jenny's rival at the time. But no black-and-gold uniform appeared. She grew nervous and impatient, and presently hurried over to the usher.

" 'Has no one asked for me?'

" 'No, Mademoiselle.'

" 'It's Wednesday, and I haven't got my violets. Did Bernard forget to send them up? Or was there some misunderstanding?'

" 'Misunderstanding, Mademoiselle? What misunderstanding? Shall I go find out from the doorman?'

" 'Yes, if you will, please . . . Or rather, no. I'll see Bernard as I leave.'

"She made fun of herself. 'What strange creatures we are,' she said to herself. 'For six months I've paid scarcely any attention to this discreet admiration, and suddenly because I miss the attention—which I've flouted—I'm as upset as if I were waiting for a lover. . . . Ah, Célimène, how you will regret Alceste when he leaves you!'

"After the performance, she stopped by the doorman's cubicle.

" 'Well, Bernard, where is my admirer? You didn't send him in?'

" 'Mademoiselle, you would think it was a conspiracy! He didn't come today. . . . The first time since you said you would see him, Mademoiselle, the first Wednesday in six months that he's not turned up for roll call!'

" 'It's very strange. Do you suppose someone could have warned him, and that he was afraid?'

" 'Absolutely not, Mademoiselle. No one knew but you and me. Did you say anything? . . . No, nor did I. I didn't even tell my wife about it.'

" 'Then how do you explain it?'

" 'I don't, Mademoiselle. So many things are possible. . . . Perhaps he's lost interest? Maybe he's been sick? Next Wednesday we'll see.'

"But the following Wednesday brought no cadet and no violets.

" 'What can I do, Bernard? Do you think one could find out from his fellow-students? Or from the Commandant at the Polytechnique?'

" 'How, Mademoiselle? We don't even know his name.'

" 'That's true. . . . Oh, how sad! Everything is ruined, Bernard!'

" 'Not at all, Mademoiselle. You've had a great season, you're leaving on tour where you'll have more successes. Nothing is spoiled, nothing at all.'

" 'You're right. I'm being ungrateful. But I did love my Wednesday violets.'

"The next day she left Paris. Henri Stahl followed her devotedly. At every hotel, Jenny found her room filled with roses. When she got back to Paris, she had forgotten her romantic mathematician."

"About a year later, she received a letter from a Colonel Genevrière, asking for an appointment on a personal matter. The letter was dignified and correct; there was no reason to refuse the request. Jenny asked the Colonel to come see her at home on a Saturday afternoon. He came in civilian clothes, and was dressed in black. She received him with that gracious ease that she owed to the stage as much as to nature, but, naturally enough, her attitude expressed an unspoken question: 'What does this stranger want?' She waited.

" 'I do thank you very much, Mademoiselle, for being willing to see me. I could scarcely explain the reason for my visit in a letter. And in permitting myself to ask you for an appointment, I was acting not as a man but as a father. You see that I am dressed in black. I am wearing mourning for my son, Lieutenant André Genevrière, who was killed two months ago in Madagascar.'

"Jenny made a gesture, as if to say, 'I am sorry with all my heart, but—'

" 'You did not know my son, Mademoiselle. I realize that. But he knew and admired you. It will seem scarcely believable to you . . . and yet what I am going to tell you is true. You were the person whom he most admired and loved in the world.'

" 'I'm afraid I don't understand, Colonel. Did he tell you this?'

" 'Tell me? No, he told his sister, who was his confidante. It all began one day when he went with her to see a performance of *Jeu de l'Amour et du Hasard*. . . . My children came back talking about you with the greatest enthusiasm. . . . "She's so delicate, so shy," they said. "She's so moving, she's like a poem!" Well, this and a thousand and one other things that were true, I don't doubt, but that the ardor of youth, their need of absolutes—my poor son was a romantic in every sense of the word.'

" 'My God!' Jenny cried. 'Then it was he who—'

" 'Yes, Mademoiselle. The Polytechnique cadet who every Wednesday for six months brought you a bouquet of violets was my son, André. . . . This also I know from my daughter. I hope this childish behavior wasn't unwelcome. He loved you— or rather the image he had made of you—so much. The walls of his room were covered with your photographs. How many excursions my daughter made to your photographers to be able to give him one more! His friends at the Academy used to tease him. "So write to her," they would say.'

" 'Which he never did.'

" 'Which he did do, Mademoiselle, and I have brought you a packet of letters that were never sent and that we found after his death.'

"The Colonel pulled a package from his pocket and gave it to Jenny. She showed it to me once. The handwriting was fine, quick, difficult. The handwriting of a mathematician and the style of a poet.

" 'You keep these letters, Mademoiselle. They belong to you. . . . And you will, I hope, forgive my rather strange request. I felt I owed it to the memory of my son. There was nothing in the feeling that you inspired in him that was disrespectful or frivolous. To him you represented perfection and grace. And I assure you that André was worthy of his great love.'

" 'But why didn't he ask to see me? Why didn't I try to meet him? Oh, I don't like myself in this, I don't like myself.'

" 'You shouldn't feel any remorse, Mademoiselle. How could you have guessed? If André applied, after graduation, to go to Madagascar, that was because of you, certainly. . . . Yes, he'd told his sister, "Either I escape from this hopeless passion thanks to distance, or I do great things there and then—" '

" 'Hadn't he already done something great?' Jenny asked. 'With that fidelity and perseverance and discretion?'

"Then, as the Colonel got up, she took both his hands in hers:

" 'I do believe I haven't done anything wrong,' she said, 'and yet—and yet it seems to me that I have a duty toward this, alas, unrequited ghost. Tell me, Colonel, where your son is buried. I promise you that to the day of my death I will go every Wednesday and place a bouquet of violets on his grave.' "

"And that is why," Léon Laurent concluded, "that is why all her life our Jenny, who passes for being skeptical, disillusioned, even cynical, has left friends or work or even love to go alone every Wednesday to the Montparnasse cemetery to the grave of a young lieutenant whom she never knew. . . . You see I was right. This story is too sentimental for us today."

There was a silence, then Bertrand Schmitt said:

"Romanticism will always exist in the world for people who are worthy of it."

A Career

ON THE THIRD SATURDAY of every month, Deputy Lambert-Leclerc, then Undersecretary of Finance, the novelist Civrac, and Fabert, the author of *Caliban Roi,* which recently opened with such distinguished success at the Gymnase, used to meet in the studio of the painter Beltara.

One evening, Beltara introduced a young man from the provinces to his friends. It was his cousin, who wanted to devote himself to a writing career.

"This child," he told them, "has written a novel that I think is no worse than a great many others and that I want to ask you, Civrac, to read. My cousin doesn't know a soul in Paris, he lives in Bayeux, and by training he's an engineer."

"Happy man," Fabert said. "You've written a book, you live in the provinces, and you don't know a soul in Paris? Your fortune is made, sir. People will fight for the honor of discovering you, and if you take care to build your legend the right way, within one year you will be more famous than Civrac

here. But let me give you one bit of advice. Keep out of sight.
. . . Bayeux! That's the best part of all, Bayeux is. Who
wouldn't seem attractive seen from the distance of Bayeux? Not
that you appear other than charming, sir, but it is human to be
able to endure genius only at some remove."

"Also contrive to be ill," Lambert-Leclerc said. "Some very
fine careers have been built on illness."

"Whatever you do," Beltara said, "never give up your job. A
job is an admirable observation post. Shut yourself up in your
study, and in one year you will be turning out books that are
competent, well-constructed, and utterly boring."

"What an ass!" Civrac said, in his rasping voice. " 'A job is
an admirable observation post.' How can an intelligent man
like you, Beltara, repeat such clichés! What do you want a
writer to observe that he can't find in himself? Did Proust go
out of the house? Did Tolstoi leave the farm? When people
asked him who Natasha was, he said, 'Me.' And Flaubert—"

"I beg to differ," Beltara said. "Tolstoi lived in the midst of
a huge family, and that was one of the elements of his strength.
Proust was a man who did, after all, go to the Ritz, who had
friends, and who got everything out of them he could. As for
Flaubert—"

"Agreed," Civrac interrupted, "but suppose that Proust had
had to do without his *mondaine* themes; he'd have found
something to say. He is just as remarkable when he's talking
about his illness or his bedroom or his old servant. I'll cite you
another case—an example of how the keenest intelligence may
be supplied by circumstance with the most unusual opportunities for observation but still cannot, alone, produce a masterpiece. Our friend Chalonnes, of course . . . Who has had more
time and opportunity than he to observe the most varied
worlds? Chalonnes has seen, and seen at first hand, painters,
writers, industrialists, actors, politicians, diplomats—in a word,
every scene in the human comedy. What has he made of it? We
all know only too well."

"Chalonnes," Lambert-Leclerc interrupted. "Whatever's become of Chalonnes? Does any one of you ever hear from him?"

"We go to the same bookstore," Civrac said, "and sometimes
I meet him there, but he pretends he doesn't see me."

The young visitor leaned toward his host and asked under his breath who Chalonnes was.

"Civrac," Beltara said, "tell this innocent about the career of Chalonnes. It could be a useful example to him at his age."

Civrac pulled himself up to a sitting position on the side of the divan, and in that biting voice of his that seemed to snap off each syllable of every word, he forthwith began his story in high form:

"I do not know, sir, whether you have ever heard of the Rhetoricians Club of the Lycée Henri IV? In 1893, it was as famous around the Panthéon as was the graduating class at the Normale—a class that, as you do know, numbered among others Taine, Prévost-Paradol, Sarcey, and Edmond About. The Club was called—as I am reminded every time I meet one of our old instructors—'a nursery of famous men,' as indeed it was, since it included Beltara, Lambert-Leclerc, Fabert, and me. Lambert-Leclerc, who was already preparing for a public-affairs career, used to spend all his afternoons with Fabert at the races—"

"Do show a little respect for my ministerial status," the Minister said.

"Your ministerial self was the only one among us whose temperament as a young man gave any hint of his future. Beltara showed no particular interest in graphics, and Fabert no aptitude whatever for the theater. Our literature professor, Père Hamelin, used to say to him. 'My poor Fabert, you will never have a real grasp of the French language.' Which was true enough, even if today's know-nothing public seems to disagree. As for me, my major artistic pleasure at the time was to fill the margins of my notebooks with sketches of Venus. Chalonnes rounded out our group.

"He was a blond fellow, with well-modeled, attractive features, who worked very little, read a lot, showed exquisite taste in poets and neckties, and, because his taste was so sure, he enjoyed great authority among the rest of us. Around that time, we were reading the history of 'The Thirteen' and their famous group trial, so we decided—Chalonnes and the four of us—to found a society called 'The Five' at Henri IV. His whole life long, each of The Five was to stand by the other four, whatever happened. It was agreed that money, influence, connections, everything that any one of The Five would acquire should be put at the service of the group. It was a fine scheme but it was only a scheme, because when we finished the *lycée,* we drifted apart. His Excellency here and I went on to study law. Fabert, who had to earn a living, went into his uncle's bank. Beltara began to study medicine. Military service scattered us even more widely, and lastly, chance. For six years, we had only very rare news of each other.

"At the 1900 Salon opening, I saw a canvas by Beltara for the first time. I was surprised to find that he had become a painter, and more surprised still to see that unquestionably he had talent. It always comes as a profound surprise to discover talent in a childhood friend. The idea that geniuses have been somebody or other's chums doesn't help us to understand that there could have been a genius among our own. I wrote to him. He invited me to go see him. I liked his studio, went back several times, and after a long exchange of letters and telegrams, I managed to organize a dinner for The Five. That evening, each man gave an account of what he had been doing since our *lycée* days.

"By a chain of rather odd accidents, three of us had shifted from the careers chosen for us by our parents. Beltara's mistress happened to be a model, and for his own pleasure he had made some sketches of her and they'd turned out well. This woman had introduced him to several painters. He had set to work, made good headway, and, after a few months, had given up his medical studies.

"Then he'd gone back to the Midi, where he had lived as a child, had painted numerous portraits of Marseilles businessmen and their wives, from which he had earned enough to permit him, on his return to Paris, to work on his own. He showed me canvases that 'revealed an artistic temperament,' as the critics used to say in those days.

"Fabert had put together and directed an amateur theatrical performance for one of his uncle's parties, and had been warmly complimented for it by an elderly author and friend of the family. At the time of our reunion, this generous man, who had taken a liking to Fabert, had just produced our friend's first play, *La Steppe,* at the Odéon. Lambert-Leclerc was secretary to a senator from the Ardèche, who was maneuvering to get him an appointment as a subprefect. As for me, I'd written some short stories that I offered The Five as required reading.

"Chalonnes had listened to us in silence. He had some perceptive and accurate things to say about my first efforts. He pointed out that the plot of one was a Mérimée subject reversed and that my style was rather too close to Barrès, whom I greatly admired then. He had seen Fabert's play, and, with an astonishing sense of theater technique, pointed out to him how one scene should be revised. With Beltara he made the rounds of the studio and talked of Impressionism with truly admirable competence. Then, for the benefit of Lambert-Leclerc, he analyzed the political situation in the Ardèche, demonstrating a very precise knowledge of the subject. Once again, all of us experienced our old impression that Chalonnes was the most brilliant member of the group, and it was with sincere humility that we asked him to tell us about the beginnings of his own career.

"Having come into a very comfortable fortune when he was eighteen, he had set himself up in a small apartment, with his books, and he was working there, he told us, on several projects.

"The first was to be a big novel on the order of Goethe's *Wilhelm Meister,* which would constitute the first volume of a *New Human Comedy.* He was also thinking of a play that would have affinities with the theater of Shakespeare, Molière, and Musset: 'You know what I mean, full of both fantasy and irony, light and profound at the same time.' Lastly, he had begun a *Philosophy of Wit* that, he said, 'was related to Bergson's ideas but that analytically would go much further.'

"Later I went to see him, and to me—I was living in a furnished hotel room at the time—his apartment seemed the most charming place in the world. Old furniture, several casts from the Louvre, a good copy of a Holbein, shelves filled with handsomely bound books, an authentic Fragonard drawing—all these made for a very 'artistic' ensemble.

"He offered me an English cigarette, of wonderful color and flavor. I asked to see the beginning of *The New Human Com-*

edy, but the first page was not quite finished. For his play he had already found a title. Regarding *The Philosophy of Wit,* he showed me a dozen or so notes. But he did show me at length a delightfully illustrated *Don Quixote* that he had just picked up in a neighborhood bookshop, several Verlaine autographs, and some art-gallery catalogues. I spent the whole afternoon with him. He was a very pleasant companion."

"Chance having thus reformed the group, The Five became more solidly knit than ever. Chalonnes, having nothing to do, ensured our staying in touch. He often spent the day here at the studio. After Beltara had painted the portrait of Mrs. Jarvis, the wife of the American Ambassador, he was very much in vogue. Lots of pretty women came to have their portraits painted, and they would bring their friends for the sittings or to see the finished work. The studio was full of dark-eyed Argentines and blond Americans and aesthetic Englishwomen who compared our friend to Whistler. Many of these women came on account of Chalonnes, whom they found attractive and amusing. Beltara had quickly taken the measure of our friend's drawing power, and skillfully turned this bait to account. Chalonnes had his own chair in the studio, with his box of cigars to the right, and his box of bonbons to the left. He refurbished the studio, and during the sittings it was his job to keep the model entertained. He had also been able to make himself indispensable because he had a kind of instinct for graphic composition. No one was better able than he to find the background and pose that best suited this or that face. He was also endowed with a rare sense of color tones, and he would signal to the painter a fugitive blue or yellow that had to be caught on the instant. 'You should really do art criticism, old man,' Beltara, who marveled at such a wealth of gifts, used to tell him.

" 'Yes, I know,' Chalonnes would reply gently, 'but I don't want to spread myself too thin.'

"In the studio, he became acquainted with Mme de Thianges, the Duchesse de Capri, Celia Dawson, Mrs. Jarvis, all of whom invited him to dine. For them, he was a 'literary man,' the friend of Beltara, and they introduced him to their guests

as 'M. Chalonnes, the well-known writer.' He became a kind of
literary adviser to the fashionable beauties of the day. They
took him to bookshops and begged him to act as their reading
mentor. He promised each of them that he would dedicate to
her one of the novels that would comprise his *New Human
Comedy.*

"Many of them used to tell him their whole life story. 'I
would love to have you tell me about yourself,' he would say,
'because I need, for this machine I am constructing, to know
how the gears mesh in the spirit of an intelligent woman.'
They knew he was discreet, and he quickly became the confidant for the most delightful secrets of Paris. He was the man
toward whom all ravishing faces turned the moment he entered
a room. As the women described their inner feelings to him,
they found him a sound psychologist. It became the customary
thing to say that 'Chalonnes is one of the most sensitive, understanding men you will ever meet.'

" 'You should write some analytical novels,' I said to him one
day. 'No one could do a kind of modern feminine Dominique
better than you.'

" 'Yes, I know, I know,' he said, with the air of a man who is
weighed down under many and diverse tasks and finds himself
forced to refuse those that it would have given him the greatest
pleasure to do. 'Only I have my big project, and one has, after
all, to concentrate.'

"Often Fabert stopped by the studio to pick him up and take
him to rehearsals. After the success of *Carnaval*, Fabert had
become a big name in the Boulevard theater. He would ask
Chalonnes to come along and offer a fresh reaction, for there
come times when actors and director are so tired of everything
that one feels they'd as soon give up and quit. In this role,
Chalonnes acquitted himself brilliantly. He had a feeling for
the movement of a scene, the sweep of an act; he could spot a
false intonation or an overinflated speech. At first, the actors
were irritated by this stranger, but they ended up by adopting
him. As against the author, who is the eternal enemy, they
loved this man who was a nobody. Presently, in the theater
world he became quite well known, first as 'the friend of M.
Fabert' and then in his own right. The box-office people got

into the habit of exchanging an orchestra seat for a smile. A
few, and presently all, secretaries put him on their dress-
rehearsal lists.

" 'You should write drama criticism,' Fabert told him. 'You'd
do it very well.'

" 'Oh, of course,' Chalonnes replied, 'but everyone should
stick to his own last, don't you think?'

"The year The Five jointly reached their thirty-fourth birth-
days, I won the Prix Goncourt with my *Ours Bleu* and Lambert-Leclerc was elected Deputy. Fabert and Beltara had been
very well known for some time. The connection among us was
in no way weakened, and so the romantic scenario that had
amused us so as students was effortlessly working out in fact.
Slowly our little group was reaching out powerful and well-
attached tentacles into the most diverse worlds. We really did
constitute one of the forces in public life in Paris, which was all
the more effective for being unofficial.

"There is unquestionably an advantage for an artistic group
to win *de jure* recognition. The reputation acquired by one
member is automatically credited in the public's mind to that
of all the others, and the name of the group, if it is well chosen,
captures public interest. A cultivated man of 1835 could be
forgiven for not knowing who Saint-Beuve was, but he had no
right to be unaware of the Romantics. However, the disadvan-
tages are no less great. Decadence is collective, just as is the
period of greatness. Doctrines and manifestos offer easy targets.
The skirmish technique of attack is less vulnerable.

"We did not follow the same professions, so jealousy did not
divide us. We formed a delightful mutual-admiration society.
The moment one of us had entrée to a new drawing room, he
delivered himself of such lively eulogies of the other four that
he was begged to introduce them. In most people, intellectual
laziness is such that they always accept their scale of artistic
values from some expert. Fabert was a great playwright because
I said so, and I was the 'most profound novelist we have today'
because Fabert kept saying as much. When we gave our Eighteenth Century Venice Fête—here in this studio—we had no trouble bringing together everyone in Paris who was worth knowing. It was an enchanting evening. Some exceedingly pretty

women put on a one-act comedy by Fabert for which Beltara did the set. But in the eyes of all our guests, the master of the house was Chalonnes. He had free time and great social ease, and he had, quite naturally, become our chief of protocol. When people spoke of 'your delicious friend,' we knew whom they meant.

"He continued to do nothing, and by that I do not mean only that his novel, his play, and his philosophical study of wit had not moved ahead by so much as a line. He literally did nothing. Not only had he never published a book, he had never written an article for a magazine or a piece for a paper or spoken in public. It wasn't that it would have been hard for him to get himself published. He knew, and knew very well, the leading book and magazine editors. Nor was it that he wanted, of his own free and considered choice, to remain a spectator. No, by nature he would have relished fame. It was rather the result of different but converging causes—an innate nonchalance, an unstable curiosity, and a kind of impotence of will. An artist is always in some aspect crippled, and it is his infirmity that detaches him from reality—that forces him to take off, to fly above life. Chalonnes was too well established in life; *living* satisfied him entirely. The perfection of his indolence mirrored the perfection of his well-being.

"Nevertheless, there was not one writer who did not call our friend 'my dear colleague' and did not send him his own books. Step by step, as one or the other of us moved up in the hierarchy of the Paris world, which, no matter how casual it seems, is so rigid, Chalonnes also advanced, and found that whatever honorary rank one of us achieved was conferred on him, too. We took pains that his self-esteem should be protected in all circumstances. It was rather like a newly promoted general who is a little embarrassed by a preferment he fears may be arbitrary and who exerts himself to get a promotion for some old friend from Saint-Cyr days.

"We were beginning to find that young people hovered around, hoping or asking for our support. To them, Chalonnes, who lived among us as an equal, was *'mon cher maître,'* for this younger generation was a prudent lot. Perhaps among themselves they asked each other: 'But what has he written, after all? Have you ever read anything of his?' Sometimes a clumsy newcomer would compliment him on *L'Ours Bleu* or *Caliban Roi*. Chalonnes would say, in a haughty, slightly offended voice, 'It is very good, indeed, but it is not mine.' Furthermore, of the five of us, he was the only one who willingly consented to read manuscripts and to give advice—useless as all advice is, but in his case always sound and perceptive.

"His gratuitous fame had grown so slowly and naturally that it didn't surprise us. We would have been surprised and shocked if people had neglected to invite our friend to one of those official ceremonies that 'bring the art and literary world together.' In any event, no one ever did forget to include him. Occasionally, when we happened to hear about the solitude and poverty of some great but unrecognized artist, who was neglected by the public and the state, we would reflect for a moment how paradoxical Chalonnes' success was. Yes, we would think, it is perhaps unfair, but what's to be done? It's always been this way. And the other man has the genius, after all; he has the better part.

"One day, as I was arriving at his house for lunch, I noticed a deferential young man off in a corner, clipping old magazines. Chalonnes introduced him: 'My secretary.' He was a very polite little fellow, fresh from the École des Chartes.

"A few days later, Chalonnes told us he was paying him three hundred francs a month and confessed that he found the expense a bit heavy. 'But,' he added resignedly, 'it is hard for men like us to do without secretaries.' "

"The war in 1914 cut like a sword into everyone's life. Beltara was in the cavalry, Fabert was a flier in Salonica. Lambert-Leclerc, wounded and honorably discharged, went back to the Chamber and snagged an undersecretaryship. Chalonnes, after serving as an infantryman second class in an army depot, was called back to Paris to work in propaganda, and finished out the war on Rue François I. When Fabert and I were demobilized, he was immensely helpful to us, for we had lost contact with Paris during our long absence whereas he, on the contrary, had made new and powerful friends.

"Beltara had been decorated, and Fabert even earlier, for

their military service. Through a colleague in Fine Arts, Lambert-Leclerc arranged for me to be on the first civilian honors list after the Armistice. The Five gave me a delightful little dinner—caviar, vodka, sturgeon—in one of the Russian restaurants that the Communist revolution seemed to have exiled among us. Musicians in silk caftans played gypsy music. It seemed to us—perhaps the effect of those melancholy songs—that Chalonnes was a bit downcast that evening.

"I walked home with Fabert, who lived in my neighborhood, and as we were going along the Champs-Élysées that fine winter night, we could talk of nothing but him.

" 'Poor Chalonnes,' I said. 'After all, at his age it must be painful to look back on a completely empty past.'

" 'Do you think he realizes it?' Fabert said. 'He's magnificently unaware.'

" 'I don't know. I think, rather, that he lives on two planes. When things are going well, when he's invited everywhere and made much of, he forgets that he hasn't done anything to deserve it. But at bottom he can't not know. It must be a forever present anxiety that rises whenever the surface is too quiet. On an evening like tonight, when all of you talked very kindly about my work and when I tried to reply, how could he not see that there's nothing to say about him?'

" 'Of course, but I don't believe that is the case with Chalonnes. For that, one would have to be either very modest and say, 'These things are not for me,' or very proud, and think: I don't want these things. Chalonnes wants the same things that everybody else wants, but he is lazier than he is ambitious. That's a painful situation to be in, I assure you.'

"We talked about this for a long time, both of us treating it rather complacently. In contrast to such sterility, our own productiveness was all the more apparent to us, and out of this agreeable awareness we extracted a measure of pity for Chalonnes.

"The next day, Fabert and I went to see Lambert-Leclerc at the Ministry.

" 'We want,' I said to him, 'to talk to you about an idea that occurred to us last evening after we left you. Don't you think it must be distasteful for Chalonnes to see all four of us decorated while he's left out in the cold? . . . It isn't important? Right, but nothing is important. It's just a symbol. And if it isn't important, then why not Chalonnes like everyone else?'

" 'Oh, I'm willing,' Lambert-Leclerc said, 'but there'd have to be some certification—' "

"What!" the Minister protested from the depths of the couch where he lay stretched full length. "I never said anything so banal."

"I'm sorry. I'll call Fabert as witness. You said, 'There'd have to be at least the semblance of certification.' "

"Maybe I said that, yes," Lambert-Leclerc said. "I wasn't in Fine Arts, so I couldn't do exactly as I'd have liked, but I did say to you that if Chalonnes wanted to stop by my office, it would be no trick to get him on the nomination list in the supply services."

"The whole thing was idiotic," the narrator went on, "but I will do you the justice of saying that you did not insist and Chalonnes did get his Cross. When I asked him to sign the application, I made the slip of telling him—because I was ever so slightly put out to see that he seemed to consider the whole business utterly natural—that we'd had a little trouble getting it arranged.

" 'Really?' he said. 'I'd have thought it would have been very simple.'

" 'Yes, if you'd had the certification . . .'

"But he was so obviously surprised that I changed the subject."

"His friends and admirers gave a little banquet for him. Lambert-Leclerc brought the Minister of Education, who turned out to be a witty fellow. There were two members of the Academy, plus a Goncourt Prize winner, some actresses, some society people. From the outset, the atmosphere at the party was excellent. Man is a well-disposed animal, on the whole, when he is not jealous or anxious. Chalonnes disturbed no one, he was liked by everyone, and since an occasion had arisen to share his happiness, everybody was glad to cooperate. At the bottom of their hearts, all the people there knew very well that the hero of the evening was nothing more than the fiction of himself that they had created. They knew that he was beholden for his existence to their goodwill, and in this rather odd flowering of his fortunes they relished the solid proof of their own influence, which had wrung this recognition out of nothing. Louis XIV loved the men who owed everything to him, and in this respect every elite is royal.

"Over dessert, a poet recited some graceful lines of celebration. The Minister gave a little speech that struck what the Goncourts would have called 'the sweet note of a touching little joke.' He referred to the discreet yet deep influence Chalonnes had on contemporary French letters, to his gifts as a conversationalist, to Rivarol and Mallarmé. At the end, he was given a friendly standing ovation. Then Chalonnes replied, with great modesty and grace. He was listened to in an atmosphere of genuinely friendly, delicate emotion. There followed some toasts, and that was that.

"When we left, I took Chalonnes home in my car, and I said to him:

" 'It went very well.'

"He smiled happily.

" 'Yes, didn't it,' he said. 'And what pleased me most was that I felt everyone was very sincere.'

"He was right."

"Thus Chalonnes' career lay open, as straight and proud as a royal highway, before our contented eyes. There was not one blot, not one failure; it is the privilege of nothingness to be invulnerable. We could already foresee our friend's rosette, followed by his collar. In certain friendly houses, there was already talk of the Institut. The Duchesse de T—— had timidly suggested this to a member of the Academy who was a great one for nominating new men, and he had replied, 'We are thinking about it, but it would be a little premature.' More and more, Chalonnes' face radiated that lovely serenity that only the purest goodness and the most complete idleness can give—indeed, perhaps they blend one with the other.

"It was around that time that Mrs. Pecks began to take an interest in him. Gladys Newton Pecks was a rich and pretty American who, like almost all rich and pretty American women, lived—actually, she still does—the larger part of the year in France. She had an apartment on Rue François I and a house in the Midi. Her husband, William Newton Pecks, being president of the Universal Rubber Company, not to mention several railroads, spent only his vacations in Europe.

"We had all known Gladys Pecks for a long time, and she had always been passionately interested in modern literature, painting, and music. She'd done a great deal for Beltara when he was just beginning. She'd bought his paintings, had him do her portrait, and had arranged for him to do the portrait of Mrs. Jarvis that launched him on his career. For two years, she talked to her friends about nothing but Beltara. She gave Beltara dinners, organized Beltara exhibits, and finally invited him to spend a winter in her house down in Napoule so that he could work in peace.

"Then success had come, and success always marks the end of Mrs. Pecks's great friendships. She is remarkably intelligent, but she brings to her love for art matters the feelings of certain speculators on the stock exchange—the ones who despise the gilt-edged investment and go only for the little stocks that are still unknown to the general public but about which they have confidential, reliable information. Mrs. Pecks loves the writer who is still in search of a publisher, the obscure playwright who has had a three-night run in some avant-garde theater, the musician on the order of Erik Satie before he ever had a disciple, or the scholar, the specialist in some recondite subject like Indian religions or primitive Chinese painting.

"But never, mind you, never are the men she takes under her patronage nonentities or even mediocrities. She is adroit, and she has taste. It's simply that fear of the popular and the banal can divert her from what is excellent. I can't conceive of Gladys Pecks's loving Tolstoi or Balzac. She dresses to perfection, buys her clothes at the best couturier house, but she stops wearing a dress, no matter how ravishing or how much she loves it, the moment she learns that it has been copied. Her writers and painters are treated in the same way. She hands them down to her maid when her friends have come around to appreciating them.

"I think I bear the responsibility for putting her on the trail of Chalonnes. I had been placed next to her at dinner one evening, at the home of Hélène de Thianges. I don't remember how, but we'd got to talking about him and I'd said, 'No, he's never published anything, but he has some big projects and even some things sketched out.'

" 'You've seen them?'

" 'Yes, but I couldn't tell you anything about them. They're scarcely more than notes.'

"I hadn't done this on purpose, but it was exactly what was most calculated in all the world to whet the appetite of Mrs. Pecks. Immediately after dinner, she got Chalonnes off into a corner, and no matter how Hélène tried to separate them—she likes people at her home to move about easily—she did not let go of him for the rest of the evening. I watched them from a distance. 'I should have foreseen as much,' I said to myself. 'Obviously, Chalonnes is the ideal author for Gladys Pecks. She looks for the unpublished and the hermetic. Who could dream of anything more closed than the public of Chalonnes, who doesn't have one, or of anything more unpublished than his work, which has never been written? The physicist who methodically rarefies the air within a balloon is moving toward the absolute void; Gladys Pecks, who rarefies the substance of the work of her successive friends, is moving toward nothingness. In Chalonnes she will find it. This is an admirable crowning of the careers of them both, and very likely I have made two people happy.'

"And, in fact, the very next day the Chalonnes phase in the life of Gladys Pecks began. It was agreed that he would dine at her home three times a week, that she would visit him to see his manuscripts, that she would take him to Napoule the following winter, so that 'he could work in peace.' For a few days, I was a little terrified to think of the first exposure of Gladys Pecks to Chalonnes' manuscripts. It seemed to me that even for her they were too meager. This was a lapse on my part and an error in judgment. I saw her the day after her first inventory, and she was enthusiastic: 'There's more there,' she told me, 'more substance in your friend's projects than in all those fat volumes of Henry James.' Everything was fine.

"This spiritual honeymoon lasted about two months, during

which Gladys informed all Paris that she was seeing to the publication of the work of a greatly neglected author—our Chalonnes. She had found a publisher; she was looking for an English translator. She introduced Chalonnes to every famous
foreigner who passed through Paris, from George Moore to Pirandello to Hofmannsthal to Sinclair Lewis. Then, having exhausted every possible promotional device, she asked Chalonnes for a manuscript.

"She would have been satisfied with a trifle—an essay, a slim
volume, a few pages. Chalonnes, naturally, had done no more
work during those two months than he normally did. He had
nothing to give her, and told her so with a serenity that nothing so far had shaken. But Gladys Pecks was not a woman to let
genius lie fallow. Ten times already in her life, she had taken
up one of these obscure, timid little men with, who knows why,
the mysterious gift of writing or painting or composing, and in
a few months' time had made him into a celebrated, sought-
after, adulated man. She took a lively satisfaction in these
transmutations. She had great and legitimate confidence in her
powers of selection and promotion. She had undertaken the
training of Chalonnes and, like it or not, Chalonnes was going
to produce.

"I don't know how she set about it—flattery, no doubt, promises perhaps, but I don't believe coquetry, because I've always
known Gladys to be cold and perfectly pure—but, in any case,
one morning I received an embarrassed visit from Chalonnes.

" 'I'd like to ask your advice,' he said to me. 'Gladys Pecks
has suggested putting her house in Napoule at my disposition
for the winter, so that I can work there quietly. I tell you quite
frankly I don't particularly want to leave Paris. Also, at the
moment I don't feel at my best for work. But it would please
her. She's terribly taken with my novel, and it is rather tempting to think that perhaps, with a few months all to myself, I
could finish it.'

" 'Finish' his novel seemed a curious euphemism to me because I didn't know that he had ever started it, but since this
was all said with the greatest seriousness, I was careful not to
touch on that point.

" 'Well,' I said to him, 'I'm delighted. Mrs. Pecks is right a dozen times over. You certainly have great talent, and every day of your life you prodigally invest whole chapters of a brilliant book in ordinary conversation. If a woman's concern and an atmosphere of confidence and admiration allow you finally to express what we all so well know you have to say, we will all be very happy for it. . . . Accept the invitation, old man. You'll be doing me a pleasure. You'll be giving us all pleasure.'

"He thanked me and a few days later came by to tell me that he was leaving. We had only a few cards from him during the winter. In February, I went to see him at La Napoule."

"The Pecks' house, which they've had restored, is utterly lovely. It's a little château, pure Provençal, that looks out over the gulf. The contrast between the rugged surroundings and exterior of the house and the nearly incredible comfort of the interior makes a fairy-like impression. The gardens are terraced —very ingeniously faked, actually, because to build them on the face of a rocky cliff, enormous quantities of cement had to be trucked up. The Pecks, at great expense, had cypresses brought from Italy, and their lofty, decorative forms framed this artificial and aggressive landscaping. When I arrived, the butler told me that Monsieur was working. He kept me waiting quite awhile.

" 'Ah, old man,' Chalonnes said, when finally I was shown into his study, 'I never knew what work could be. I'm writing with such zest, producing so much! The ideas just flow—they besiege me, make me dizzy. My pen can't keep up with the images, recollections, reflections that gush up from memory. Do you find that kind of thing happens to you?'

"I confessed humbly that such crises of superabundance were fairly rare with me—but to me it seemed natural, I added, that he rather than I should be elected for such visitations, and that his long silence must have allowed him to accumulate materials in a way that would not have been possible for the rest of us.

"I spent the whole evening with him alone. (Mrs. Pecks was still in Paris.) I found him curiously changed. Until then, one of his great charms had been the wide range of his conversation. For me, who have little time to read, a man like Chalonnes, who read everything, was a godsend. It was through him that I had discovered the most interesting people of the younger generation. Since he went out every evening, either to the theater or to parties, no one in Paris knew more stories and private dramas and current *bons mots*. Above all, Chalonnes was one of the rare friends with whom you could always talk about yourself and your own work, and feel that it really interested him, that while you were talking, he wasn't thinking about himself. All this was very agreeable.

"But the Chalonnes of La Napoule was a changed man. For two months he'd not opened a book, he'd seen no one. He no longer talked about anything—literally, anything—but his novel. I told him the latest news of our friends. He listened for a moment, then took a little notebook from his pocket and jotted something down.

" 'What are you doing?' I asked.

" 'Oh, nothing. Just an idea I had then for my book, and I don't want it to slip my mind.'

"A moment later, as I was repeating an amusing remark of one of Beltara's models, the notebook reappeared.

" 'Again! But this is a mania!'

" 'No, it's because I have a character who in some ways is like Beltara. What you've just been telling me could be useful.'

"He had that terrible professionalism of the neophyte, the zeal of the convert. I had a few chapters of my new book with me that I'd brought along to read to Chalonnes and to get his opinion, as I habitually did. I couldn't get him to listen to me. I decided he'd become an unbearable bore. And in the end, he irritated me by the scornful way he criticized or dismissed writers whom we'd always respected.

" 'You think so?' he said. 'Stendhal's innate gift? . . . Well, yes . . . You think it's so great, do you? But after all, essentially it's serial writing—the *Chartreuse* and the *Rouge* both. I think that one can do much better than that. . . .'

"I was almost glad to leave."

"When I got back to Paris, I immediately recognized signs of Gladys Pecks's admirable managerial talents. People were already talking about Chalonnes's book, and it was the right kind of talk. None of the vulgar, overstated publicity that puts people off. This woman seemed to have discovered the secret of intimate publicity—she knew how to cast a kind of obscure glow over a name. Paul Morand used to say she knew how to unseal the hermetic.

"Everywhere I went, people asked me, 'You're back from the Midi? Did you see Chalonnes? It seems that his book is quite remarkable.'

"Gladys Pecks spent March at La Napoule, and she told us that the book was almost finished but that Chalonnes hadn't wanted to show her any part of it. He said that his work formed an entity, and that to let isolated fragments of it be seen would violate it.

"Finally, in early April, she informed us that Chalonnes was coming back to Paris and that, at his request, she was summoning us for one of our Saturday evenings at her house for a reading of the novel.

"That reading! None of us, I think, will ever forget it. The drawing room on Rue François I had been prepared with the skill of a stage designer. All the lights were off except for a great Venetian-glass lamp that cast a soft, milky light on the reader, the manuscript, and a charming plum branch in a Chinese-porcelain vase placed behind Chalonnes. The telephone had been shut off. The servants had been instructed not to disturb us on any account. Chalonnes was nervous, artificially gay, and quite the conceited ass. Mrs. Pecks was radiant and triumphant. She sat him down, placed a glass of water beside him, and adjusted the venetian blinds. He put on a pair of heavy tortoise-shell-rimmed glasses, cleared his throat, and began to read.

"After the first half-dozen sentences, Fabert and I looked at each other. There are art forms in which a mistake is possible, where novelty of vision or style can disconcert or mislead one's judgment, but a few words are enough to reveal a writer. Here the worst was revealed to us instantly: Chalonnes could not write, could not write at all. A child can have a simple freshness and ease of expression. Chalonnes was flat and inane. From this man who was so sensitive and aware we would have expected perhaps excessive complications. But it was just the opposite—what we used to call 'shopgirls' fiction'—and it was

didactic and boring and puerile to boot. The revelation of the
nonexistent form was followed, within the space of two chapters, by the revelation that content also was nonexistent. We
looked at each other in despair. Beltara shrugged imperceptibly and his eyes said to me, 'Would you believe it!' Fabert was
shaking his head, as if he were muttering, 'Can this be?' I kept
watching Gladys Pecks. Did she also realize the real worth of
what we were hearing? At first, she had listened with an air of
great satisfaction, but soon she began to shift about uneasily in
her chair, and now and then she would look questioningly at
me. What a catastrophe! I thought. What am I ever going to
say to her?

"The reading lasted more than two hours, during which time
no one opened his mouth. A bad book is such a pathetic thing,
and so transparent. Excellent intentions are handled with such
childish awkwardness. The author's naïveté of spirit is so fully
revealed. Listening to Chalonnes, I was amazed suddenly to
find in him a whole world of disappointments and despond-
ency and repressed sentimentality. It occurred to me that it
would be amusing to write a book in which the hero would be
the author of a bad book, and to provide the full text of his
book, which would open new and surprising perspectives on
his character. Chalonnes read on with obvious emotion that,
given the abominable clumsiness of the form, made one think
of the touching, absurd loves of the fairy-tale monster.

"When he had finished, the silence was unbroken for a moment. We were hoping Gladys Pecks would rescue us. After all,
it was her home and it was she who had wanted this evening.
But she seemed somber and hostile. Beltara, who owes a heroic
sangfroid to his native Midi, finally saw that it was up to him
to sacrifice himself and he improvised a decent speech. He
attributed our wordlessness to emotion, thanked Mrs. Pecks,
without whom this fine book would never have been written,
and, turning to me, concluded: 'Civrac will be very proud indeed to offer it to his publisher.'

" 'Oh,' I said, 'my own or another . . . I believe Mrs.
Pecks—'

" 'Why another?' Chalonnes said quickly. 'I like yours very

much, he's very capable. If you want to take care of approaching him, I'll be delighted.'

" 'Certainly, old man, nothing easier.'

"Mrs. Pecks's silence was becoming painful. She rang and had orangeade and *petits fours* brought in. Chalonnes cast about for more definite reasons to be content with his evening.

" 'What do you think of the character of Alice?'

" 'Admirable,' Beltara said.

" 'The reconciliation scene rings very true, doesn't it?'

" 'The best scene in the book,' Beltara said.

" 'Oh, no,' Chalonnes said, 'I don't think it's the best. The best is perhaps the meeting between Georgiana and Silvio.'

" 'You're right,' Beltara said, soothingly. 'That one's even better.'

"Mrs. Pecks drew me aside into a corner.

" 'Please,' she said, 'be frank. It's ridiculous, isn't it? Utterly?'

"I nodded.

" 'But how is it possible?' she went on. 'If I could have supposed . . . He seemed so intelligent.'

" 'But dear Mrs. Pecks, he is very intelligent. Creation and conversation are two different worlds. It's so easy to make a mistake.'

" 'No, no,' she said, 'it's unforgivable. Above all, the book must not be published. After all I've said about it . . . He has to be told, hasn't he, that it's idiotic, that it's a disgrace?'

" 'Wait, please wait. You don't know how you're going to hurt him. Tomorrow, when we're alone, I'll try. But spare him this evening. I assure you, it's very important that you do.'

"Next day, at my first attempt to criticize a minor detail, Chalonnes received my timid little comment with such anger and scorn that I felt how raw his nerves must be and lost all my courage. Long experience had taught me how futile such efforts are, anyhow. Why repeat *Le Misanthrope*, Act I, Scene 2? I knew I would just bring down on my head 'And I, I assure you that my poetry is very good,' and that I wouldn't be cruel enough to quote the rejoinder. Better to beat a retreat forthwith. I went off with his manuscript under my arm and took it to my publisher, to whom I gave it without comment, saying simply that it was by Chalonnes.

" 'Really?' he said. 'This is Chalonnes' book? Why, I'm delighted to have it! I've heard a lot about it. I'm very grateful to you for having thought of me. Don't you suppose I'd do well to sign him up on a ten-year contract right away?'

"I persuaded him to wait a little. I was still nourishing some hope that he would read the book and turn it down. But you know how these things go. My name, Chalonnes' name—they were enough for him. He sent the manuscript off to the printer without a reading, and this news consoled Chalonnes for the attitude of his patroness.

"Mrs. Pecks had waited three days to give my move time to produce some results. When she learned the outcome, like an honest, stern Protestant, she had reproached me for my weakness and had written Chalonnes a curt note, which he had showed me the following day with stunned indignation. He spent a long time searching for a motive to which he could attribute such an unfair judgment. Finally, he fastened on an utterly absurd notion, but one that spared him humiliation: he fancied that Gladys Pecks had recognized herself in the character of a rather silly Englishwoman who figured in his book. With that, he recovered his peace of mind and gave her no further thought."

"Three months later the book came out.

"The reviews were not bad. Chalonnes was too well liked by everyone for anyone to want to cause him pointless pain. Critics who were friends alluded to the book discreetly, and the others kept silent.

"But word-of-mouth comment made the rounds with brutal speed. After a few days, I couldn't meet a person who didn't say to me, 'How about Chalonnes? Have you *read* it? Really, such things shouldn't be allowed!' Within a month, all Paris knew without having read the book that there was no point in reading it. In bookshop windows, the bright-yellow jacket turned lemon pale, and slowly darkened. At the end of the year, almost the entire first printing was returned to the publisher, who lost his investment and whom Chalonnes accused of being a bandit.

"For the book's failure to sell had greatly embittered him.

He now divided humanity into two classes: 'People who have
been good about my book' and 'People who have not been
good about my book.' It made social life very difficult. When
one wanted to arrange a dinner:

" 'Not him,' Chalonnes would say. 'I can't stand him.'

" 'Why?' Fabert would ask. 'He's very witty and he's not malicious.'

" 'Is that so?' Chalonnes would retort. 'He didn't write me
one word about my book.'

"This man, once so modest and so agreeable, had become
insufferably vain. He carried around in his pocket the clipping
of a favorable little comment I had managed with great difficulty to arrange for, and he read it to everyone he met. When a
critic enumerated the gifted novelists of our generation, he was
amazed not to find his name among them. 'That Bidou is a
scoundrel!' he would say. Or 'I would never have expected that
of Jaloux.' Soon—like the deranged souls who accuse the whole
neighborhood of persecuting them and end up believing that
their wives and children are also enemies—he took it into his
head that The Five hadn't been really 'good' about his book,
and he gradually drifted away from us.

"Perhaps, in a new, less informed milieu, he found again the
respectful, gratuitous confidence that we had extended to him
for so long. Three times in a row, he did not come to our
reunions. Beltara wrote him and got no reply. Finally, it was
decided that I would be dispatched as ambassador of The Four
on a mission to see him.

" 'Because, after all, the poor devil,' we told each other, 'it's
not his fault that he has no talent.'

" 'I found him at home and he saw me, but his manner was
very cold.

" 'No, no,' he said to me, 'the truth of it is, people are beastly
and you're no better than the others. So long as I was your
adviser and open-mouthed admirer, you were my friends. The
moment I wanted to create something myself, the moment that
you in particular felt I was a possible rival, you buried my book
in silence.'

" 'I?' I said to him. 'But if you knew the things I tried to do
to help you—'

" 'Yes, I know how one buries people while seeming to praise them to the skies.'

" 'But good God, Chalonnes, you are really too unfair! Do you remember the day you came to see me and tell me that you were leaving for La Napoule, that finally you wanted to work? You were hesitating, you didn't feel in good form. If I'd held you back, you would have stayed. But no, I encouraged you, congratulated you—'

" 'Exactly,' he said. 'And that is what I'll never forgive you or Gladys Pecks for.'

"He stood up, went to the door, opened it to show me that the audience was over, and sent me off with this wonderful closing line:

" 'You made me ruin my career.' "

"The most wonderful part of it," Beltara said, "the most wonderful part of it all is that that was true."

Ten Years Later

"Do you know who phoned me this morning, Bertrand?"

"How should I know?"

"Intuition should have told you. . . . It was a woman you were very much in love with once."

"Is there a woman in the world aside from you whom I've ever been very much in love with?"

"What an ungrateful man you are, Bertrand! What about Béatrice?"

"Béatrice who?"

"Béatrice who? Really, what a fraud you are! So you don't remember Béatrice de Saulges anymore?"

"Oh, that Béatrice . . . I thought she was in China or Japan or God knows where. Isn't she making a tour of the world?"

"She's made it. She got back to Le Havre last evening."

"And why in the devil did she phone you first thing this morning?"

"To be back in touch . . . She's been away a long time, she wants to see her friends again. That's only natural."

"I didn't know that we were friends of hers."

"Bertrand! . . . When I think that I almost left you on account of that woman . . . Oh, yes! I said to myself, 'If he doesn't care about me anymore, if he needs another woman, why should I hang on to him? We have no children. My duty, I suppose, would be to get out of the way. . . .' I even went to see my friend Lancret to ask him how one goes about getting a quiet, unobtrusive divorce. He listened to my tale of woe and advised me to be patient. Then, after a while the sacrifice seemed too great. So I stayed."

"Happily."

"Yes, happily. But who could foresee, dearest, that you would make such a rapid recovery? Have you forgotten that ten years ago you could not live one hour away from Béatrice? How you used to wait every day for her to call, and at a word from her cancel important appointments or break the most solemn promises? . . . Oh, that morning telephone ring! I can still hear it. My heart used to pound every time. And if you happened to be in my bedroom, Amélie would resort to such a guilty, conspiratorial tone of voice to say to you, 'Someone wants Monsieur on the telephone,' and you would look uncomfortable and idiotically proud. . . . Oh, it was horrible."

"Ridiculous, I'd have thought, more than anything else."

"Probably. But at the time I was too unhappy to see the funny aspects. . . . Remember, Bertrand? You weren't interested in anything in the world except Béatrice. If her name came up in conversation, your face was transformed. It was painful but also touching to watch. You liked people if they knew her, and things because she liked them. At one point, I saw you—the most rational, the least superstitious of men—suddenly curious about fakirs and fortunetellers and miracle workers. You used to run around with her to all kinds of strange little holes in the wall. . . . And you'd never let me have a cat, but you spent hours on end choosing for her a Persian that she wanted. Well, it was simple enough. You were at her beck and call. She could whistle, and you would come running like a puppy."

"You exaggerate."

"I am not exaggerating. You used to change plans three times a day because she was so capricious. Our vacations depended on her whims. One summer you dragged me all the way up to North Cape—me, who hates the cold worse than death—because Béatrice had gone off to Norway on the Jameses' boat, and you hoped that they might put in at some port where you could meet her. . . . I wept my way through most of that trip. I was cold and sick and sick at heart. But you didn't even notice. . . . What are you thinking about now?"

"I'm trying to recapture how I felt then. . . . It's true, all the same. I was mad about that woman. One wonders why, really."

"That's rather low of you, Bertrand. She was charming. She still is."

"Hundreds of women in Paris are prettier."

"Maybe . . . but she had a grave, an almost childish grace that was all hers. And she was very witty."

"You think so?"

"You told me so, Bertrand."

"Could I have been much of a judge? When I see her now, I don't know what to say to her. It seems to me that she gets by on a half-dozen clichés she picked up from me and some stories she heard from Salviati. . . . It's annoying."

"Bertrand, do you remember the day Gaudin operated on her? You were white with worry. I couldn't help but pity you. That morning, I did my best to be sublime. I called Rue Puccini three times myself to ask after her. The reports were good, and I passed them on to you and said, 'Don't be afraid, dear. It's not too serious.' "

"I'd forgotten that."

"What a pity! The noblest act of my life, and he doesn't even remember! . . . Tell me, dear. Have you also forgotten that when she went off with Salviati, you wanted to kill yourself?"

"I didn't want to very badly since I didn't do it."

"You thought about it. You even started a letter to me in which you told me what you were planning. One day, when we were filing papers, you handed it to me. Would you like to see it?"

"Certainly not."

"Yes, yes, you should. . . . Here it is: 'My dear little one, I know that I am about to hurt you frightfully. Forgive me. I have no more courage to go on living. But before drawing the final curtain, I want to explain many things that you must not have understood. It seems to me that I will soften your grief, if I can show you that our marriage has always been different from what you've imagined—' "

"Isabelle, this is painful for me."

"You think it's so pleasant for me? . . . 'The secret of an attitude that must so often have seemed strange to you is that when we met, I was already in love with Béatrice de Saulges. Why did I single you out, court you, marry you? Because Béatrice herself had just married, because I hoped to forget her, because I found in you a tenderness that she had never given me, and, finally, because man is not a simple creature and I very sincerely believed—' "

"That's enough, Isabelle. Burn that letter."

"I never burn anything. Furthermore, it's very healthy reading. Healthy for both of us. To please you, I'm skipping two pages, but listen to this: 'Your great mistake, Isabelle—because you, too, have been at fault in this miserable affair—your greatest mistake was that strange visit to Béatrice, when you begged her to discourage me and to give you back your husband. That day, my poor Isabelle, you succeeded only too well. You aroused remorse in a woman who is, at bottom, very good. You separated her from me, but you also separated me from you. It was after that maneuver, Isabelle—I didn't know about it for a long time, but I guessed from a hundred signs—it was after that that I felt Béatrice moving away from me and toward Salviati. And it's because of that maneuver that I shall die—' "

"What a disagreeable, theatrical tone!"

"Just muddled, Bertrand . . . But I still want you to hear the last paragraph: 'Don't regret anything. My life, in any event, is finished and I've never wanted to live to an old age. Welcome this step, as I do, with all sincerity. You will be loved again, Isabelle. You deserve to be. Forgive me if I've not been able to make you happy. I was never cut out for marriage, but I've had a real affection for you. No doubt, if circumstances had allowed me to live, I should have become more and more attached to you. One word more: when Béatrice comes back, with or without Salviati, be friendly to her. And if—' "

"Show me that letter. Did I really write those idiotic things?"

"Yes, Bertrand, you did."

"How strange . . . I tell you, I can't even recall the man who thought those things. 'I've never wanted to live to an old age!' And here I am, dear Isabelle, on the threshold of that old age."

"Discontented with life?"

"No, happy to grow old with you."

"Which proves, Bertrand, that one must not die for love or despair of a conquest."

"Do you believe that examples constitute proofs in the realm of emotions, Isabelle? Everything is always possible. Your approaching Béatrice succeeded. It could have failed. It could have killed me."

"One has to take risks, and you are very much alive. But you haven't told me what I shall say to the lady—"

"What does she want?"

"To see us. To have lunch or dinner—whatever you like."

"She'll tell us all about her trip—Bali . . . Angkor . . . Honolulu . . . It will be a deadly bore. Find some excuse."

"That's not possible, Bertrand. She'd think I bear a grudge. . . . And, furthermore, it rather amuses me."

"What pleasure can you find in meeting a woman you tell me made you suffer so bitterly?"

"The pleasure one finds in being on firm ground again after a rough voyage. The sight of Béatrice will recall to me my past suffering and make me appreciate my present security all the more. And then, I do find your friend very nice, you know."

"You hated her."

"I hated her when she was running after you, when she was upsetting you, when she was taking my place. Now I see that she is a delightful woman and that you had very good taste. . . . And that I enjoy."

"You know, Isabelle, at this moment I am very tired and

more than anything else I dread useless conversations. Don't force them on me."

"I'll spare you all the others provided you grant me this one—"

"You're not going to tell me, Isabelle, that I should see Mme de Saulges in order to be agreeable to *you?*"

"Why, yes, Bertrand."

Tidal Wave

"Drop his mask?" Bertrand Schmitt said. "Do you really believe it's often desirable for a man to drop his mask? I don't. I think that except in the case of a few rare and wonderful friendships, it is our masks—and only they—that make our life together bearable. . . . Sometimes circumstances force one of us to suddenly reveal the whole truth to people from whom we've habitually concealed it. But we're quick to regret such sincerity. After the fact, it seems very rash."

Christian Ménétrier intervened.

"I remember a disaster in England," he said. "A dozen miners had been trapped at the bottom of a mine by a fire-damp explosion. At the end of a week, they never expected to see the light of day again and believed they were lost, so they indulged in a kind of public confession. You can imagine how it went: 'Well, since it's all over with, I don't want to die without saying, et cetera . . .' Then, contrary to every expectation, they were rescued. And they never wanted to see each other again.

Instinctively, each man avoided the others, because they knew too much about him. Each mask had been restored, and society preserved."

"Yes," Bertrand said, "but one can imagine other reactions. I remember that while I was on a trip in Africa I was, quite involuntarily, witness to an overwhelming confession scene."

He cleared his throat and looked at us with some hesitation. It is odd, but Bertrand, who has done so much public speaking, is a timid man. He is afraid of boring people. But that evening, since none of us gave any sign of wanting to take the floor from him, he ventured on:

"You've all forgotten, I'm sure, that in 1938 I went on a lecture tour for the Alliance Française—to French West Africa, French East Africa, and some other overseas territories. English, French, Belgian colonies—back in those days one still said 'colonies'—I've been all over, and I've not regretted it. Visitors to those places were rare then, and I used to be royally received —or what was better, fraternally. I shan't tell you the name of the little capital I'm going to talk to you about now, because the heroes of my story are still alive. My characters are a governor, a man of about fifty, close-shaven, with silvery hair; his wife, much younger than he, a blonde, with dark eyes, lively and very witty. To make the telling easier, let's say their name was Boussart. They'd offered me the hospitality of the 'palace,' a big villa set among red rocks that might have been designed by some army engineer and that was very exotically furnished. I spent two pleasantly relaxed days there. On the living-room table—it was an ebony table that stood on a tiger rug—I found copies of *La Nouvelle Revue Française* and *Mercure de France,* and the latest novels. I complimented the young aide-de-camp, a Lieutenant Dugas, on the way the house was run.

" 'Heavens,' he said, 'I've nothing to do with all the things you like about it. It's Mme Boussart. That's her province.'

" 'Mme Boussart has literary interests?'

" 'Very much so. You must have noticed. Giselle, as we say here rather irreverently, was graduated from the École Normale in Sèvres. Before she married the Governor, she was professor of literature in Lyons. That's where he saw her again, while he was on leave. I say "saw her again" because he was already acquainted with her. She was the daughter of one of the Chief's best friends. He fell in love with her, and she agreed to follow him out here. It seems she'd been attached to him for a long time.'

" 'In spite of the difference in age?'

" 'Well, I must say that the Governor was extremely attractive then. People who knew him before his marriage say he had great success with women. He's older now.'

" 'That kind of marriage is hard on the blood pressure.'

" 'Oh, not only his marriage. The Chief has never had an easy life. Thirty years in Africa . . . The climate, constant troubles, working like a dog . . . He's a first-class man, the Chief is. Two years ago, when he arrived here, the tribes living in this immense jungle were completely primitive. They were starving to death. Their witch doctors were always stirring them up to kill each other off, kidnap women and children, offer human sacrifices to their idols. The Chief pacified the tribes, got them to work together, showed them that they could raise cacao here. . . . Not easy, I assure you, to persuade people who couldn't even conceive of the idea of a future to plant trees that would bear fruit only after six years.'

" 'They don't regret their old freedom, their old lazy ways? How do they feel about the Governor?'

" 'They feel affection for him—or veneration, rather. The other day I accompanied him on a visit to a very primitive tribe. The chief came out to kneel before him. "You have dealt with me as with a ne'er-do-well son," he said, "and you have done well. You have awakened me. Today I am rich." They're very intelligent, as you'll see, and easy to teach if you know how to handle them. But one has to be a kind of saint to win their respect.'

" 'And your chief is a saint?'

"The young lieutenant looked at me and smiled.

" 'What is a saint?' he asked.

" 'I don't know. . . . A perfectly pure man.'

" 'Ah, yes, that the Chief is. I don't know that he has any vices, not even any appetites, except perhaps on one score. He is ambitious—not for notoriety but for the work that's to be done. He loves administration, and what he hopes is to govern bigger and bigger territories.'

" 'Like Lyautey, who said, "Morocco? A big village . . . I need a world." '

" 'Exactly. The Chief would be delighted to be called on to govern our whole little planet. And he'd do a better job than the rest of them.'

" 'But your saint was a Don Juan.'

" 'So was St. Augustine. The transgressions of youth . . . Since his marriage, he has been the most exemplary of husbands. And God knows, in his position opportunities aren't lacking. I, who am only his shadow—'

" '*You* take advantage of them?'

" 'I am neither governor not saint, nor am I married. I enjoy all the advantages of my obscurity. . . . But let's talk about your trip, *mon cher maître*. You know that the Chief intends to accompany you tomorrow as far as your next stopover?'

" 'The Governor has offered, yes, to take me in his private plane. He told me he has an inspection to make on the coast, and a monument to unveil. Will you be coming?'

" 'No. Aside from the Governor and you, there will be only Mme Boussart, who doesn't like her husband to fly without her, plus the pilot, and the regimental commander, Colonel Angelini, who must take part in the inspection.'

" 'Have I met him?'

" 'I don't believe so, but you'll like him. He's a brilliant man, very entertaining. . . . And an ace, from the military point of view. A former intelligence officer in Morocco, one of your Lyautey's trainees. A colonel very young . . . great future ahead of him . . .'

" 'Is it a long trip?'

" 'Oh, no. An hour over the jungle down to the delta, then about sixty miles of beach, and you're there.' "

"My last dinner at the palace was pleasant. Colonel Angelini had been invited, to help prepare for the trip. This lieutenant colonel was really young for his rank—young in face and in heart. He talked a lot, and well. He had a paradoxical, at times aggressive, turn of mind, and was very cultivated. About native customs, and their totems and taboos, he knew more than the Governor, and, to my surprise, Mme Boussart kept up her end of the conversation very competently. The Governor listened to his wife with obvious admiration, and from time to time he would steal a glance at me to see what impression she was making on me. After dinner, he took Angelini and Dugas into his study, to settle some urgent matters, and I remained alone with 'Giselle.' She was coquettish, which is a game I play easily, but as soon as she was at ease, she began to question me about the Colonel.

" 'What do you think of him?' she asked. 'As a writer, you should like him. He is very precious to us. My husband swears by him. And to me, since I am a bit of an exile here, he brings the air of France—and of the world. If you have the chance, ask him to recite some poetry for you. He is a walking anthology.'

" 'That will be something for the plane trip.'

" 'No,' she said. 'The propeller drowns out voices.'

"Around ten, the Governor and the Colonel rejoined us, but we separated almost immediately, because our departure the next morning was set for 4 A.M. on account of the temperature.

"When the native boy woke me, the weather was not good. A quite stiff wind was blowing from the east. I've flown thousands of hours in my lifetime and I board a plane with no apprehension. Even so, I'm not too fond of those flights over virgin forest where it would be impossible to land or where, if by some miracle one did set down in a clearing, one would have little chance of being rescued. I went down to breakfast and found Dugas at table.

" 'The weather report is bad,' he said, with some concern. 'The pilot's suggested postponing the trip, but the Chief won't hear of it. He says he's got the *baraka* and that anyhow the weather forecast is always wrong.'

" 'I hope so,' I said, 'because I have to give a lecture this evening at Batoka. I've no other way of getting there.'

" 'It's all very easy for me to be brave,' Dugas said. 'I'm not going. But I do agree with the Chief. The disaster that is foretold is the disaster that never happens.'

"A moment later, the Governor and his wife came down. He was in a white linen uniform, and his decorations stood out vividly. Mme Boussart, very elegant and *sportive,* looked like her husband's daughter. She was scarcely awake, and said very little. At the airfield, an immense clearing hacked out of the forest, we found the Colonel, who was looking at the stormy sky with an air of ironic defiance.

" 'Do you remember,' he said to me, 'those descriptions of St.-Ex's of air pockets in the mountains? Well, they are much worse over the jungle. Be prepared for a good bouncing about. . . . You should really stay, Madame,' he said, turning to Mme Boussart.

" 'That's out of the question,' she said, emphatically. 'I'll stay if everyone else stays. If everyone else leaves, I leave.'

"The pilot had saluted the Governor and had walked with him somewhat apart from our group. I guessed that he was arguing in favor of a postponement and that he was meeting with some resistance. After a moment, the Governor came back toward us and said dryly:

" 'We're leaving.'

"A few moments later, we were flying above a sea of trees, and the propellers were making such a racket that conversation was difficult. Under the wind blasts, the jungle was trembling like the withers of a thoroughbred horse. Mme Boussart had closed her eyes. I had taken out a book, but soon the plane was bucking so that I had to give up trying to read. We were flying about three thousand feet above the forest, through dark clouds, and a heavy rain enclosed the plane. The heat was heavy, oppressive. Now and then, the plane dropped like lead and landed on denser air layers with a shock that made one wonder whether the wings would hold out.

"I'll not try to describe the nightmare of that trip to you. Just imagine a hurricane that was growing more and more violent, a bucking plane, a pilot glancing back at us now and then with a worried frown. The Governor was calm. His wife did not open her eyes. More than an hour went by like that. Suddenly the Colonel seized me by the arm and pushed me toward the porthole.

" 'Look!' he shouted in my ear. 'A tidal wave! You can't see the delta anymore!'

"What I saw was extraordinary indeed. At the point where

the black mass of the forest stopped, only the sea was visible—a yellow sea, as if it had been filled with mud. A furious wind was hurling it against the forest wall. The beach had disappeared entirely. The pilot scribbled a few notes in pencil and, half turning, handed the paper to the Colonel, who showed it to me: 'No landmarks. No radio signal. No idea where to land.'

"The Colonel got up. Staggering under the jolts of the plane and clinging to the seats, he took the message to the Governor.

" 'Is there fuel enough to turn around and go back?' he asked.

"The Colonel went to ask, and returned.

" 'No,' he said, calmly.

" 'Then have him drop lower and see if there is some island or sandbank still above water. That's our only chance.' And to his wife, who had just opened her eyes: 'Don't be afraid, Giselle. It's a tidal wave. We're going to try to land wherever we can. We'll wait there for the storm to blow over and for them to come rescue us.'

"She accepted this alarming news with a disconcerting, stoical calm. The plane dropped very low. I could clearly see the enormous yellow waves and, in a murky light, the trees bent low by the wind. The pilot was following the coast along the line where forest and sea met, searching for a clearing or a patch of beach. I didn't say anything, but I was thinking that we were lost beyond recall.

"Why? I thought. What did I get into this hellhole for? To talk to two or three hundred people who couldn't care less. How idiotic these useless trips are! . . . But then what? One has to die sometime. If it weren't here, it would be under a truck on some Paris street or from some germ or a stray bullet. . . . Let's see what happens.

"Don't think I'm boasting when I say I was resigned. The truth is, hope is hard to kill and, the evidence notwithstanding, like every other man I didn't believe death might be near. My reason told me it was; my body did not agree. The Colonel had gone to sit with the pilot, and together their eyes scanned the yellow sea. I saw the Colonel stretch out his arm. The plane veered. The Colonel turned around. His face, which until then had been impassive, was transformed.

" 'A small island,' he said.

" 'Big enough to land?' the Governor asked.

" 'I think so. . . .'

"After a moment, he said:

" 'Yes, definitely. Let's go, Bohec.'

"Five minutes later, we landed on a sandbank, no doubt one of those in the delta, and the pilot had maneuvered so well or chance had served us so well that the plane had come to a stop wedged between two palm trees, which allowed it to withstand the wind. The wind was blowing with such violence that it would have been impossible to leave the plane. And why try, for that matter? To go where? To the right and left of us, there was about a three-hundred-foot stretch of wet sand. Ahead and behind, the ocean. For the moment, we were saved; short of a miracle, we were not saved for long.

"In this almost hopeless situation, I admired our companion. She was not only courageous but calm and gay.

" 'Is anyone hungry?' she asked. 'I've some sandwiches and fruit. . . .'

"The pilot, who had joined us in the cabin said it would be sensible to ration provisions, for God only knew when and how we'd be got out of there. He tried once again to transmit his position by radio but got no response. I looked at my watch. It was eleven in the morning.

"In the afternoon, the wind fell a little. Our palm trees had held firm. The Governor was dozing. I myself felt worn out. I closed my eyes and then, involuntarily, half-opened them because that instant I'd sensed a curious emanation of warmth and strength. And I caught a glance exchanged between the Colonel and Giselle, who were sitting perhaps ten feet apart. The expression on their faces was so tender, so uninhibited, that it left no room for doubt; those two were lovers. I'd had a presentiment of it the evening before—I don't exactly know why, for their behavior was irreproachable. I quickly shut my eyes, and I was so tired that I fell asleep.

"I was awakened by a gust of wind that shook the plane so hard I thought it would be ripped from its flimsy support.

" 'What's going on?' I asked.

" 'The storm's picking up, and the sea is rising,' the pilot said, with a kind of bitterness. 'This time we're lost for sure, sir. In an hour, the water will have covered this sandbar—and us with it.'

"He looked at the Governor with an air of reproach—or of rancor—and he added:

"'I happen to be a Breton and a believer. . . . I'm going to pray.'

"I had learned the night before from Dugas that the Governor passed for being anticlerical, out of his political traditions, but that he was well disposed toward missionaries, who were very useful to him. He did not react now, either to imitate the pilot or to blame him. At that moment, we heard a splintering noise: a blast of wind had split the palm on our left. The end seemed only a question of minutes. It was then that Giselle, very pale and as if carried away by passion, ran to the young Colonel's side.

"'Since we're all going to die,' she said, 'I want to die in your arms.'

"Turning to her husband, she added:

"'Forgive me, Eric. . . . I've done everything to spare you this so long as— But now everything is finished, for me as for you. I can't lie any longer.'

"The Colonel, shaking, got to his feet and tried to push the hysterical woman away from him.

"'Your Excellency . . .' he began.

"The din of the hurricane kept me from hearing the rest. Seated six feet away, the Governor seemed fascinated by this couple. His lips were trembling, but I don't know whether he was really speaking or was trying helplessly to form words. The terrifying pallor of his face made me fear he was about to faint. The plane, which was now secured to the ground only by the one wing wedged against the palm on the right, was crackling in the wind like a flag. I should have been thinking only of the mortal danger we were all in, and of Isabelle and my family, but the spectacle before me was so extraordinary that I was galvanized by it.

"Up ahead, the pilot was kneeling, with his back turned toward us, murmuring his prayers. The Colonel appeared to be torn between the love that commanded him to gather the imploring woman in his arms and grief at humiliating a superior whom he quite evidently worshiped. As for me, braced to resist the jolting, I was doing my best to stay apart from this drama and to disturb them as little as possible. For that matter, I think they'd forgotten I was there.

"The Governor, clutching at the seats, managed to go over to his wife. In this dreadful cataclysm, which was destroying both his existence and his happiness, he preserved a strange dignity. No anger distorted his fine face, but his eyes were wet. When he was quite near, he leaned on me, and spoke to her in a voice so gentle it was heartbreaking:

" 'I had no idea, Giselle, no idea. . . . Come back and sit beside me. . . . Giselle! Please . . . I order you, come!'

"She had thrown her arms around the Colonel and was trying to draw him to her.

" 'My lover, my lover,' she kept saying, 'why hold back? Everything is over. I want to die with my mouth against yours. . . . Oh, my darling, don't sacrifice our last moment together to some scruple. As long as it was necessary, I obeyed you, you know that. . . . You respected Eric, you loved him. . . . So did I. . . . Yes, it's true, Eric, I loved you. . . . But since this is the end!'

"I don't know what piece of metal, ripped off by a stronger wrench of the plane, struck her in the face. A line of blood, very fine, was outlined on her cheek.

" 'Save appearances!' she said bitterly. 'How many times have you said that! And we saved them, my darling, we saved them. . . . But now? It's not appearances we must save now, but these poor, these last few moments. . . .'

"Then, in a low, dull voice:

" 'Coward! Coward!' she said to her lover. 'We are going to die, and you stand there at attention in front of a ghost!'

"Her husband leaned down, a handkerchief in his hand, and gently, skillfully, wiped the bleeding cheek. Then he looked at the Colonel with a kind of sad firmness but without hostility. I thought I understood what the look meant: 'Take this unhappy woman in your arms. I am beyond all suffering. . . .' The other man, overwhelmed, seemed to answer in the same mute way: 'No. I respect you too much. Forgive me.' I felt as if I were watching Tristan and King Mark. I've never witnessed a more pathetic scene. One heard only the whistling of the wind, and, like a distant murmur, the pilot's prayers; through the porthole, only the lead-gray sky and the white manes of shredded, livid clouds were visible—and, if one leaned down, the yellow waves that kept rising higher and higher.

"Then there was a brief respite. The woman, clutching the officer's dolman, was able to right herself. With a kind of savage defiance, she kissed him full on the mouth. He defended himself for a second or two and then, surrendering either to pity or to desire, he returned the kiss with passion. The Governor turned even more ashen, fell back on the chair, and seemed to faint. Out of some instinctive decency, I shut my eyes."

"How long did our group remain like this? I don't know. The only thing I remember with any certainty is that after minutes or maybe hours I thought I heard the sound of a motor boring through the storm. Was it an hallucination? I listened intently and glanced around me. My companions, like me, were listening. The Colonel and Giselle had moved apart. She had taken a step toward her husband. The Governor was leaning toward the porthole. The pilot, on his feet, was listening with intense concentration.

" 'Do you hear that, sir?'

" 'I hear it. Is it a plane?'

" 'I don't think so,' the pilot said. 'It's a motor, all right, but lighter than a plane's.'

" 'Then what?' the Colonel asked. 'I don't see anything.'

" 'Maybe a Navy vedette?'

" 'How would she know we're here?'

" 'I don't know, sir, but the noise is getting louder. They're coming nearer. The sound is from the east, so it's from the coast. . . . Look, sir, look at that gray spot—there! there!—on the waves. It *is* a vedette boat!'

"He broke into hysterical laughter.

" 'My God,' Giselle sighed, and she moved a step nearer her husband.

"With my face pressed against the porthole, I now could see the vedette very clearly as she came toward us. She was fighting painfully against the mounting tide, and now and then she disappeared among the waves, but she was making headway. The sailors took a quarter of an hour to reach us, but to us the time seemed interminable. When they were within reach and secured near us by a boat hook thrown into the palm tree, the transfer became the difficult problem. The gusts of wind that shook our plane made every move dangerous. The vedette itself was bouncing on the water like a cork. Finally, the pilot opened the door and managed to toss a rope ladder to the sailors, who caught it. Even today I don't know how we managed to disembark without one of us falling into the sea.

"Wrapped in oilskins, we looked back at our plane from the vedette with a surge of terror. To anyone seeing it from the outside, it was obvious that that miracle of balance could not last much longer. With surprising calm, Giselle was trying to smooth her hair. The midshipman who was in command of the little craft told us that a lookout had seen our plane set down and that they'd been trying to get through to help us since morning. Three times the violence of the sea had forced the rescuers to give up. The fourth time they'd succeeded. The sailors informed us also that the tidal wave had inflicted terrible damage in villages along the coast and in the port of Batoka.

"The local administrator met us on the dock. He was a young colonial officer, rather intimidated by the problems that the disaster confronted him with. But Governor Boussart, the moment he set foot on land, had become the 'Chief' again. And as he ordered the necessary measures to be taken, he acted like a true leader. He needed Colonel Angelini's help in organizing the cooperation of the rescue squads, and I was struck by the manner of the two men. To see them working on a common task, no one would have suspected any resentment or remorse between them. Mme Boussart had been escorted to the administrator's house, where his young wife gave her tea and loaned her a raincoat. With that, she also insisted on working and taking care of the wounded and the children.

" 'About the dedication of the monument, sir . . .' the administrator said.

" 'We'll worry about the dead when the living are all safe,' the Governor said.

"There could be no question of my giving my lecture. I sensed that all the actors in this little drama were in a hurry to get me off on the next lap of my journey. It was agreed that I should travel by train. I went to bid Mme Boussart good-bye.

" 'What memories you're going to have of us!' she said.

"But I don't know whether she meant the terrible flight or the lovers' tragedy."

"Did you ever see them again?" Claire Ménétrier asked.

"Wait," Bertrand Schmitt said. "Two years later, in 1940, I was called up, and one day I met Dugas, who was a captain by then, at the field mess of a colonial division commander on the Flanders front. He talked to me about that dreadful flight. 'You had a narrow squeak,' he said. 'Your pilot told me the whole story. He was furious with the Chief, because he'd warned him before you took off that there would be a disaster.'

"After a moment's rather heavy silence, Dugas went on:

" 'Tell me, *mon cher maître,* what happened that day? No-body ever said a word to me about it, but a cloud seemed to hang over them when they got back—over the Governor and his wife and Colonel Angelini. The Colonel asked for a transfer soon after, you know, and he got it. What surprised me was that the Chief seconded his application very strongly.'

" 'Why surprised?'

" 'I don't know. He thought a lot of the Colonel. I'd have expected some move to try to keep him.'

" 'On whose part? Giselle's?'

"Dugas looked at me very attentively.

" 'She was the most insistent of all about his leaving.'

" 'So what happened to Angelini?'

" 'He became a full colonel, of course. Now he's commanding an armored tank regiment.' "

"Came the debacle. Five years of fighting and suffering and hoping. Finally, I saw—as did you all—Paris return to life. Sometime early in 1947 Hélène de Thianges asked me one day:

" 'Would you like to lunch with the Eric Boussarts? They say he's going to be appointed Resident General in Indochina.

He's a remarkable man, a little cold, very cultivated. Do you know, last year he published a book of poetry under a pseudonym? . . . His wife is beautiful.'

" 'I know her,' I said. 'Before the war, I stopped over with them in one of the African colonies where he was governor. . . . Yes, I'd be curious to see them again.'

"I wondered whether they would be pleased at this meeting. Was I not sole witness to what had no doubt been the greatest drama of their lives? However, out of curiosity I agreed to go to lunch.

"Had the war and all the troubles it brought transformed me so? The Boussarts didn't recognize me immediately. I went over to greet them, but since they were looking at Hélène with that politely inquiring air that seems to beg for enlightenment, she introduced me by name. The Governor's closed face relaxed and his wife smiled:

" 'Of course,' she said. 'You visited with us in Africa.'

"She sat next to me at lunch. I tiptoed among her thoughts rather the way one walks on ice, prudently trying to sound out her resistances. Finally, when I saw that she was completely serene and at ease, I ventured to recall the hurricane on the delta.

" 'That's true!' she said. 'You were on that absurd expedition. . . . What an experience! We very nearly didn't survive it.'

"She paused a moment, because the butler was offering her a platter, and then went on in a natural tone of voice:

" 'But then you would have met Angelini at our house. . . . You know that he was killed, poor boy?'

" 'No, I didn't know. . . . In the war?'

" 'Yes, in Italy. He was in command of a division at Monte Cassino, and there he remained. . . . It's a pity. He had a great future ahead of him. My husband thought very well of him.'

"I looked at her in surprise, wondering to myself whether she realized how her words had amazed me. She had that innocent, detached, decently regretful air that one assumes in speaking of the death of a stranger. Then I understood that the mask had been so firmly restored that it had become the face itself. Giselle had forgotten that I knew."

Transference

"No, no!" Irène said to herself. "It can't go on. Raymond *has* to change or I'll get to hate him. And that would be unfair. He's so sweet. He loves me, I'm sure. . . . Ouf! Perhaps that's why I don't love him. Raymond falls in with every whim of mine. With me, he's weak. . . . Weak, yes, and that's what I can never forgive in a man. Last evening he did so want to have dinner in the Bois. I suggest Montparnasse. What happens? He gives in without another word, and we go to Montparnasse. Afterward he wanted—and I knew it perfectly well—to come back here, but the moment I said vaguely that I'd like to see the new Garbo film, he gave in and we went to the movies!"

Stretched out on her bed, her eyes closed, listening to the sounds of Paris that rose from the street, she reviewed in her mind the men she had really loved. Salviati, a professional Don Juan, who had picked her up and almost immediately dropped her; Fabert, the playwright, amusing, violent, cynical; Bernard

Quesnay above all, a friend of Raymond's, a rigid, severe young industrialist who had, all unconsciously, been very hard on her.

But, she thought, there was something charming about Bernard's egotism, while Raymond is so submissive. . . .

Raymond Lambert-Leclerc owned, together with his father and brothers, one of the largest manufacturing concerns in the country. He was rich and, in his own world, powerful. But Irène derided money and power. She had, on the other hand, a great need to admire. Having spent her childhood in Russia, in the days of the revolution, and followed her family into exile, she had been marked for life by those terrible experiences. For a long time she believed herself incapable of experiencing more normal emotions. "I am a warped person and always will be," she used to say mournfully to herself. Then, one day, she met Dr. Marolles.

Marolles was one of the first French medical men to have studied in Vienna under Sigmund Freud. Thirty-five years old at the outside, with a closely shaven face, penetrating eyes behind horn-rimmed glasses, and a soft, firm voice, he exercised an extraordinary influence over his patients, especially the women.

Patiently, in the course of three sessions a week, he had reconstructed Irène piece by piece. He had taught her to look squarely at her past, and not to be afraid of other women; he had restored her appetite for work, and her self-confidence; he had instilled in her an authority such that, in the couturier house where she was working, she had quickly become the favorite assistant of the director. However, Marolles said, she had still to learn to stop attaching herself by preference to men who were unfaithful and unfeeling and who made her suffer, and she had to come around to seeing that she could now get along without him, Marolles.

"You don't need me any longer," he would say to her. "These sessions are expensive for you. You aren't rich. Why spend your money uselessly? I'll be very glad to go on seeing you as a friend. But the doctor is letting you go. Other people have more right to my time."

"Please keep me on," Irène would answer. "If you let me go, I'll fall right back into the old insecurities and terrors and thoughts of suicide. . . . No, I'm not strong enough to face the world alone."

Several times, Marolles had acquiesced, because Irène was beautiful and touching, and because the authority he enjoyed over her flattered him. Only to him had she confided that Raymond Lambert-Leclerc, heir to the great Cambrai factories, wanted to marry her.

"Marry me!" she said. "As if I were cut out for marriage . . . Raymond is a good little boy. He wants a home of his own, a family. I don't blame him, but how can he believe that I would make him happy in those ways? It isn't that he's unaware of my past, since we met at Bernard's. And yet he has confidence in me, in himself, in the future of a ménage that we would make together. . . . Really, men are so strange."

"Don't hesitate," Marolles had said. "There's precisely the marriage that will reintegrate you into a stable society. Ever since childhood you've suffered from the destruction of the social world you would have belonged to. So join a French one."

"I would never really belong," she said. "I think I'd always feel unwelcome in his family. All those Lamberts and Leclercs . . . I'm beginning to know them a little from what Raymond says about them. They're middle-class North of France people, very conservative, very upright, very dull. . . . 'That half-touched Russian,' they'll say. . . . And then, I don't love Raymond."

"Are you sure? You tell me he's young, well-bred, very intelligent, that he's got a charming face—"

"Oh, he's pleasant enough and, given his background, quite cultivated, and he has an exquisitely considerate nature—too considerate. He even suggests that, if I'm afraid of living in the provinces, we live in Paris the year round. He could manage the sales end of the business here. It's tempting, of course it is. All my family urges me to say yes. But—"

"But what?"

"But I don't love him. Why not? You know me so well, Doctor, I scarcely need tell you why. Because he is too kind, because he is weak, because he is not a very good lover. He has a soft body, white white skin, and the shoulders and arms of a girl. No muscle . . . I tell him so. I'm very mean to him, and he never reacts. That's not the kind of a husband I need—if I need a husband—as you very well know, Doctor. I'm looking for a man who lays down the law for me and who doesn't allow me to deviate from it."

"Someone who'll beat you up!" Marolles said.

"I don't absolutely insist on the beating part! But I'd prefer that, certainly, to a man who trots along obediently at my heels."

He looked at her, smiling. They had become very good friends.

"You told me once," Marolles went on, "that the only time you thought you were very close to loving him was when he almost betrayed you with one of your friends."

It was her turn to smile.

"That's true. . . . Because that day he made me feel he was —oh, daring. Also, because he'd made me suffer a little. But it didn't go any further than that. Raymond had scruples; he let my friend slip through his fingers—and me, at the same time."

"You know," Marolles said, "the person who should be in analysis is no longer you but Raymond. You should give up your sessions to him. Bring him here, and I'll make the kind of man out of him that you could love."

"Do you believe that?"

"I am sure of it," the doctor said.

"He'd never have time to see you three hours a week. . . . And who told you I want to love him?"

"You did," he said.

At the time, she had rejected the proposal but now, stretched out on her bed and thinking of Raymond's finely chiseled face, she could not help reverting with a certain smugness to Dr. Marolles' suggestion.

"He's saved me from myself," she told herself. "Why mightn't he turn Raymond into a different man?"

She tried to imagine Raymond on Marolles' blue couch, recounting his dreams and childhood.

It would be terribly difficult, she thought. Frenchmen, this breed especially, have very little genuine taste for confession.

But Marolles, of course, would know how to put him at his ease. . . . And who knows?

When Raymond came back from Cambrai the following day, and while they were dining together at the wineshop on Avenue d'Italie, where once a week the owner prepared a prime *steak au poivre* for them, she talked to him about Dr. Marolles.

"I've often told you how much good he's done me. And you've seen it for yourself. . . . Well, what do you suppose? The other day, when I was talking about you and about your wanting to marry me—"

"What!" Raymond said. "You talk to him about things like that?"

"I talk to him about everything, of course. Otherwise, an analysis would be impossible."

"Analysis, analysis!" he said. "I detest the word. . . . Don't you see the treatment is endless? Your doctor's been telling you how to live your life for two years, to the tune of a hundred and fifty francs a week."

"Raymond, don't say things like that! You're unfair and you know it. Marolles has ten times more patients than he can handle, and in order to treat me he gives up patients who can pay him infinitely more than I can. Furthermore, if it were simply up to him, my analysis would be finished. . . . He seems to think from what I've told him that it's you who might need his guidance now."

Raymond looked both shocked and intractable.

"Me! What an idea! I'm not sick," he said. "And what's more, I have a horror of that kind of charlatanism."

"There's no charlatanism about it. . . . Neither was I *sick*. I was—like you—indecisive. I had no self-confidence. Marolles built up my will again."

"I know very well what I want."

"You know what you want in business, in your work, but with your family, and especially with women, you are timid, clumsy. . . . This is not a reproach, dear, it's a statement of fact."

He flushed. He knew she was right.

"What do you expect? I spent my youth in a provincial city, surrounded by middle-class people in whose lives love plays a very small role. . . . I lack experience, initiative. That's all. And that isn't in a doctor's bailiwick. Also, timidity will make me a faithful husband, so don't complain."

"Oh, I'm not complaining about anything," Irène said.

In the weeks that followed, she came back to the charge so often, and talked about Marolles so much that, in the end, she convinced him. One day, she took him to the doctor's, and it was agreed that he would go back alone not three times but once a week.

"It's very little," Marolles said, "but we'll see what we can do."

"I'm so glad," Irène said to Raymond, as they were leaving. "You're a darling."

And she kissed him, right in the middle of the street. Raymond looked around wildly for fear someone "from up North" might have seen them.

After two meetings with Marolles, he was as enthusiastic as she.

"I can't tell you how grateful I am to you for having given me that advice."

"I know," Irène said. "He's a wonderful man."

"Yes," Raymond said. "And extremely intelligent. He goes straight to the point. I think he'll do me a lot of good."

"I find you changed already," she said.

After three months, the effects of the treatment became quite apparent.

"You don't realize, Raymond," Irène would say, "but you're no longer the same man. Now it's possible to talk with you frankly and directly without bumping into your complexes, your shell. You dare look at yourself in the face and recognize what you really are and what you want. I find you a hundred times more attractive—yes, I really do."

"I know that I feel very different," Raymond said. "The one thing that bothers me now is that Marolles wants me to see other women. He says my life with the family at home has made me a poorly adjusted person, that I should widen my experience before I settle down in a marriage."

"He's right, of course," Irène said. "Marolles is always right. Do what he tells you. But save a little of your time for me."

296 : THE COLLECTED STORIES OF ANDRÉ MAUROIS

"I'd like nothing better than to save all my time for you," he said tenderly. "You know that. . . . Only Marolles—"

"Do what he tells you."

At the next session, Raymond confessed to Dr. Marolles that in Paris he had only very boring business contacts.

· "What about Irène's circle?"

"You know she lives more and more to herself, and she loves to create an atmosphere of mystery. . . . Never, not to this day, has she been willing to introduce me even to her mother or her sisters."

"Well," Marolles said, "I'll undertake to introduce you to some lively young couples who will amuse you and wake you up a bit. For that matter, Irène can come along. I don't in the slightest wish to take you away from her. . . . Emphatically not! What I want simply is for both of you not to wrap yourselves up, always alone, in your cocoons of scruples and insecurities."

To Irène he said:

"I know your Raymond very well now, and the day you two marry I promise you the most perfect conjugal adjustment."

The doctor organized a little dinner for six: himself and his wife; Wanda Nedjanine, another young Russian whom he had saved from despair, and the pianist Rosenkranz, whom Wanda was in love with. Rosenkranz, who was possessed of a completely uninhibited verve, made the evening. He was a marvelous mimic, and he imitated, in succession, the rages of his impresario, the passionate fervor of his admirers, and the playing of his fellow musicians. At Odette Marolles' request, he sat down at the piano and improvised musical parodies of Wagner, Debussy, and Chopin. When they were parting much later, Raymond said to Irène:

"Marolles' wife's very pretty."

Irène made a little face.

"Nice rather than pretty. No, Wanda's the one I think is beautiful, with that wild, strange air of hers."

"Maybe, but she's got eyes only for Rosenkranz. She looks at him with those sheep's eyes of hers, hangs on every word he says. At least Odette Marolles realizes that other people exist. . . . I like that short, curly hair—and she's got a fine bosom."

"How do you know that?"

"Well, she was wearing a very low-cut dress. . . . Lucky Marolles!"

"Oh, come," Irène said. "Lucky Odette. She's the lucky one, to have a husband whose shoes she is not worthy to unlace."

"You're being pretty hard on her," Raymond said. "I didn't find her stupid at all."

"She never opened her mouth."

"Nobody opened his mouth! . . . Neither you nor I nor she nor anybody else. With Rosenkranz, who talks all the time, that's not possible."

"Nor desirable," Irène said. "Rosenkranz is a very amusing man."

"You like him?"

"Yes," she said. "To be quite frank, that's the kind of man who could be dangerous for me. But he hasn't the slightest wish to bother about little me. Fortunately."

The following week, Raymond returned the Marolles' invitation, but at the last moment Odette came alone, the doctor having been called to a consultation. Odette had a very animated conversation with Raymond. They had discovered that they shared a passion for hunting. Irène, amused at first, quickly wearied as she listened to them talk about hare and partridge, deer and wild boar.

"I didn't know you were such a good shot," she said to Raymond, when they were alone in the car.

"You don't really know me," he said. "When I used to spend every Sunday in the country, hunting was my one pleasure."

"You're more of a sportsman than I'd have believed."

"Yes, I'm very good in sports. Why shouldn't I be?" Raymond said, a little vexed.

"I don't know. You don't have an athletic body."

"You'd be surprised at my endurance," he said. "In the army, I amazed all the other men. I'm more solid than I seem."

"Maybe," Irène said. "I wouldn't have thought that. But if you say so . . ."

Raymond continued to go to Marolles every Tuesday. At the end of six months, the doctor said to Irène:

"It seems to me that our friend is on the right track."

"Oh, indeed!" she said. "The transformation is almost unbelievable. Do you know that he's become authoritarian, demanding, difficult? My little Raymond, whom I used to twist around my little finger! You've given me back a very nearly aggressive man."

"Isn't that what you asked me for?" Marolles said. "It's indispensable for a man to have some aggressiveness in his makeup, otherwise he's crushed. You yourself have done better since you became aggressive."

"Yes," she said reticently, "but there are limits beyond which one shouldn't go. Now Raymond and I clash sometimes. We had a quarrel yesterday and he was hateful. . . . And then, this aggressiveness sometimes takes a form that is a little ridiculous. Raymond was modesty itself, and suddenly he believes he is irresistible. . . . I'm not joking. Now he thinks all women are interested in him, and he flirts with them all."

"Any success?"

"I don't know," she said. "He's also become very secretive."

After a moment's silence, she said to him casually:

"Do you and Odette still go out with him?"

"What a question!" Marolles said, with surprise. "I'd have let you know. . . . No, now that he's launched, I leave him to his own devices. Furthermore, I don't think he needs me much longer. I've brought about the change you wanted. It's up to you to manage the ending."

"The ending?"

"Well, yes. The marriage."

"Oh," she said. "I don't know that I will marry Raymond."

"Irène!" Marolles said. "I'm not going to let you slip back into your old hesitations. That, no!"

But she left rather abruptly. She no longer had exactly the same confidence in Marolles. She knew that Raymond and Odette were seeing each other very often. At the beginning, Raymond had admitted as much to her, with a pride that she had found sweet and naïve. At that point, he was having innocent appointments with Mme Marolles in restaurants in the Bois, where they would have a glass of port. Or they went boating on the lake. Then he had stopped mentioning Odette to Irène entirely, but she noted that he was stealing evenings from her on the excuse of business appointments. Finally, he had disappeared for a whole weekend, and a benevolent woman friend had told Irène that Odette Marolles and Raymond Lambert-Leclerc had been seen in one of those out-of-the-way forest lodges that were habitual hideaways for clandestine couples. "So much for the famous doctor!" Irène told herself. "So much for the strong man who considers us all so many puppets whose strings he can pull as he chooses! So much for the marriage counselor! The expert in matrimonial relations! His own wife is deceiving him under his nose with a mere boy whom he introduced to her. And Marolles doesn't even know what's going on!"

This revelation hurt Irène seriously. She derived her strength from Marolles. When she saw him duped and ridiculous, she collapsed. In her confusion, she talked too much and put the doctor on the scent. He discovered the truth in his turn. No doubt about it. His wife was this boy's mistress. When he questioned Odette, she confessed, left town precipitately, and went to live in a country house outside Cambrai. The shock was such that Marolles had to stop work entirely and ask a colleague to agree to treat him.

"Poor Marolles!" Dr. Bias said. "He's really down. He'll have to go through an analysis himself once more before he'll be able to practice again."

Little by little, everything got adjusted. After several months in retirement, Marolles recovered his equilibrium and was promptly reconciled with his wife, whom he adored. The affair had been known only to a few close friends, and in the worldly circles where Marolles now recruited his patients, he kept his prestige intact. Raymond Lambert-Leclerc went back to Irène. He never again offered to marry her, but she was only too happy to take him back without conditions.

The cure had, after all, worked.

Flowers in Season

ÉTIENNE CARLUT got out of the taxi in front of the main gate to the Montparnasse cemetery. He was carrying a bunch of chrysanthemums aflame with all the fires of autumn, from rust red to vivid yellow. As he passed the two caretakers who guard the entrance, one of them saluted. Encumbered by his flowers, he replied merely with a nod.

"You know him, chief?"

"A little, yes. He's a professor. They buried his wife over in Section 7, end of July. He comes every Thursday—he has no classes that day. He told me that—at the beginning."

"Too young to be a widower. He won't be coming long."

"You never can tell. No, you never can tell. It depends on the kind of person."

If they had questioned him about it, this man dressed in black, with a short beard, who carried his chrysanthemums so awkwardly, now in his arms like a baby, now behind his back, he would have replied that he would be coming every Thursday until the day of his death, which day he hoped would not be too far distant. The sudden disappearance of Lucile had been for him an irreparable disaster that his mind refused to accept. They had been married five years, and she had transformed his life. Before knowing her, he had been a serious man (a little boring, women said) to whom nothing mattered outside his work. He loved teaching, correcting papers, preparing his own doctoral thesis. The outside world scarcely existed for him.

Then, in a mountain hotel where he was spending his vacation, he had met Lucile. She had such rare beauty, with her golden hair and violet eyes, her arching throat and softly rounded shoulders, that for all those five years he had found it hard to believe she was real. Even when he held her naked in bed and she looked up at him, a consenting victim, she seemed to him a creature out of a legend or fairy tale. For him she evoked Shakespeare and Musset. When he made such associations, he reproached himself for being even in love the unregenerate professor, the pedant. No, Lucile was not a facsimile of imaginary heroines, but a tenderly smiling woman, with an expressive face, and a fresh, supple body. She was flirtatious, and sometimes she had teased him, upset him. Now he remembered only her inimitable charm.

"I have lost more than I possessed," he said to himself, as he walked toward the grave that was sacred to him.

Third south, second west. The first weeks he had needed these signs to find his way. Now he could go straight to the ashgray marble stone, on which one read simply, "Lucile Carlut, née Auban, 1901-1928." For a moment he had considered a Latin inscription—"*Conjugi, amicae*"—but she would not have approved. To reach the grave, he passed by the vaults of powerful families, hideous monuments in Gothic or Egyptian style, that bespoke the wealth of some steel or grocery magnate. He much preferred the unified, plain slab, the last gift he had lovingly chosen for his wife. The last? No, not entirely, since he had these chrysanthemums whose burning colors she would have praised. Was it possible that she was beneath this stone? He thought he could hear her voice:

"You've brought me flowers again? How sweet of you!"

He remembered his own disbelief, his passionate denial when the doctor, after leaning down over Lucile's heart, had said, "It's all over." How could she have left him alone! It was so unlike Lucile. She was so attentive, thoughtful; she never lost hope.

He laid his chrysanthemums slantingly under the inscription, then stood by the stone, lost in thought. Every week, he forced himself to evoke the stages of their happiness: their engagement, honeymoon, long nights of making love; the delicious intimacy when, sitting at his work table, he would look up to meet that furtive, conspiratorial smile; then the moving experience of awaiting their child. They had agreed about everything—from the furnishing of their apartment to the choice of plays they wanted to see. She read his thoughts so well that she would answer a question before he had voiced it. Now he had neither wife nor son.

"Poor Lucile! Your last words were to reassure me. Then, in the middle of a word—"

Throughout the winter, he came back every Thursday. Each time he brought different flowers, showing as much imagination to charm the dead woman as he had formerly to please the living. At Christmas, he remembered the childlike joy that the tiny illuminated tree used to give Lucile, and the presents he placed one by one under the boughs; he decorated her grave with evergreens, holly, and heather. Then the days, week by week, grew longer. He began to find new flowers on the carts. One March day, he brought a bouquet of violets and primroses. The sky was limpid, the air already warm; the light played over the marble. He felt a kind of well-being and immediately reproached himself for it.

As always, he slipped into a reverie. "You used to love the spring," he said to her. "The first day you could go out without a coat, with a flower pinned to your jacket, you had such a triumphant air—every year. I will never see you again, walking like a goddess—" In spite of himself, he turned his head. A young woman dressed in black had just turned into the path; she stopped before a grave perhaps thirty feet away from him. She was carrying a sheaf of flowers in her arms, which she laid gracefully on the stone. Then she kneeled on the stone pediment.

Her hat partly hid her face. Étienne waited for the moment when she would turn her head, and when she got up, he saw that she was crying. The outline of her face was pure and grave. Black hair framed a high forehead. Her coat, a long fitted jacket, emphasized her slender waist. She did not glance around her before walking away. Slipping between the graves and vaults, she rejoined the main path. When he heard the sound of her footsteps on the gravel fade away, he went to look at the stone before which the young woman had kneeled. He read: "Antoine Constant, 1891-1928." So she was weeping for a husband, not a father or son. Then he thought: Or perhaps for a lover. But he did not believe it.

The next Thursday, without realizing that he hoped to see her again, he came at exactly the same time. She did not appear. He waited a long time, and his meditation was more melancholy than usual. He was filled with pity for himself. His life was completely empty. He had no close friends. Lucile and he had kept their families severely at a distance, so as not to let them invade two lives that were sufficient unto each other.

What a difference, he thought, between what our evenings were then and my loneliness now. What a miserable thing it is to eat quickly, without appetite, and to get back to your armchair to read the evening papers, or to try to become interested in some book, then to wait hours for sleep that doesn't come.

His work had interested him passionately when he was sharing it with his wife. He would read her a sentence and wait for her reaction, which was always sensitive and intelligent. When the time came, they would go to their bedroom. How adorable she was in her nightgown, with her hair undone. Would he be forever deprived of that most intense of all pleasures?

Never again! He had to say "Never again" to love, for the idea of remarrying, even of courting another woman, seemed to him a sacrilege. How could he repeat to another woman words that he had found for this one? How could he introduce an intruder into a home that he had consecrated totally to the memory of Lucile? There were portraits of her on every table. In the closets, her clothes hung where she had put them. Mme

Auban, his mother-in-law, who lived in the provinces, had suggested after the funeral that he give them to some charity.

"Why, yes. Of course . . . You can't make any use of them, my poor boy. They'll only depress you."

The very idea had seemed to him vile and unforgivable.

An old woman walked by. She was carrying water in an aluminum container, no doubt to revive some flowers. A cloud passed over the sun. Étienne shivered and, with one last glance at the gray stone, he left. Without intending to, instead of going directly to the main path he made a turn and passed by the grave of Antoine Constant. A bouquet of iris, still fresh, lay on the stone. The stranger had come the evening before, or perhaps that morning.

Two more Thursdays, and he did not see her. The third, when he arrived, she was already there. Étienne had the impression that she glanced quickly out of the corner of her eye at the flowers he was unwrapping. They were red and yellow tulips. No, not right for mourning, he thought, not at all . . . but you would have loved them. You used to say, "We must wake up this monk's cell!" Ah, all that I want to awaken is you, your fragrant cheeks, your warm forehead. Then, glancing in turn toward the woman in black, he observed what she had brought. Like him, she had chosen bright colors that day, but hers were carnations, not tulips.

After that, he saw her every Thursday. Sometimes she came before he did, sometimes later, but she kept faithful to Thursday. "It can't be because of me," he told himself. Yet he would wait for her arrival with some faint emotion. Each took great care in his choice of flowers, and now they noticed more openly what the other was offering his ghost. A kind of competition developed between them, from which the dead profited, for the quality of the bouquets kept rising. Simultaneously they brought the first roses of the season, but the lady's were red, while Étienne's were tea roses. Then they produced some genuine fireworks with multicolored gladiolas.

He would wait until she was quite far off before he himself left, fearing that he would embarrass her if he seemed to be following her, or trying to speak to her. She evidently did not wish that, for she would walk off quickly without looking back.

One day in May, as he turned into the path of the moneyed sepulchers and was walking toward Lucile's grave, he heard a voice and saw the caretaker, whom he knew, holding by the arm the old woman he himself had noticed several times as she went by carrying a receptacle full of water. She was struggling to get free. The guard seemed to be calling the young woman in black as witness, and when he saw Étienne, he said:

"Wait, here is the gentleman, he's in this, too."

Étienne, his flowers in hand, came up to the group.

"What's going on?"

"What's going on," the guard said, "is that I've caught this woman stealing flowers. . . . Yes, Madame. She's taken yours, among others, and yours, too, sir. I've been watching her for several weeks, but this time I caught her redhanded."

The young woman seemed much upset.

"Let her go," she said. "It doesn't matter to me at all. The flowers were faded. I came today to replace them."

"Faded?" the guard said. "Not all of them. She knows how to choose in each bouquet the ones that will last a little longer. . . . Look, you can go to No. 107 in Section 8 and see how she manages for herself. She's got a bunch of violets in her jar that didn't cost her very much, I assure you. They've come from all over the place."

"What is the harm of that?" the young woman said. "She doesn't take them to sell them."

"Why did you do it?" Etienne asked the old woman.

He looked at her more closely; it was not a vulgar face. The woman lowered her eyes.

"Why do you do it?" he asked again. "You don't have any money to buy flowers. Is that it?"

She raised her head.

"Of course that's it. . . . What else could it be? What would you do, Madame, if you had your son's grave over there—and a husband so stingy that he won't give you a lily of the valley, not even a bunch of violets? . . . Eh? What would you do?"

"I would do the same as you," the woman in black said sturdily.

"All right," the guard said, "but I've got a job to do."

Lifting his cap, he let go of the old woman, and called Étienne to witness.

"After all, sir . . . You've been in the army, naturally? A duty is a duty. I'm no harder than the next man, but service—"

"Since there's no charge against her," Étienne said. "Madame and I come here every Thursday and change our flowers. If someone can find a few that are still good, so much the better!"

"All right, all right," the guard said. "If you're satisfied, everybody's satisfied."

And turning to the malefactor, he said:

"You can go."

Étienne gave the woman a little money, and the lady in black wanted to add something. Then, like every other week, Étienne went to meditate by Lucile's grave. But he had been disturbed by the incident, and he could not concentrate as intently as usual. The familiar images that he tried to evoke escaped him. When the lady in black left, he deliberately rejoined her.

"Thank you," she said. "It was so lucky that you came. A man has more authority."

"Poor woman. We understand, you and I, better than anyone her need to do something, no matter how small, for someone she's loved."

"Yes," she said. "One does it for them and for one's self."

"To keep them alive within us."

She looked at him, surprised and grateful.

"You feel about it exactly as I do. Actually, I've noticed for a long time with what—what tenderness your flowers are chosen. You loved your wife very much, M. Carlut?"

"You know my name."

"One day when you weren't there, I looked. . . . I saw that she died when she was twenty-seven. . . . So dreadful."

"Dreadful, yes. She was so perfect—beautiful, gentle, intelligent."

"It is the same with me. I lost the best husband in the world. I don't know any woman who was loved with such delicacy and protected by such kindness. . . . Almost too much. Antoine did everything for me, and his death has left me absolutely broken."

"But he died so young! . . . Yes, I admit: I, too, out of a feeling of . . . curiosity . . . and sympathy, read the inscription. I saw the dates 1891-1928. . . . What happened?"

"An auto accident. They brought him back to me one evening unconscious. He had left me that morning in perfect health and spirits. He'd just been promoted to department chief."

"He was in the Civil Service?"

"No. A large chemical-manufacturing plant. At thirty-seven, he had become third man in the top management. He would have been head of it very soon."

"You have children?"

"I haven't even that consolation."

They were approaching the main gate. The chief guard saluted them rather mockingly.

"So," he said to his assistant, when they had passed. "See those two. . . . Things are looking up, eh?"

The following Thursday, as if it were a convention henceforth agreed upon, they took the same path after their visits to the graves. Étienne talked about his life. He was senior professor in a large *lycée* in Paris; he was also writing. A magazine had just invited him to be its literary critic.

"Just before my wife died, I'd begun a play. I haven't had the courage to pick up and go on with it."

"You must," she said. "Your wife would have wanted you to."

He said, with sudden animation:

"Oh, of course! She always encouraged me to try to find my way in that direction."

Mme Constant said that she also loved the theater. She had completed quite advanced studies in literature—two *bachots* and a degree in English literature.

"But that's very good! The business world didn't bore you?"

"No, not as long as Antoine was living. To please him I used to entertain anyone. As far as my own tastes went, I'd have preferred to meet writers and painters, but with him . . ."

He asked whether she had seen the monuments to Sainte-

Beuve and Baudelaire in the cemetery. She didn't know them, and he offered to show them to her. She found them hideous.

"No," he said, "it's a matter of period."

This detour had prolonged their walk and, talking together with great animation, they had not noticed that the sky was darkening and did not even hear the distant rumbling of a storm. As they came up to the main gate, big drops of rain were falling.

"I'm going to take a cab," she said. "There's a stand a little farther on."

"I will, too. This isn't a rain, it's a cloudburst."

They walked on quickly, and as their clothing became soaked, they ran. At the taxi stand there was one cab.

"Get in quickly," he said.

"And you?"

"I'll wait. There'll be another one along."

"In this weather? That's not so sure. Can't I drop you on the way?"

"Where are you going?"

"Home," she said. "Avenue Mozart."

"That's a happy coincidence. I live just beyond, Rue de la Pompe. I'll drop you."

There followed a little skirmish of generosity, then she surrendered and gave him her address. When they realized they were together in a cab, both people felt suddenly timid. Each drew into his corner and neither spoke. He was remembering an evening when he had accompanied a woman colleague home on foot and Lucile had met them. She had been angry. "If I hadn't seen you, would you have told me?"

He had answered, "Of course. She wasn't feeling well and had taken my arm. I couldn't just leave her. . . . Anyhow, she's twenty years older than you."

"What does that prove? She is still very attractive."

"What would you say," he was silently asking Lucile as the taxi went by the Montparnasse station, "what would you say if you saw me shut up in a cab with a young, beautiful woman?" Who is alive, he thought to himself. . . . "I feel as if you were here with me, as if your breasts were swelling under that black sweater. Oh, I'm ashamed to feel ready to come back to life! I need you so. . . ." He sighed. The woman in black looked at him with a sad, understanding air.

"You are unhappy," she said. *"We* are unhappy."

"You live alone?"

"Yes. Well, with an old servant, Amélie. . . . Oh, she is perfect. She brought Antoine up. She does everything about the house. And you?"

"I am alone, too. A maid comes in mornings. She goes at five, but she leaves me a cold supper."

He spoke with some difficulty, unable to confess his real thoughts or the emotion aroused in him by the presence, so close, of this female body. The sun had come out and the gilded Invalides dome was sparkling.

"How beautiful it is now!" he said. "Do you ever feel what I feel—a kind of black bitterness because the world is still beautiful, while—"

She said passionately:

"I could never have put it in words, but I feel it."

He asked if she came by taxi every week.

"Yes, on account of the flowers. When my husband was living, we had a car, but only he drove."

"I take a taxi, too, for the same reason. The flowers . . ."

He hesitated a long time, then said in the same low, timid voice:

"Would . . . well . . . It may seem odd to you, but since we make the same trip, and on the same day, couldn't we share a taxi? I would come to fetch you."

"That's very kind of you. But I shouldn't want Amélie . . . Heaven only knows what she would think if she saw me leaving with you."

"Let's do it the other way. Take a taxi at your house and pass by to pick me up. I'll wait out in front of the house."

"That would be better. . . . But *they*—do you think they would approve?"

"Why not? We are going to fulfill the same duty of respect and love."

"Let me think about it. In any case, I won't agree to let you pay for the taxi."

"That's not a problem. We'll share the fare, if you like."

"I'll see," she said. "Here is my house."

She took off a glove and held out a hand with long, very white fingers, on one of which she wore a ring.

The following Thursday, they came to the cemetery each by himself, but, without any mention of it, on leaving they went together to the taxi stand and took the same cab. On the way, she said, "I've thought about your very kind offer. I think I can accept. It's true that it's silly to pay for two cabs every week. And it does me good to be with you. Next week I'll come by to pick you up."

It became a rite. She would arrive at Rue de la Pompe, holding her flowers in her lap; he would be waiting, his sheaf of flowers in his arms. The taxi would stop. Étienne would get in. They had decided not to go as far as the cemetery gate, so that the caretaker would not see them arrive together. They used to get out before that corner, and from there on proceed at a discreet distance from each other, after saying, with an air of complicity that concealed the hint of a smile, "Until later."

Since they made so many trips together, they began to talk of everything. Flowers had been one of their first subjects of conversation. They both loved summer flowers and bouquets of wild flowers—bluebottles mixed with wild oat, for example. Now they composed their bouquets for the poor dead, no doubt, but also for each other.

Étienne, whose duties as a critic led him to read widely, guided the young woman's reading and lent her books. When she returned them, he was struck by the soundness of her judgments. She was of a more serious turn of mind than Lucile. The instant this thought occurred to him, he was full of self-reproach.

By mutual agreement, they scarcely left Paris over the summer, except for visits of a few days to their families in the provinces. The first anniversary of Lucile's death was to be observed in July. He was touched to see, modestly seated in the last row in the church, Gabrielle Constant. For now he knew the first name of the lady in black.

"I don't like it," she'd said to him, "but it's a family name."

In August, since the weather was very hot, she permitted herself to wear mourning with a touch of white.

"Antoine didn't like to see me in black," she said, by way of explanation and excuse.

One evening, he had invited her to have dinner with him out of doors, not far from town. Sitting at a small table in the shadows, they had talked freely and openly.

"Antoine loved to dine like this in the Bois, and it's true, it is delightful. . . . Paris and forest in one . . . Often he would come home from the office and say, 'Come, we're going to the Bois!' He was a wonderful husband."

"That must not have been too hard, with a woman like you."

"Why?"

"You have everything—beauty, intelligence, character—"

"Don't go too far. You don't know me. Sometimes I made terrible scenes for poor Antoine."

"Really? I can scarcely see you in that role."

"Oh, yes . . . Poor Antoine. He was desperately, unhealthily jealous. And because I was sure of my own fidelity, I sometimes played with fire. My husband would get angry, and I would answer back. . . . I'm sorry for all the times I irritated him. But often it was his fault."

Suddenly, struck with remorse, she looked at Étienne with terror, pleading, and love.

"My God, what have I just said to you! Please forget it. The evening is too beautiful; it makes one slip into confidences, even dangerous ones. On an evening like this," she added despairingly, "I need so to feel him here, near me. . . ."

In the shadows, she turned away and brushed the tears from her eyes.

"After all, I am young, very young, and my life is finished. . . . I am the most unhappy woman in the world."

He laid his hand on hers.

"No," he said, "it isn't true that everything is finished for you. Life isn't like that. . . . The seasons return every year, each with its own flowers. It isn't healthy or wise to give one's self up to an obsession with the past. That deflects memories from the role they should play in our lives. . . . Yes, yes. They are meant to make us live, not to prevent us from living, to give us courage, not to take it from us. Because you and I have each been happily married, we know that a harmonious marriage is possible. . . . Don't you believe that?"

She did not withdraw her hand. She looked at him questioningly through her tears, then shook her head.

"No, I don't believe it. The sad thing is not sorrow itself but the possibility that one could stop being sad. Only I have sworn to be faithful."

"I, too," he said, almost fiercely. "The pain is still the pain of love."

The maître d'hôtel came up for them to choose dessert. She ordered sugared strawberries, and guided the conversation toward more neutral subjects.

The next day she came to pick him up, as usual, to go to the cemetery. They were both ill at ease and constrained during the drive. The hoarse-voiced, grumbling driver never stopped complaining about pedestrians or the police or the weather. Their solitary meditations before the two graves were longer than other weeks. As they were leaving the path, they passed a pile of broken stones. There were shafts of columns, bits of inscriptions: "ETERNAL REG— . . . TO MY DEAR WI— . . ." She stopped.

"Étienne," she said. It was the first time she had called him by his first name. "I find that so sad. These dead who have no one anymore, no one who cherishes their memory. They die a second death."

He took her arm, and she pressed against him.

When they were in the taxi on the way back, they spoke of a book he had promised to lend her, and he suggested stopping at his house to get it. For the first time since she had known him, she went to his apartment. Photographs of Lucile were on all the tables, walls, and on the desk.

"Do you feel how this dead house returns to life the moment you come into it?" he said.

She sensed that he was going to ask her to marry him, and thought that she would not want it to happen in a room dedicated to the memory of another woman.

"What are you doing this evening?" she asked.

"I've no plans. Would you like to have dinner together?"

She nodded yes, held out her hand, which he kissed, and she fled.

Alone in the street, she wandered about for a while before going to her own house. Her head was whirling, but she was happy and astounded that so much appetite for life was flowing back into her.

Surely, she thought, Antoine would not have wanted me to give up love forever at my age. . . . He would have advised me to remarry. And he, if I had died . . .

That was all true, but she had adopted an attitude, an inflexible mourning, that would make it difficult, after so short a widowhood, to announce to friends and family a quite contrary decision. And what would Amélie say? Undoubtedly she would be full of reproaches. But did one live for others? It would have to be a very simple, quiet wedding, kept to the indispensable ceremonies. She envisioned the dress she would wear that day—gray, with a white, stand-up collar, and a touch of white at the waist.

The Will

THE CHÂTEAU DE CHARDEUIL having been bought by an industrialist obliged by illness and advancing age to seek a rural retreat, all Périgord was soon talking of nothing but the munificence and taste with which this house, abandoned for a century by the Marquises of Chardeuil, had been restored. Above all, the gardens, people said, were admirable. A landscape architect had come from Paris and had dammed the valley of the Loue to create an artificial lake and make of Chardeuil a second Versailles.

Beautiful gardens are rare in this poor and rustic province where most château owners follow the example of the Saviniacs, who converted their park into a vegetable garden. The flower beds of Chardeuil aroused intense curiosity as far as Brive, and beyond to Périgueux and even as far as Bordeaux. However, when, after a year-long restoration, the new owners came to live in the area, callers were less numerous than one could have expected. The Périgordian does not welcome newcomers indiscriminately, and no one knew who this Mme Bernin was.

She appeared to be no more than thirty-five years old, whereas her husband was at least sixty-five. She was quite pretty, and even in her present solitude changed her costume three times a day. This did not seem natural, and at first the châteaux thought that she must be not the wife of Bernin but his mistress. When Mme de La Guichardie, the social arbiter of the environs, who knew her Paris thoroughly although she had lived in the provinces since the war, affirmed that Mme Bernin was indeed Mme Bernin and that she came from a modest but self-respecting middle-class family, the châteaux accepted this version, for on such a subject no one would have dared contradict a powerful and well-informed woman. However, many families continued privately to profess a heretical doctrine, holding that if Mme Bernin was really Mme Bernin, she was nonetheless merely a mistress married late in the day.

Gaston and Valentine Romilly, the Bernins' nearest neighbors, since one can see the towers of Chardeuil from the Preyssac hill, considered that they had less right than other people to appear stiff, and since the Bernins had left cards at Preyssac, and since Mme de La Guichardie had given them every license to be polite, they decided to return the call.

They were the more cordially received for being among the first visitors. Not only did the new owners keep them until teatime but they offered to show the Romillys the house, the gardens, and the outbuildings. Gaston and Valentine Romilly sensed that these two poor people were beginning to suffer from possessing such perfection without being able to exhibit it.

Bernin preserved from his days of ruling over a business a somewhat authoritarian tone and the habit of delivering himself of trenchant opinions on the subjects he knew least about, but he seemed a good sort. Valentine was touched by the tenderness he showed his wife, who was a little blond woman, plump and gentle and lighthearted. However, during a visit to the second floor, where Mme Romilly praised the amazing transformation of the house in so short a time, admired the bathrooms, which were recessed in the thick old walls, and the elevators installed in the towers, she was shocked to hear Mme Bernin reply:

"Yes, Adolphe wanted everything to be perfect. For the moment, of course, Chardeuil is only a country house for us, but Adolphe knows that I intend to live here after he dies—as late as possible, naturally—and he wants me to be as comfortable here as in a house in the city. . . . You know, perhaps, that he has several children from a previous marriage? So he has taken his precautions. Chardeuil has been put in my name and belongs entirely to me."

In a meadow next to the house, some old farm buildings had been converted into stables. Gaston admired the handsome horses, the perfect condition of the harnesses, and the impeccable stable boys.

"Horses are my greatest pleasure," Mme Bernin said animatedly. "Papa did his military service in the dragoons, and he had us children in the saddle while we were still in the cradle.

"Obviously," she went on, "it will be a great expense to maintain this stable, but Adolphe has thought about that. In his will, he has provided for a special foundation that will undertake to improve breeding practices here at Chardeuil. It will be entirely nonprofit—won't it, Adolphe—so that on this score, you see, I won't have to pay any taxes."

The gardens were not yet finished, but already one could discern the general plan of the flower beds. Beautiful statuary marked the points toward which the architect wished to direct the eye. In the middle of a long, rectangular pool, some workmen were setting up romantic columns on an artificial island of reinforced concrete. The visitors and their hosts strolled along a wide path bordered by chestnut trees. This opened onto a group of little houses, built in the style of the Périgord farmhouses and roofed with old tiles.

"I never knew there was a village here," Valentine said.

"It's not a village," Mme Bernin said, laughing. "These are the servants' quarters. It was Adolphe's idea to have them built this way, like separate houses. And you'll see how ingenious it is for the future, as far as I am concerned. We have some servants who are devoted married couples whom I intend to keep on, even when I am alone. Well, Adolphe will bequeath each couple the house it is occupying, with a clause annulling the bequest if they leave my service. In this way, not only are they bound to me but they are partially paid without my having to spend a sou. It's a marvelous protection for me. And tax exempt, naturally. And his children can't say a thing."

"Do you think so, Madame? Is it legal?" Gaston Romilly asked.

"Oh, Monsieur, you don't know Adolphe. He and his lawyer spent hours looking for the right formula. You can't imagine how thoughtful he is, for all his bearish manners. Isn't that so, Adolphe?"

She slipped her arm under the old man's, and he grunted tenderly. It was a long walk, for the visitors were spared neither the farm nor the model dairy nor the hen house built for rare breeds, where hundreds of wonderfully white chickens were clucking. When the Romillys were finally alone in their car, Valentine spoke up.

"Well, what do you think of them?"

"I like Bernin," Gaston said. "He's brusque and he thinks too well of himself, but I think he's a genuinely good man. . . . She's a little strange."

"Strange?" Valentine said. "I think she's terrifying. The will here, the will there . . . 'When I am alone . . .' 'As late as possible, naturally . . .' All this talk in front of the poor man about what will happen when he dies! Really, it was painful. I didn't know what to say."

They sat for some time without speaking, while the car passed by the mist-enfolded meadows and poplars in the valley. Gaston, who was driving, watched the road carefully, for groups of children were walking home from school. Finally he said:

"All the same . . . it's quite reasonable, his taking all these precautions so that his wife can be perfectly secure after his death. As I listened to him, I was thinking of us. I've been wrong not to make a will. I'm going to attend to it right away."

"What an idea, dear! It sends chills down my spine. And in the first place, I'm going to die first."

"Why? You know nothing about it. You're younger than I am. You have nothing wrong with you physically, whereas I—"

"Be still! You are a hypochondriac. You're in wonderful health, and furthermore, if you died I wouldn't want to survive you. What would my life be without you? I'd kill myself."

"How can you talk such foolishness, Valentine? That's absurd. You know very well people don't die of grief, no matter how painful it is. And then, you don't have only me in the world. There's Colette and her husband, and the grandchildren."

"Colette has made her own life. She doesn't need us anymore."

"Exactly. That's one reason for my taking some steps to protect you."

Again they were silent, for the car was passing through a denser fog bank. Then Valentine went on in a very low voice:

"It is true that if misfortune willed it that I should survive you by a few months, I would be more at ease in my mind if I had—oh, not a will. That would seem like a bad omen to me. No . . . Just a simple paper specifying that Preyssac—the house and the land—should remain in my possession until my death. Our son-in-law is a very nice boy, but he's a Saviniac. He takes after his father. He loves land. He'd be quite capable of wanting to add to his own at my expense, and packing me off to live in some little house, who knows where. . . . That would make me very unhappy."

"Things must be arranged so that that's impossible," Gaston said, a trifle somberly. "I'm quite ready to sign any papers you want, and even to leave you Preyssac in a will. . . . Only, is it legal? I mean, isn't the value of Preyssac greater than what your share should be?"

"A little, but that's easily adjusted," Valentine said, "whenever you want to."

"What do you mean?" he said. "Have you already asked Maître Passaga about this?"

"Oh, just by chance," Valentine said.

The Campaign

"Chief, I'm sorry to disturb you, but—"

"No one, I said."

"I know, sir, it's the time for your editorial. But this is so serious. . . . Havas just telephoned us that Brignac is dead."

"Brignac! . . . My God! How? Suicide?"

"No, Chief, not at all—"

"Then what? Murdered? Speak up, man!"

"Nothing like that, Chief . . . A natural death, almost instantaneous . . . After lunch, he left his house as usual to go to the Ministry. When he got to the corner of Rue de Varenne, he staggered, and the newspaper woman there saw him fall to the sidewalk. A chauffeur who was driving by picked him up and took him to the police station. It was all over."

"Cause of death?"

"It seems he had an old heart condition that had become very much aggravated in the last six months. It would have been strange if it hadn't—"

"Yes . . . So there's no way to present this as a suspicious death?"

"None at all, Chief. The police have apparently been extremely cautious. The Chief of Police himself had the body examined by three doctors. Furthermore, last week Brignac had gone to see Debrie for a checkup, and the doctor had warned the family there was trouble in the offing. And what's more, the son is insisting on an autopsy. Everything's in order—more than in order!"

"Well, well . . . That's the end of that campaign. Too bad. But we'll find something else. . . . It was wearing a little thin, after all. Things could be worse."

"So what are we going to do, Chief? Headline on page one?"

"Of course. What else is there this evening?"

"The Austrian business . . . Earthquake in Japan."

"Hmm. Nothing, in other words . . . So, a big headline—three columns—'BRIGNAC DEAD' . . . No 'Monsieur' and no first name. Photo on page one. Make a note of this—not the good ones. Use the one we dug up when the story broke, the one where he looks like a bandit. And then the facts. Have enough details for three columns?"

"Oh, sure, Chief. And anyhow, it's easy to blow up an obit. But after all, Brignac was President of the Council twice, Minister six times, and then, to round it out, we've got this lurid death. . . . We're not short of material."

"Of course not. But check over the copy yourself. What we want is straight facts, no comment. . . . And remember that French readers are very punctilious about good form when it comes to death. Attacks from us that would have delighted them yesterday we would be criticized for today. . . . 'Unseemly attitude' . . . I know all about that one."

"What if we did just the opposite, Chief? . . . 'We bow before this premature grave. . . . Death puts an end to all polemic. . . . The right to judge Brignac belongs to Him who . . .' All this said much better, of course. No platitudes. But something in this tone?"

"Are you crazy, boy? . . . What are you talking about? For one year I have been waging the most violent campaign in the history of modern journalism against this man. I pulled him down, I destroyed him! I set the whole of France yapping at his heels. I saw to it that he was booed out of his own constituency. I had the doors of every decent hotel in the country closed to him. And with this campaign, in the space of six months I doubled the circulation of a paper that was half dead when I took it over. And now you want me to reverse myself?"

"It isn't a question of that."

"Listen to me. What is it a question of, if not of that? Or are you wanting me to make honorable amends to Brignac on the pretext that his mitral valve or his aorta has supplied him with an out? Well, that's a great idea you've got there. What kind of credit would we be left with if we were to back down like that? I repeat—and this is an order—the facts, the facts as they come in over the agency wires. And if you want, send one of the younger fellows to interview the witnesses. Bertrand could do you a good piece on the newspaper woman, if she's willing to talk. . . . But no one, understand, no one is to go to the Brignac house. There'll be too many people signing the callers' book with their condolences, and I don't want to have to give any lists. . . . Especially since all our fine associates, in the face of this, are going to desert us. . . . Oh, I know them. So, a simple, very factual news story, and that's all. Understand?"

"Yes. That is—"

"What?"

"Nothing. I understand."

"So—get going!"

"Right. I'm off. . . . You really don't want anything more?"

"Here we go again! What's the matter with you, boy? You look all upset, you're sulking. . . . Is it this same business? Or is there something you haven't told me?"

"I've told you everything, everything I know. Which isn't much. But it's true, Chief, I am—I don't know—I'm more than upset. Brignac died of a heart ailment, and it's our campaign for sure—or at least the results of that campaign—that helped to hasten his death. Don't you think so?"

"That's very possible. No one will ever be certain. In any case, to me that is something that couldn't matter less."

"It would be all the same to me, too, I guess, if I were sure Brignac was guilty. But that's what I'm not sure of, I'm not sure of it at all. I told you from the very first day, Chief, that I didn't like this business. When I came back from down there, after my first trip to check into things, at the very beginning of this whole business I remember pointing out to you how strange the attitude of the local police was, and how they were obviously hostile to Brignac. I pointed all that out in my first report. You didn't let it go through."

"Why should I? Brignac was a political opponent, the most dangerous of them all. It wasn't up to us to suggest arguments in his favor when chance was handing us the means to get rid of him."

"Maybe not . . . But it wasn't up to us, either, to accuse him when the courts, in spite of all our pressure, refused to— Look, Chief, let's suppose for a minute that Brignac was completely in the clear and that we killed him."

"Don't use big words to talk about little things. We did *not* kill him. We have killed nobody. We have done our job, politically, for our own side. He did the same for his all his life."

"Excuse me, Chief, but the words I'm using are the right words. We have killed him. And not only killed but tortured and persecuted him, until his heart gave way. I don't know if our role in this business isn't much dirtier than his."

"What little fairy tale is this you're telling me? Now, that's about enough, young man! If any other one of my editors had said such things to me, I'd have shown him the door long before this—and invited him to find a job somewhere else. But I value you; we've built this paper up together. But just understand this: I have nothing to be ashamed of in this affair. Quite the opposite. I've done my job as best I could. It's not our responsibility to correct injustices. That's up to the courts. Our job is to satisfy the wishes of a certain public that is *our* public. Now, this public *wanted* Brignac to be guilty."

"They wanted it because we told them it was so."

"Not only because we said it was so but for much deeper reasons . . . Because Brignac was the symbol of forces that we hate—that it is our duty to hate. And now it is no longer the newspaperman but the politician who is talking to you. . . . One year ago, we were heading toward an intolerable election. We knew that the opposition, once it got in power, was determined never to give it up. So it was a question of preventing them, whatever the cost, from taking over. The Brignac affair will prove to be for us, and for our friends, our salvation. It decided a great many decent people who until then had been hesitating, who were on the fence. Brignac's dead, but maybe we'll be indebted to him for a miraculous restoration of public order. . . . And what is one man? A military leader—hasn't he got to sacrifice millions of lives to ensure victory? . . . You shake your head. You don't believe that?"

"No, Chief, a thousand times no. How can you compare war to political battles that may be hot and hard but that, all the same, are between citizens of the same country? Between people who may find tomorrow that they have to unite to defend that country? . . . And furthermore, how can I admit that lies— No, no, between you and me there's no place for hypocrisy. We know they were lies—"

"Not at all. Hypotheses . . ."

"An hypothesis that you give out as true is a lie. Well, why suppose that these lies will bring us victory better than truth would have done, or sincerity or loyalty? The Brignac affair, you say, rallied decent people to our side. Do you believe we'll be able to hold them when they find out what the Brignac affair really was? And find out they will. Everything comes out, eventually. I believe that the surest way of rallying people to our support is through honesty. . . . I'm sorry, Chief, to be so emotional about this. . . . But I have the feeling that the future of our ideas—perhaps even of the country—depends on the position we take today. I believe that it's a mistake, that it's foolish to stir up the kind of fight in which the truth is all on the other side. Because one day that truth will win out. . . . Every political defeat in history has come about for that reason. We belong, you and I, to the same party—"

"But not to the same school of thought."

"Right. And the strange thing is, Chief, that it's you, the man—the man of experience who—"

"You can say 'the old man.' Where we stand, niceties aren't—"

"Well, that you, the mature man, believe in violence, while I, who am younger, want something else. . . . Something worthier . . . A reconciliation between Frenchman and Frenchman, some great work that can be done together—"

"Then you are of the opinion that our opponents wage their campaigns in good faith, that one could stand up and answer them with arguments in good faith?"

"God, no, Chief! Our opponents are as guilty—they're guiltier than we are. But I do believe that we won't defeat them by trying to outdo them in bad faith. Nor will we win them over that way. I believe that violence 'doesn't pay.' "

"That's quite remarkable. In postwar Europe violence doesn't pay! Have you looked, by any chance, at what this Europe really is? Violence didn't work for Lenin? Violence didn't make an unknown Hitler into Chancellor of the German Reich?"

"Hitler and Lenin, to conquer the masses, had something more than personal attacks against individuals. They had an ideology—whether true or false doesn't matter for the moment. . . . They were offering an ideal, they pointed to some goal, they offered some hope. . . . But our party people have been simpleminded enough to believe that we'd seduce the people by slandering their leaders."

"And what leaders!"

"That's not the point! Even if you operate on the basis of the most cynical realism, can you imagine a clumsier tactic! When the rank and file was beginning to get sick and tired of these men, our attacks had one immediate effect, which was to regroup their troops around them."

"I say again, the attacks of Lenin and of Hitler did not result in rallying the Russians around Kerenski or the Germans around Brüning."

"Russia and Germany aren't France, Chief. You've argued that point yourself in your articles, and with far more skill than I have. . . . France is a country whose unity is constantly threatened. Traditionally, the country is divided and it must take care not to split itself in two. Now, for ten years—"

"I do believe, may God forgive me, that you are about to deliver a lecture on the political-party system in France! . . . Thanks. Now, come on, this is enough. I have a piece to write, you have an order to carry out. . . . And tomorrow you will hand over the management of the news desk to Bertrand. I'm sorry to have to let you go, boy. Sometimes I'd dreamed I would leave this paper to you. . . . Yes, that's the truth. I never spoke to you about it, but I thought about it often. . . . Well, that's the end of that. You know I never fight by retreating. You'll give in or you'll leave."

"I'll leave tomorrow, Chief—or at the end of the month. Let me know which you'd rather. . . . And I should like you to know what friendship I feel for you, how grateful I am. . . . You've taught me this job. . . . You've treated me like a son."

"Brutus said that, I believe?"

"I'm not making speeches. I have had and I always will have a great affection for you. . . . That's all."

"I believe you mean it. And in twenty years, you'll concede that I've been right. But I won't be here to know that."

"Good night, Chief."

"Good night, boy. . . . Tell Vincent I don't want to see anyone. And it's understood—right? Three columns on page one: 'BRIGNAC DEAD.' "

The Life of Man

Fragments from a history of the world published by the University of Timbuktu in 1992

Chapter CXVII

1954—Crises on Earth
1959—Publication of the Uranian edition of *The Life of Man*
1982—First Earth edition

LATE IN 1970, as soon as friendly relations had been established between Earth and the majority of the large planets, Earth scientists were eager to compare their scientific principles and hypotheses with those of their colleagues in other worlds. The comparison often proved to be difficult, because, as we know, the eminent physicists of Venus, Jupiter, and Mars are not sensitive to light or to sound, and live in an environment of radiations of which we were until recently quite ignorant. However, the theory of sensorial equivalents made rapid progress and today, in 1992, it may be said that we are able to translate into Earth language all the other tongues of the solar system, with the exception of Saturnian.

One of the most interesting developments in our period has been the discovery of works written about us Earth dwellers by the scholars of foreign planets. Men were far from imagining that over millions of years they had been observed, with the aid of instruments far more powerful than their own, by the natural scientists of Mars, Venus, and even Uranus. Earth science was very much behind that of neighboring stars, and since our sensory organs are unreceptive to the radiations utilized by these observers, we could not know that in even the most private moments of our life we were at times within the range of a celestial ultramicroscope.

Any specialist can now consult these works in the Library of the League of Planets, and any young man who wishes to devote himself to a career in science must be urged to read them —first, for their great intrinsic interest, and also because of the feeling of humility they cannot fail to evoke. When one realizes what incredible errors of interpretation were committed by beings so intelligent and so marvelously armed for research, one cannot help but review certain of our own human interpretations and ask whether we have not observed animals and plants as the Martians once observed us.

One case in particular has seemed to merit the most careful study. It is that of the Uranian scholar A.E. 17, who, in 1959, published *The Life of Man*.[1] Up until the war, his was considered the authoritative book on the subject by Uranians, as well as by the Venusians and Martians, who had translated it. It is readily accessible to us, since the Uranians, alone among our coplanetarians, are endowed, like us, with the sense of sight, which makes their vocabulary very close to our own. Fur-

---

[1] The original Uranian edition is dated 1959; the first Earth edition appeared in 1982.

thermore, the experiments performed and here reported on were of such a nature that they threw Earth into turmoil for some six months, so that we find parallel Earth accounts in the newspapers and memoirs of the period.

Here we propose (1) to describe briefly several verified incidents that occurred on our planet in 1954; and (2) to show how the famous A.E. 17 interpreted his related experiments.

The Mysterious Spring

Starting in March, 1954, in the Northern Hemisphere, many observers pointed to unusual atmospheric conditions. Although the prevailing weather was fine and normally cool, storms of great violence were occurring suddenly in narrowly delimited zones. Ship captains and airplane pilots were reporting to the Central Bureau of Meteorology that their compasses were perturbed for seconds at a time for no conceivable reason. At several places, something like the shadow of a vast cloud was seen to pass over the ground, although the sky was clear and no cloud was visible. The papers published interviews with leading meteorologists, who explained that they had foreseen the phenomenon, that it was caused by sun spots, and that it would stop with the equinoctial tides. But when the equinox came, it brought with it still stranger events.

The So-called Hyde Park Incidents

On the third Sunday of April, 1954, while an audience of men and women crowded into the path leading to the Marble Arch to listen to the open-air orators, they suddenly saw pass over them the shadow of an invisible obstacle mysteriously placed between the Earth and the Sun. A few moments later, from the gate to as far as three or four hundred yards inside the park, the ground was suddenly lifted, trees were uprooted, people were knocked over and even buried, while those who were on the periphery of the upheaval saw with stupefaction that a crater at least three hundred feet deep had been hollowed out, and that the soil from this had been heaped to one side to form a hill of comparable height.

"It all happened," a policeman testified the next day before the coroner, "as if a giant had taken his shovel and scooped up a piece of the park. That's exactly what it was like, the scoop of a shovel, because one side of the crater was straight and smooth, while the side of the new hill was crumbly clods of earth, with heads and bodies cut in half sticking out of it."

More than three hundred Sunday strollers had been buried alive. Those who had been covered by a relatively light layer of earth fought their way free with great difficulty. Some were deranged by shock, and rushed down the steep slope of the new hill, uttering horrible screams. At the top of the hillock, on-lookers saw the figure of one of the Salvation Army's chaplains rear into view; it was Captain R. R. Ward, who, with amazing presence of mind, began to shout, as he shook the dirt from his hair and clothing:

"I told you so, brethren! Because you have sacrificed to false gods, the Lord is angry with His people and the hand of the Lord now lies heavy upon you. . . ."

The inexplicable event did, in fact, bear such strong resemblance to various divine punishments, as these are described in the Bible, that several skeptics among those present were converted on the spot and began a life of religious observance that they have continued ever since.

The incident provided an opportunity for the public to appreciate the caliber of the London police. Three policemen were among the victims, but a dozen others rushed to the scene and with great courage set about clearing the site of the disaster. A phone call was placed immediately to the House Guards and to the Fire Department; the Superintendent of Police, Clarkwell, took charge of the rescue squads, and in less than four hours Hyde Park had resumed its normal aspect. Unfortunately, the casualties numbered two hundred victims.

Scientists offered widely differing explanations for the catastrophe. The earthquake hypothesis—the only rational one, unless one wished to invoke a supernatural cause—seemed scarcely plausible. No seismograph had registered any tremors. The public, however, was in general satisfied to learn that it was an earthquake, although one of a very special kind, to which the seismologists gave the name "vertical monoform seism."

The House on Avenue Victor-Hugo

The Hyde Park incident was followed by a rather large number of similar occurrences. These attracted much less public notice, because they did not involve the loss of human life, but at different points on our planet strange hills were seen to form, always with the same rapidity and always flanked by a cleanly scooped-out chasm. In certain localities these hills still exist; we may mention in particular those at Ayen, in Périgord, France; at Rosznov, in Walachia, Romania; and at Itapura, in Brazil.

But the mysterious Spade that seemed to be operating on open ground was now to attack human habitations. On April 24th, around midnight, a strange noise, which was compared by some witnesses to that of a whistling knife blade, and by others to the sound of a very thin, powerful steam jet, startled passers-by in the section of Paris that is bordered, roughly, by the Arc de Triomphe, the Avenue de la Grande Armée, Avenue Marceau, and Avenue Henri-Martin.

People who happened to be opposite the building at No. 60, Avenue Victor-Hugo, saw an enormous, slanting fissure open in the façade; the building was rocked by two or three shocks, and suddenly the whole mansarded top floor, where the servant quarters were located, seemed to crumble as if under tremendous pressure. Terrified tenants appeared at windows and on balconies. Fortunately, the building, although it was literally cut in half, did not collapse. Halfway up the inner stairway, rescuers came upon the fissure produced by the invisible instrument. It looked exactly as if a giant blade had cut through the carpeting, floor, and iron balustrade, following a rectilinear path. Everything along its way—furniture, rugs, paintings, books—had been neatly cut in two, with one clean stroke. The servant quarters were empty, because it was dinnertime. A young girl lying in bed on the fourth floor had seen her bed cut in two obliquely; the blow had passed right beside her. She had felt no pain, only a shock such as would come from a faint electrical charge.

Once again, numerous explanations were offered. The term "seism" reappeared. Some papers accused the architect and owner of the house of having used poor material in construction. A Communist deputy demanded an investigation. The government promised to take measures to prevent the reoccurrence of such accidents, and called for a vote of confidence, which was passed by a simple raising of hands.

The Sky Riders

Like the incident in Hyde Park, the one on Avenue Victor-Hugo was followed by several others quite similar in kind, which we will not describe but which, it now seems to us in retrospect, should have indicated to observant minds that a hidden will was at work in pursuit of a definite plan. In numerous countries, houses both small and large were sectioned by some invisible power. Several small country cottages—one in Massachusetts, one in Denmark, one in Spain—were lifted from the ground, dropped, and crushed, their occupants with them. In New York City, an office building on Madison Avenue was cut in two. Some fifty men and women were killed in these incidents, but because they occurred in different countries and each individual case involved only a few victims, and, above all, because no one could offer any intelligible explanation for them, people talked about them as little as possible.

This did not hold true for the series of incidents that followed, and that kept the whole planet in a state of extreme agitation during the months of May and June, 1954. The first victim was a young Negro woman of Hartford, Connecticut.

She was coming out of her employer's house when a postman, the only witness to the accident, saw her suddenly lifted shrieking into the air. She rose to a height of three hundred feet, fell to the ground, and was crushed. The postman reported seeing no flying machine of any kind above her.

The second sky rider was a customs officer in Calais, who was also seen to rise vertically in the air, and then move rapidly in the direction of the English coast. He was found a few minutes later on the Dover cliffs, dead but without visible injury. From his appearance, one would have said that he had been deposited gently on the ground; his skin had the bluish tinge of a hanged man.

Thereupon followed the period of the so-called "happy-ending flights." The first of the "fliers" to end his voyage alive was an elderly beggar seized by an invisible hand as he was reaching for a handout on the square of Notre Dame and set down ten minutes later in the middle of Piccadilly Circus at the feet of a consternated bobby. He had suffered no ill effects, and had the impression that he had traveled in a closed cabin where neither light nor air entered. The witnesses of his takeoff had observed that he became invisible the moment he had been lifted from the ground.

These "flights" continued for several weeks. As soon as they were recognized to be relatively harmless, they were found rather funny. The greatest fantasy seemed to guide the choice of the invisible hand. Once it was a little girl from Denver, Colorado, who was recovered on the steppes of eastern Russia; another time, a dentist from Saragossa was recovered in Stockholm. The flight that aroused the widest comment was the experience of the venerable President of the French Senate, M. Marc Lefaut, who was picked up in the Luxembourg Gardens and set down on the banks of Lake Ontario. He took advantage of this fact to make a tour of Canada, and on his return to France was given a triumphant welcome at the Bois de Boulogne station; it is likely that this involuntary publicity contributed greatly toward assuring his election as President of the Republic in 1956.

It was observed that when they "landed," the "fliers" were besmeared with a reddish liquid that stained their clothing; the cause of this was never discovered. It was the only real inconvenience in these otherwise inoffensive adventures. The incidents stopped after about two months, and were followed by a new and even stranger series that opened with the so-called "two-family" episode.

The Two-Family Episode

The first of the two famous families was a young French couple living in a little house in Neuilly, just outside the gates of Paris. The husband, Jacques Martin, was a professor at the Lycée Pasteur, a university athlete, scholar, and author of a remarkable critical study of Paul Morand. The couple had four children. On July 3rd, toward midnight, Mme Jacques Martin had just fallen asleep when she heard the steam-whistling that we have already described; she felt a slight shock, and had the sensation of rising into the air at great speed. Opening her eyes, she was stupefied to see pale moonlight flooding the room, one whole wall of which had disappeared. She realized that she herself was lying near the edge of a bed that had been cut in half, and that on her left, where a few seconds before her husband had been lying, there was a bottomless void above which the stars were shining. She was terrified; she threw herself toward the still solid side of the bed and was astounded—as well as reassured—to confirm that it was not toppling over, although it was standing on only two feet. Mme Martin sensed that she was no longer climbing but was being propelled forward at high speed; then she felt her heart skip, rather the way this may happen in a too fast elevator, and she realized that she was losing altitude. She supposed that her fall was going to end in a crash, and closed her eyes in anticipation of the fatal landing. However, contact with the earth was accomplished with elastic gentleness. When Mme Martin looked about her, she could see nothing. The room was pitch dark. What happened next follows in her own words:

> The chasm seemed to have closed over. I called to my husband. I thought I'd been having a nightmare. I was terribly upset and wanted to tell him about it. I reached out and I felt a man's arm, and then I heard an unfamiliar, resonant voice saying in English:
> "Oh, darling, you startled me."
> I shrank back and reached for the light, but I couldn't find the switch.
> "What's wrong?" the strange voice asked.

He turned on the light. We both let out a cry. Beside me I saw a young Englishman, with a short, straight nose, slightly myopic, and still half asleep; he was wearing blue pajamas. Down the middle of the bed there was a slit; the bed clothing, bolster, and mattress had been cut in two. There was a difference of five to ten centimeters in height between the two parts of the bed.

As soon as he had collected his wits, my extemporaneous bed companion behaved, in these difficult circumstances, in a way that gave me great respect for the British people. After the briefest and certainly most excusable moment of bewilderment, he was as correct and as urbane as if we had met in someone's living room. I speak English, so I told him my name, and he told me his—John Graham. The place where we were, he said, was Richmond. Looking around, I saw that one whole half of my bedroom had followed me. I recognized my own window, my cerise-colored drapes, the large photograph of my husband on the dresser, the small reading table piled with books beside the bed, and on top of the books, my wristwatch. The other half—his half—was unfamiliar. On his bedside table there was the portrait of an exceedingly pretty woman, photographs of children, magazines, and a pack of cigarettes. John Graham looked at me at length, then examined the background in which I appeared to him, and finally he said very seriously:

"What are you doing here, Mrs. Martin?"

I explained that I didn't know, and, pointing toward the large photograph, I said:

"This is my husband."

He pointed:

"This is my wife."

She was ravishing, and suddenly it occurred to me that she might at this very moment be in Jacques's arms.

"Do you think," I said to him, "that half of your house may have been moved over to France while half of mine was coming here?"

"Why?" he said.

That irritated me. Why? How would I know? . . . But

there was a kind of natural symmetry in the whole affair.
"This is rather strange," he said, shaking his head.
"And how is it possible?"
"It isn't possible," I said. "It's—"
At that moment, a sound of crying seemed to come
from the floor below, and we both had the same thought:
The children?
John Graham leaped out of bed, ran barefoot to a
door, and opened it. I heard crying, coughing, and the
vigorous voice of the Englishman mingling words of comfort with curses. I got up quickly and looked at myself in
the mirror; it was my own usual face. I tidied my hair a
little. Then I noticed that my nightgown was cut very
low and I looked around for my kimono, but remembered that I had hung it in the half of the room that had
not followed me. While I was standing in front of the
mirror, I heard a distracted voice behind me:
"Please come help me!" John Graham said, beseech-
ingly.
In the nursery, the wails were redoubling, mixed with
coughs and cries for help.
"Certainly . . . But would you have one of your wife's
dressing gowns? And some slippers?"
"Oh, of course."
He gave me his own bathrobe and showed me the way
to the nursery. The children were wonderful but they all
had whooping cough. The youngest, a handsome and
adorable blond baby, seemed to be the sickest. I took his
hand, and he accepted my being there.
We spent two hours like that in the nursery, both of us
in a state of mortal anxiety, he thinking of his wife and
I of my husband.
I asked whether one couldn't telephone the police. He
tried, and came back to report that his telephone had
been cut off, and likewise the antenna of his wireless.
The moment light began to dawn, John Graham went
out. The children had fallen asleep. A few minutes later,
he came back and said I should go down with him, that
the façade of the house was something worth seeing. It

was. The unknown author of this miracle had evidently wanted to choose two houses of the same height, divided more or less in the same way, and he had succeeded, but our house in Neuilly was a brick building, very simple, with high windows surrounded by a stone molding; the English house was a small white-and-black cottage, with bow windows. The juxtaposition of these two unlike halves formed the oddest whole. It was a Picasso harlequin.

I urged Mr. Graham to dress and go send a wire to France to find out what had become of his wife. He replied that the telegraph office did not open until eight. He was such a phlegmatic creature! He seemed to find it inconceivable that, in such special circumstances, one might infringe on regulations and arouse the telegraph operator. There was no use in my pushing him; all I could get out of him was "It doesn't open until eight!"

Finally, around seven-thirty, as he was about to go out, we saw a mounted policeman arriving. He stared at the house in amazement; he was the bearer of a telegram from the Prefect of Police in Paris, wanting to know whether I was there and announcing that Mrs. John Graham was safe and sound in Neuilly. . . .

There is no point in quoting this classic account in its entirety. Suffice it to say that Mrs. John Graham had cared for the children of Mme Jacques Martin as well as the latter had tended the little English children; that the two couples declared themselves enchanted by the good grace with which their companions had shared the adventure; and that the two households remained very close for the rest of their lives. Mme Martin was still living, ten years ago, in Chambourcy (Seine-et-Oise), in the family house.

The scope allowed to this chapter in the overall plan of the present book does not permit us to recount similar adventures that astonished mankind during that month of July, 1954.

The list of "divided houses" is even longer than the list of "fliers." More than a hundred couples were switched in similar fashion, and these exchanges became a favorite subject with novelists and film makers. They contained elements of sensuality and of fantasy that greatly appealed to the public. Furthermore, it was amusing to see—as actually did happen—a queen wake up in the bed of a policeman, and a Russian dancer in that of the President of the United States. Then, this series stopped abruptly and made way for another. It seemed that the mysterious beings who were diverting themselves by upsetting the lives of men were capricious and quickly tired of their games.

The Cage Episodes

Early in September, the hand whose power the whole world now recognized fell on some of the finest minds of the period. A dozen men, almost all of them physicists and chemists of great distinction, were simultaneously snatched up in civilized countries all over the globe and transported to a clearing in the woods at Fontainebleau.

A group of young people who were in the habit of going to the forest of a Sunday for rock climbing noticed some elderly men wandering disconsolately among the trees and rocks. Seeing that they were in difficulties, the young people started toward them but, to their surprise, were abruptly halted by a transparent but impassable barrier. They attempted to skirt the obstacle, but after they had gone the whole way around the cirque, they realized that it was completely surrounded by an invisible rampart. Several of these young people recognized one of the figures as a professor of theirs, and they called out to him, but he evidently did not hear them. So not even sound passed through the barrier. The elderly celebrities were like so many wild animals in a cage.

However, they rather quickly appeared to make the best of their predicament. They could be seen stretching out on the ground, or producing pieces of paper from their pockets and jotting down long notations, or talking animatedly among themselves. One of the young spectators had gone to alert the authorities, and around noon a number of curiosity seekers began to arrive. By this time, the scholars seemed quite disturbed. They struggled painfully—they were all advanced in years—to the rim of the cirque and, realizing that their voices could not be heard, they made signs asking for food.

A few army officers were at the scene. One of them proposed feeding the unfortunates by a food drop, which seemed an excellent idea. Two hours later, the roar of a motor was heard, and with great skill the pilot swept over the cirque and released some food packages directly over the center of the area. Unfortunately, about sixty feet above ground the boxes were seen to stop in their fall, bounce, and at last come to rest, although suspended in the air. The cage had a roof, made of the same invisible radiation.

Toward evening, the old men became desperate. They indicated by signs that now they were really suffering from hunger and that they were afraid of the night chill. The spectators were filled with pity but helpless. Would they have to witness such a remarkable group of great minds perish?

At dawn, the following day, it was believed at first that the situation had not changed, but on closer look a whole new decor was seen to have been created in the middle of the cage. The invisible hand had devised a new set. The food packages dropped by the pilot were now suspended at the end of a cable about fifteen feet above ground; a short distance away, a second cable hung to the ground. For any young man, it would have been easy to swing back and forth and reach the packages, which represented survival. Unfortunately, there was little hope that any of the elderly scholars, all at least in their seventies, could perform such gymnastics. They could be seen circling around the cables, measuring their strength, but none of them ventured to try them.

One whole day went by in this way. Night came. Slowly, the merely curious drifted away. Toward midnight, a young student had the idea of checking whether the radiation barrier was still there. To his great surprise, he encountered nothing and with a shout of triumph, he hurried forward. The cruel powers that had been playing with mankind for two days had consented to spare their victims. The scholars were fed, warmed, and none of them succumbed after their ordeal.

These are the principal events marking this period on Earth. They were inexplicable at the time, but today we know that they corresponded to a phase of Uranian experimentation. We shall now cite a few and, in our judgment, the most important fragments from the book of the famous A. E. 17.

The reader will understand that we have had to find Earth equivalents for Uranian words that cannot be translated literally. Uranian time is comprised of years much longer than ours. Wherever possible, we have transposed time into Earth terms. Furthermore, the Uranians use a phrase to designate us which is uselessly complicated—"apterous [wingless] bipeds" —and we have substituted for it almost everywhere the word "men" or "Earthmen." Similarly, the bizarre word they use to designate our cities we have rendered as "manhills," which, it seems to us, suggests fairly well the associations of analogous ideas. Lastly, the reader must not forget that although the Uranian is endowed with sight, like us, he is ignorant of sound. Uranians communicate among themselves thanks to a special organ composed of a series of tiny colored cells that flash on and off. Seeing that man is not provided with this organ and lacking any concept of what a word is, the Uranians naturally concluded that we were incapable of communicating ideas.

We can give here only a few short selections from the book of A. E. 17, but we warmly recommend that every student read the book in its entirety. It is available in an excellent scholarly edition prepared, with notes and appendices, by Professor Ah-chou, of Peking.

A. E. 17 is not, as we believe the reader will have understood, the Uranian name of the author but the designation chosen for him in Dr. Ah-chou's nomenclature.

THE LIFE OF MANKIND
by
A. E. 17

When, with the aid of an ordinary telescope, one examines the surface of the small planets and in particular that of Earth, one detects large patches that are much more variegated than areas of sea or lake. Observing these spots over a period of time, one notes that they increase in area over several Earth centuries, attain a maximum size, after which they decrease and sometimes even disappear. Many observers have assumed that this was a matter of some soil disease. The phenomenon does resemble nothing so much as the development and re-absorption of a tumor in a living organism. Since the invention of the ultratelemicroscope, however, it has been recognized that we are here in the presence of a mass of living matter. The earlier telescopes, being imperfect, permitted us to see only a confused swarming, a kind of animate hoarfrost, and some extremely competent observers—H. 33, for one—maintained that these were actually terrestrial colonies of animals joined to each other and living a common life. Our present instruments enable us to see immediately that this is not so. Individual forms are readily distinguished from each other, and it is possible to follow their independent movements. The spots observed by H. 33 are in reality immense nests that might roughly be compared to Uranian cities, and we call them man-hills.

The minute animals [men] that inhabit these cities are apterous bipeds, mammals, and are equipped with an inferior pilose system, large areas of the body surface being generally covered with an artificial epidermis. For a long time it was supposed that they secreted this supplementary skin. My studies allow me to state definitely that this is not the case; rather, some instinct impels them to collect certain animal or vegetable fibers that they piece together to form a protection against the cold.

I have used the word "instinct," and thereby wish to indicate very clearly at the outset of this book my view on a question that should never have been raised and that, especially in recent years, has been treated with incredible frivolity. A strange fashion has come to be established among our younger naturalists of attributing to these terrestrial molds an intelligence on the order of the Uranian. We shall leave to others the task of emphasizing how scandalous, particularly from the religious point of view, such a thesis is. Here I shall show how absurd it is purely from the scientific point of view. Undeniably, when we contemplate one of those particles of frost under the microscope for the first time and suddenly witness hundreds of lively, interesting scenes taking place—long streets where Earthmen pass each other and where they sometimes stop and appear to communicate; a tiny individual nest where a pair watches over its brood of young; armies on the march; construction workers on their job—the beauty of the spectacle is such that enthusiasm is excusable. But a fruitful study of the psychic mechanism of these animals requires the observer not merely to take advantage of circumstances provided by chance. He must know how to create other and more favorable conditions for observation, and to vary them as much as possible; in a word, it is necessary to experiment and thereby to construct a body of scientific knowledge based solidly on facts.

This is what we endeavored to do in the course of the long series of controlled experiments reported on here. Before beginning my account, I must ask the reader to visualize and measure the immense difficulties that such a project entails. Unquestionably, long-distance experimentation has become relatively easy since we have had at our disposal the W-rays, which enable us to seize, manipulate, and even transport bodies across interstellar space. But when one is dealing with organisms as small and fragile as men, W-rays are very clumsy and brutal instruments. In our first attempts, it too often happened that we destroyed the tiny beasts we wished to observe. What we needed was an emitting apparatus of extraordinary precision that would allow us to aim directly at the target and to handle sensitive living matter with the required delicacy. In particular, when we began to transport men from one place to another on the surface of the globe, we neglected to take into account the animals' powers of resistance. We caused them to move too rapidly through the thin layer of air that surrounds Earth, and they died of asphyxiation. Accordingly, we were obliged to devise an actual ray box in which they could be transported without the speed of displacement's producing any harmful effects. Similarly, when we first wanted to bisect and displace nests, we did not adequately take into account the construction methods employed by Earthmen. With experience, we learned to buttress the nests after bisection by causing massive currents of radiation to pass through them.

The reader will find here a summary map of that area on Earth's surface where we conducted our major experiments. We should like to draw attention particularly to the two large manhills where we made our initial attempts and to which we gave the names, since adopted by astrosociologists, of Rigid Manhill and Random Manhill.

These names were chosen because of the very different aspects of the two manhills, one of which immediately strikes the observer because of the regularity of its plan, whereas the other is a complicated network of quite torturous roads. Between Rigid Manhill and Random Manhill there stretches a brilliant line that may be assumed to be a sea. The largest manhill on Earth is Geometric Manhill, which is even more systematic in plan than Rigid Manhill, but is set apart and separated from the other two by a broader, brilliant surface.

First Attempts

What was the most suitable place on Earth for us to begin our work? How should we intervene in the existence of these animals in order to obtain revealing reactions from them? I confess to being deeply stirred when, for the first time, armed with an apparatus of sufficient range, I was ready to begin my study of Earth.

I was surrounded by four of my students, who were also much moved, and we looked in turn through the ultratele-microscope at those charming, diminutive landscapes. We had trained the apparatus on Random Manhill, and had searched for an area sufficiently exposed for us to see more easily what would develop from our action. Some very small trees were glowing in the spring sunshine, and we could see a multitude of motionless insects forming irregular circles in the midst of which stood an isolated insect. We tried briefly to analyze this game but, being unable to, decided to attempt a ray application. The effect was dumfounding. A hole was formed in the ground, and several insects were buried under the debris. Instantly, an amazing activity was unleashed. One would really have said that these animals were capable of intelligent organization. Some rescued their buried companions and others went to look for help. The damage was quite quickly repaired. In next applying our rays, we tried to choose uninhabited spots insofar as possible so as not to endanger our subjects at the outset of our studies. We learned how to reduce the strength of our rays and to employ them more skillfully. When finally we were sure of our methods of operation, we decided to begin the first series of our experiments.

My plan was to take individuals from one manhill, mark them with an identifying sign, transport them to some other spot, and verify whether the individual so transported found the way back to his original manhill. At the outset, as I have said, we encountered great difficulties, first because the animal would die in transit, and later because we had neglected to take account of the artificial epidermis that Earthmen fabricate for themselves. Since they are able easily to divest themselves of it, we would lose track of them as soon as we had deposited them on the ground in the middle of a manhill. In later transports, we attempted to mark them directly on the body, after removing the supplementary skin, but as soon as the animal reached the manhill, he made himself a new skin.

With a little practice, my students finally learned to follow an animal through the ultratelemicroscope and not to lose it from sight. They determined that in ninety cases out of a hundred the man returns to his starting point. I undertook to transport two males from Random Manhill to the one we call Geometric Manhill, which is a long distance away. After ten Earthdays, my warmly cherished disciple E. X. 33, who had followed them night and day with incomparable devotion, showed them to me returning to Random Manhill. They had returned home despite the fact that I had transported them to a location unknown to them. However, these two were individuals of home-loving habits (we had observed them at length) who obviously were seeing the region to which we had taken them for the first time. How had they found their way back? Their transportation had been so rapid that they could not have observed the route. What, then, guided them? Certainly not memory, but some special faculty which we can discuss only in terms of its astonishing effects without pretending to explain it, so far removed is it from our own psychology.

•

The transports posed another question. At the time of his return, would the individual be recognized by the others? It seems that he is. Generally, one observes great excitement in the nest when the absent one returns. The others put their arms about him and sometimes even place their lips on his. In certain cases, however, the emotion manifested has seemed to be one of dissatisfaction or anger.

These early experiments demonstrated that some instinct enables the apterous bipeds to recognize their own manhills. The second question we put to ourselves was to learn whether there could exist between these creatures emotions similar to those of Uranians—whether, for example, love, either conjugal or maternal, exists on Earth. Such a supposition, which attributes to Earthmen the refined sentiments that the Uranian has achieved after millions of years of civilization, seemed to me absurd. But the duty of the experimenter is to approach his subject with an open mind and to carry out all his tests without prejudging the result.

At night, the male Earthman generally rests near his female. I asked my students to cut some nests in two, so as to separate the male from his female without injury to either, then to re-knit Half A with Half B and see whether the little animals would notice the change. For the experiment to be carried out in normal conditions, it was indispensable that the nests chosen should resemble each other. Accordingly, I recommended that my laboratory workers choose two nests containing broods of the same number and cells of the same size. E. X. 33 triumphantly showed me in Random and Rigid Manhill two nearly identical nests, each containing one pair and four young. Bisection and transportation of the dwellings were executed by E. X. 33 with consummate skill. The results were conclusive. The two couples that we had artificially united exhibited, on awaking, a very slight surprise that the recent motion and shock would, together, suffice to explain. In both instances, the new couples stayed together, and their attitudes and behavior seemed normal. One very nearly incredible fact: both females undertook to care for the strange brood, exhibiting neither horror nor disgust. Evidently they were incapable of recognizing that the young were not their own.

We repeated this experiment numerous times. In ninety-three cases out of a hundred, care and attention were given to the nests by the new-formed couples. The Earthman's female retains a tenacious sense of the functions she should perform, but with no idea of the individuals toward whom she owes this duty. Whether the offspring belong to her or not, she labors for them with equal fervor. One might assume that such confusion results from the close resemblance between the two nests. However, as we progressed, we chose nests of dissimilar aspect, joining, for example, the half of an impoverished nest with the half of a rich one of a different kind. The results were approximately the same: the Earthman makes no distinction between his own and another's nest.

Having thus demonstrated that insofar as feelings are concerned, the Earthman stands very low on the scale of being, we sought to measure his intellectual faculties. To accomplish this, we decided to isolate a few individuals in a ray-enclosed cage and to put food within their reach—so placed, however, that they could seize it only after performing more and more complicated actions. For this experiment, I flirted with the notion of choosing some Earthmen in whom my colleague X. 38 claimed to have discovered signs of scientific intelligence. The details of the experiment are to be found in Appendix B. They indicate beyond possible doubt that the Earthman's sense of time is extremely limited, as regards both the past and the future; that he forgets immediately; and that he is incapable of devising solutions to the simplest problems that differ only slightly from those he has hereditarily been able to solve.

After a long period of experimentation with individual Earthmen, my assistants and I became sufficiently familiar with the behavior of these animals to be able to observe them in the course of their ordinary life without our having to intervene. Nothing is more interesting than to follow, as I have done, the record of a manhill over a period of several Earth years.

The origin of human societies is unknown. Why and how did these animals renounce their freedom to become slaves of the manhill? We do not know. One may hazard the guess that in such groupings they found support in their struggle with other animals and against natural forces, but it is a support for which they pay very dearly. No other animal species is less familiar with leisure and the joy of living. In the large man-hills, and especially in Geometric Manhill, activity begins at dawn and continues on into the night. Were this activity essential it would be comprehensible, but man is a limited animal, so dominated by his instincts that he labors and produces far in excess of his needs. In ten different instances, I have observed how objects accumulate in a manhill's reserve depots to such an extent that men seemed inconvenienced thereby; nevertheless, only a short distance away, another group was continuing to fabricate these very same objects.

The division of Earthmen into castes is also little understood. It is certain that among these animals some work the land and produce almost all the food; others manufacture the supplementary epidermises, build nests, etc.; still others appear to do nothing other than to move rapidly over the surface of the planet, and to eat and to mate. Why do the first two castes consent to nourish and clothe the third? This for me remains obscure. E.X. 33 has undertaken a remarkable study to prove that this tolerance is of sexual origin. He has demonstrated that when individuals of the superior caste assemble in the evening, workers flock to the entrances of these celebrations to see the seminude females. According to him, what they derive from this spectacle is an aesthetic pleasure, which is, in effect, compensation or reward for their sacrifices. I find the theory ingenious but not solidly enough established for me to accept it as true.

I would prefer to look for the explanation in the Earthman's amazing stupidity. It is the greatest folly to seek always to explain the actions of Earthmen in terms of Uranian reasoning. This is an error, a profound error. The Earthman is not guided by a free intelligence. He obeys unconscious, ineluctable stimuli; he does not possess the power to do what he should do; he somehow rolls along, propelled by an irresistible, predetermined propensity in order to reach his goal. A case in point: I have found it rather diverting to follow the individual existence of several Earthmen for whom the functions of love appear to be the essential thing in life. I would notice how, by dint of conquering one female, the Earthman burdens himself with all the responsibilities for a nest; not content with this initial encumbrance, my male would go in search of a second companion for whom he set up a second nest! These simultaneous love involvements led the unfortunate animal into dozens of difficulties, as I myself witnessed. They made little impression on him; his successive troubles apparently taught him nothing, and he continued to pursue his little adventures, seemingly no wiser by the tenth than at the first.

One of the strongest proofs of this inability to retain the past and to imagine the future was supplied me by frightful struggles I have been able to observe between individuals of the same species. To us, the idea that a group of Uranians could attack another group, hurl objects intended to wound them, and attempt to asphyxiate them with poisoned gas—to us such things seem absurd.

Nevertheless, this is what happens on Earth. In the course of several years of study, I have been able to observe, now in one, now in another corner of that planet, compact masses of men confront each other. Sometimes they fight out in the open; at other times, sheltered in burrows, they attempt to demolish nearby burrows by spraying them with heavy masses of metal; sometimes, they rig themselves up in rudimentary wings in order to drop projectiles from the sky. Note that simultaneously they themselves are being sprayed in the same fashion. This is a fearsome and ridiculous spectacle. The scenes of horror one must perforce witness at such times are such that, had these animals the slightest faculty of memory, they would avoid any repetition of them, at least for several generations. However, within the life span of the same men, short as that is, they can be seen hurling themselves, twice, three times, into the same murderous adventure.

Another striking example of the Earthman's blind obedience to his instincts is the manner in which he untiringly builds manhills at certain sites on the planet where inevitably they will be destroyed. In this connection, I closely observed a heavily populated island on which all the nests were demolished three times in the space of eight years by a cracking of the terrestrial crust. To any sensible observer, it is obvious that animals living in these places should emigrate. Earthmen do nothing of the sort. With various ritual gestures, they seize the same pieces of iron and wood and zealously rebuild a man-hill that will be destroyed again the following year.

"Even so," my opponents say to me, "while the objective of this activity may be absurd, it is ordered activity nonetheless, which proves that there exists a directing power, an intellect."

This I hold to be a further error. Men who have been thrown into confusion by an earthquake swarm about, and their movements are similar to those of gas molecules. If one observes the latter individually they are seen to describe complex, broken trajectories, but because of their great numbers they produce unified effects. Similarly, when we destroy a man-hill, millions of insects collide, rush about in the most haphazard way, and obstruct each other, yet at the end of a given period of time, the manhill has been rebuilt.

Thus there is the singular intellectual point of view, fashionable today, that discerns here a replica of Uranian intelligence. However, fashions pass and facts remain, with which we are brought back to the solid, old-fashioned virtues of the Uranian spirit and its manifest, privileged destiny. I consider myself fortunate to have been able, by a few experiments modestly and prudently conducted, to contribute toward discrediting pernicious doctrines and to restore to their proper place in the great chain of being animals that are assuredly strange and worthy of study but that also, by the very naïveté and incoherence of their actions, are calculated to make us measure the abyss established by the Creator between the Uranian soul and the bestial instinct.

Death of A.E. 17

Happily, A.E. 17 died in time not to witness the first interplanetary war, the establishment of diplomatic relations between Uranus and Earth, and the discrediting, in the light of later knowledge, of his entire work. He enjoyed his fame, which was great, to the end of his life. He was a good, simple

Uranian, who grew irritable only when contradicted. An interesting detail for us: the monument that was erected in his honor on Uranus bears on its pedestal a bas-relief that was carved after a telephoto; it represents a mass of men and women swarming against a background suggestive of Fifth Avenue.

The Corinthian Porch

DURING THE FORTY YEARS of their married life, Lord and Lady Barchester had lived in the same house on Park Lane. After the war, however, they found themselves in straitened circumstances. They had made some bad investments; one of their sons had been killed, and his widow and children left for the parents to support; and the income tax had risen to five shillings on the pound. Lord Barchester was obliged to recognize that he could not keep both the family seat, in Sussex, and the Park Lane town house. Finally he decided to speak to his wife about his difficulties. For a long time, he had hesitated for fear he would depress her. Thirty years before, their marital life had been stormy, but age had brought with it a mutual ease, indulgence, and tenderness.

"My dear," he said to her, "I'm frightfully sorry, but I see only one way for us to live out our life without being quite ruined, and I know that you will find it most disagreeable. So I will leave it entirely up to you to accept or reject. Here it is:

the land bordering the Park has become very valuable. A promoter needs our corner lot, which forms an enclave in property he has already acquired. He is offering me a price that would not only allow us to buy a house in the same area but also leave a comfortable margin as security for the few years remaining to us. But I know that you love Barchester House, and I do not want to do anything that could upset you."

Lady Barchester agreed to the sale and, a few months later, the elderly couple moved into a new house only a few hundred yards from the one they had had to give up, which workmen had already begun to demolish. Every day, when Lord and Lady Barchester left their new house, they would pass by their old home, and it made a very strange impression on them to watch a shape slowly dissolve that, for them, had been the most essential, most stable aspect of the universe. When they saw their home roofless, they felt as if they themselves were exposed to the wind and rain. Lady Barchester suffered especially when the front wall was staved in, exposing, as if it were on a stage in public view, the bedroom of Patrick, the son she had lost, and her own bedroom, where she had spent most of her days for forty years.

From the street, she looked at the glazed chintz with the black background that had covered the walls of her room. She had so often contemplated it in moments of mourning, illness, and happiness, too, that the pattern of the material had come to seem to her like the very background against which her life had been painted. A few days later, she had a great surprise. The workmen had ripped off the chintz, and a black-and-white paper appeared underneath that she had forgotten but that immediately, and with an impact she could scarcely understand, evoked for her her long affair with Harry Webb. How many mornings had she dreamed away, hour upon hour, staring absently at those designs of Japanese pagodas, after she had read the beautiful letters Harry used to write her from the Far East. She had loved him very much. Now he was Sir Henry Webb, His Majesty's Ambassador to Spain.

Presently the rain loosened that black-and-white paper, and under it still another appeared. This was a rather ugly flower design, but Lady Barchester remembered having chosen it with much devotion at the time of her marriage, in 1890. In those days, she wore blue serge dresses and yellow amber necklaces; she was striving to resemble Mrs. Burne-Jones and she used to go to Sunday tea at old William Morris'. So long as patches of this rose-and-green paper were visible, she would pass by the house several times a day, because the design brought back her youth and the days of her great love for Lord Barchester.

At last, the walls themselves came down and one day, on their way out for a walk in the park, Lord and Lady Barchester saw that nothing remained of the house but the small Corinthian porch that had sheltered the front entrance. It was a strange, sad sight, for this porch at the top of the front steps now opened onto a desolate landscape of rubble heaped under a wintry sky. For a long moment, Lady Barchester watched the clouds scudding between the white columns, and then she said to her husband:

"That porch is bound up in my memories with the saddest day of my life. I have never dared talk to you about it, but we are so old now that it doesn't matter anymore. It was when I was in love with Harry, and you with Sybil. One evening I went to a ball to meet Harry, who was coming back from Tokyo. I had been looking forward to that meeting for weeks, but it seems that Harry had asked for special leave to become engaged, and all evening long he danced with a young woman, and pretended not to see me. In the carriage coming home I cried. I got to the house. My face was so disfigured by tears that I felt I hadn't the courage to show myself to you in such a state. I pretended to ring, let the coachman drive off, and then I leaned against one of those columns, and I stood there a long time. It was raining very hard. I was sobbing. I knew that you also were thinking of someone else, and it seemed to me that my life was finished. That's what that little porch, which is about to disappear, reminds me of."

Lord Barchester, who had listened to this little story with great interest and sympathy, took his wife affectionately by the arm.

"Do you know what we're going to do?" he said. "Before they demolish the porch, which is the grave of your memories, we'll go together and buy a few flowers and we'll lay them on the steps."

The old couple went to a florist, brought back roses, and laid them at the foot of one of the Corinthian columns. The next day, the porch disappeared.

The Cathedral

In 18——, a student stopped in the Rue Saint-Honoré before an art dealer's window. A canvas by Manet was on display: the "Cathedral of Chartres." At that time, Manet was admired only by a few amateur art lovers, but the passerby had a sure taste. The beauty of this painting enchanted him. A few days later, he came back to see it again. Finally he dared go in and ask the price.

"My word," the dealer said, "that's been here a long time. You can have it for two thousand francs."

The student did not have that much money, but he came from a provincial family that was not without means. When he was setting out for Paris, an uncle had said to him:

"I know what the life of a young man is. In case of urgent need, write me."

The young man asked the dealer not to sell the painting for a week, and he wrote to his uncle.

The young man had a mistress in Paris, who was married

to an older man and who was bored. She was rather vulgar, quite stupid, and very pretty. The evening of the day the student asked the price of the painting, this woman said to him:

"I'm expecting an old school friend to arrive tomorrow from Toulon. She is coming to visit me. My husband has no time to go out with us. I shall count on you."

The friend arrived the next day. She was accompanied by still another friend. The student had to show these three women around Paris for several days. Since he was paying for meals, cabs, and theaters, his monthly allowance melted away. He borrowed from a fellow-student and was beginning to be very much worried when he received a letter from his uncle. Enclosed were two thousand francs. This was a great relief. He paid his debts and bought a gift for his mistress. A collector bought the "Cathedral" and, much later, bequeathed his paintings to the Louvre.

Now the former student is an old and famous writer. His heart has stayed young. He still stops, deeply moved, before a beautiful landscape or a beautiful woman. Often, as he is leaving his house, he meets in the street an elderly lady who lives in the house next door. This woman is his former mistress. Her face is deformed by folds of fat; her eyes, which once were beautiful, are underlined by puffy bags; her upper lip is shadowed by a gray fuzz. She walks with difficulty, and one can imagine her flabby legs. The writer bows to her but he never stops, for he knows she is malicious and he does not like to think that he ever loved her.

Sometimes he goes into the Louvre and climbs up to the gallery where the "Cathedral" hangs. He looks at it a long time, and he sighs.

The Ants

BETWEEN TWO SHEETS OF GLASS, taped together at the edges by strips of paper, a colony of little brown monsters was bustling about, busily at work. The shopkeeper had given the ants a bit of sand, in which they had traced converging pathways. In the center, nearly motionless, sat a creature plumper than the others. This was the queen, whom the ants fed with great deference.

"They're no trouble," the shopkeeper said. "You just have to give them a drop of honey here, through this little opening, once a month. . . . Just one drop . . . The ants take care of carrying it away and dividing it."

"One drop a month!" the young woman said. "One drop is enough to keep the whole population alive for a month?"

She was wearing a large white straw hat and a dress of flowered mousseline. Her arms were bare. The shopkeeper looked at her mournfully.

"One drop is enough," he said again.

"How charming," she said.

And she bought the transparent ant nest.

"Darling," she said, "have you seen my ants?"

She was holding the thin glass sheets between her white fingers with their tinted nails. The man seated beside her was admiring the curve of her throat.

"You make life so interesting, my sweet. With you, everything is new and always different. . . . Last night, Bach; now these ants . . ."

"Darling, look," she said, with the childish enthusiasm he, as she well knew, loved. "You see this giant ant? That is the queen. The workers serve her. . . . I feed them myself. And would you believe it, darling? One drop of honey a month is enough for all of them. Isn't that a poem in itself?"

At the end of a week, her lover and her husband were both tired of the ant nest. She hid it on the mantelpiece in her bedroom, behind the mirror. At the end of the month, she forgot the drop of honey. The ants died of hunger slowly. Up until the end, they kept a tiny bit of honey for the queen, who was the last to die.

The Postcard

"I WAS FOUR," Nathalie said, "when my mother left my father to marry her handsome German. I loved Papa very much, but he was weak and resigned, so he didn't insist on keeping me with him in Moscow. Presently—quite against my will—I began to admire my stepfather. He was very affectionate with me. I refused to call him Father, and finally it was agreed that I would call him Heinrich, like my mother.

"We stayed three years in Leipzig, and then Maman had to go back to Moscow to settle some business affairs. She phoned my father, had a quite friendly conversation with him, and promised to send me to spend a day with him. I was excited at the thought of seeing him again and also of being back in the house where I'd played so much and which I remembered as being utterly wonderful.

"I wasn't disappointed. The porter was standing at the door, the great courtyard was filled with snow—everything looked the way I had remembered it. As for my father, he had made prodi-

gious efforts so that the day would be perfect. He had bought
me new toys, ordered a marvelous lunch, and for the evening
he had prepared a little fireworks display in the garden.

"Papa was a very kind man, but he was also infinitely clumsy.
Everything he had organized so lovingly was a fiasco. The new
toys only revived my longing for old toys that I asked for and
he could not find. The fine lunch was poorly prepared by
servants who had no woman watching over them, and it made
me sick. One of the firework fuses fell on the roof and down
the chimney of my old room, where it set the carpet afire. To
put out what would have become a real blaze, the whole household had to form a bucket brigade and my father burned his
hand, so that the day he had wanted to be so jolly left me with
the memory of terrifying flames and the dismal smell of medical
dressings.

"When my fräulein came to get me that evening, she found
me in tears. I was very young, but I was very sensitive to shades
of feeling. I knew that my father loved me, that he had done
his best, and that he had failed. I was sorry for him, and at the
same time a little ashamed of him. I wanted him not to know
what I was thinking, and I tried to smile, but instead I cried.

"When the time came to leave, he said to me that in Russia
it was the custom to give one's friends decorated cards at
Christmas, and that he had bought one for me, and that he
hoped I would like it. Today, when I think of that card, I know
that it was dreadful. But I believe I loved it then. It had
spangly snow made of sodium bicarbonate, and red stars pasted
behind a transparent midnight-blue sky, and its sleigh was attached by cardboard hinges—remember?—so that it seemed to
be galloping off the card. I thanked Papa, kissed him, and we
left each other.

"Fräulein took me back to the hotel where we were staying.
My mother and stepfather were dressing to go out to dinner at
the home of friends. Maman, in a white evening gown, was
wearing a heavy diamond necklace. Heinrich was in a tuxedo.
They asked if I'd had a good time. I said defiantly that I had
spent a wonderful day, and I described the fireworks without a
word about the fire. Then, no doubt as proof of my papa's
magnificence, I produced my postcard.

"My mother took it and immediately went into gales of laughter.

" 'Great heavens!' she said. 'Poor Pierre, he hasn't changed. . . . What an addition to the Museum of Horrors.'

"Heinrich, who was watching me, leaned toward her, and his expression was displeased.

" 'Come, come,' he said, under his breath. 'Not in front of the child.'

"He took the card from my mother, smilingly admired the snow, made the sleigh move on its little hinges, and said:

" 'It's the most beautiful card I've ever seen. You must take good care of it.'

"I was seven years old, but I knew that he was lying, that, like Maman, he thought the card was dreadful, that they were both right, and that out of pity Heinrich wanted to protect poor Papa.

"I tore the card up and from that day forward I detested my stepfather."

Poor Maman

BERTRAND SCHMITT was opening his mail. Nearby, his wife, Isabelle, was amused to watch the contents bring in turn smiles and frowns to his face.

"Well!" he said. "A letter from Pont-de-l'Eure . . . They're becoming pretty rare."

He looked for the signature.

"Germaine Guérin? . . . Oh, yes, the mother of Denise Holmann. Now what does she want?"

Mme Guérin was announcing the death of her mother, the Baroness d'Hocquinville, in Rouen, Rue Damiette, in her eightieth year. ". . . I wanted to write you this sad news myself, since you are friends of my dear little girl and in days past knew poor Maman. I remember when Denise used to bring you to Rue Damiette, and how much pleasure it gave poor Maman to listen to the two of you chatter away. Denise was a remarkable little girl, even then, and you . . . I do not want to make compliments, but I do want you to know how much poor Maman thought of you. . . . I shall miss her terribly. For more than thirty years I have been going to Rouen to see her every week. Despite her age, she was for me a cherished mentor. My grief would not be bearable, I believe, if I were not sustained by Georges, who is, as always, admirable, and by the affection of my children. . . . If chance brings you back to our Normandy someday and if you do not fear the ramblings of an old woman, do stop to see me. I would be happy to show you a few mementos of poor Maman. . . ."

"Did you know Mme d'Hocquinville?" Isabelle said.

"Hardly at all! I remember going once or twice with Denise to that house in Rouen, which even then was very old and run-down."

"Then why does her daughter write you such an emotional letter?"

"To be pitied," Bertrand said. "She's one of those creatures who find a reason for self-glorification in every misfortune. It's all the more comical since she treated 'poor Maman' very harshly indeed while she was alive."

" 'Harshly'—how?"

"The d'Hocquinvilles had lost all their money, but Mme Guérin, who had made two good marriages, one right after the other, had a lot. She gave her mother enough to live on—just enough—but she made her pay for her dole in humiliation. . . . It was pretty awful."

After a moment's reflection, he added:

"And not only in humiliation. In obligations, too."

"What do you mean?"

"It's an old story. . . . Mme Guérin had been married first to a poor sort of fellow by the name of Herpain, who was Denise' father. She'd been unfaithful to him, first with some officer, then with Guérin himself—he was a bachelor at the time. But she needed alibis to cover up her rendezvous. Poor Maman was well trained, and she used to cover for her daughter. I'm not sure she didn't meet her lovers at her mother's house. . . . There was something of the procuress in poor Maman."

"There's something of the procuress in almost all women," Isabelle said, dreamily.

"In the case of Mother d'Hocquinville," Bertrand went on, "that kind of complicity isn't surprising. As a young woman, she had passed for being what they used to call in that part of the country 'an easy thigh.' My father was an austere man, and he spoke very disparagingly about her. . . . But she wasn't that bad. She was stupid."

"You have to write a note of sympathy, Bertrand."

"You think so? . . . What do you want me to say? Nothing could matter to me less."

"Yes, I know, but it's a question of civility."

Bertrand sighed, sat down at the table, and took a sheet of paper.

"Dear Madame," he wrote. "Your letter has touched me deeply. How good of you, in the midst of your great grief, to think of writing yourself to give me this sad news. Yes, I remember with nostalgia my all too rare visits to Rue Damiette. The beauty of the grounds, the gracious and still youthful gaiety of your mother, her kindness to the child I then was— all these are for me perfect and quite unforgettable memories. I know how greatly devoted you were to your mother, and I can well understand how only the affection of your husband and daughters will reconcile you to life. If I have the opportunity to be in Pont-de-l'Eure, I shall certainly talk with you of the past. Please accept, dear Madame, my respectful sympathy. . . ."

He handed the note to Isabelle.

"Read it," he said. "I find it ridiculous."

Isabelle skimmed rapidly through the letter, and with grave satisfaction handed it back to Bertrand.

"It is exactly what is called for," she said.

The Green Belt

"BERTRAND," said Isabelle, "could you be home this afternoon at tea time? I'd be so relieved if you could. I'm expecting poor little Nathalie and it will be hard for me to see her alone. Also, in her letter she said she would like to ask your advice about something."

He consulted his appointment book and shook his head impatiently.

"It upsets my whole afternoon," he said.

"I'm sorry to insist, Bertrand, but I dread this meeting more than you can imagine. We haven't seen Nathalie since her husband died, and what happened to him seems so dreadful to me that I don't understand how she lived through it. . . . The tragedy of it—his losing his mind, his life ruined—and hers, too! It's too much for one person. What kind of human comfort can one offer? Truthfully, I don't know what to say to her."

"Neither do I," he said. "Don't you think in such cases the

best thing to do is to say very little? I imagine that when she
sees you again, she'll break down and cry. And you will cry.
Then take her in your arms, kiss her. . . . Let your instinct
guide you."

After a moment, he added:

"I do understand that it will be a painful meeting. I'll
arrange to be here with you."

Late that afternoon, a few minutes before the appointed
time, he came into Isabelle's little sitting room.

"I'm so nervous," she said. "I try to read but I can't think
of anything but this poor woman. I stare at the door I know
she'll be coming through and the words fly straight out of my
head. This is awful."

"Try to be calm," he said. "You must never try to prepare
for a difficult moment. Dive into a painful conversation the
way a swimmer jumps into icy water. That is Stendhal's advice.
Have you ordered tea?"

"Yes, I told Maria to bring in the tea things five minutes
after Nathalie arrives. I'm hoping that if a strange person ap-
pears, it will stop her crying and after that conversation will
be easier."

Bertrand picked up a book, opened it, and closed it with a
sigh. They sat without speaking. A short, timid tinkle of a
bell broke the silence. Isabelle stood up.

"That's Nathalie," she said.

"Do sit down," Bertrand begged her.

They heard a clear voice in the vestibule.

"It's so pleasantly warm! I'll leave my coat here."

The door opened and Nathalie appeared on the threshold,
her pretty face a bit thinner and paler, but scarcely changed
and very young.

"Hello," she said. "Oh, Bertrand, how good of you! . . . I
didn't dare hope you'd have time to see me. . . . How com-
fortably warm your house is, Isabelle."

When, an hour later, Bertrand came back to the sitting room
from having shown Nathalie to the door, Isabelle burst out:

"It's incredible! Don't you find it is, darling? To think that
I was afraid to see her again. Did she say one word about her
troubles?"

"A few vague references," Bertrand said. "Now and then she slipped in something like 'in my situation.' But nothing direct, actually. I don't understand at all why she hoped I would be here. She wanted to ask me for some advice, you said? Well, she didn't ask me a thing."

"That isn't my fault, Bertrand. I repeated her message to you word for word. . . . I can't get over it. Have you ever seen anything like it? That interminable dissertation on the puffed sleeve! By the by, did you really like her sleeves as much as you told her you did? I thought you countenanced only form-fitting dresses?"

"Naturally," Bertrand said. "But you were sitting there without saying a word and I wanted to help you out."

"I tried twice to speak about her husband," Isabelle said. "Each time she brushed it aside with some very cold remark and came back to this plan for a trip to Greece. this cruise she wants to go on. At the bottom of her heart, she never loved him."

"Who knows?" Bertrand said.

"And her children? . . . You heard what she answered when I said they would be a comfort to her? . . . 'You think so?' she said. 'You like children? I don't. . . . I go into their room. If they're playing, they don't even notice me. It makes me feel rather sad. . . .' I didn't know what to say. On the other hand, she was irreproachable on the subject of your latest book."

"That's no crime," Bertrand said. "It was obvious that she'd read it carefully."

"Which is exactly what I can't forgive her for," Isabelle said. "How can one concentrate on reading when one ought to be in despair? . . . And then, the green belt! Did you notice?"

"Yes," Bertrand said. "It was pretty, for that matter. A touch of live color against all that black."

"Pretty! Bertrand! . . . Well, perhaps, but it was more scandalous than anything else. . . . Why? Because she lost her husband a mere three months ago, in tragic circumstances, and she doesn't even wear deep mourning! . . . Oh, I know, I know you don't attach any importance to these details. . . .

Nor do I. But all the same, there are certain decencies. . . . That green belt! I couldn't take my eyes off it."

"Poor Isabelle," Bertrand said, taking her by the arm. "You really were upset by that young woman, weren't you?"

"Not that she deserved it. . . . And what she managed to tuck away! At first, I scarcely dared offer her a cup of tea. But she had a second helping of everything—cakes, biscuits. . . . 'Your pimiento sandwiches are a poem,' she said. I didn't know what to answer."

Bertrand smiled.

"Who would believe," he said, "that this morning I found you practically in tears because of her and that a little while ago, when you were waiting for her, you were trembling like a leaf! . . . You see I was right to say that one should never think about the future. Everything is always different than in our dreams, simpler than we have imagined."

A few days later, they learned that Nathalie had swallowed three bottles of Veronal and that she was dead.

The Neuilly Fair

"BONNIVET was five or six years older than I," Maufras said, "and his career had been so brilliant, he'd risen so rapidly, that I always thought of him as a patron rather than as a friend. I owed him a great deal. It was he who invited me to join his department when he became Minister of Public Works, and when the Ministry fell, again it was he who got me a wonderful spot in the administrative setup of the Prefecture.

"When he came back to power, he took over Colonies. I had a very agreeable job in Paris at the time, and I asked him to let me stay on in it. We continued to have a very friendly relationship, and our two families often had dinner together at one or the other's house. Nelly Bonnivet was a woman of forty, maybe, but still pretty. Her husband adored her, and she made the perfect minister's wife. I'd been married for ten years, and you know how happy Madeleine and I have always been.

"Early in June, the Bonnivets invited us out to dinner at a

restaurant in the Bois. There were six of us. The evening was very gay and, come midnight, no one wanted to break up. Bonnivet was in a high good humor, and he proposed going to the Neuilly Fair. When he's in office, he loves to play Harun al-Rashid and hear people say as he goes by, 'Say, there's Bonnivet!'

"The spectacle of three middle-aged couples trying to recapture a childish delight in silly games is rather dismal. In various lotteries we won some macaroons, an assortment of spun-glass boats, and some animal spice cakes. The three men played that game of knocking down revolving pipes—remember that?—and the eggshells that are held up by feeble little jets of water. Finally, we came to a circular railroad. It made a couple of turns under an open sky, and then a canvas roofing was raised over it, making a kind of tunnel. Nelly Bonnivet suggested a ride. Madeleine didn't look as if she found the game very amusing or the seat cushions very clean, but she didn't want to spoil the fun, and we got tickets. In the confusion of going aboard, our group was separated and I found myself alone in a seat with Nelly Bonnivet.

"That little train traveled very fast, and the curves were designed so as to throw the occupants of the cars against each other. At the first turn, Mme Bonnivet almost fell into my arms. Then the canvas tunnel plunged us into darkness—and I could never explain to you what happened in the next few moments. Sometimes our bodies do act without any check from the brain. However that may be, I felt Nelly lying half in my lap and realized that I was embracing her the way a twenty-year-old soldier might behave with some girl he's taken to the village fair. I tried to find her lips, really without knowing what I was doing, and the moment I found them—without meeting any resistance—the light came back on. With one accord, we wrenched apart and looked at each other, dazzled and stunned.

"I remember trying at the time to understand the expression on Nelly Bonnivet's face. She smoothed her hair, looked at me gravely, and did not say a word. The awkwardness lasted only an instant. The train was slowing down, and a moment later we rejoined Bonnivet, Madeleine, and the two others on the circular platform.

" 'This is really a little too young for us,' Bonnivet said, sounding bored. 'I think it's time for bed.'

"Madeleine seconded him and we headed back for the Porte Maillot, where the group disbanded. As I kissed Nelly's hand, I tried to see her eyes; she was talking brightly to Madeleine and left without a sign.

"I couldn't sleep. This unforeseen adventure was unsettling my very stable, very balanced life. I'd never been a man to run after women, and much less than ever since my marriage. I loved Madeleine with all my heart, and our relationship was one of tender, unreserved trust. For Bonnivet I felt not only affection but sincere gratitude. The devil of it was that in spite of everything, I was on fire to see Nelly again and to learn what her expression meant the moment after we'd both let go. Was it surprise? Pique? You know how fatuous the most modest of men can be at heart. I was imagining some long, wordless passion that had suddenly broken out thanks to chance. In her twin bed next to mine, Madeleine was sound asleep, breathing gently.

"The next day I was very busy and scarcely had time to think of the odd escapade of the night before. The morning following that, the telephone buzzed.

" 'They are calling you from Colonies,' a voice said. 'Hold on, please, the Minister wishes to speak with you. Hold a moment, please.'

A chill ran down my back. Bonnivet never telephoned himself. Invitations and replies were transmitted by our wives. This could have to do only with that stupid adventure.

" 'Hello!' Bonnivet's voice said suddenly. 'Is that you, Maufras? . . . Could you come over to my office? . . . Yes, it's urgent. . . . I'll explain when you get here. . . . Right away? Thanks.'

"I hung up. So Nelly belonged to that odious breed of women who lead men on—for it was she, I'd have sworn, who deliberately fell into my arms—and then complain to their husbands: 'You're making a mistake, you know, to trust Bernard. . . . He's not the friend you think he is. . . .' Hateful race of female!

"While I was looking for a taxi to go over to Bonnivet's, I asked myself rather wildly what would happen. A duel? I'd have welcomed that. It would have been a simple solution, at least, but since the war it wasn't done anymore. No, Bonnivet was going to heap reproaches on my head, and inform me that our connections were at an end. It would be the end of a precious friendship and also the end of my career, no doubt, for Bonnivet had influence. And how was I going to account to Madeleine for this unaccountable rupture?

"These and thoughts still more dire were racing through my mind as I drove to the Ministry. I reached the point where I understood how suicide could be considered an escape by all the unfortunates who find themselves in situations they haven't the courage to face.

"I waited awhile in an anteroom crowded with solicitors and process servers. My heart was beating irregularly. I remember I kept staring at a fresco that portrayed the Annamites at harvest time. Finally, a guard called my name and I got up. Bonnivet's office door was before me. Should I let him speak? Or forestall the scene with a complete confession?

"He got up and shook hands. The warmth of the reception stunned me. Perhaps he had had the intelligence to realize that the whole incident was unintentional, an accident?

" 'First of all,' he said, 'excuse me for having called you over so urgently, but as you'll see, it's a matter of making an immediate decision. This is what it's all about. You know that Nelly and I have to go on a longish trip to West Africa next month. An inspection trip for me, tourism and discovery for her. I've decided to take along not only some people here in the Ministry but also a few journalists. It's high time the French get to know their empire. I hadn't thought until now of talking to you about this project, since you've got nothing to do with colonial affairs and you aren't a journalist, and you do, on the other hand, have your own job. But last evening, Nelly was pointing out to me that our trip coincides, give or take a week, with your holiday, and that you would be—you and your wife—much closer and pleasanter companions for her on the trip than my cortege of civil servants. We thought that perhaps this chance to see West Africa in rather unusual circumstances might appeal to you. So, if you agree, you two will be part of the safari. . . . Only, I do have to know right away, because my office is drawing up the lists and schedules.'

"I thanked him and asked for a few hours to consult my wife. At first, I had been tempted. But the moment I was alone, I visualized how awkward and distasteful it would be to carry on a vague affair under the watchful eyes of Madeleine and as Bonnivet's guest. Nelly was beautiful, but I took a dim view of her behavior in this. Over lunch, I told Madeleine about the offer without saying, naturally, what had provoked it, and I cast about with her for some way to refuse without being impolite. She easily conjured up some previous engagements, and we did not go to Africa.

"I know that ever since, Nelly Bonnivet has spoken about me not only ironically but with a touch of hostility. Our friend Lambert-Leclerc mentioned my name in front of her recently as a possible appointee to the Seine Prefecture. She made a face. 'Maufras!' she said. 'What an idea! He's terribly nice, but he has no drive. He is a man who doesn't know what he wants.'

"Bonnivet replied, 'Nelly's right.' And I have not been appointed."

The Birth of a Master

THE PAINTER Pierre Douche was finishing a still life—
flowers in a pharmacy jar, eggplants on a platter—when the
novelist Paul-Émile Glaise came into the studio. Glaise stood
for a few moments watching his friend work; then he said
emphatically:

"No!"

Surprised, the other man looked up and stopped polishing
an eggplant.

"No," Glaise said. "No! You'll never make it. You have the
craft, you have the talent, and you're honest. But your painting is flat, my friend. It doesn't dazzle, it doesn't shout. In a
show of five thousand canvases, nothing is going to make the
half-asleep spectator stop in front of yours. . . . No, Pierre
Douche, you are never going to make it. And that's a pity."

"Why is it?" Honest Douche sighed. "I paint what I see. I
try to express what I feel."

"That's it, my friend. You have a wife—a wife and three

children, each of them needing three thousand calories a day. But there are more paintings than there are purchasers, and more idiots than connoisseurs. The question is, Pierre Douche, how does one emerge from the crowd of the anonymous and the failures?"

"By hard work," Pierre Douche said, "and sincerity."

"Be serious. The one way, Pierre Douche, of waking up the dolts is to operate on a big scale. Announce that you are going to the North Pole to paint. Walk about town dressed like an Egyptian pharaoh. Found a school. Toss off clichés—exteriorization, dynamism, subconscious, nonrepresentational—and write manifestos. Denounce motion or repose, white or black, the circle or the square. Invent neo-Homeric painting, which admits nothing but red and yellow, or cylindrical painting, octahedral painting, four-dimensional painting. . . ."

At that moment, a sweet, exotic perfume announced the arrival of Mme Kosnevska. Mme Kosnevska was a beautiful Pole whose violet eyes Pierre Douche deeply admired. Subscribing to expensive magazines that reproduced, at great cost, the masterpieces of three-year-olds, she did not find anywhere in them the name of honest Douche, and she despised his paintings. Sinking down on a divan, she considered the most recent canvas, shook her blond head, and smiled with faint disdain.

"Yesterday," she said, in her rolling, singing accent, "I went to see an exhibit of African art—all work from a good period. Ah, what sensitivity, what modeling. What power!"

The painter brought out a portrait that he was satisfied with, and showed it to her.

"Nice," she said. With which, disappointed and rolling and singing and perfumed, she disappeared.

Pierre Douche threw his palette into a corner and dropped down onto the couch. "I," he said, "am going to become an insurance examiner, a bank teller, a policeman. The painter sits on the lowest rung of the work ladder. Success is created by fools and goes to frauds. The critics don't respect the serious painters; they encourage the barbarians. I've had enough. I'm quitting."

Paul-Émile listened, lighted a cigarette, and thought for a long moment.

"Do you think you would be capable," he said finally, "of announcing with pontifical seriousness to Kosnevska and a few others that for the past ten years you have been preparing a change of style?"

"Who? Me?"

"Listen. . . . I'm going to write two well-placed articles, alerting our friends 'in the know' to the fact that you are founding the ideo-analytical school of painting. Until you came along, portrait painters, in their ignorance, have been studying the human face. Foolishness! No, what really represents the man are the ideas he evokes in us. Thus, the portrait of an Army colonel is a blue-and-gold background, crossed by five enormous stripes of braid, a horse in one corner, and crosses in the other. The portrait of an industrialist is a factory smokestack, a closed fist lying on a table. Do you understand, Pierre Douche, what you are bringing into this world? And could you paint me about twenty ideo-analytical portraits in, say, a month?"

The painter smiled wanly.

"In a day," he said, "and the sad part is, Glaise, that with another man that kind of thing might work."

"Let's try it."

"I can't manage that kind of glib talk."

"Well, my man, every time someone asks you to explain your work, you will take a moment, you will relight your pipe, you will blow a little puff of smoke in the person's face, and you will say these seven simple words: 'Have you ever looked at a river?'"

"What's that mean?"

"Nothing," Glaise said. "And therefore they will find you tremendous. And when they'll have discovered you, and explained you, and touted you to the skies, we'll spill the whole story and have a good laugh at their expense."

Two months later, the Douche exhibit opened on a note of triumph. The beautiful lilting, rolling, perfumed Mme

Kosnevska could not tear herself from the side of her new great man.

"Ah!" she said, over and over. "Such sensitivity! Such modeling! Such power! My dear, how did you ever achieve such astonishing syntheses?"

The painter took a moment, he relighted his pipe, puffed hard, and said, "Madame, have you ever looked at a river?"

The lips of the lovely Pole trembled, promising rolling, lilting delights to come.

In his fur-collared topcoat, the brilliant young critic Strunsky was holding forth to a group. "Very strong!" he was saying. "Very strong! But tell me, Douche, how about this revelation? Where did it come from? From my articles?"

Pierre Douche took quite a long moment, blew a triumphant puff of smoke in the other man's face, and said, "My dear fellow, have you ever looked at a river?"

"Admirable," the other man said, approvingly. "Admirable!"

At that moment, a prominent dealer, having finished a tour of the studio, seized the painter by the sleeve and dragged him off into a corner.

"Douche, my friend," he said, "you're a sharp fellow. This stuff can really be promoted. Give me exclusive representation. Don't change your style until I give you the word, and I'll buy fifty paintings a year. All right?"

Douche, enigmatic, puffing on his pipe, said nothing.

Slowly the studio emptied. Paul-Emile Glaise went to close the door after the last visitor. Out in the hallway, the admiring murmur faded into the distance. Alone with the painter, the writer thrust his hands joyously into his pockets.

"Well, my fine friend," he said, "we really took them over, didn't we? Did you hear that young sprout in the fur-collared coat? And your lovely Pole? And those three young women—pretty, eh?—who kept saying, 'So new! So new!' Ah, Pierre Douche, I thought human stupidity had no limits, but this goes beyond my wildest expectations."

He was overcome by a fit of helpless laughter. The painter frowned, and as the other man shook with convulsive gasps, he said sharply:

"Idiot!"

"Idiot!" the writer shouted, furious. "When I've just pulled off the best fraud of the century!"

The artist's eye swept proudly around the twenty ideo-analytical portraits, and he said with a quiet emphasis that bespoke conviction:

"Yes, you are an idiot. There is something in this kind of painting."

The writer stared at his friend, stupefied.

"But this is too much!" he howled. "Douche! Do you remember who dreamed up your new style?"

Pierre Douche took a moment, and, drawing hard on his pipe, blew a tremendous puff.

"Have you," he said, "ever looked at a river?"

Black Masks

FOR A LONG TIME, I'd wanted to meet Walter Cooper. I loved his books. No one since Kipling has written better about animals. However, in Cooper, you find not the Asian jungle but the Southern County woodlands—moist, glowing with flowers, and peopled by rabbits and foxes.

English authors are hard to meet. Many of them live in the country and never come up to London. Literary people there do not form a guild, as they do in France, complete with apprentices, canons of excellence, and rules, and even in a society which is so respectful of every freedom, Walter Cooper passed for a savage.

"You'll have trouble snaring him," Lady Shalford had told me. She was also one of his admirers. "He lives down in Suffolk with his wife in a little cottage. Both families were Puritan, and two of the grandfathers were Nonconformist ministers. Miriam Cooper wears dresses that go down to her ankles and have no shape at all. . . . She is very beautiful. I believe she never speaks."

This description whetted my wish to know the Coopers. One day, I took advantage of the fact that I was traveling by car to stop off in their village. The villagers I questioned had no idea that a man of genius was living in their midst. However, the butcher was able to tell me the address of the Coopers, who were customers of his.

"You do mean Walter Cooper the writer?" I asked.

"I wouldn't know about that," he said, "but he's the nephew of old Miss Cooper."

I followed the road that the butcher had indicated and that wound endlessly between hedgerows. It brought me finally to an open gate. Beyond the gate, a path led one through a woods sown with flowers. Pink, orange, fiery-red, and rose rhododendrons had been planted under the trees with an art all the more refined because its effects seemed so natural. The house, tiny and deliciously shabby, was roofed with thatch.

It was Miriam Cooper who came to the door. She was wearing, as Lady Shalford had said, a long dress of mousseline and over it an apron. Her face was of a disturbing, almost inhuman purity. She listened to my excuses as if she were not understanding me and suddenly, in the middle of a sentence, she fled like a frightened animal, crying:

"Walter!"

Walter Cooper's long body moved awkwardly, his yellow waistcoat was spotted and nobly frayed. He accepted my explanations with mute benevolence and waved me into the room where he worked. Shelves of wood painted white were loaded with books. As we came in, a man who was glancing at the titles turned around. Cooper introduced him; the man was a famous critic. They resumed the conversation I had interrupted. They were discussing peonies and the proper depth at which to plant the bulbs.

It may seem surprising, but that visit was the beginning of a friendship. The Coopers came to see me when they were passing through Paris on their way to spend the winter in Tamaris. I went again to their home in Suffolk for a weekend. But in spite of the friendliness and the evident pleasure they had at seeing me again, I knew little more about this couple than I did the first day. For that matter, they seemed as incapable of communicating with each other as with a stranger. During an evening in their little house, they would sit side by side on a couch in front of the fire, and pat each other on the back. I believe they loved each other.

I did not see them at all during the war. Around 1920, Lady Shalford wrote me that she was giving a masked ball for a hospital benefit, and, if I were in London at the time, it would be a pleasure to have me come. Before going into the ballroom, one paused behind a screen, removed one's mask to greet the lady of the house, and then put it back on for the rest of the evening.

"Good evening," Lady Shalford said to me. "How was your crossing? . . . Not too bad? . . . I want to introduce you right away to a woman who will interest you."

She took me by the arm, abandoned her post, and for a long time searched among the crowd.

"Ah," she said finally, "there she is."

She sat me down beside a very tall woman, masked in black like the others, and disappeared.

Disconcerted and ill at ease, I said:

"This is all a bit difficult. As my accent tells you, I am a Frenchman. . . . Almost certainly I will never see you again. . . . I am going to speak to you of all the hidden, unhappy things one tells to the ghosts of one's dreams."

My companion had fluid, expressive hands. She entered into the game with spirit. I found her at first a little too daring for my taste. She confessed to savage desires in that rather naïvely scientific language Freud and his disciples had just supplied to the Anglo-Saxons. But presently she spoke so well of the animal nature of women, then of the connections between love and our physical nature, and of books that she cherished—all strange and sensual—that she won me over completely.

"Who are you?" I begged. "Some of the things you say would make me think you know me. But I've never heard your voice. . . . Wouldn't you lift your mask for a second? You could turn your head. . . . No? Shall I never see you again? No conversation has ever given me such pleasure."

"I have had a very fine evening," she said, as she got up. "Very. But here is where it must end."

She was lost in the crowd and I made no attempt to rejoin her.

It was ten years later that Lady Shalford revealed to me that my masked companion had been Miriam Cooper. I had seen her again several times in the interval, and had found her as always—mute, friendly, and wild.

As for Walter, I discovered last week that he, too, talks when he is drunk.

Irène

"I'M SO GLAD to be going out with you this evening," she said. "It's been a hard week. So much work and so many setbacks. But now you're here, and I won't think about it anymore. We're going to see a wonderful movie."

"Don't think you're going to drag me to the movies tonight," he said sulkily.

"That's a pity," she said. "I was looking forward to seeing the film with you. . . . But it doesn't matter. I know a new nightclub in Montparnasse that's got some marvelous Martinique dancers—"

"Oh, no!" he said violently. "No Negro music. I'm up to here with it."

"What would you like to do?" she asked.

"You know perfectly well," he said. "Have dinner in some quiet little restaurant, talk, come back to your place, stretch out on a couch, and dream—"

"Oh, no!" she said, in her turn. "Oh, no. You're too selfish, you really are! . . . You look surprised? That's because no one has ever told you the truth. No one. You've got into the habit of seeing women fall in with your wishes as if they were laws. You're a kind of modern sultan. And your harem is wide open —it extends over ten countries. But it's a harem, all the same. Women are your slaves—your wife more so than all the others. If you want to daydream, they must watch you daydream. If you want to dance, they must bestir themselves. If you've written a half-dozen lines, they must listen to you read them. If you want to be amused, they must turn themselves into Scheherazades. . . . Once more, my dear, no! There will be at least one woman in this world who will not give in to your whims."

She paused, and then went on more gently:

"Oh, how dismal, Bernard! . . . I was looking forward so to seeing you. I thought you'd help me forget all my woes, and you turn up thinking only of yourself. . . . Go along now. And come back when you've learned that other people exist in this world, too."

The whole night long, lying sleepless in bed, Bernard pondered dismally over what Irène had said. She was right. He was odious. Not only did he deceive and virtually desert Alice, who was sweet and faithful and resigned, but he deceived her lovelessly. Why was he made like this? Why this need to conquer and dominate? Why this inability to "learn that other people exist"? Thinking back over his past, he remembered his difficult adolescence, how inaccessible women were. There was an element of revenge in his egoism, timidity in his cynicism. It wasn't a very noble feeling.

Noble! he thought to himself. I'm slipping into platitudes. One had to be hard. In love, he who does not devour is devoured. Still, it must be a relief sometimes to surrender, to be the weaker, to find one's own happiness in the happiness of another.

Single cars, spaced by longer and longer silences, were returning to their garages. . . . Find his happiness in the happiness of another? Was he not capable of that? Who had condemned him to be cruel? Did not every man have the right at any moment to begin a new life? And could he, in this new role, find a better partner than Irène? Irène was so touching, with her one evening dress, her mended stockings, her seedy coat. Irène was so lovely and so poor. So generous in her poverty. A dozen times he'd caught her coming to the rescue of Russian students, all poorer than she, who would have died of hunger without her. She worked six days a week in a department store—she who, before the revolution, had been brought up as a princess. She never spoke of it. Not Irène. How could he have haggled with her over the simple pleasures of her one free evening?

The last bus rumbled by, rattling the windowpanes. Now no further noise would pierce the long stillness of the night. Weary of himself, Bernard sought escape in sleep. Suddenly, a great peace flowed through him. He had made a resolution. He would devote himself to Irène's happiness. He would be for her a tender, thoughtful, submissive friend. Yes, submissive. The decision so calmed him that he fell asleep almost immediately.

The next morning when he awoke he was still altogether happy. He got up and as he dressed he sang, something that had not happened to him since he was a boy. This evening, he thought, I'll go see Irène and ask her to forgive me.

As he was knotting his tie, the telephone rang.

"Hello!" It was Irène's lilting voice. "Is that you, Bernard? . . . Listen. . . . I couldn't sleep, I was so full of remorse. . . . The way I treated you last evening. Please forgive me. I don't know what was the matter with me—"

"No, no," he said, "it was me. All night long I swore to myself I would change."

"You're mad," she said. "Above all else, don't change. . . . No, no! What women love in you, Bernard, is just that—the whims, the demands, the little spoiled boy. . . . It's so good to have a man insist on one's making sacrifices for him. . . . I wanted to tell you that I'm going to be free this evening and that I will not impose any plans on you. . . . I'll do whatever you like."

Bernard, as he was hanging up the receiver, shook his head mournfully.

The Letters

"FIVE YEARS AGO," she said, "I was Fabert's mistress. I was very much in love with him. He makes a woman's life so exciting, so full of miseries and joys, that women who have tasted this poison cannot do without it. He kept me on a very tight leash, for no reason except to prove his own power. I was glad to obey him. Every morning, around six, he used to telephone me. At that hour, my husband would be asleep and, in his bedroom, didn't hear the bell, which I had muffled, in any case, by putting a wad of cotton wool under the hammer.

"Within a few months, the affair became a public scandal. My parents-in-law urged my husband, who adored me, to threaten a divorce, and for the sake of the children I finally agreed to break off. I promised never to see my lover again. For two years, I thought I would die. Fabert did everything to get me back; I left France; I kept my address secret. At last, I felt stronger and I came back. During all those trips, I had grown close to my husband again. He was very gentle and indulgent toward me. He never referred to the affair, and, as far as the world was concerned, we passed as being a happy couple. But I was depressed, life seemed to me to have no point, and I only wanted to grow old quickly. Two more years went by like this.

"One morning, while I was still asleep, in a dream I thought I heard the telephone ring. I dreamed that Fabert was phoning me and that he was speaking to me in the passionate, incoherent way that had first conquered me. I woke up. The real phone was ringing by the bed. I lifted the receiver, and I heard a voice that seemed to be reciting rather than talking. It seemed to me that it was Fabert's voice, but I couldn't catch what he was saying. After a moment, I realized that he was reading. What he was reading was very beautiful. It was letters from a woman in love. They seemed to me absolutely and sublimely heartrending. I thought of the letters of Lespinasse or Sor Marianna Alca Forado. Finally, one even more beautiful phrase made me cry out:

" 'Fabert, please! . . . Stop! I can't bear any more. What are you reading?'

" 'Stop?' he said. 'Why? I'm reading you your own letters, the ones you wrote me only a few years ago. Don't you recognize your own thoughts?'

"Then I realized what a different, what a humdrum woman peace of heart had made of me. The next day, I went back to him. I see him every day."

The Cuckoo

GENERAL BRAMBLE asked me to come spend the Christmas holidays in the country. "This year I am inviting only my brother-in-law, Lord Tullock, and my sister-in-law, so it will not be very jolly, and I am sorry for that. But if you are not afraid of either solitude or the English winter, we will be happy to have you with us and to talk of old times."

I knew that earlier in the year my friends had suffered the loss of an eighteen-year-old daughter; the girl had been killed in a fall from her horse while hunting. I was sorry for them and wanted to see them, so I accepted.

Lord and Lady Tullock terrified me a bit, but as soon as I got to know them, I was glad they were there. General Bramble is capable of sitting by the fire for three hours on end, smoking his pipe and saying not one word. Mrs. Bramble embroiders or does needlework, also in silence. Lord Tullock proved to be a pleasant conversationalist; he had served as ambassador to several countries and, amazingly enough, seemed actually to have seen and understood them. His wife was attractively plain and altogether suitably nondescript in her dress.

Mrs. Bramble's face was streaked with tears, but she did not mention her loss to me. Only the first evening, as I was going upstairs to bed, she stopped a moment by the bedroom before mine. "That was her room," she said, and turned her head away.

Christmas Eve we spent in the library. A log fire was burning high in the fireplace, and the vast room was lighted only by candles. Through leaded windowpanes, one could see by moonlight that fresh snow was slanting down on the white garden. The General was smoking his pipe; Mrs. Bramble was busy with her needlework; Lord Tullock talked about Christmas Eve.

"Fifty years ago," he said, "many old farm people in my county still believed that on this particular night of the year animals talked like human beings. I remember hearing my nurse tell the story of a farmhand who couldn't believe this, so he hid in the stable to put the legend to the test. The moment the first stroke of midnight sounded, one of the horses turned its head to the other. 'We'll be having some work to do within the week,' it said. 'Yes,' the other answered, 'and he's heavy, that servant is.'

" 'He's heavy,' the first horse went on, 'and the hill up to the cemetery is a hard pull.' One week later, the farmhand was dead.

"Humph," the General said. "Had your nurse actually known the fellow?"

"Known him very well. He was her brother," Lord Tullock said.

He sat for sometime in silence. I was watching the high flames that crackled on the hearth like flags in a storm. The General did not stir. Mrs. Bramble's needle was distributing brightly colored dots over her canvas.

"In Sweden," Lord Tullock went on, finally, "I've often seen the peasants of Dalecarlia prepare supper for the ghosts. There, on Christmas Eve, the dead return to the houses where they have spent their lives. Before the country people leave each other for the night, they build a great fire, light fresh candles, put snow-white linen on the table, dust the chairs, and leave the place to the shades. The next morning, one always finds a little earth scattered over the floor, plates and glasses have been moved, and a strange odor is floating through the air."

"Humph," the General said softly.

It seemed to me that Lord Tullock was being tactless. I glanced at Mrs. Bramble. She seemed quite composed, but I wanted to change the subject.

"My idea of Christmas Eve is more on the order of Shakespeare's," I said. "You remember? 'And then, they say, no spirit dare stir abroad,/ The nights are wholesome, then no planets strike,/ No fairy takes, nor witch hath power to charm.' "

"But we happen to know that Shakespeare was quite mistaken about that." Lady Tullock spoke in utter seriousness. "Edward dear, would you tell the story of our Tullock Castle adventure?"

"I'd love to hear it," I said.

"Well," Lord Tullock said, "it was exactly five years ago, Christmas Eve, 1920. I had a touch of headache, and since the weather was cold and dry, around midnight I wanted to take a bit of a walk in the open air, so I went outdoors. Beyond the grill gate to the park, I took a little path that is bordered by fairly high shrubbery. That night it was well lighted by a very brilliant moon and a sky filled with stars. I'd walked perhaps half a mile when I noticed some distance ahead a dark line crossing the path, which was white with frost. When I came up to it, I saw to my surprise that it was blood, and, looking about to discover where this trickle of blood was coming from, I noticed that at that point the hedge formed a kind of reverse angle, and that a body was lying there half concealed. I went over. It was a dead body. I ran back to the house on the double and called the servants. I sent several off to alert the police, and told the others to get their torches and to follow me. We went back over the same path and we walked for a long time—far too long, it seemed to me—but there was nothing to be seen. Finally, after at least two miles, I said, 'This is impossible. I certainly hadn't come this far. We must have passed the spot. Let's go back.' We went back. 'Now, let's see,' I said. 'It's easy enough to find the place. It's the point where the hedge forms a reverse angle.' None of the servants remembered ever seeing the place I was describing. We walked on, skirting the hedge, but as far as we could go we found it absolutely straight."

Lord Tullock paused. Outdoors, the snow continued to fall with implacable slowness. The only sounds were the faint squeak of the needle passing through the canvas and the crackling of the fire.

"Had you had an hallucination?" I asked.

The General turned his head and looked at me but said nothing.

"For a long while I thought so," Lord Tullock said. "I questioned the police, the neighbors, and all possible passersby, but to no point. No crime had been committed that night along Tullock Road, and there'd been no accident. Four years went by, and I'd long since conceded that that evening my senses had been briefly deranged, when I received from a friend of ours, an archaeologist by profession, a letter that gave me a great deal of satisfaction. 'Dear Lord Tullock,' he wrote, 'This morning, in the course of some research I am following up at the British Museum, I came upon a curious fact that is quite evidently connected with a strange story you told me the last time I had the pleasure of spending a weekend with you. In connection with my research, I have had to glance through some old papers from your county, and in one I read that, on December 24, 1820, six hundred yards from Tullock Castle, one Sir John Lacy, a Catholic gentleman who was going alone to midnight Mass, was set upon by highwaymen. To spy on passersby, the bandits had hidden themselves behind the hedge, which in those days here and there formed a reverse angle. That was also where, after robbing their victim, they concealed his corpse. As a result of this incident, the lord lieutenant of the county ordered these angles to be removed. Since then, the hedge that borders the road has been straight.' "

"I wish you could have seen Edward's joy when he read that letter," Lady Tullock said.

"Quite understandable," the General said gravely.

"Yes," Mrs. Bramble said. "Quite understandable."

I looked at them all in amazement.

"Why?" I said. "Do you believe the dead man came back for the centenary of his murder?"

"You don't believe it?" Lord Tullock asked, disturbed.

General and Mrs. Bramble looked at me with such a reproving air that I kept still. Then I thought that no doubt stories of talking animals and ghosts' banquets would find a welcome from such hospitable souls. I got up and excused myself, saying that I was going to bed.

In my bedroom, a huge fire of pine logs was burning. The air was filled with a transparent smoke. One could sense outside the cottony plop of the snow against the windowpanes. When I had put out my candle, only the dancing flames animated the warm, luminous haze. I was so warm that I could not sleep. I kept thinking about the strange stories. Presently, in the bedroom beside mine, a cuckoo clock struck midnight. I was weary and slightly on edge, but at the same time my insomnia seemed somehow pleasant. It was rather as if a mysterious, impalpable presence had brought an atmosphere of intimacy and tenderness into my room. I heard the cuckoo strike every hour until sunrise, at which point I fell asleep.

When I went down the next morning a bit late for breakfast in the great rough-oak-paneled dining room, Mrs. Bramble, who was already at the table loaded with porridge and haddock and marmalade, asked me how I had slept.

"To be quite honest," I said, "I didn't sleep a great deal. But it wasn't unpleasant, and the cuckoo kept me company."

"What?" the General said sharply. "You heard a cuckoo? . . . You understand, Edith?" he said with emphasis, turning to his wife.

"Why . . . yes," I said, surprised by the tone in which he had uttered the longest sentence I had ever heard come out of his mouth. Then I saw that Mrs. Bramble was looking at me intently. Clearly she was much moved; her eyes were filled with tears.

"I must explain to you," she said. "In the bedroom next to yours there is indeed a cuckoo clock. My daughter received it as a gift when she was a little girl, but she always loved it and always wound it herself every evening. Since our dear child's death, no one has touched her cuckoo—no one will ever touch it again—so that we supposed it was silent forever. But last evening, you see, last evening was Christmas Eve. . . ."

The House

"TWO YEARS AGO," she said, "when I was so sick, I realized that I was dreaming the same dream night after night. I was walking in the country. In the distance, I could see a white house, low and long, that was surrounded by a grove of linden trees. To the left of the house, a meadow bordered by poplars pleasantly interrupted the symmetry of the scene, and the tips of the poplars, which you could see from far off, were swaying above the linden.

"In my dream, I was drawn to this house, and I walked toward it. A white wooden gate closed the entrance. I opened it and walked along a gracefully curving path. The path was lined by trees and under the trees I found spring flowers—primroses and periwinkles and anemones that faded the moment I picked them. As I came to the end of this path, I was only a few steps from the house. In front of the house, there was a great green expanse, clipped like the English lawns. It was bare, except for a single bed of violet flowers encircling it.

"The house was built of white stone and it had a slate roof. The door—a light-oak door with carved panels—was at the top of a flight of steps. I wanted to visit the house, but no one answered when I called. I was terribly disappointed, and I rang and I shouted—and finally I woke up.

"That was my dream, and for months it kept coming back with such precision and fidelity that finally I thought: Surely I must have seen this park and this house as a child. When I would wake up, however, I could never recapture it in waking memory. The search for it became such an obsession that one summer—I'd learned to drive a little car—I decided to spend my vacation driving through France in search of my dream house.

"I'm not going to tell you about my travels. I explored Normandy, Touraine, Poitou, and found nothing, which didn't surprise me. In October, I came back to Paris, and all through the winter I continued to dream about the white house. Last spring, I resumed my old habit of making excursions in the outskirts of Paris. One day, I was crossing a valley near l'Isle-Adam. Suddenly I felt an agreeable shock—that strange feeling one has when after a long absence one recognizes people or places one has loved.

"Although I had never been in that particular area before, I was perfectly familiar with the landscape lying to my right. The crests of some poplars dominated a stand of linden trees. Through the foliage, which was still sparse, I could glimpse a house. Then I knew that I had found my dream château. I was quite aware that a hundred yards ahead, a narrow road would be cutting across the highway. The road was there. I followed it. It led me to a white gate.

"There began the path I had so often followed. Under the trees, I admired the carpet of soft colors woven by the periwinkles, the primroses, and the anemones. When I came to the end of the row of linden, I saw the green lawn and the little flight of steps at the top of which was the light-oak door. I got out of my car, ran quickly up the steps, and rang the bell.

"I was terribly afraid that no one would answer, but almost

immediately a servant appeared. It was a man, with a sad face, very old. He was wearing a black jacket. He seemed very much surprised to see me, and he looked at me closely without saying a word.

" 'I'm going to ask you a rather odd favor,' I said. 'I don't know the owners of this house, but I would be very happy if they would permit me to visit it.'

" 'The château is for rent, Madame,' he said, with what struck me as regret, 'and I am here to show it.'

" 'To rent?' I said. 'What luck! It's too much to have hoped for. But how is it that the owners of such a beautiful house aren't living in it?'

" 'The owners did live in it, Madame. They moved out when it became haunted.'

" 'Haunted?' I said. 'That will scarcely stop me. I didn't know people in France, even in the country, still believed in ghosts.'

" 'I wouldn't believe in them, Madame,' he said seriously, 'if I myself had not met, in the park at night, the phantom that drove my employers away.'

" 'What a story!' I said, trying to smile.

" 'A story, Madame,' the old man said, with an air of reproach, 'that you least of all should laugh at, since the phantom was you.' "

ABOUT THE AUTHOR

ANDRÉ MAUROIS needs no introduction. Just for the record, he was born at Elbeuf, France on July 26, 1885. He holds a doctorate in philosophy from the University of Caen and has been awarded countless honorary doctorates in literature from universities in England, Scotland, the United States, and Peru. A member of the French Academy, he is considered to be the greatest living French literary biographer. His first biography, *Ariel: The Life of Shelley,* became an immediate success. It was followed by biographies of Dickens, Disraeli, Dumas, and Sir Alexander Fleming; Hugo, Napoleon, Proust, George Sand, and Voltaire. *Prometheus: The Life of Balzac,* his latest book, has received instant acclaim everywhere. All these as well as his novels, stories, and plays have been translated into most European languages. THE COLLECTED STORIES have been most successful in France, Germany, Spain, and the USSR. Maurois has lectured widely throughout the United States and is a familiar figure on French television, the BBC, and on CBS.

ABOUT THE TRANSLATOR

ANDRIENNE FOULKE is on the editorial staff of *The New Yorker* magazine.

She is a gifted translator, equally at home in French and Italian. Among the authors she has translated are François Mauriac, Saint-Exupéry, and Simenon; Morante and Sciascia.

Miss Foulke is the author of that succinct and invaluable handbook, published by Pocket Books, *English for Everyone*.